WITHO

MERCY

Siobhan Dunmoore Book 5

Eric Thomson

Without Mercy
Copyright 2018 Eric Thomson
First paperback printing October 2018

Published in Canada
By Sanddiver Books
ISBN: 978-1-775343-29-5

Sanddiver
Books

— One —

Carrie Fennon carefully opened the hidden compartment's hatch a few centimeters and listened, eyes narrowed in concentration. Her ears, finely attuned to *Kattegat Maru*'s background noise, picked up no suspicious sounds. Her nose, however, detected a faint, almost feral alien scent and the unmistakable tang of blood mixed with the freighter's natural aroma of metal, ozone, and lubricants.

She pushed the hatch aside and stuck her head out of the shielded cubbyhole hidden behind a stack of environmental recycling pumps. Somehow, Carrie knew she was the only living being left. *Kattegat Maru* no longer seemed as alive as she did a few hours earlier before the pirates struck not long after they dropped out of hyperspace. A shiver ran down Carrie's spine, and she felt nauseous at the idea everyone else could be dead, that she shared the ship with seventy corpses, including that of her mother.

After a short scramble up through the opening, Carrie stood on the main engineering compartment's dull, scuffed deck. She paused again to listen, then cautiously crept around the pump stack, nervous eyes looking for evidence of violent death.

But engineering was empty, its crew vanished without a trace. A quick glance at the status display, twin to the one on *Kattegat Maru*'s bridge, told her that the freighter still traveled at sub-light speed on the same heading as before; that her systems still functioned, and that her compartments were pressurized, save for the hangar deck. The space doors were open, a clue that no one remained to close them after the pirates left.

Why didn't they take *Katie* with them? Or destroy her? Why did they just leave? Sure, she was old, but she could still outsail most ships her size.

Carrie gingerly stepped into the main corridor running along the freighter's spine from engineering to the bridge. No untoward sounds disrupted the starship's familiar, soft purr. Nothing triggered a subconscious alert.

Members of multi-generation spacer families such as the Fennons developed an almost symbiotic rapport with the starship that was both their home and their livelihood. Other than the oppressive sense of emptiness, *Katie* felt eerily normal, as if everyone had stepped off for an hour or two so they might play a prank on the captain's daughter.

Merchant crews who spent their lives in interstellar space were partial to practical jokes, anything that might relieve the boredom of a long crossing. But not if they carried a full complement of passengers. Or at least they wouldn't carry out a prank that might in any way involve them. Captain Aurelia Fennon wouldn't stand for it. *Kattegat Maru*'s reputation was precious to her, as it had been precious to Carrie's grandfather, the late Nemo Fennon, who first sailed *Katie* off the slipways and into deep space.

She passed the circular stairwell connecting the freighter's decks. Upward led to the passenger cabins, downward to the crew quarters and the hangar deck wedged between the forward and aft cargo holds.

Though *Kattegat Maru* could land on worlds whose gravity didn't exceed one point two standard gees, Aurelia Fennon preferred to shift goods via shuttlecraft where there was no orbital station with transshipment facilities. It spared her ship the stress of repeated takeoffs and landings and prolonged her life.

Carrie glanced up and down the stairwell, knowing she would eventually have to visit every deck, then continued forward to the bridge, stopping every few steps to listen. But she heard nothing out of the ordinary. *Katie* was humming along as she usually did between faster-than-light jumps.

A smear of blood on the scuffed deck greeted her just before the bridge's open door. Carrie paused again, suddenly fearful of entering her mother's domain, one forbidden to her unless she stood watch in her capacity as an apprentice merchant officer.

She took a deep, steadying breath and then entered. The bridge, like engineering, was devoid of life, with nothing to show it was crewed only hours earlier. A small, almost unnoticeable blood spatter covered the helm console as if someone had struck the duty quartermaster's head. The captain's chair sat as empty as the others.

Carrie reached out to touch it, to see if she could still sense her mother's warmth, but the seat was cold. Fear transfixed her with its icy spear, and she fought the urge to hyperventilate.

After a few minutes, during which her thoughts seemed to enter a state of suspended animation, she studied each of the bridge consoles in turn and realized everything seemed intact. The pirates, or whoever their attackers might be, didn't carry out the orgy of destruction conjured by her fevered imagination while she hid in the shielded compartment, invisible to even naval grade sensors.

Carrie retraced her steps to the circular staircase. She cautiously climbed its metallic treads, careful to make no sound, and stepped off one deck higher, where an open door piercing the airtight bulkhead gave admission to the passenger accommodations. She still keenly felt that sensation of emptiness, of being alone.

The first door to her left opened onto the saloon and she finally saw evidence of human occupation. Half-empty drink bulbs, food wrappers, and other assorted items littered the tables as if someone hustled the occupants away without warning. The cabins, on the other hand, appeared as desolate as the bridge, with nary a personal item in sight. Forty-five paying guests gone without a trace.

They weren't wealthy, to be sure. Those with money traveled on one of the liners crisscrossing the Commonwealth. Or if they had urgent business in a part of the human sphere threatened by Shrehari incursions, found berths on fast traders capable of outrunning Imperial warships. But the price suited budget-conscious travelers or those for whom anonymity was more important than comfort.

The crew quarters proved to be just as devoid of human life, but personal belongings, including her own, remained in evidence as if the attackers didn't give her shipmates time or even permission to pack. The crew's mess, however, appeared as spotless as it should be between meals.

Carrie wound her way down the staircase until it ended on the hangar deck, just outside the control room. One glance through the thick, armored window told her *Kattegat Maru*'s shuttles were gone.

She closed the space doors but didn't bother pressurizing the hangar. Then, Carrie visited each of the six cargo holds. All but one seemed undisturbed. Cargo hold C, used for small, high value items, was empty. When she accompanied the first officer on his daily rounds a day earlier as part of her apprenticeship, it had been filled with standard, albeit small cubic containers.

The nervous energy that kept Carrie going since she left the cubbyhole ebbed away and she slumped to the deck, her back against a bare metal bulkhead. Tears welled up in her eyes, and when one rolled down her cheek, she wiped it away with a brusque gesture.

After a while, the urge to cry subsided and a ghostly voice, that of her mother, reminded Carrie she was a Fennon, a spacer born and bred. Someone trained from infancy to survive anything the galaxy could throw at her, including pirates who turned *Katie* into a ghost ship.

She climbed to her feet and, with deliberate steps, returned to the bridge. Since the mysterious attackers didn't shoot everything up, maybe the subspace transmitter still worked. There must be a Navy ship somewhere within a short FTL jump, considering how closely *Kattegat Maru* skirted the frontier. And if that didn't work, she would get to sail solo a year before completing her apprenticeship.

— Two —

"The ghost has struck again, Lord."

Acting Strike Group Leader Brakal raised his angular, bony head, crowned by a strip of bristly fur, and speared Urag with eyes of unrelieved black. The Shrehari officer's mouth opened in a semi-feral snarl, exposing cracked, yellowed fangs.

Left in charge of the strike group by dint of seniority when the Admiralty recalled its commanding officer, Admiral Hralk, to the capital, Brakal quickly sank into the quagmire of administrative minutiae. In despair, he took to patrolling the stars with his cruiser *Tol Vehar*, its brother *Tol Vach* and two *Ptar* class corvettes instead of moldering aboard a misbegotten orbital station at the hind end of nowhere.

"What has the poxed human done this time?"

"Convoy *Yulin* Twenty-One vanished after sending out a distress signal that an unidentified ship, which seemingly appeared out of nowhere, attacked them."

Brakal's gloved hand slammed down on the metal desk.

"May the demons of the Underworld rip out their throats. That makes three more transport ships and one *Ptar* class corvette lost to this damn apparition in the last ten days."

"*Yulin* Twenty-One carried our monthly resupply."

"I know that." Brakal's sneer twisted a face that could be considered handsome by Shrehari standards but would remind a human of nothing so much as a demented gargoyle. Urag, who'd become inured to his commander's moods long ago, didn't reply.

"Send a message to the staff. I want a full briefing on the event and recommendations within the day. Let us see if they can propose a practical course of action, or if they're merely good enough to deliver bad news."

"As you command." Urag vanished into the corridor.

Alone once more, Brakal turned his seat toward a thick porthole and stared out at a faint red star in a part of space the humans called, not without justification, the Rim.

Ever since his return from the distant human colony with the unpronounceable heathen name, he and *Tol Vehar* had been engaged in fruitless patrols designed to probe Commonwealth defenses on the far flank of the war zone. Then, Shrehari ships began to disappear without a trace.

The sparse distribution of inhabited systems at this end of the Rim sector meant shipping was mostly an isolated business, without any secure, acknowledged star lanes. Yet this ghost kept not only finding Shrehari vessels that should be hard to detect, it even seemed to operate with impunity inside Imperial space, if the latest little disaster was any indication. The Empire could ill afford a war of attrition, not after the most recent, thoroughly unsuccessful attempts to break a stalemate that just wouldn't end.

Adding to Brakal's long list of grievances, the ghost was directly responsible for Admiral Hralk's recall to Shrehari Prime so he might explain why ships were vanishing in his area of responsibility with no human prize or wreckage to show for the losses. It left the squadron's senior commander in charge of the sclerotic, unimaginative Strike Group Khorsan staff who seemed to delight in tormenting him with bureaucratic nonsense.

After several weeks in their company, Brakal suspected the Deep Space Fleet's staff officer corps was the Empire's real enemy, not the humans. So he fled aboard his ship, now under Urag's temporary command. Yet their baleful influence kept reaching out across the void to torment him.

At least no one protested his appointment of *Tol Vehar*'s secret police spy as Strike Group Khorsan's chief political officer. It allowed him to leave the incumbent on the orbital station with the rest of the staff and went a long way to make sure the latter kept their plots against him as innocuous as possible.

Should Regar's superiors on the home planet find out their agent's loyalty belonged to Brakal instead of the Empire's secret police, they might suffer a collective brain aneurysm. If they possessed brains in the first place. Regar certainly never missed a chance to express his opinion of the *Tai Kan*, albeit in private, and would occasionally go on at length about the stupidity of the entire organization.

However, if the ghost wasn't run to ground soon, Brakal would follow Hralk into the Admiralty's hallowed halls, perhaps never to emerge again this time, whether or not his loyal spy kept watch. But it was the devil's ion storm that brought no one good tidings. At least Urag seemed to enjoy being one of the rare Deep Space Fleet captains with no *Tai Kan* officer looking over his shoulder at all hours, something the thrice-damned humans didn't have to countenance.

As if summoned by the demons themselves, Regar's cynical features appeared in the open doorway. He too wore a warrior caste ruff of fur across the top of his ridged skull, a reminder he preferred to think of himself as the Fleet officer he'd been years earlier rather than a political watchdog.

"The staff should soon be stirring like an *iragan* blasted from its century-long slumber," he said. "Your ill humor at the latest news will travel at speeds unheard of if Urag has any say in the matter. And with a tone so pungent it will give them a century of indigestion."

Brakal grunted.

"Trying to cheer me up, miscreant? Bring me the head of the ghost ship's captain. Then perhaps I can inherit Hralk's robes along with his endless chores."

"Sorry. The only heads I can bring you sit on Shrehari shoulders and most in Strike Group Khorsan aren't worth harvesting. Although," he took on a thoughtful expression, "I might take a few for simple enjoyment. Your benighted chief of staff, for instance. No doubt he still believes the mantle of command should have been his upon Hralk's departure. You might find things working better without his constant interference. I mention it merely as something to consider when we return to base."

"I wish it were that easy. Until he openly defies me, his position must remain secure. The Honorable Gra'k has many connections inside the nobility, and cannot fall to a casual assassin's knife, not even if it's wielded by a *Tai Kan* officer."

"Pity. If you showed fewer scruples, you might be further ahead."

"If I were less scrupulous, I wouldn't be the warrior I am. The uninhibited exercise of power corrupts without limits, Regar. You should be intimately familiar with that idea."

"And yet it will take warriors with fewer scruples to force this farce of a government onto its knees and make them sue for an armistice with the humans. Four more ships gone without a single loss inflicted on the enemy, and deep within our sphere of control too. If these small defeats are generalized throughout the war zone, our shipyards will not keep up, and soon the advantage of numbers will fall to the hairless apes."

"Your words need hearing in the Imperial Palace and the Admiralty, not in this miserable office. I know the humans are slowly gaining on us. The imbeciles back home, however, refuse to see the truth."

Regar's bitter laugh echoed off the bare metal bulkheads.

"And you think they would listen to a *Tai Kan* officer whose true allegiance lies with the Fleet? They'd just as soon slit my throat."

"Then barring a sudden intellectual awakening on the homeworld, let us hope we can do something about the demon scratching at our door before *Tol Vehar* is the only Imperial ship left in this sector."

"You forget *Chorlak*, although it is under *Tai Kan* control."

Brakal made an obscene gesture.

"Bah. A damned pretend-corsair fraternizing with human outcasts and traitors in the Unclaimed Zone. What good is he to the war effort?"

"His crew might help us find the ghost, Commander." When Brakal didn't reply, Regar said, "I can use *Tai Kan* lines of communication to pass the word of a human that appears out of nowhere, looks nothing like a proper ship of war, and strikes without mercy. Allow me private access to *Tol Vehar*'s otherspace device so I may use *Tai Kan* codes and interrogate the nearest retransmission array."

A grunt.

"Do it. But make sure I don't end up owing the diseased *Tai Kan* any favors."

"You won't."

— Three —

"Bridge to the captain."

Siobhan Dunmoore, engrossed in a particularly well-crafted nineteenth-century mystery, looked up with a start. She put her book down on the day cabin's desk, careful to avoid damaging the precious paper pages and frowned with displeasure. This was her first chance to relax since *Iolanthe* wiped out the Shrehari convoy after stalking it for days.

"Yes?"

"Officer of the watch, sir." Dunmoore needn't ask for a name. Astrid Drost, *Iolanthe*'s navigation officer, or as the traditionalists called it, sailing master, owned a distinctive, lilting voice. "We're picking up a distress call on the emergency subspace channel, sir, from a freighter by the name *Kattegat Maru*. Pirates made off with everyone aboard save a single survivor. An apprentice ship's officer by the name Carrie Fennon. I looked up *Kattegat Maru* in Lloyd's Registry. She's an old Skeid class freighter commanded by a Captain Aurelia Fennon. No adverse notations, no indications she's a shady operator. Normal complement is twenty-five crew, and she can take up to sixty passengers. According to the distress signal she was carrying forty-five passengers at the time of the attack."

"Distance?"

"According to the coordinates she's transmitting, approximately zero point two parsecs. A little over thirty hours sailing time if we push the upper interstellar hyperspace bands. Rin is already working on the navigation plot." Sub Lieutenant Rin Pashar was *Iolanthe*'s junior navigator and Lieutenant Drost's understudy. "Do you want us to reply?"

"No." Dunmoore shook her head even though she was alone in the day cabin. "If this isn't on the up-and-up, I'd rather not give warning of our arrival. Make sure we drop out of FTL at a safe distance, just in case."

"Already factored in, sir."

Dunmoore could almost see Drost's pleased smile.

"In that case, when you're happy with the plot, take us FTL. Warn Commander Holt and Major Salminen we'll need a boarding party and a prize crew ready to go. A lonesome apprentice ship's officer won't be taking something the size of a Skeid class freighter anywhere on her own."

A few minutes later, Drost's voice echoed through the ship.

"Now hear this. *Iolanthe* will go FTL in five, I repeat five minutes. That is all."

Soon after that, a soft chime wafted through Dunmoore's day cabin, announcing someone wished to enter.

"Come."

The door slid aside with a sigh to admit a tall, good-looking blond officer in unadorned Navy battledress, wearing a piratical eye patch and an almost permanent sardonic smile. Commander Ezekiel Holt, *Iolanthe*'s first officer, was still resisting the notion of three months ashore to regrow the eye lost in battle years earlier when he was Dunmoore's executive officer in the corvette *Shenzen*. But at least the leg lost at the same time was now as good as new.

"What's this I hear?" He headed for the coffee urn almost out of reflex and picked up a cup. Part of the ship's bespoke crockery, it featured an angry, sword-bearing faerie in full flight along with the ship's hull number and name. He filled it with the rich black brew always on tap in Dunmoore's day cabin and turned to face her. "A distress signal from an apprentice merchant officer, sole survivor of a pirate attack? Sounds a little loopy. Pirates wouldn't leave a captured ship behind, let alone a witness."

He dropped into a chair across from Dunmoore.

"Perhaps they damaged the freighter during their attack and it's no longer spaceworthy. As for witnesses? I can think of several explanations why they might have missed someone, especially if they weren't scanning for life signs."

"Still." Holt made a face. "I hope you intend to be cautious."

"To a fault, Zeke."

"What about HQ?"

"I'll report once we know more about the situation. There's no sense getting everyone worked up over something that might not actually be important. I'd rather avoid a protracted back and forth submitting report after report. I swear even Special Operations Command is being overrun by bureaucratic gnomes intent on stifling the efficient prosecuting of this damned war. And with a potential prize in play..."

"Ah, yes. That misbegotten idea of growing the Q-ship inventory with seized merchant vessels rather than slip custom builds such as *Iolanthe* into the shipbuilding cycle. It's a wonder the Guild hasn't raised holy hell with the Senate yet."

The public address system came on again, drowning out Dunmoore's reply.

"Now hear this, FTL in one minute. That is all."

Precisely thirty seconds later, a shrill klaxon sounded three times, and Holt placed his half-empty coffee mug on Dunmoore's desk. Then both braced themselves for the inevitable transition nausea.

It surged and ebbed as quickly as always. Dunmoore stood and stretched, then ran a gloved hand through her silver-tinged red hair. Though not quite forty yet, her watchful gray eyes radiated the thousand parsec stare of a veteran twice her age. They and her lean, almost predatory features were a result of humanity's exhausting war against the Shrehari Empire.

Of her three permanent and one acting commands before *Iolanthe*, only the latest, *Stingray*, was decommissioned with proper ceremony. The Shrehari were responsible for wrecking the others, with attendant loss of life. If she never faced the task of writing grieving families again, it wouldn't be too soon.

"Chess?" Holt asked. "Emma will assemble a suitable prize crew since she knows merchant ships better than any of us, so I can afford to waste a bit of time."

Lieutenant Commander Emma Cullop, *Iolanthe*'s second officer, was a civilian starship officer before the war and joined up for the duration, though Dunmoore suspected she would stay on afterward. The lifestyle suited her, and she displayed all the right attributes for a warship command at some point.

"Sure, why not?" Dunmoore reached over and retrieved a mahogany box. "Do you want to choose a color or see what chance gives you?"

"I'll take white, thank you very much. Anyone facing an opponent who thinks chess is a blood sport needs every little advantage he can get."

**

"That's a Skeid class freighter all right," Chief Petty Officer Marti Yens, *Iolanthe*'s sensor chief said once the first scans came back. "Looks to be in reasonable shape for a fifty-year-old tub. Though sailing it in these parts is just asking for trouble."

Dunmoore, seated in the combat information center's command chair, leaned forward and studied the video feed. Though *Iolanthe*, a battlecruiser disguised as a bulk freighter, boasted analytical systems so modern and advanced they would make most admirals salivate with envy, Dunmoore still took counsel from her tactical instincts. And so she let her mind reach out to pick up the subliminal clues that could mean the difference between reacting to a hidden threat in time and finding herself on the back foot.

Around her, the members of the duty watch worked silently and efficiently at their consoles, monitoring the ship's ordnance, her systems, the sensors, and everything else that made *Iolanthe* a finely tuned weapon of war.

A three-dimensional holographic projection occupied the CIC's center and currently showed two small icons, one blue, and one green, with the former closing in on the latter.

"Power emissions are consistent with the type," Yens continued in her usual tone. "She appears undamaged and isn't leaking radiation. Her gun ports are closed."

"Life signs, Chief?"

"Though it's hard to be sure at this distance, I'd say only one." A pause. "And unless the assorted scum, boneheads included, who call this part of the galaxy home finally mastered the art of masking emissions, I'd say there's no one else around. At least not close enough to try for an ambush."

Between the Q-ship's sensors and Chief Yens' own instincts, it was as reliable a situational assessment as any captain could wish. Even her combat systems officer,

Lieutenant Commander Thorin Sirico, found nothing to add.

Dunmoore settled back in her chair though her eyes never left *Kattegat Maru*'s image. Much smaller than the freighter *Iolanthe* mimicked, she was also sleeker and more rounded, befitting her ability to land on planets hospitable to human life. As Yens said, she seemed in good condition for something that was crossing the star lanes over ten years before Dunmoore's birth.

If she had indeed fallen victim to pirates, there was scant evidence her crew fought back. Which begged the question why they didn't take her. From here it was only a few jumps before vanishing into the galactic badlands, a sector of space that both the Commonwealth and Imperial navies stopped patrolling after the war's onset years earlier. Who knew what mischief was brewing out there?

"Do we go as a privateer or a Fleet transport?" Ezekiel Holt asked from his station on the bridge where he controlled the helm and navigation.

"If I were a terrified apprentice ship's officer, I dare say a Navy unit would reassure me more than some scummy privateer, even if she carries a letter of marque from the Secretary-General of the Commonwealth. We'll put up rank insignia and switch on our naval beacon. But unless hostile starships show up unannounced, we won't turn *Iolanthe* into the Furious Faerie."

"I agree, Captain."

Dunmoore swiveled her chair to face the signals console.

"Open a link on the standard emergency band, please. Identify us as the Commonwealth Starship *Iolanthe*, naval transport."

— Four —

The unexpected sound of a male voice, business-like, neither kind nor unkind, erupted from the bridge speakers. It yanked Carrie Fennon out of her funk-induced trance. The young woman's head whipped up while her eyes darted everywhere, looking for the source of the unexpected interruption. Then, Carrie's brain caught up with her reflexes. The Navy. Thank God — the Navy.

"*Kattegat Maru*, this is the Commonwealth Starship *Iolanthe*. We received your distress signal. Please respond." The same words rang in her ears two more times before she reached out and touched the controls embedded in the command chair's arm. Her mother's command chair.

"This is *Kattegat Maru*." No other response came to mind. Nothing about her condition, how relieved she was to no longer be alone in interstellar space close to Shrehari patrol routes. Only 'this is *Kattegat Maru*.' A tiny part of Carrie Fennon, the part that desperately wanted to slash the word apprentice from her official designation blushed with embarrassment.

The rest of her simply wanted someone, a grownup with a merchant spacer's watch-keeping ticket, to come aboard and take over so she could sleep. Thirty hours awake, gripped by an equal measure of terror and despondency took a toll.

"Stand by."

A pause, then a woman's vibrant alto, only slightly marred by the rough edge of abused vocal chords, filled her ears.

"Apprentice Officer Carrie Fennon, I'm Captain Siobhan Dunmoore, commanding officer of the Navy transport *Iolanthe*. We are approximately one million kilometers aft of your position and closing. What is your status?"

Alone, scared, with no idea what to do next. "My systems are functioning. I have hull integrity and apparently no battle damage. But I'm by myself, and *Katie* isn't exactly a single hander."

"Are you perchance related to Captain Aurelia Fennon whom the Lloyd's Registry lists as master and owner?"

"She's my mother. *Kattegat Maru* is our family's ship. Most of the crew are either Fennons or related to the Fennons."

"I see."

Carrie tried to imagine what this Captain Dunmoore looked like, but her mind's eye kept conjuring the image of another captain, the one in whose command chair she sat.

"Here is what I propose to do, Apprentice Officer Fennon. I will approach your ship, match velocities, and send over a boarding party along with a prize crew."

"No!" The word escaped Carrie's throat before she could think. "You will not send a prize crew. *Kattegat Maru* is not a derelict, nor did you capture her in battle. I am a Fennon and will not relinquish ownership."

Dunmoore's chuckle sounded amused rather than mocking though it still raised Carrie's hackles.

"Of course, Apprentice Officer Fennon. My apologies. I misspoke. The Navy has no intention of challenging your right to *Kattegat Maru*. As you are a member of the owner's family and still in control, she's not a derelict and therefore not salvageable under the law. Let me rephrase what I said. I will send a relief crew under one of my officers, Lieutenant Commander Emma Cullop, to help you sail your ship. She served in merchant vessels before the war and is familiar with civilian protocols. But I insist on a detachment of Marines accompanying them to provide security."

Carrie swallowed her reflexive outrage at the thought of turning *Katie* over to the Navy and said, "In that case, thank you, Captain." She was aware her reply sounded stilted and grudging and hated herself for it. For the way it made her sound callow.

"Would you be amenable to opening a video link, Apprentice Officer? It will be a while before we match velocities so I can send the relief crew over and I'm interested to know what happened."

"I would." Carrie touched the command chair's control screen, accepting an enhanced connection.

The woman whose face swam into focus on the main bridge display did not resemble the picture in her mind. Dunmoore's rich voice seemed at odds with her lean and prematurely aged features. Even the thin white scar running along her jawline looked out of place.

Penetrating eyes beneath arched copper brows studied Carrie, and she knew instinctively this was not someone with whom you trifled. This was a professional spacer like her mother, capable of detecting bullshit from a hundred parsecs. What Dunmoore saw in return wasn't obvious. Her expression gave nothing away.

"Pray tell me, Apprentice Officer Carrie Fennon, what the hell happened to your crew and passengers?"

"I don't know, sir." She took a deep, calming breath and exhaled. "About thirty minutes after we dropped out of FTL to check our position, tune the drives and calculate the next jump, three ships appeared out of nowhere almost on top of us. I was working a shift in engineering as part of my training cycle when it happened. One of the ships fired a warning salvo and ordered us to prepare for boarding. We couldn't go FTL since the hyperdrives were still cycling, and shaking them off at sub-light speeds was impossible. As for fighting? *Kattegat Maru*'s shield generators and guns are ancient. One pirate ship, perhaps. Three? Never.

"My mother figured it would be best to let them plunder our cargo in the hopes they'd let us go afterward. My uncle Steph, he's the chief engineer, wasn't as optimistic. He shoved me into a shielded cubbyhole beneath the main engineering deck and told me to stay there until he gave the all-clear."

"But he never did."

"No." Carrie shook her head. An anguished expression twisted her youthful features. "Once I no longer felt any strange vibrations run through the ship, I poked my head out of the cubbyhole only to find myself the last person aboard. Everyone else is gone. Some probably didn't go voluntarily. I saw blood stains, but no bodies."

"And your cargo?"

"That's what's strange, Captain. Cargo hold C is empty. That's where we put the high value, small volume stuff. They didn't touch the others. Our shuttles are gone as well. And it appears the passengers left with their personal stuff, but the crew didn't."

Dunmoore slowly nodded, her face taking on a thoughtful cast.

"That is bizarre. Why didn't they simply take *Kattegat Maru*? You said she was spaceworthy, but could you have missed something that might prevent her from traveling FTL? Perhaps your mother sabotaged her ship to frustrate the pirates."

"Maybe. I didn't run a full survey, or any sort of survey, other than seeing if anyone remained aboard." Carrie felt herself blush with embarrassment. She should have checked *Katie's* hull, frames, and systems from stem to stern instead of sinking into a funk.

If Dunmoore noticed Carrie's discomfiture, she thankfully didn't remark on it.

"Understandable. *Kattegat Maru* is a big ship, and you're alone. And an apprentice at that. I'll ask Lieutenant Commander Cullop and the relief crew do so. Did your mother log anything about the pirates? Imagery, telemetry, sensor readings? If we're to find them, we must know what we're hunting."

"You intend to chase the pirates?"

"Of course. They took seventy humans, presumably to sell them into slavery or hold them for ransom. Either way, it's my duty to find your crew and passengers."

Carrie couldn't hide her incredulity.

"But you're a transport, not a frigate, or a cruiser."

"True, yet *Iolanthe* is also the only Navy ship close enough to do something useful. If we know what we're chasing. Did you check the logs?"

Another surge of embarrassment set her cheeks on fire.

"No."

"Could you please do so now, Apprentice Officer?" Her tone was kind but uncompromising.

"Yes, sir." Carrie called up the relevant files, then bit back a curse that might make Captain Dunmoore frown. "They wiped the logs. Not everything, just from when we dropped out of FTL onward. There's nothing about the pirates."

"Sometimes, we can recover these erasures with the right tools." Dunmoore studied Carrie again. "Do you need medical care?"

Carrie shook her head.

"No, sir. I'm fine. I can stay at my post."

Another amused chuckle.

"That wasn't a ploy to get you off your ship. The Navy will not claim it, mainly because we wouldn't find much use for a fifty-year-old Skeid class transport, and frankly, they're not worth much on the used starship market. Certainly not enough to warrant the effort. But you've been through a traumatic experience."

"I'll be fine, sir." Her reply held more than a hint of petulance.

That amused smile returned.

"I'm sure you will." Dunmoore glanced to one side. "Is there anyone we can notify? Corporate headquarters? Family?"

"Although *Kattegat Maru* is incorporated, we don't have a shore office. My mom is the chief executive officer as well as her captain. I have grandparents, but at this point, I'd rather not worry them."

"If there's nothing else you want to discuss, I'll leave you to prepare for the relief crew. But should anything come up before they arrive, call us on this channel, okay? Anything at all."

"Thank you, Captain Dunmoore. I will."

The screen went blank, and Carrie Fennon found herself alone once more. She would prefer to keep an open link with *Iolanthe* until this Lieutenant Commander Cullop and her people arrived, if only for even a hint of human contact.

But that would be undignified. She was the last Fennon in *Katie* and therefore the owner's legal representative.

— Five —

"Did everyone hear that?" Dunmoore asked. "Zeke, Emma?"

"Aye," both replied simultaneously from the bridge.

Iolanthe's combat systems officer, Thorin Sirico, and her Major of Marines, Tatiana Salminen, both of whom were at their stations in the CIC, nodded silently.

Although titled Major of Marines, Salminen was actually an Army officer from the Scandia Regiment whose company found itself drafted into the Q-ship during the Toboso incident. Fleet HQ made the assignment official shortly after that.

"Opinions?"

"There is a lot not right with this situation, Captain," Lieutenant Commander Cullop said. "*Kattegat Maru* is a family ship, which means her captain's been aboard since before she was Carrie Fennon's age. She would have learned long ago to choose her intervals between jumps at random in interstellar space. There's no way that pirate attack was opportunistic. Not out here and not if they appeared almost on top of Fennon's ship. *Kattegat Maru* was betrayed. Either at her last port of call or by someone aboard. Those pirates tracked her. There's no other way. And that's just the beginning."

"What else, Emma?"

"Not taking the ship. Okay, so *Kattegat Maru* is an old Skeid class transport. If she's still sailing along the frontier, it means her captain kept her well maintained and provisioned. Why not simply put a prize crew aboard and head off into the wilds? Pirates either wreck their prey or take it with them. They don't leave an intact ship just like that. Or at least, I've never heard of it happening."

"We don't know yet she's intact," Holt cautioned.

"Agreed, sir. Then there's the matter of taking everyone off. We know there's slave trading out beyond our and the Shrehari's spheres of influence, but nowhere near as much as in the Coalsack sector. And why did the passengers take their belongings but not the crew? You'd think the crew would own more items of value since that ship is their home."

Dunmoore nodded.

"That and what in cargo hold C caught the pirates' interest? As you said, Emma. There is a lot off-kilter here."

"What if they did it with a purpose in mind," Salminen suggested. "Had their chief engineer not stashed the young lady in a shielded cubbyhole, someone would eventually have found *Kattegat Maru* abandoned but intact. And with nothing to show what happened, no one to tell the tale, and no evidence she was carrying anything more than her regular crew. If there's no shore office to keep records, the passengers might by now be non-persons, people who vanished without a trace after being last seen at whatever port they joined *Kattegat Maru*."

Lieutenant Commander Sirico emitted a low, but appreciative whistle.

"Give that soldier another commendation. I do believe she's got it."

"Someone trying for a *Mary Celeste*," a new voice from the bridge, that of Chief Petty Officer First Class Guthren, *Iolanthe*'s coxswain and therefore the senior enlisted man aboard said. "Mister Devall would relish telling us about it in excruciating detail."

Dunmoore let out an involuntary snort. Her former second officer in *Stingray*, and now first officer in *Jan Sobieski*, the frigate commanded by her then first officer, Gregor Pushkin, was an avid collector of maritime and deep space mysteries.

"Before anyone asks," she said, "look it up. But Major Salminen is right. As is Mister Guthren. We, and by that I mean the collective Navy we, were meant to find an enigma, something more puzzling that a simple disappearance. Ships go missing every day, thanks to rogue wormholes, ion storms, enemy action, and the odd bit of piracy. If *Kattegat Maru* didn't make her next scheduled port call, no one would know why. Finding her abandoned is a whole order of magnitude more perplexing."

"Except they didn't count on one young apprentice officer who can't be a day over seventeen remaining aboard unbeknown to the pirates and calling for help."

"Except for that, Emma."

"I may have a wild idea to propose."

Dunmoore glanced at Salminen with an eyebrow cocked in question.

"Propose away, Tatiana. You already scored what everyone agrees is a direct hit."

The Scandian, a lean, tall woman with short dark hair and intense blue eyes gave Siobhan the shy smile she'd never quite managed to shed.

"Could it be the pirates were after one or more of the passengers but wanted to turn their disappearance into a mystery?"

"Assuming they expected salvagers or the Navy to find *Kattegat Maru* in interstellar space before the end of this damned war."

Salminen gave Sirico a half shrug.

"The pirates might have planned on somehow informing the Navy or one of the shipping companies sailing in this sector, or even on accomplices pretending they're honest spacers finding her. As I said, it's a wild idea."

"No," Holt replied. "I think Tatiana's on to something. We should obtain a copy of the passenger manifest and see if any names catch our attention."

"Provided the pirates didn't wipe it along with the log."

"True, Captain. If Tatiana's theory holds water, then they'll have taken that precaution as well. But maybe Chief Day can work his magic on the manifest along with the log. And Carrie Fennon should be able to provide at least a partial list from memory."

"I'll make sure he gets a copy of *Kattegat Maru*'s database the moment we board. And on that note, I want to brief the relief crew and the Marines coming with us."

"You're getting Karlo Saari's platoon, Emma. They'll be waiting on the hangar deck, equipped to live in *Kattegat Maru* for however long they're needed."

"Excellent. Karlo's always good for a laugh when things become dull."

**

"The hangar deck is pressurized, the space doors are closed, but so is the airlock," Petty Officer Third Class Gus Purdy, the lead shuttle's pilot said. "No reception committee. You want me to drop the ramp, Commander Cullop?"

"Hang on a second." *Iolanthe*'s second officer could have sworn she saw a shadow in *Kattegat Maru*'s hangar deck control room. "I think our Apprentice Officer Fennon is cagey, and I don't blame her." She switched to the general frequency. "Folks, I will step off first. Alone. Otherwise, I think we might scare Fennon into opening the space doors and turn our friendly arrival into an unpleasant emergency decompression. That means no Marines stamping down aft ramps, weapons at the ready, shouting barbaric Scandian war cries."

"It's Suomi, not barbarian, Commander, but considering where you're from, the confusion is understandable. And if I may say so, you take the fun out of boarding parties."

"And you would scare the life out of Shrehari Marines, let alone a young woman trying to keep what's left of her nerves from fraying, Command Sergeant Saari."

"There is that, of course," he replied in a rueful tone. "I seem to have a rather unfortunate effect on civilians."

"Damn straight, Karlo. You're not the prettiest thing to be whelped in Kollsvik," Sergeant First Class Maki Mattis, Saari's platoon sergeant said to undisguised guffaws from the rest of 1st Platoon, E Company, 3rd Battalion, Scandia Regiment. "On the contrary."

"Pardon my soldiers' lack of manners, Commander Cullop. You can take them away from where the dire-wolves roam, but you can't keep them from marking their territory. I will bow to your greater judgment."

The Scandia Regiment's crest, a loping wolf on a stylized snowflake obviously inspired Saari's quip. He saw Mattis give him a good-natured rigid digit salute out of the corner of his eyes.

"Okay. Everyone stays in the shuttles, buttoned up until I give the word." Cullop, wearing battle armor like that of the boarding party's soldiers, climbed to her feet, checked her suit's integrity, then gestured aft. "Let me out."

She walked down the ramp with a deliberate, unhurried stride and headed for the inner door. When it didn't open at her approach, she stopped three paces short and, after one last check that the hangar deck's air was breathable, she unfastened her helmet and removed it.

"Hi. I'm Emma Cullop." She pointed at the two-and-a-half stripes of her rank in the middle of her chest. "I'm a lieutenant commander in the Commonwealth Navy these days. But before the war, I was a merchant officer, just like you. In fact, I believe I'm still a member of the Guild. They kept everyone who volunteered for the Navy on the books at no cost."

Cullop heard a mechanical clang as locking bars moved out of the way. Then, the thick door shifted backward and to one side, revealing an airlock whose other door was already gaping wide.

A tall, gangly, almost coltish young woman with short dark hair and big brown eyes stood inside, a wicked-looking blaster in her hand, barrel pointed downward, finger on the trigger guard. Her posture and her expression signaled caution, distrust, and perhaps even an undercurrent of fear. Cullop raised both hands.

"I'm unarmed, as you can see, Apprentice Officer Fennon. Will you grant me permission to come aboard?"

Carrie seemed momentarily thrown by Cullop's question and merely stared at her as if she'd expected the Navy to barge in rather than follow the customary courtesies.

"Um, yes. I suppose." She stepped back and waved Cullop into the airlock.

"I brought twenty naval crew and twenty-five soldiers with me, Officer Fennon. They'll stay aboard the shuttles until you let them disembark. Captain Dunmoore assigned me the role of *Kattegat Maru*'s relief captain until we recover your crew or dock at a suitable port, since an apprentice officer can't legally act as master. *Kattegat Maru* will temporarily hold the status of a Fleet Auxiliary vessel and you that of a temporary civilian Fleet employee, so I can run her as a naval unit without breaking any laws. But your family's ownership remains unchanged."

A dubious frown creased Fennon's smooth forehead.

"Does that mean I must obey your orders?"

"It does."

"But it's my ship."

"And that makes you no different from any other ship-owner who doesn't hold a merchant officer's certificate. You may consider yourself a supercargo if you prefer."

Fennon considered Cullop's suggestion for a moment, then nodded.

"Understood." A pause. "Captain."

— Six —

Carrie Fennon wondered whether she would remember every name and rating as Cullop took her through the ranks and introduced *Kattegat Maru*'s relief crew. They, in turn, met her gaze with the professional confidence she expected from her ship's regular complement, and she saw no hint of unkindness in their eyes.

When Cullop guided her to Command Sergeant Karlo Saari's platoon, formed up beside the relief crew, and introduced him as coming from the Scandia Regiment, Fennon blurted out, "You're not Marines, are you?"

Saari gave her a broad, friendly grin.

"No, Officer Fennon. We're Army through and through. The Marine Corps needed help, and they sent us to show them how it's done."

Fennon didn't know whether he was pulling her leg, so she smiled and nodded once.

"Welcome."

"Don't mind Karlo," Cullop said. "He's blessed with a questionable sense of humor. I understand it's a Scandian thing."

"And so it is, sir. As you might remember, Scandia is known as the happiest place in the galaxy." That statement drew a few muffled groans from the soldiers behind him.

"If you'll follow me, I can introduce you to those blessed by that happiness."

Another bewildering round of names, ranks, and functions jostled for space in Carrie's head. But these strange, smiling soldiers seemed to exude the same quiet competence as the spacers, and for the first time since her uncle Steph shoved her into the shielded cubbyhole, Carrie felt a glimmer of hope.

"Might I suggest we head for the passenger cabins so the relief crew can settle in, Officer Fennon?" Cullop asked after the introductions were over. "When everyone's stripped off their tin suit, you can show us around *Kattegat Maru*. Not everybody at once but in small groups, spacers first. And I'm really curious to see where you hid."

Fennon noticed how carefully Cullop worded the request, reinforcing the notion she and the others were temporary, here to help until *Kattegat Maru*'s rightful crew could return. It gave her mood an unexpected lift.

"Please follow me, Captain." This time she neither paused nor hesitated before giving Lieutenant Commander Cullop the proper courtesy title.

**

"So?" Dunmoore raised a questioning eyebrow moments after the video link between *Iolanthe* and *Kattegat Maru* went live.

"Yulia confirms there's nothing wrong with the ship, sir." Cullop was referring to Lieutenant Yulia Zhukov, one of the Q-ship's engineering officers, and for now, the freighter's relief chief engineer. "She should be able to accelerate, decelerate, go FTL, or maneuver on thrusters. Her environmental suite is clean and functional, as are the secondary systems. Chief Henkman checked the shield generators and guns, and they too are functional. If we were the ones to find her with no Apprentice Officer Fennon aboard, we'd be scratching our heads right now. For a ship older than most of *Iolanthe*'s crew, she's in remarkably good condition."

"What about the logs?"

"Wiped, as Fennon said. The captain's log, the navigation log, and the sensor log all stop right after *Kattegat Maru* emerged from her last FTL jump. And the passenger manifest is gone."

"What are the chances of recovering something?"

Cullop, a slim, short-haired, prematurely gray woman in her late thirties was alone on the bridge, sitting in Captain Aurelia Fennon's command chair. She shrugged.

"That's Chief Day's domain, sir. I fired a copy of everything over to him a few hours ago. If he's made any progress by now, we'd have heard."

"Do you expect problems sailing *Kattegat Maru*?"

"No." Cullop looked around the small bridge with its efficient layout. "As I said, she's in good condition. Apprentice Officer Fennon is proving to be extremely useful in helping us figure everything out. I don't doubt she'll pass her watch-keeping certification on the first try."

"Good. Now what we need is figure out our next destination. If Chief Day can't restore anything useful from the erased logs, I'm afraid we'll need to make for the nearest port."

"Perhaps I could offer a suggestion or two, sir. Talking with Carrie Fennon about *Kattegat Maru*'s regular ports of call got me thinking. You know most merchant ships working the frontiers visit places that aren't officially run by the Commonwealth, right? At least those ships not belonging to the big companies such as Black Nova. I'm talking about outposts and stations established under private charters with private money and no permits from the Colonial Office. No one talks about them, and they're not listed in any official registers."

"Yes."

Cullop fancied she could see Dunmoore's brain already working out the implications, thanks to the familiar gleam in her gray eyes. It was the same one the CIC crew always saw when she worked out tactical angles before a battle.

"If we take it as a given the attack wasn't opportunistic but deliberate and planned well ahead of time, our pirates might come from one of the unauthorized outposts hidden away in this part of the frontier. They would offer the perfect opportunity to place a subspace tracking device or even an infiltrator aboard *Kattegat Maru*."

"Did she visit any of these shady places recently?"

A wry smile twisted Cullop's face.

"The logs mention nothing, sir. Which is what I expected. While it's not exactly illegal to trade with unregistered colonies, the government likes to collect its share of taxes from commercial transactions. If the tax collectors can't take them from those outposts, they will squeeze merchant shippers instead. Therefore, neither visits nor transactions are logged. And so far, Apprentice Officer Fennon is being extremely cagey about discussing the matter. But I'll keep trying to convince her we would only use the information to look for her crew, not to sic the government on *Kattegat Maru* over accounting mistakes."

"You mentioned a subspace tracking device or infiltrator. Did you see evidence of either?"

"No. Nor would I expect any. If the goal was to create a mystery, they'll have removed the evidence."

Dunmoore nodded.

"Of course. How do merchant captains store the navigation instructions to find those hidden gems, Emma? Assuming they don't want government inspectors to discover them because keeping the locations confidential is part of the deal with it comes to docking or landing there, right?"

"Correct, sir. Confidentiality is big with unregistered outposts. Portable storage would be my guess. A memory chip embedded in jewelry for example. Captain Aurelia Fennon would have been wearing or carrying her confidential navigation instructions when the pirates took *Kattegat Maru*, meaning we won't find them. I'm not even sure Carrie would know, but I'll keep trying for an answer to that question as well."

"Did you ever visit an unregistered colony before the war?"

"No. I didn't work on independent merchantmen inclined to veer off regular shipping lanes for undeclared trading, but one hears things in the Guild saloons when booze is flowing. There will be hidden outposts in this area, but don't ask me where or what their names are. It's been years since I last listened to a captain with questionable ethics discuss the most profitable ports no one knows about."

"Understood. Keep at it, but remember we don't enjoy the luxury of time. Either we go after the pirates to find *Kattegat Maru*'s crew, or we head for the nearest port. The Admiralty won't thank me for sitting here doing nothing while the war is still on. Was there anything else?"

"Not at the moment, sir."

"Dunmoore, out."

Cullop sat back and exhaled slowly. Time for another chat with Apprentice Officer Fennon. Though the young woman seemed happy that competent professionals now safeguarded her family's ship, she still had a long way to go before trusting them with family secrets. And Cullop knew how that felt.

She too was raised aboard a family ship, leaving it only at her parents' behest so she could gain experience on corporate vessels. After it vanished without a trace one day with her entire family when she wasn't yet twenty-five years old, Cullop remained with the same shipping line right until the war. There was little else she could do under the circumstances.

**

"Would it be impertinent of me to ask when you plan on informing Special Operations Command of the *Kattegat Maru* business?" Holt asked once Emma Cullop's face faded from the day cabin's main display. "At some point, we need to account for our movements, if only so HQ can ping the right subspace array. You know, in case someone with stars on his or her collar feels the urge to send us fresh orders or asks for a copy of our patrol log."

Dunmoore gave her first officer a wry smile.

"I've been struggling with that question, Zeke, believe it or not. And that struggle will become more intense if Emma gets Carrie Fennon to talk about *Kattegat Maru*'s undocumented forays into the unclaimed frontier zone."

"Share the burden, Skipper. It might not feel half as heavy afterward, but at least you'll make me just as miserable as you are."

"I'm afraid if I tell HQ we picked up a crewless Skeid class freighter in good condition, they'll order me to hand it over so that SOCOM can increase its flotilla of irregular starships."

"We didn't find *Kattegat Maru* completely abandoned nor did we seize her in battle, so the Navy can't call on the normal salvage rules and make a claim."

"For the bureaucratic gnomes of this galaxy, it's a mere detail, Zeke. They wouldn't care that I gave my word to Carrie Fennon. The war will be over, and young Carrie an old age pensioner before the lawyers sort things out."

Holt grunted disconsolately.

"Why must we always keep in mind our superiors might do what's expedient instead of what's right?"

"SOCOM needs hulls for undercover work and converting a prize is the quickest, most cost-effective way. I doubt we'll see another *Iolanthe* any time soon, if ever. Regular Fleet admirals probably howled at the idea of a special ops battlecruiser in the first place. So I can't quite discount the justification of wartime requirements trumping private ownership, let alone our betters overriding the word of a captain who didn't have the authority to give it."

"What are you going to do?"

"Hope we somehow find a lead in the next forty-eight to seventy-two hours. Then, I can claim hot pursuit. If we find Fennon's crewmates, we can turn the ship back to them, no harm, no foul."

"You'd take *Kattegat Maru* along on a hot pursuit? She's not a warship under the skin like *Iolanthe*."

The question wasn't so much skepticism on Holt's part, but more his doing a first officer's job by analyzing the factors and forcing her to do the same.

"I'm open to alternative suggestions, Zeke, but yeah. We can't just leave her here or send her off to port by herself."

"I suppose not. Although, it might be instructive if only to see who shows up to find her if our working theory is correct."

"Or we could leave a stealth probe that'll do the same job without exposing *Kattegat Maru* to any new dangers."

"Or we could do that. I'll have one prepared, just in case."

— Seven —

Cullop found Carrie Fennon alone in the crew mess, nursing a lukewarm tea. The young woman glanced up and put on a weak smile, then turned her eyes back at the milky brown dregs in her cup. Cullop went to the samovar, poured herself a healthy serving and, disdaining any additives, wandered over to where Fennon sat at a scarred plastic table. It probably dated back to *Kattegat Maru*'s original configuration, well before either of them was born.

"Care for company?"

"You're the captain, Captain." Fennon jerked her chin at a vacant chair without looking up.

"How's your morale, Carrie?"

Fennon essayed a dismissive shrug. It came across as a jerky, unconvincing gesture.

"I'm breathing air instead of vacuum, I'm surrounded by the Navy and the Army, and so far my family still owns *Kattegat Maru*. For an independent trader picked over by pirates, it couldn't be better."

"Things could always be better. Or worse. At least that's been my experience. I was a starship baby too. My parents, they owned a nice little two-hander called *Juliette* and raised me to be a merchant spacer. I passed my watch-keeping certificate six weeks after turning seventeen. The Guild examiner was impressed. Then, the day I turned eighteen, my parents farmed me out to Smyrna Shipping as the sixth officer on a container ship, to get experience in the big leagues before they retired and gave me *Juliette*. I made it to third officer before those damned boneheads invaded. The Navy took my ship into service as an auxiliary transport, along with the entire crew. And that was the end of my civilian career."

"What are your folks doing these days?" Fennon's question seemed pro forma as if to show she wasn't snubbing her new captain, though Cullop knew she would rather be left to fret about her mother in silence.

"They're probably dead. Or at least I hope they are and not serving as human chattel for some alien asshole hundreds of light years away. *Juliette* vanished a long time ago out in the Shield Sector. I figure reivers caught up with her."

Fennon's head came up, and she stared at Cullop in stunned silence for a few moments.

"I'm sorry."

"So am I. But my father enjoyed taking chances. He pushed the odds by going where no one else would because it paid so well. Until his luck ran out. If they hadn't sent me to work for Smyrna, you and I wouldn't be talking, so he made at least one good decision in his life, other than marrying my mother."

"What will you do after the war?"

"Stay in the Navy, if they'll keep me. It's been a good hitch so far, and anyone could do a lot worse than serve under Captain Dunmoore. She's not exactly a by-the-book skipper."

Cullop took a sip of tea and repressed a grimace. It wasn't particularly good. Over-brewed, bitter and excessively tannic.

"But she gets things done. And right now, what she wants to do is find *Katie*'s crew and passengers. Problem is, we don't know where the pirates went, and without at least a clue, the captain will receive orders to bring your ship to the nearest port before returning to her regular duties. What happens after that will be between your lawyers and the Navy's."

Fennon's face twisted into a scowl. "I'm not giving *Katie* to the Navy. I'll scuttle her before that happens."

"Then help Captain Dunmoore help you, Carrie. She doesn't want to give your ship away either, but she's a Navy officer, and we're in a war. Personal preferences don't come into it."

A derisive snort. Then, "How the hell am I supposed to help? I was stuck in a damned cubbyhole."

"We think the pirates tagged *Katie* and followed her here, where they could ambush you with no one noticing. And it probably happened at one of the outposts that aren't supposed to exist, the sort where merchant captains make their profits off the books. Pirates hang around those places between raids."

When Cullop saw Fennon's expression turn to stone, she chuckled.

"I overheard a lot of talk in various Guild saloons during my time with Smyrna Shipping. Never visited them myself. Smyrna didn't sail beyond the Commonwealth sphere, and *Juliette* worked along the Shield Sector's outer edge, not around here. Want to know what I think? Your crew and the passengers are headed for one of those outposts right now. Maybe the same one where the pirates tagged this ship."

Carrie gave Cullop a defiant stare but *Iolanthe*'s second officer merely smiled.

"Help Captain Dunmoore help you. Tell me at which of the unregistered outposts *Kattegat Maru* docked before the pirate attack."

"What would you do with that information? *If* I could answer." Still defiant, but with uncertainty in those big brown eyes.

"Go there and find your mother, her crew, and the passengers."

"Just like that. With a supply ship resembling an idiotically slow bulk freighter instead of a frigate or a destroyer?"

Cullop nodded, still smiling.

"Yep. Just like that. *Iolanthe*'s bite is a lot bigger than you might expect. The Navy lets its replenishment ships sail without an escort for a good reason, Carrie. Think about it."

"And if Captain Dunmoore goes chasing after my mother and the rest, what happens to us? To *Katie*? We're not a Navy ship."

"We're an auxiliary naval vessel now."

Fennon's face briefly took on an exasperated air, as if she thought Cullop was deliberately obtuse.

"You know what I mean, sir."

"We follow *Iolanthe* wherever she goes, but stay out of her way. At least that's what I figure Captain Dunmoore intends. She can't just leave us here, or send us to the nearest civilian port by ourselves."

"Why wouldn't she send us to a port?"

Cullop explained their theory the pirates left *Kattegat Maru* as a mysteriously abandoned vessel for someone to find so she might cover a specific abduction or serve as a message. When she fell silent, Fennon seemed lost in thought, eyes staring once more at the dregs in her cup.

"Kilia."

"Beg pardon?" Cullop asked.

"Kilia Station. That was our last port of call. It's one of those rogue places on the frontier, a hollowed-out asteroid in a dead star system. My mother didn't enjoy heading there, but cargoes to and from Kilia pay well, and we can always use the money."

**

"Sorry." Lieutenant Astrid Drost looked up from the navigation console and turned to Dunmoore. "There's no Kilia Station listed. I tried every possible spelling variation."

Dunmoore glanced at the bridge's main display.

"Carrie Fennon can't tell us in which system we might find this station, nor does she know where her mother keeps the navigation instructions for the special places, right, Emma?"

Cullop shook her head.

"No. Captain Aurelia Fennon kept that information to herself, so no one could accidentally say the wrong thing after one too many drinks at the Guild or in a spaceport bar. Or when a federal inspector came calling. And it's a reasonable fear. I discovered the existence of outlaw colonies precisely because of unguarded talk in the Guild saloon."

"That doesn't help us much."

A faint smile appeared on Cullop's lips.

"No, but Carrie says the system in question is a three day FTL jump from this location. Seventy hours from the system's heliopause, give or take. Her mother always made a long leg coming out of the frontier region, to throw off anyone with bad intentions."

Holt made a face.

"It didn't work this time. But that's another bit of evidence the attack wasn't random. The pirates most certainly tracked them."

Drost silently worked the navigation plot for a little longer, then said, "Depending on how hard Captain Fennon was pushing her drives, there are eight star systems within seventy hours of our current position. None with known outposts or colonies. At least not officially. All have planets, most of them hostile to human life. A few terrifyingly so."

"It'll take weeks to search every system, Skipper. We might hit the jackpot and find Kilia on the first try. But the Admiralty won't let us go off on our own for that long if it turns out we're not lucky."

"True. We need more clues." Dunmoore glanced at Cullop again. "Keep talking with Carrie and see if she remembers anything else."

"And search the navigation logs, Emma," Drost said. "Even if they erased anything related to this Kilia Station and replaced it with fake data to show they never came near the place, mistakes are always possible. The tiniest thing might give us added data to narrow down the possibilities."

"That was my next task. Carrie Fennon is trying, Captain. The Almighty knows she's trying. Once she internalized the notion that leaving *Kattegat Maru* at the nearest port to be fought over by lawyers might represent the end of the Fennon family transport emporium, she talked. But Aurelia Fennon seems to keep many things from her daughter. It wouldn't surprise me to find she engaged in illicit activities as a way of boosting profits. Nothing which might entail a twenty-year sentence on Parth, but illicit commerce that comes with a stiff fine and confiscated cargo. Keeping an old ship such as this in such good condition takes money."

"Understood. If you think my speaking with Carrie Fennon in person might help, I'll gladly come for a visit."

"And satisfy your curiosity about *Kattegat Maru*," Holt muttered. The devilish glint in his one eye and his teasing tone brought a brief but rueful smile to Dunmoore's face. "You know you want to."

"Guilty. But let's focus on the mission, not my curiosity."

She looked at each of her principal officers in turn, silently asking if they wanted to add anything else. When the last, Cullop, shook her head, Dunmoore stood.

"Let's do it, then. We'll regroup at the end of the watch and assess our progress at finding this mysterious Kilia Station."

"CIC to the bridge."

Dunmoore held up her hand, ordering everyone to stay, including Cullop. Lieutenant Commander Sirico, who listened in on the conversation from his regular duty station, wouldn't interrupt unless it was urgent.

"Dunmoore."

"Chief Yens picked up a hyperspace trail heading in our general direction from the frontier."

"Tatiana's theoretical finders already?" Holt glanced at his captain with a raised eyebrow.

"Perhaps. It's been what? Almost four days since the attack. And this isn't near any charted star lane. Or it could be another merchant ship heading home after making a few more creds by trading with quasi-outlaws." Dunmoore thought for a moment, gloved hand stroking the scar on her jawline. "All right. Here's what we'll do, in case this is someone who knows where the pirates left *Kattegat Maru*. Emma, put everyone in battlesuits so their life signs are dampened, then make like you're a derelict."

"I have no suit for Carrie, meaning it's back into the shielded cubbyhole."

"Whatever works. *Iolanthe* will rig for silent running right away and then quietly go to battle stations without unmasking. If, and that's a big if, these are people interested in *Kattegat Maru*, I want to lure them close and then pull a partial Furious Faerie transformation, but as our privateer alter ego, *Persephone*. That means you, Emma, are running a privateer's prize crew and Sergeant

Saari is now back in the Varangian Company. If we play this right, perhaps they can tell us where Kilia Station is hiding. Questions?"

When no one answered, she clapped her hands.

"Let's move, people." Dunmoore gestured at the officer of the watch. "Call it, please."

Moments later, Sub Lieutenant Rin Pashar's voice rang out over the public address system.

"Now hear this, *Iolanthe* will rig for silent running immediately. I repeat, *Iolanthe* will rig for silent running immediately. That is all."

— Eight —

"I can still pick up faint life signs from *Kattegat Maru*," Yens reported once Cullop called in to confirm her ship was ready. "But since we're almost alongside, I know where she is, and my sensors can beat the pants off any civilian grade stuff, that's not surprising."

"You, however, vanished from my crappy civilian grade sensors, Chief," Cullop said over the tight-beam comlink between both ships. She wore her battlesuit, complete with helmet, but her visor was still raised. "Watching *Iolanthe* turn into a hole in space was an interesting experience. I can still see you on visual because I know where to look and you're blotting out the background stars, but that's it. Someone dropping out of FTL nearby will only see an abandoned *Katie*."

Dunmoore nodded her approval. "And that's how we want it. How's Carrie Fennon?"

"She understandably resisted returning to the cubbyhole. But Yulia rigged a way for me to keep in touch and let her see what's happening from the bridge perspective without compromising the cubbyhole's shielding. Crisis averted. Oh, and just so you know, Carrie remembered at the last moment she found the hangar deck depressurized and the space doors open, so we're replicating that as we speak."

"Excellent. Tell her I said good catch. If that was it, Emma, say bye-bye."

"Bye-bye." Cullop's smiling face faded from the secondary display.

With nothing else to do, Dunmoore mentally ran through every scenario she could think of, her eyes fixed on the CIC's holographic tactical projection. The fish tank as some called it. Two blue icons represented *Iolanthe* and *Kattegat Maru.* A third, this one green, was the hyperspace trail picked up by Chief Yens' long-range sensors. Even if the ship making that trail kept going on its merry way, calculating the possible point of origin based on her current vector might narrow down the star system hiding Kilia Station. If that ship came from Kilia Station. So far, everything was a supposition.

Pirates abandoning a perfectly good freighter could be for reasons other than a grand scheme with unknown objectives. Perhaps something scared them away. Or they didn't want an old Skeid class and couldn't bring themselves to destroy it. Or they left her as a ghost ship out of sheer devilment, to mess with any potential salvagers. Even pirates loved to play pranks although few honest people would find them funny.

"Emergence, four hundred and fifty kilometers aft. One ship." The green icon turned purple.

"Extraordinarily precise for something that should be random, such as choosing where to drop out of FTL in interstellar space so one might tune the engines and recalculate one's course," Holt remarked in a dry tone from his station on the bridge.

"Based on the emissions signature," Yens continued, "it's either a high-powered fast trader or someone less honest keeping his emissions dampened. I have a visual."

The image of a sleek starship with swept back hyperdrive nacelle pylons appeared on a side display. Its hull was matte black, with no markings, but liberally pitted and streaked by atmospheric re-entries. Small bumps precisely distributed along its topside and keel could only be one thing: retracted gun turrets. Of course, *Kattegat Maru* was equally well equipped and she was an ordinary, inoffensive merchantman.

"Clearly of human construction rather than Shrehari, although it could be crewed by anyone."

"I doubt the Shrehari would bother taking something of ours into service, Chief. They'd find it a tad cramped."

"Aye, but the boneheads have subject species that aren't as big as they are. Although the buggers don't let them play without supervision, I suppose." A red pointer appeared on the display and hovered over a larger, flatter bump near the ship's nose. "That could hide missile launchers. And if so, it's not an honest trader."

"Agreed, Chief." Dunmoore's eyes narrowed as she studied the intruder. Anti-ship missiles were expensive. Too expensive for honest traders who preferred evading danger through speed and stealth rather than brute force.

"No beacon, which isn't unusual out here. He's decelerating."

"And the only reason would be *Kattegat Maru*."

"How do you intend to play it, Skipper?" Holt asked.

"If he comes near enough without spotting us, we do a partial reveal. Only the tier one guns he'd expect from a privateer. It should suffice to put his captain in a talkative mood."

"Emma just reported that he's pinging *Kattegat Maru* with his sensors," Thorin Sirico said. "Let's hope he's sticking to a narrow cone. Otherwise, he'll pick up evidence of a ghost. A huge ghost."

The minutes ticked by as they watched the newcomer adjust his course to match *Kattegat Maru*'s while decelerating.

"Looks as if he'll be coming alongside her at about ninety degrees from us on the zee axis. That's almost ideal." Sirico sounded like a man about to enjoy himself. "Although I can't believe he hasn't spotted us yet."

Dunmoore made a dismissive sound.

"Confirmation bias. Since he's not expecting *Kattegat Maru* to be found so quickly out in the dark, he's not expecting anyone else to be around. The sensor scans are probably out of reflex, to make sure the target's status hasn't changed."

"That'll cost him, Captain."

She shrugged.

"So far, he's done nothing wrong, and if he's on the Navy's most wanted list, Chief Yens would have found a match in the database by now. Yes, he knew where to find her, but that doesn't prove he's guilty of piracy. Not yet. Let's watch and wait."

More time passed while the intruder maneuvered to close with *Kattegat Maru*, still oblivious to the large mass moving in tandem with their target.

"I always love these moments," Sirico said. "Scaring the crap out of unsuspecting bastards when we suddenly show up on their sensors, looking like the angel of death."

Major Salminen gave him a broad grin.

"Should I worry that you seem to love your job so much?"

He made a dismissive hand gesture.

"Certainly not. You may be a pongo, but you're still one of the favored few serving the Furious Faerie."

"Favored few? I suppose it's better to do the scaring than be the one running for the heads."

"You said it, sister." Sirico rubbed his hands with glee. "Just a little closer, my pretty, so I can show you my big guns."

Dunmoore, a smile tugging at her lips, gave *Iolanthe*'s combat systems officer a mock exasperated glare.

In return, Sirico put on a contrite look as insincere as it was exaggerated.

"Okay, okay. I'll enjoy these sublime moments more quietly in future." He composed himself and sat back in his chair. "This is me, basking in quiet pleasure."

"I still can't believe they didn't spot us yet," Salminen said.

"We won't be invisible for much longer." Dunmoore nodded at the tactical projection, now scaled up to show three ships within the same fifty cubic kilometers of space. "Once they match velocity with us, I'll sic Thorin on them."

"Maybe it'll be even funnier if we let them board, Skipper," Holt suggested. "I'm sure between them, Emma and Sergeant Saari can prepare a warm welcome. Then we light up. With part of their crew away, they'll hesitate just long enough for the situation to sink in."

"If they don't spot us first."

"As you said, the bastards don't expect an interloper, so they're not looking for one. Let the candidates for interrogation come to us instead of us trying to pry them out of their hull."

Dunmoore mulled over the suggestion, eyes fixed on the approaching ship's image, weighing the pros and the cons.

Then Sirico raised his hand to attract her attention.

"I asked Emma. She's good with the idea. Sergeant Saari is even more enthusiastic."

"I suppose there's no harm in trying. Tell Emma to go ahead. But let's make damned sure they don't catch on we're Fleet."

"I sent Karlo across in gear with no identifying marks," Salminen said. "He'll play Varangian Company mercenary without letting on it's a sham."

An air of anticipation cloaked the CIC while they watched the unknown ship come to a relative rest five kilometers from *Kattegat Maru* and a mere thirty from *Iolanthe*, its velocity matching theirs.

"Here we go," Yens said. "It doesn't get better than this."

"Sure it does, Chief." Sirico gave her a bloodthirsty grin. "Wait for it."

"No need to wait, sir. They launched a shuttle. Unmarked, of course, and no beacon. Standard civilian model with add-on weapon pods. That thing can carry twenty warm bodies, max."

"Which it won't. Twenty could easily represent half of the crew. They're not expecting to face a platoon of the Scandia Regiment's finest aboard a supposedly empty starship ripe for salvage."

"Don't let Karlo Saari know you've called him and his people the regiment's finest, even if it was in jest, Captain. Otherwise, the entire company will never hear the end of it."

Dunmoore gave Salminen a wink and a grin.

"Don't worry."

"Emma reports ready to capture boarders. Apparently, Sergeant Saari and his soldiers are giggling with glee."

Salminen sighed.

"I doubt that's even close to being an exaggeration. They've not seen much action in recent weeks, and we ground pounders love a good ambush."

"The shuttle is lining up with the hangar doors," Yens said.

And still nothing to show the newcomers were aware of a Q-ship watching them with hungry eyes.

— Nine —

"This seems almost too easy," Emma Cullop whispered, eyes on the bridge's main display as she watched a small spacecraft pass through the open doors with exquisite care. Then she realized how asinine whispering was. Everyone on the bridge, everyone aboard for that matter except Carrie Fennon, wore a tightly buttoned battlesuit. She could scream inside her helmet, but with both crew and soldiers on strict radio silence, no one would hear.

A secondary display showed Karlo Saari's troops hidden away in the corridor leading to the hangar deck airlock. Another gave her a glimpse of those waiting in readiness behind the stacked containers that hid *Iolanthe*'s shuttles. They were prepared to seize the intruding craft once its occupants entered through the airlock.

The newcomer, an ordinary civilian model common throughout human space with multi-barrel gun pods on either side and on the top, settled gently in the center of the deck. Its aft ramp dropped to disgorge six figures in armored pressure suits as unmarked as everything else.

They carried backpacks, slung carbines, and blasters holstered at the waist. She recognized the carbines as obsolete military variants, the sort still in use by various national guards and planetary militias.

One of the figures, perhaps the leader, broke away from the group and headed for the airlock with a determined pace. There, he entered the code in use at the time of *Kattegat Maru*'s capture. It proved they or someone they knew had recently been in contact with the freighter's crew.

Cullop unlocked the door remotely from the bridge, to give the illusion that the old code still worked. It pulled back and to one side without a sound, opening on an empty airlock that appeared as it was when the pirates left days earlier. The leader motioned his crew in, then closed the outer door again before triggering the pressurization cycle.

When the panel glowed a soft green, he opened the inner door and stepped into the corridor which ran along the bulkhead separating the hangar from the ship's forward half before turning at ninety-degree angles on both the port and starboard sides.

One of Sergeant Saari's fire teams waited behind a half-closed door in the control room, next to the airlock. Two more fire teams hid around each corner while Saari and a fourth fire team waited in the storage compartment across from the airlock.

Sergeant First Class Mattis and two more fire teams were on the hangar deck, waiting to seize the shuttle which still sat with its ramp open.

The six intruders cautiously turned right and headed for the bend. Almost immediately, Saari broke radio silence and yelled out the 3rd Battalion's beloved war cry.

"*Hakkaa päälle.*"

In a matter of seconds, the boarding party found itself boxed in by nine menacing soldiers in battle armor who pointed lethal weapons at their helmet visors, a suit's most vulnerable point.

"Surrender or die." Saari's voice boomed through external speakers loud enough to deafen anyone without hearing protection.

After exchanging glances with his men, the leader barked out an order, and they carefully placed their carbines on the deck before raising their hands.

Back on the bridge, Cullop gestured toward Chief Henkman at the technical console.

"Close the space doors."

She switched her gaze to the display showing *Kattegat Maru*'s hangar deck just in time to see Mattis and her teams rush the shuttle. Moments later, they pushed a pressure-suited prisoner down the ramp and shoved him toward the airlock.

Seven for seven. And a shuttle to boot.

As prearranged, Saari took the prisoners to cargo hold C, where they stripped off their pressure suits and clothes before being searched, and handed black coveralls.

Carrie Fennon, released from her cubbyhole by Lieutenant Zhukov the moment Cullop sounded the all-clear, watched the scene with undisguised satisfaction. The soldiers then shackled their prisoners at the ankles and wrists and left them to stew while Captain Dunmoore dealt with their ship.

**

Sirico pumped a fist in the air. "And one for the Furious Faerie's sidekick, our lovely *Katie*. Emma reports seven boarders in the brig, one shuttle seized, no shots fired."

"Meaning we can go up systems and become, if not quite the Furious Faerie, then something almost as frightening. Ping him hard with your targeting sensors, Thorin. Let him know we're here and when he looks, let him see our tier one ordnance."

Dunmoore would have enjoyed seeing the other captain's face when a starship of *Iolanthe*'s size suddenly appeared out of nowhere without warning.

"Signals, open a channel. I want to speak to the ship's captain. Audio only. And bring Lieutenant Commander Cullop in on the link. She should hear everything."

A few minutes passed before an angry, rumbling voice spat, "Who the fuck are you and what the fuck do you want."

"I could ask you the same question," Dunmoore replied in honeyed tones. "But without using crude expletives. They make one sound like such an uncouth space rat, don't you think. And just so you understand the situation, my guns are locked onto your ship and will shred it if you so much as annoy me. At this close range, I won't even waste a missile. Now, let's try this again. Who are you and why did you send people to board my prize?"

"*Your* prize?" His outrage sounded only partially feigned.

"Mine. I found her abandoned, the crew gone without a trace, so under Commonwealth salvage laws, I claimed her as mine. Your boarding party is, as we speak, in *Kattegat Maru*'s brig under guard while we establish whether they're pirates and should be spaced without a trial." She paused, then in a commanding, almost cruel tone she snapped, "State your name, the name of your ship and the nature of your business here. Don't try my patience because it will be the last thing you do."

"Kotto Piris," the man finally replied in a grudging tone. "My ship is the fast trader *Kurgan*. And you are?"

Her voice softened again.

"Shannon O'Donnell, of the privateer *Persephone*."

"A fat tub such as yours with a letter of marque?" Piris exploded. "Did the imbeciles at the Admiralty finally lose what little was left of their minds."

"I could point out you're under my guns and unable to flee without suffering fatal damage," she replied in a reasonable tone. "That means my fat tub trumps your fast trader, which is what really counts. Why are you here, in interstellar space, attempting to recover a ship that was abandoned only days ago? We stumbled across her by accident, but you came out of FTL almost dead on."

"And ambushed me, damn you. Why not send out a friendly warning before we boarded *your* prize?"

Piris' attempt at sarcasm made his increasing annoyance clear.

"I wanted to see what you would do. Now that I have, I can only conclude you came specifically to recover her and aren't here by accident since your boarding party entered the correct the airlock entry code."

Dunmoore heard sounds resembling a muffled curse over the comlink.

"That's two points against you, Captain Piris. One, you knew where to find her and two, you knew how to board her. I'd say there are grounds to suspect you're in league with whoever kidnapped the crew and took off a cargo hold's worth of valuable items. My letter of marque covers dealing with pirates, so I'd be within my rights to seize your ship and crew, or simply blow you up, depending on how I feel when this conversation is over. Even if I do overstep my limits, the Admiralty won't mind. Not when it comes to pirates."

"You're playing a dangerous game, O'Donnell, messing with powerful forces that don't fear the Navy, let alone a mangy privateer with delusions of adequacy."

"Care to explain, so I can judge whether I should be afraid? Threats only work if there's something to back them up. Your powerful forces don't have their guns on me right now. I, on the other hand, can wreck you with one salvo."

Piris was silent for almost a minute. Then he said, "Tell you what. Give me that nasty old tub, and we'll call it even. I won't mention you exist, and you can go make someone else's life miserable. Final offer."

"Do you like your people, Captain Piris?" Dunmoore's menacingly honeyed tones were back. "And more importantly, do they respect you? My prize crew has seven of them in custody. I merely need to give the order, and they'll space one of your men. Or more, if that's my fancy. And they'll keep doing so until your entire boarding party is dead. Unless you tell me what I wish to know. Then, we can call it even."

A written message shimmered before her eyes.

Emma says Sergeant Saari can dummy up the boarders' pressure suits so that if you want to fake tossing a few of them out, they'll do it. He'll make the dummies look as if there's a head suffering catastrophic decompression behind an open helmet visor.

Dunmoore glanced at Sirico and nodded once. He gave her thumbs up.

"Are you still there, Captain Piris? What's your answer? Will you make your crew happy or nervous? It's all the same to me. Signals, tell the prize captain to select a prisoner and stand by for my orders. It doesn't matter who. Unless Captain Piris has a preference." Dunmoore paused before asking, "Is there anyone you wouldn't miss, Kotto? Or are they equally useless to you?"

When he didn't reply, Dunmoore said, "The prize crew is to shove a prisoner out the main airlock. Perhaps that will get Captain Piris' attention. Or better yet, that of his crew, which will find itself with one less comrade in the mess tonight. Watching a mutiny unfold could be entertaining."

— Ten —

"No. Wait." Piris' voice held a hint of panic. At that moment, Dunmoore knew he wasn't a dread pirate or a soulless reiver. A small-time mercenary, perhaps. A smuggler most certainly. But not one of those maladjusted personalities who find an outlet for their appetites by preying on others. "What do you want to know?"

"Let's start with my first question. Why are you here?"

"I'm on a contract, okay. Just a damned contract. Someone hired me to find an abandoned tub by the name *Kattegat Maru* — last known coordinates here — claim her as salvage, and bring her to Scandia where a lawyer is waiting. He's supposed to pay me the second half of my fee and take charge of the ship."

"Who paid you the first half?"

"A guy on Kilia Station who doesn't want his name spoken aloud."

"Who? Or do I start the first round of fatal spacewalks?"

Piris sighed.

"Enoc Tarrant. He's a big man on the frontier. Owns a lot of the action, if you know what I mean."

Dunmoore didn't, but it wasn't worth the aggravation to ask.

"Why did he hire you?"

"Not a fucking clue. But the money was good, the work was easy, and I'm between jobs."

And he made a good fall guy, but she didn't have the heart to tell him there wouldn't be a second payment. An arrest, perhaps, on suspicion of piracy.

"Fair enough. Second question. What are Kilia Station's coordinates?"

Piris laughed.

"A privateer who doesn't know about the most important independent outpost on the frontier? Who are you really, O'Donnell?"

"I'm the one who's seconds away from tossing one of your dummies out the door."

"Okay, okay. Don't be so damned hasty. My crew and I, we want to make money. Sometimes we skirt the law a little, but we're not pirates, so there's no reason to kill anyone. I'll give you Kilia Station's coordinates. Just do me a favor and tell whoever asks that you never met me or my ship, okay? We'll forget about whatever your monster is called and go look for odd jobs elsewhere." A pause, then, "I transmitted the navigation instructions to guide you there. Now, do I get my boarding party back?"

"Once we check those navigation instructions. If you're trying to con me, it'll be the last thing you ever do, so sit tight."

"We're good," Holt said from the bridge.

Dunmoore made a chopping motion with her hand, instructing the signals petty officer to cut the link.

"We're clear, Zeke."

"Astrid is checking those coordinates, Skipper. Give her a few minutes. But let me ask you this. Do you trust Piris?"

"No. But I didn't give him time to dummy up a plausible fake location, and I don't see a reason why he'd keep one in his back pocket, ready to toss at gullible privateers. Piris doesn't strike me as a hardened criminal. A liar, sure, and a slippery customer. But a real pirate keeping a sworn secret would let me wipe out the entire boarding party while he thought of a way to escape. And the rest of his crew wouldn't say a word. We'll take a full scan of his emissions signature. If he pulls a fast one, we'll find him again."

"I wish I shared your optimism."

"It's not so much optimism as a realistic appreciation of human nature, Zeke. Piris isn't a genius. Cunning perhaps, but he's slow in other ways. Do you think there really is a lawyer on Scandia waiting to pay him the second half of the salvage fee?"

Holt was silent for a few seconds.

"If there is, he's probably from the firm Dewey, Cheetam, and Howe. In other words, no. At best, he'll face arrest. At worst, a quick death. This is not the sort of scenario where loose ends can be tolerated, and Piris is a very loose end."

"Precisely," Dunmoore said. "He's a link back to Kilia and Enoc Tarrant, who seems to be a man with plenty of juice. Whoever thought up this scheme will have made sure to eliminate any and all links. Piris doesn't know it yet, but we're doing him a favor."

"Should I worry that you dreamed up this twisty theory without my finely honed ex-counterintelligence analyst's instincts?"

"No, you should be proud of teaching your formerly straight-laced captain how to come up with twisty theories."

"Then consider me delighted by my pupil. Ah, Astrid has something for us."

The tactical holo in the CIC swirled until it settled into the representation of a star system, copying the bridge's navigation plot. Drost rattled off a Guide Star Catalog designation that meant nothing to Dunmoore or anyone else.

"It's well outside what we consider the Commonwealth sphere and far enough from the Shrehari Empire to be reasonably safe. The Survey Service passed through this system about half a century ago. It found no inhabitable worlds, though it has three outer gas giants, two inner rocky planets, and a large debris disk that might still, one day, coalesce since this is a very young star. Apparently, this Kilia Station is inside a large asteroid at the edge of the debris disk."

A new image flashed on the CIC's main display, that of a somewhat oval rock. But with no immediately visible points of reference, judging its size was impossible.

"Kilia either already had enough spin to create something approximating one gee, or they imparted spin with impellers." A red pointer appeared. "That seems to be an entrance, a big one. There are no visible docking facilities, and the instructions provided by Captain Piris merely discuss rules about orbiting Kilia. And that's it, Captain."

"Thank you, Astrid. What's your gut feeling about this?"

"Could the instructions be fake? Sure. But the system they reference exists, and the navigational markers match what the Survey Service reported."

Dunmoore sat back in her command chair and studied the unremarkable rock that might hold answers to the *Kattegat Maru* mystery. "Open a channel with Captain Piris. Audio only again and make sure Lieutenant Commander Cullop is still linked in."

This time, Piris answered right away. "So, are you happy?"

"Provisionally. I will return your boarding party and shuttle in a moment but first I want you to listen carefully, Kotto Piris. If I don't find Kilia with those navigation instructions, I will find you and kill you. Should you discuss our encounter with anyone, I will find you and kill you. If you want to live and con someone else another day, forget this happened. Tell anyone who asks you didn't find *Kattegat Maru*. Perhaps figure a way to return the initial payment on your contract. Then quit this sector and find a new playground. You're done here. Don't come back. Understood?"

"Yeah, yeah. Understood."

"You may not realize it yet and perhaps you never will, but meeting me saved your life and the lives of your crew. This Enoc Tarrant wasn't about to let you live after delivering *Kattegat Maru* to Scandia. I'll let you think about that. O'Donnell, out." When the signals petty officer nodded, she said, "Emma?"

"Here, Captain."

"Tell Sergeant Saari I'm sorry we didn't use his idea, but it's something to remember if we're ever in a similar situation."

"He does seem a little sad right now. I gather we should release the boarding party and send it home to mother."

"If you would. I'm calling this one no harm, no foul, so be gentle and let them leave with their possessions."

"Will do. Could you ask Astrid to send me a copy of those navigation instructions, please? I assume we'll be sailing there as a mismatched space rat flotilla."

"Of course. I can hardly send you to the nearest starbase now that we finally have a lead on *Kattegat Maru*'s kidnapped crew and passengers."

**

"Captain Piris has recovered his shuttle and is accelerating away," Holt announced as he entered Dunmoore's day cabin. "Do you think he'll take your warning to heart?"

She made a dismissive hand gesture.

"I doubt it'll matter to us one way or the other, but he struck me as the sort to consider discretion the better part of valor. He didn't seem frightened enough of this Enoc Tarrant to run back and warn him, but wary enough to stay out of his reach now that he didn't carry out his contract."

"Keep in mind Tarrant must be quite wealthy, powerful, or well-connected. Or all three. That his little empire escaped inclusion in the naval database implies folks within the Commonwealth government or even the Navy itself are hiding Kilia's existence from general knowledge." Holt filled a coffee mug from the urn and dropped into a chair. "What about HQ? Will you tell them we're headed into the wild frontier in the hot pursuit of kidnapped Commonwealth citizens?"

She let a sly smile tug at her lips.

"Of course. I'll send my report shortly before we go FTL."

The first officer snorted.

"Let me guess, you'll phrase it as one of those 'unless ordered to do otherwise' missives. Then, by the time HQ decides differently, we'll be too far from the nearest subspace array and won't get the reply. Sneaky. Though it's pretty telling that you feel the need to do this."

"Captains dodging admirals whose agendas they don't trust is a time-honored naval tradition. Except for a brief period between the invention of the radio and the establishment of the first space navy, when captains couldn't avoid daily if not hourly reports to the flagship or shore HQ."

"Thank the Almighty we've never discovered a way to make interstellar communications instantaneous."

Dunmoore shivered theatrically.

"Heavens forfend. It would have caused even greater disasters than those which befell the Fleet in the war's early years. Can you imagine our intellectually sclerotic, utterly unimaginative, but politically safe flag officers on Earth trying to micromanage some of those engagements? The mind boggles. No. I'll gladly take the inconvenience of not having instantaneous communications over the even greater inconvenience of reporting to HQ every time I feel the need for a bowel movement."

Holt cocked an amused eyebrow at her.

"Surely it's not that bad."

She made a face.

"I exaggerate, true. But not by much. There are seniors officers in SOCOM — I won't name anyone — who make micromanagers look like mission command devotees. Pray that none of them ever gets a command running special ops in deep space."

A playful glint appeared in Holt's single eye.

"Apparently, something similar is said about you, Skipper. But for very different reasons." Before she could think of a biting reply, he drained the mug and sprang to his feet. "I'll make sure we're ready to leave, so you can send that report."

— Eleven —

"*Kattegat Maru* kept almost perfect station," Chief Yens reported once human nausea and machine disorientation evaporated, allowing her systems to reach out. "She's doing a good job at running silent. Kudos to Commander Cullop and Lieutenant Zhukov. I see her only because I know where she is. Anyone who doesn't, won't."

Five minutes later, Yens declared no threat within range and Dunmoore ordered the ship to stand down from battle stations, confident Cullop was doing the same without prompting. Their brief conversation between FTL jumps gave Siobhan confidence *Iolanthe*'s second officer had *Katie* well in hand, to the point of continuing Carrie Fennon's education and training to prepare her for the Guild examination boards. Perhaps with even more intensity than her mother might prefer.

"Commander Cullop is calling, sir."

"Put her on."

"Good evening, Captain. Or at least my universal timekeeper says it's just past six bells in the dog watch. *Iolanthe* made a good passage, I trust?"

"Perfectly adequate, Emma, and your timekeeper is correct. How does *Kattegat Maru* fare?"

"Also adequate, though Sergeant Saari's soldiers are getting a little stir crazy. As I mentioned when we last spoke, he set up a parkour course through the ship to keep them in fighting trim and is using the hangar deck for simulations. But it's not *Iolanthe,* and there's precious little for them to do here. If it weren't for the fact we're deep inside the badlands and *Kattegat Maru*'s no warship, I might suggest we dispense with a Marine detail, but as it is... Perhaps we could switch 1st Platoon out for another one and give Saari's lot a break."

Dunmoore glanced over her shoulder at Salminen, who nodded and said, "I figured we'd switch platoons around at some point. Aase Jensen's people can be ready whenever you want, sir."

"Before our jump inward, so sometime in the next few hours, while we make sure this is the right system and no one with bad intent is lurking nearby."

"Roger that," Cullop said. "I'll have Saari and a shuttle readied. We can do it before the end of the evening watch. On a related note, since *Kattegat Maru* is to loiter at the hyperlimit, running silent while you visit Kilia Station, Carrie asked whether she could shift to *Iolanthe* and come along." Cullop must have sensed Dunmoore was about to object because she added, "It's not a bad idea, sir. She's been here before, she knows people, and she might be able to identify the pirate ships. Yes, Carrie's young, but her life has not been without risk, and on her current career path, it will stay that way. I can send her over with Karlo's platoon."

Dunmoore swallowed her intended reply, conscious that Cullop would not make such a suggestion without giving it a lot of thought. She'd been in Carrie Fennon's boots twenty years ago and knew how quickly starship children grew up.

"Agreed."

"Thank you, sir. Carrie will be thrilled. And just so you know, I explained *Iolanthe* sometimes pretends to be a privateer so she can carry out hush-hush missions for the Fleet. I pretty much had to after she heard your exchange with Kotto Piris."

Dunmoore mentally shrugged. Fennon was bound to find out *Iolanthe* wasn't really a supply ship.

"Thanks for the warning, Emma, and it's just as well. That means we won't need to go through endless contortions in the name of keeping our true identity a secret."

"That's what I figured. Chances are good the Furious Faerie will eventually show her full strength while Carrie is looking."

**

Dunmoore watched Saari's soldiers march off the shuttle and form in three ranks beside Command Sergeant Jennsen's 4th Platoon from her usual place in the control room alongside Petty Officer First Class Harkon. Since it was pressurized, the atmosphere kept in by a force field blanketing the open space doors, helmet visors were up, and both platoon leaders could exchange words without using E Company's radio net. And that meant Dunmoore couldn't hear what they were saying. But judging by the raucous laughter, it was amusing.

A solitary figure in a civilian pressure suit, carrying a spacer's duffel bag, exited the shuttle and stood awkwardly beside 1st Platoon, as if unsure of her welcome. Carrie Fennon.

Dunmoore gave Harkon a friendly nod and left the control room for the hangar deck's main inner door. As soon as she appeared, Saari stopped speaking with Jennsen and wandered over to Carrie. He pointed at Dunmoore, gave the young woman a comradely thump on the shoulder, and propelled her toward *Iolanthe*'s captain.

Not wanting to interfere in the handover between platoons, Siobhan put on a welcoming smile and waited for Carrie to join her rather than walk out onto the deck. To her surprise, the young woman came to an almost perfect halt as soon as she was three paces away and saluted.

"Apprentice Officer Carrie Fennon, Merchant Vessel *Kattegat Maru*, reporting to Captain Dunmoore as ordered. Permission to come aboard, sir?"

Dunmoore returned the compliment.

"Permission granted. At ease, Apprentice Officer, and welcome aboard. I'm glad to finally meet you in person."

Clearly, someone, she suspected it was Command Sergeant Saari, coached Fennon on proper etiquette if for no other reason than to boost her confidence.

"Likewise, sir." She sounded shy, tentative, but her eyes rarely rested on the same spot for more than a second or two.

"If you'll follow me, I'll take you to your quarters where you can dump the tin suit and settle in. There's also enough time for a quick tour before going FTL on our last jump to Kilia's hyperlimit."

"Yes, sir."

Carrie fell into step beside Dunmoore as she led her to the crew quarters.

"I understand Emma told you we're not an ordinary replenishment ship and sometimes work undercover."

"She did." Carrie hesitated, but then her next words came out in a rush. "That explains everything, sir, and now I'm delighted you found me instead of a frigate stuck on a patrol route."

Dunmoore smiled at her.

"Chasing pirates is what we do for a living. We do it extremely well, and none live to tell the tale, so no one knows the privateer *Persephone* is a Navy ship called *Iolanthe*."

"The Furious Faerie."

"That's right. The original Iolanthe was a faerie from a nineteenth-century operetta, but she wasn't furious. Our ship's crest, however, shows an armored faerie brandishing a flaming sword, so the nickname came naturally, especially since we can turn from harmless transport into a something with a serious bite at a moment's notice."

"Sounds fun."

Dunmoore chuckled.

"For us, it can be. For enemies of the Commonwealth, not so much. We're more often than not the last thing they see before joining their ancestors."

"Yet you let this Piris guy and his crew go."

"He's a small-time smuggler, a grifter, and no threat to shipping, let alone the Commonwealth. Since he chose to cooperate rather than fight, it was the right thing to do."

"But he wanted to steal my ship." Fennon's indignant tone brought another smile to Dunmoore's face.

"He believed *Kattegat Maru* was abandoned and therefore legitimate salvage. Under the law, it doesn't matter if a ship is abandoned because its crew was kidnapped. The fact someone paid him to retrieve her and gave him the precise coordinates doesn't mean he deserves a pirate's fate."

Dunmoore stopped at a door, one of many piercing both sides of the quiet corridor not far from her own suite.

"This section has the officer's quarters. My cabin is the one by the airtight bulkhead over there, and this one, reserved for guests, will be yours while you're with us." At her touch, the door panel slid aside with a soft sigh.

Carrie stepped across the threshold and froze as her eyes took in the compartment's size and amenities.

"Wow. Even my mother's quarters in *Kattegat Maru* aren't this nice, and because I'm the most junior crewmember, I get what we call the broom closet. Space only for a bunk, a locker, and a chair. No private heads either."

She examined the cabin with almost comical awe before carefully placing her duffel bag by the freshly made bed. Dunmoore showed her the closet then watched as she stripped off the pressure suit to reveal a dark blue merchant officer's shipboard uniform, with an apprentice's thin silver stripe at the collar. Once her gear was stowed, Dunmoore took Carrie in quick succession to the wardroom, the CIC and the bridge, introducing officers, petty officers, and ratings along the way.

The young woman once again felt her head swim at the onrush of new names and faces, everyone friendly and welcoming. But few seemed particularly naval in their privateer's guise, especially the bearded, rather bloodthirsty looking lieutenant commander who was *Iolanthe*'s combat systems officer.

Or the even more piratical Commander Holt, with his eye patch and roguish smile He shook Fennon's hand as if she were a full-fledged officer.

"Welcome aboard, Apprentice Officer Fennon. I hope you'll enjoy your time in *Iolanthe*." Holt turned to Dunmoore. "Both ships are ready to go FTL for Kilia's hyperlimit, Skipper. Since the CIC hasn't picked up anything of note, perhaps in the interests of time we should jump now."

"Agreed. And since we're already here, maybe our guest can observe how a Navy ship does it. Would you enjoy that, Officer Fennon?"

Her eyes lit up with curiosity. "Yes, sir."

Dunmoore indicated unoccupied stations at the rear of the bridge.

"Why don't we sit there?"

Holt went to stand beside Astrid Drost, the officer of the watch.

"Are both ships synchronized?"

"They are, sir."

"Then you may go FTL at your discretion."

Seconds later, the usual warning sounded throughout the ship, then, once the timer hit zero, everyone's universe shifted.

**

"*Iolanthe* is impressive, Captain. Almost frighteningly so." Fennon's eyes, still darting everywhere as they had throughout the evening, tried to take in all of Dunmoore's day cabin at once. "But it doesn't feel like a Navy ship."

Dunmoore gestured at a chair by her desk.

"Please sit. Not seeming as if we're Fleet is the whole point of an undercover naval vessel, Carrie. If we can convince the bad guys we're a scummy privateer whose only interest is making money, and to hell with the rest, or a helpless civilian freighter with a frightened crew, we can lure them close enough to land a fatal blow. Often, we don't even go hunting for Shrehari raiders or human marauders. We let them come to us by imitating a big, fat, juicy target."

"That must be hard on the nerves." Fennon cautiously sat on the edge of the chair as if afraid it might break.

"Ours or the enemy's?" Dunmoore gestured at the urn. "Can I offer you a coffee, or if you want something else, I can call the wardroom."

"Coffee's fine, sir. Black, no additives. We drink it like that in *Katie*. Or at least we used to." An anguished expression briefly replaced that of awe and wonder she'd worn since arriving. "I meant your nerves, waiting for someone to attack."

"It can become interesting, for sure." Dunmoore busied herself with two cups, each bearing *Iolanthe*'s crest. "But by now we're used to setting and springing traps on every species of nasty customer, so it's become old hat. You may get a taste of it if we ever face a fight in trying to recover your crew and passengers. Here."

"Thank you." She took a sip. "Nice. Much nicer than what I'm used to drinking."

"Emma tells me you've been to Kilia before, I mean inside the station."

Fennon nodded.

"Not this time, but the time before that. Although no further than their hangar. Mother didn't allow liberty on any of the unregistered outposts, so only she and another officer ever went beyond the docks, and then only on business if absolutely necessary."

"Wise woman. Tell me about Kilia's hangar."

She nibbled on her lower lip, eyes staring down at the deck, as she formed words to describe her memories of the place.

"Huge. It takes a bit of doing to match the habitat's spin so you can fly in without problems because they have no tractor beams to help. It's not pressurized, but there are cargo and people-sized airlocks inside. Passenger-only shuttles can connect via a pressurized gangway tube if they have the right sort of hatches. Otherwise, you wear a tin suit. Unless you make friends in high places, the sort that'll see your shuttle admitted to one of the smaller, pressurized auxiliary hangars. Those are my mother's words, by the way, that bit about friends in high places." Carrie looked up at Siobhan. "Do you think she's there? In Kilia? Along with everyone else?"

Dunmoore put on a reassuring expression.

"We'll see soon enough. And if they're not, I'll turn the place upside down until someone tells us where to find them."

"Commander Cullop said you usually get what you're after, sir."

"Did she now? I hope Emma also mentioned it's always a team effort. *Iolanthe* has one of the best crews in the Navy, and we hold one of the highest kill records of any ship currently in commission."

Fennon gave her a solemn nod.

"She told me precisely that, sir." A shy expression took years off her already youthful features. "Everyone you sent to *Katie* seems really proud about serving in *Iolanthe*. Even the soldiers."

"Esprit de corps is a wonderful thing." When she saw the blank look in her eyes, Dunmoore added, "it's what we call the intangible spirit that lifts men and women above themselves for the good of the unit, or in this case, for the good of the ship."

"Oh. Like morale, then?"

"Something of the sort." Dunmoore took a sip of coffee while Carrie processed the notion, then said, "If this isn't a bad moment, I'd be grateful to learn more about you and your family, Apprentice Officer Fennon."

"Certainly, sir. What do you want to know?"

— Twelve —

The door chime's melody wrenched Dunmoore away from a world long vanished, and she reluctantly placed her book on a side table. Reading one of the pre-diaspora classics in her collection before turning in was a long-standing ritual. She suspected the visitor outside her quarters came for another, less frequent and more recent one.

"Enter."

The door slid aside to reveal a smiling Ezekiel Holt. He held a green bottle in one hand and two small glasses in the other.

"Care for a nightcap, Skipper?"

"If that's your eighteen-year-old single malt, you are most welcome. If it's wardroom plonk, go away."

Holt stepped in.

"Would I dare offend your delicate sensibilities with anything less than the best?"

"In a heartbeat."

She motioned toward the other chair, but instead of sitting right away, Holt handed her a tumbler and poured a healthy dram. He served himself and raised his glass.

"To a successful infiltration." Both took a sip. Holt smacked his lips appreciatively. "Good thing I bought several bottles the last time we touched port. Otherwise, we might need to cut this patrol short." He dropped into the chair and crossed his legs. "How's our guest?"

"Overtired, overstimulated, overeager, and overly worried about her mother and *Kattegat Maru*'s crew."

"That's a lot of over for someone who's underage."

"Yet she's remarkably steady and self-possessed for an apprentice yanked out of her comfort zone and thrust into a naval anti-piracy operation to recover her own family. I'm not sure the teenaged me would have been able to act like a junior officer rather than a frightened girl."

"As Emma said, starship kids grow up fast."

"True, but she's been surrounded by her extended family since birth. From what she told me, the Fennons are strict but loving and took great pains to care for the crew's youngest member. Knowing they're in the hands of pirates is bound to cause trauma, yet she's holding up remarkably well."

"Then Carrie's extended family also took pains to help her become resilient. It speaks well for them." Holt took another sip. "That's the good stuff. What do you intend once we reach Kilia?"

"That'll depend on what ships we find orbiting the place. Chief Day finally reconstructed fragmentary images from *Kattegat Maru*'s erased sensor logs. Yens is running them against Lloyd's Registry and the threat database. Perhaps we'll find a reasonable match."

"So I heard. No progress on the other logs though."

Dunmoore shook her head.

"No. And Day's not optimistic."

"What if we find no suspects orbiting Kilia?"

She made a noncommittal gesture. "I go ashore with a landing party and ask questions."

Holt's face turned to stone the moment he heard the words 'I go ashore.'

"Must we do this again, Skipper? A captain's place is in her ship, not with a landing party."

"Yes, we must. Navy captains can afford to stay on their thrones and work via remote control. Civilians, especially privateers, not so much. It would look strange if Shannon O'Donnell sent her first officer or anyone else to represent *Persephone*. If we're to play the game, we play it properly, and that means I go ashore, not you, or Thorin or Tatiana. But I will take a few of her finest with me. If I'm surrounded by hulking, foul-tempered Scandian mercenaries, I'll be less of a target."

Holt knew better than to take this discussion past a pro forma objection but felt someone must say it. He nodded once.

"I don't enjoy the idea, but I suppose your point is valid."

"There's no suppose about it, Zeke. Though I understand you wishing to stick with the first officers' union rules."

"And returning to our original subject, did you learn more about *Kattegat Maru* from young Carrie? Such as why someone targeted them?"

Dunmoore grimaced.

"Not much of use. She mentioned her mother seemed no more nervous than usual when they visited Kilia just before the pirate attack. No one save Captain Fennon and the second officer, responsible for cargo handling, went ashore. They stayed maybe an hour and came back with a half dozen containers and four new passengers."

"Let me guess. Fennon put those containers in cargo hold C, the one emptied by the pirates."

"Precisely."

"Finally, a glimmer of a clue in this murky mess. Want to bet one of the containers she took aboard hid a subspace tracker?"

"It's plausible."

"And perhaps one or more of the new passengers worked as insiders for the pirates, which would explain how they seized her so easily."

"Again, plausible, Zeke. But why would someone use a complex plan to set *Kattegat Maru* up as a victim of piracy by infiltrating people and equipment at Kilia, then wait until she was in interstellar space to seize her?"

"If we knew that, we'd know who and why. Mind you, it could be something as prosaic as the masters of Kilia forbidding piracy in their realm on pain of excommunication or death."

"True." She drained her glass and yawned. "We won't solve those questions tonight. Thanks for the drink. I'd better turn in and catch a few hours of sleep before we jump toward what Yens assures me is a spinning asteroid with unnaturally high power emissions."

Holt climbed to his feet, collected the glasses, and gave Dunmoore a formal nod.

"Enjoy your rest, Captain."

"Try to grab a few winks yourself, Zeke. First officers don't run on coffee and professional pride alone."

"I will. After my usual tour of the ship." He grinned. "Union rules. A first officer doesn't go to bed unless he's made his presence felt to discourage shenanigans while he sleeps."

**

Holt found *Iolanthe*'s chief engineer, a gray-bearded, stocky man in well-worn black coveralls munching on a sandwich in the otherwise empty wardroom. It was just past one bell in the night watch, thirty minutes after midnight, and the other officers were either at their duty stations or in their quarters, asleep.

Though in space the concept of night and day was academic, the human body still craved a regular cycle. Except for Commander Renny Halfen, who cheerfully worked at any hour, sleeping here and there when the need overtook him.

The chief engineer looked up at Holt and nodded once. Then he swallowed and said, "Shouldn't you be in bed by now, Zeke?"

"I could ask the same." Holt opened the cold storage pantry and pulled out a juice bulb. He held it up. "I'll hit my rack after this."

"Worried about Kilia Station?" Halfen shoved the rest of the sandwich into his mouth and chewed as he patiently waited for Holt's reply.

"Only a fool doesn't worry about the unknown, Renny." Holt sat across from him and sighed. "Our Siobhan intends to go ashore with an escort from Tatiana's mob."

"Did you talk her out of it?"

"This is one of those times where she's right. Unfortunately." Holt drained half of the juice bulb in one gulp.

"Then you'll not thank me for giving you another thing to worry about. I studied the images and sensor readings Chief Yens posted on the threat board just now. You can probably expect Kilia to have heavy ordnance hidden away under fake rock lids."

"How so?"

Halfen made a face.

"The place has one big mama of a power plant, and what I believe are four auxiliaries, each of which puts out twice, if not more than what our fusion reactor can manage at full rate. More than enough to feed whatever you want — plasma cannon, lasers, grasers, masers, you name it — on top of environmental systems and everything else. And high-powered versions too. Putting large reactors and big guns on a spinning asteroid is easy as pie, compared to balancing out the mass-power-ordnance ratio of a starship. After doing the hard work of turning a big rock into a space station, giving it adequate firepower is child's play. And they'll likely be protected by kick-ass shield generators to cover the most vulnerable spots, which shouldn't be hard since the habitat cavern only occupies a tiny fraction of that oversized lump."

"I doubt the captain intends to storm Kilia with guns blazing, Renny."

"Aye, but Kilia might take exception to the captain and greet us with guns blazing. Best think of it as a Fleet orbital station. Too tough for anything less than a full task force and capable of hammering even *Iolanthe*'s shields into overload before we can move out of range. Since Kilia survived this long where few honest spacers venture, two things are sure." Halfen took a sip of his coffee before continuing. "First, they're well protected. Enough to discourage the most ambitious reiver or the most aggressive Shrehari corsair."

"And second?" Holt asked when the chief engineer paused for more coffee.

"There's more money out here than you or I can fathom. Kilia must be raking in millions per day merely in docking and transaction fees. It's the only way to finance that sort of habitat. Trying to imagine the quantity of ill-gotten plunder that passes through there must be mind-boggling. I hope the captain's ready to plunder our precious metals reserve." Halfen drained his cup. "I'll post my observations on the threat board." Then he stood and sketched a salute with his calloused right hand. "That's me heading back to my dungeon. Enjoy your night, Zeke."

"You too, Renny."

Holt finished his juice bulb but didn't immediately get up to leave. Instead, he stared at the Furious Faerie crest dominating the starboard bulkhead. A delicate faced woman in a knee-length coat of mail, armored leggings and a spiked helmet, she had diaphanous wings that seem incongruous, more so than the flaming crusader's sword held high in her right hand.

Iolanthe, condemned to death by the Queen of the Faeries, a sentence the latter commuted to lifetime banishment before lifting it altogether, started off as a romantic operetta character six hundred years earlier. How she ever ended up as a warship's namesake, looking anything but romantic, still puzzled Holt. He stood and stretched before tossing the empty bulb into the wardroom recycler.

The coming twenty-four hours would be interesting indeed, even for a ship and crew that experience more than their fair share of unusual situations as a matter of course.

— Thirteen —

Dunmoore, no longer resembling a merchant officer, never mind a Navy captain, entered the bridge shortly after four bells in the morning watch, or oh-six-hundred according to Major Salminen and her soldiers. Like the rest of her crew — but not Salminen's company — she'd gone full privateer.

In Dunmoore's case, it meant a rakish, silver-trimmed quasi-uniform of black trousers tucked into knee-high boots, a black tunic with a hem reaching halfway down her thighs and a white, collarless shirt. A menacing blaster in an open holster at her hip and intricate earrings, among other jewelry items, complemented her distinctly non-naval appearance.

Lieutenant Magnus Protti, *Iolanthe*'s assistant combat systems officer, and currently the officer of the watch, jumped out of the command chair and nodded politely at the captain. In his late twenties, with longish black hair, a black chin beard, and dark, hooded eyes, Protti appeared even more villainous than Dunmoore although his privateer's clothing wasn't quite as stylish.

"All systems are green and nothing else to report, sir."

"Thank you, Magnus."

She took the command chair and opened the overnight log entries. Renny Halfen's comments on the threat board caught her immediate attention. She silently chastised herself for not giving Kilia's defensive potential more thought. But that's why she had instituted a threat board, among other public fora. So that many minds could cover the senior officers' inevitable blind spots, including hers.

The door to the bridge opened behind her, and a tentative voice asked, "Permission to enter, sir."

Dunmoore swiveled her chair around and gave the serious-looking young woman standing at attention on the threshold a warm smile. She still wore her merchant officer's tunic with the thin silver apprentice stripe, making her the only one present in any sort of uniform. When she saw Dunmoore's privateer disguise, her eyes widened. Lieutenant Protti's amused chuckle caught Carrie's attention, and her eyes grew even larger at his disquieting appearance.

"Welcome aboard the privateer ship *Persephone*, Officer Fennon. And yes, you may enter." Dunmoore waved at an unoccupied station. "Sit. You're probably wondering why the fancy costumes now when we didn't use them with Kotto Piris and his gang, right?"

Carrie nodded as she sat.

"Simple. The only people with whom Kotto Piris' folks came into contact were Sergeant Saari's villainous mercenaries and a few ship's officers who could belong to anyone. Kilia will be a more difficult target since I intend to go ashore with a suitable escort under the guise of looking for work. And that means anyone who might be seen by outsiders, including the bridge crew, should we establish video contact, must look the part."

"Understood, sir. If you prefer, I'll change right away."

"Later is fine. As long as it's done by the time we drop out of FTL at Kilia's hyperlimit in about three hours. Did you sleep well?"

Carrie hesitated, then shook her head.

"The bunk is way more comfortable than my own in *Katie,* but I've slept nowhere else in years, so I spent a lot of the night tossing and turning. However, the wardroom served an amazing breakfast, and the officers were kind to me, though none of their clothes looked like yours."

"Yet. But they will the next time you see them. Or most will. Commander Halfen and his engineering crew spend their days in black coveralls whether we're sailing as a Navy vessel or whether we're pretending to be a privateer."

"Are Commander Cullop and the relief crew also disguised?"

"If you mean more than simply as the civilian spacers you last saw, then no. I don't intend to take *Kattegat Maru* closer in than the hyperlimit so she can jump out at a moment's notice in case things turn against us." Anticipating Fennon's next question, Dunmoore said, "Should anything happen, Commander Cullop will go to a meeting point on the edge of this system and wait twelve hours. If she doesn't hear from us by then, she'll take your ship to the nearest starbase."

"Oh." Carrie Fennon seemed torn between the desire to follow Dunmoore and keep an eye on her family's ship.

"Emma will make sure no one touches *Kattegat Maru* until I — we — return."

"Good." Fennon, clearly eager to join the crew in doffing her uniform to become a false privateer, jumped to her feet. "With your permission, I'll return to my quarters now and change, Captain."

"Please do so and join me in my day cabin for a cup of coffee afterward."

A timid smile crept across Carrie's face.

"I will. Thank you."

**

"*Kattegat Maru* is still keeping station but has gone silent. I doubt Kilia picked up her emergence signature so close to our larger and fully visible one," Chief Yens reported shortly after carrying out her usual post FTL checks. "I can make out six ships in orbit, one of which shares general characteristics with the fragmentary sensor log images we recovered." She let out a muffled curse. "There's also a damned Shrehari corsair."

"And we know at least half of all Shrehari corsairs are Imperial Deep Space Fleet or *Tai Kan* intelligence-gathering ships," Sirico said.

"If not more, Thorin. This adds an interesting twist to our situation. Two sworn enemies at the same outlaw station. Although Kilia would insist on keeping this system neutral, and if Renny is correct, can enforce said neutrality at least out to the maximum range of its guns."

"Good thing we came in as *Persephone* and not the Commonwealth Starship *Iolanthe*," Holt remarked from the bridge. "Does that corsair change your intentions, Skipper?"

"No. Unless they're somehow involved with the *Kattegat Maru* business, in which case we may no longer be talking about simple piracy by humans. Mind you, because they're Shrehari and perhaps even Imperial Fleet, if I see a chance to destroy them, I will. But not around here."

"We're being hailed, sir. Audio only."

"Kudos to their sensor watch for spotting us so quickly at this range." Sirico's voice held grudging respect.

"It stands to reason, sir," Yens said. "If trouble is coming, they'll want to know the moment it drops out of FTL."

Dunmoore made a go-ahead gesture at the signals petty officer.

"Put them on."

A flat female voice of undetermined origin came through the CIC speakers.

"Unknown vessel approaching Kilia Station, identify yourself and state your business."

"This is the mercenary ship *Persephone,* and I'm Captain Shannon O'Donnell. We heard Kilia is a good place to find private military contracts."

"If you can afford our docking and transaction fees, it can indeed be a good place to find a contract, Captain O'Donnell. How will you be paying?"

Dunmoore cocked an amused eyebrow at Thorin Sirico. Straight to the point.

"Precious metals."

"That is acceptable. Please listen to the following. Our guns will cover you at all times. We will meet any hostile act with instant force. Kilia and its star system are neutral in the war between the Commonwealth and the Shrehari Empire. As a result, we will not tolerate acts of aggression between visitors from either entity. The minimum punishment for violation of our rules can include fines, forfeiture of cargo, or ejection with no right to return. Maximum punishment can entail destruction. All decisions are final. There is no right to appeal. I will shortly transmit a copy of the Kilia Station Regulations. Do you understand and accept these conditions? If not, you are free to leave the system."

"I understand and accept them."

"Thank you, Captain O'Donnell. You may approach and enter Kilia orbit. We will provide further instructions upon your arrival."

After a moment, the signals petty officer said, "They dropped the link, Captain."

"Not much for small talk, are they? Give me *Kattegat Maru.*"

Emma Cullop's smiling face appeared soon afterward.

"I assume you're off and we're playing invisible starship?"

"Indeed. I don't know when we'll be able to speak again. It would probably be too risky calling you from Kilia, but keep an eye on the place. It looks as if there's a Shrehari corsair in orbit and it more than likely means undercover Imperial Fleet."

Cullop made a face.

"Wonderful. As if we need the added complication."

"So if you see us do something sudden and unexpected, head for the rendezvous point."

"Will do."

"Take care, Emma. We have an apprentice officer here who really wants to board her ship again."

"No worries, sir. Go get 'em."

"I aim to do so. *Iolanthe*, out."

**

Up close, Kilia Station appeared unprepossessing. Built inside a potato-shaped asteroid forty kilometers long and eight kilometers wide spinning on its long axis, almost nothing of the habitat was visible to the naked eye. It took up only a small part of the interior where early surveyors found an extensive cavern network, much of it filled with ice, alongside seams of valuable ore.

Its most prominent artificial surface feature was the large opening that marked the entrance to the main shuttle docks. But *Iolanthe*'s sensors found a dozen gun emplacements, eight missile launchers and twenty-four shield generators cunningly camouflaged by low domes that blended seamlessly with the surrounding rock.

As proved by *Iolanthe*'s threat detectors, Kilia's own sensors studied the Q-ship with undisguised interest as she approached the station and entered orbit.

Of the other ships present, five came from human shipyards and resembled Kotto Piris' *Kurgan*. Sleek, capable of landing in an atmosphere, with oversized drives and plenty of gun blisters, they were not primarily designed to haul bulk cargo.

The sixth couldn't be mistaken for anything but Shrehari. Its shape was too reminiscent of the Imperial Deep Space Fleet's basic design, an elongated wedge with broad, almost wing-like hyperdrive nacelle pylons. But contrary to naval vessels, it bore elaborate markings instead of the military's stylized dragon. Or what human eyes interpreted as one.

Chief Yens let out a soft grunt.

"Folks around here must be trusting. None of those suspiciously piratical tubs are giving off the power emissions you'd expect from ships at high alert. But they are looking us over. Especially the bonehead. He's no corsair. You can take that as a given. His sensor signature comes from Imperial standard-issue electronics." She shook her head. "I can't believe we're within touching distance of a fucking bonehead and not at battle stations."

"And he's probably stewing with impotent frustration at being within touching distance of a fat, *untouchable* human prize." Sirico grinned at her. "That's the joy of a neutral port which can enforce its rules."

"Aye. Perhaps we can wait for him at the edge of the system once we're done here. And then..." Yens made a chopping gesture at the main display. "One less Shrehari intelligence-gathering garbage scow."

Dunmoore gave Sirico an amused glance.

"I'll keep the suggestion in mind, Chief."

"We're receiving instructions," Holt said from the bridge. "And not just for our parking orbit. Since this is our first visit, they're demanding a representative come ashore to meet with the Kilia administration and pay a deposit on the harbor fees as a gesture of goodwill. We must do this within six hours of entering orbit. Otherwise, we'll be told to leave.

No doubt with a few large bore plasma cannon poking up our skirts."

An ironic smile creased Major Salminen's usually earnest countenance.

"Truly a money-making proposition, this rogue outpost."

"Please prepare a shuttle, Zeke. I'll go ashore with the harbor fees in an hour."

"And with a suitable escort," Holt said. "To include Vincenzo, because excluding him is ill-advised, Chief Guthren, because he said so and he's the chief of the ship, as well as a platoon from E Company."

"Sergeant Saari's platoon," Salminen interjected.

"He seems to draw every interesting assignment these days."

"This time, it was luck. The platoon leaders played a hand of poker to decide who goes ashore with you first, and Karlo won."

"Gambling? In my ship?"

She put on a feigned expression of shock.

The soldiers shrugged. "It was poker or drawing straws, and poker is more entertaining for spectators."

— Fourteen —

The knot of people waiting by one of the shuttles on *Iolanthe*'s spacious hangar deck came to attention in unison when Dunmoore walked through the inner door. Two of them, Leading Spacer 'Vince' Vincenzo, bosun's mate and Dunmoore's self-appointed bodyguard, and Chief Petty Officer First Class Kurt Guthren, *Iolanthe*'s coxswain stood out from the rest.

Guthren was a barrel-shaped man whose close-cropped blond hair and short gray beard framed a worn but kindly face that reminded many of a favorite uncle — until he let the ferocious side of his personality take over. Watchful brown eyes beneath thick brows tracked his captain's approach.

Vincenzo, by contrast, was lithe, almost wiry, with dark, wavy hair, a luxuriant mustache, and an intense gaze. Both wore their adaptation of a privateer's dark-hued quasi-uniform. But where most of the crew appeared villainous, Guthren and Vincenzo came across as menacing, an impression strengthened by the oversized blasters and long-bladed knives hanging from wide leather belts.

Sergeant Saari and the dozen soldiers from 1st Platoon, E Company, on the other hand, had the appearance of solid, disciplined mercenaries. They wore dark green uniforms with subdued mercenary-style rank insignia derived from those of the Commonwealth's regular Armed Services, as well as light body armor and load-bearing harnesses. In addition to pistols and knives, they carried either a plasma carbine or a scattergun and plenty of spare ammunition and power packs.

"Good morning, everyone," Dunmoore called out as she came within earshot.

A reply, belted out by good-humored voices speaking as one, crashed over her with unexpected force.

"Good morning, Captain."

"Who has the precious metals to pay our deposit?"

Guthren raised his hand. "Vince and me, sir." He gestured at the small, black pack slung over his shoulder. "Lieutenant Biros figured it would be better to split the stash in two. Less conspicuous that way."

Joelle Biros, *Iolanthe*'s supply officer, was the guardian of their untraceable funds, precious metals included. What the coxswain didn't add, because he knew Dunmoore would understand right away, was that their carrying the funds gave them a perfect excuse to always be at her side.

"Vince and I are also amply supplied with listening devices," he added. "We can seed the place for sound at will. If they're not running active countermeasures, of course."

"Somehow, I doubt they'll be able to block the latest in surveillance tech. Even the Navy outside special ops doesn't know it exists. Who's flying us?"

As if on cue, a smiling face looked out through the shuttle's thick cockpit windows, and a hand waved in greeting.

"Eve Knowles," Guthren unnecessarily said, since Dunmoore recognized the petty officer, one of the bosun's mates qualified as a pilot.

Dunmoore waved back, then asked, "How did you choose which of your platoon's sections were coming on this mission, Sergeant Saari? Poker?"

The soldier gave her a toothy grin.

"Shooting competition in the simulator between the section sergeants, sir. Games of chance are for command ranks only. We wouldn't want to corrupt our juniors."

"Very considerate, I'm sure." She let her eyes run over the assembly, then said in a louder voice, "We don't know what's waiting for us in there. But Kilia Station makes its profits by providing a space where shady beings can conduct business without fear of getting shot. However, General Order Eighty-One is in effect. If things go pear-shaped, Commander Holt will not risk the ship to rescue us. Consider your weapons and menacing scowls as props designed to give those with evil intent second thoughts, and give me added prestige as the leader of a secretive, but highly effective mercenary force. Opening fire will be the last resort. If something happens to me, Chief Guthren is in charge of the landing party, and he will immediately take you back to the ship. Any questions?"

A hand shot into the air.

"Yes, Corporal Vallin."

"What happens if we run across Shrehari assholes in there? Those fuckers rained a crap load of hurt on Scandia before we kicked their bony butts back into space."

"Avoid them, ignore them. Pretend they don't exist. Any boneheads you see are probably our counterparts, undercover Deep Space Fleet officers and ratings, or worse yet, *Tai Kan.* They won't be anxious to start something with humans in the first place. And please do nothing that might provoke their ticklish sense of honor. We're here to find *Kattegat Maru*'s missing crew and passengers, not hunt Shrehari."

"So we can't combine business and pleasure, then?" Vallin asked, earning himself a few amused chuckles from the ranks.

"Sorry. Not this time. Any other questions?" When no one else raised a hand, she gestured at the shuttle. "Climb in. Let's go sightseeing."

**

As they neared it, Dunmoore realized the entrance to Kilia Station's hangar was huge. A careful pilot might even thread something the size of a standard sloop through the opening. It posed no challenge for Petty Officer Knowles.

Once inside, a traffic control droid with the name *Persephone* on a display panel as broad as the shuttle led them to a berth with a flexible gangway tube that seemed to vanish through a smooth stone wall.

Though they saw at least a dozen small spacecraft sitting at various docking stations, including one that could only be Shrehari, the immense, brightly lit hangar cavern seemed empty.

Shortly after Knowles set her shuttle down to the traffic control droid's satisfaction, which it expressed by erasing the ship's name from the display panel and trundling off, a gangway tube stiffened and snaked out. It settled precisely over the starboard personnel airlock with a muted thump. A few moments later, Knowles gave Dunmoore, who was sitting in the cockpit beside her, thumbs up.

"It's pressurized and I've unlatched the door, sir."

"Thanks. Once I'm out of the cockpit, seal yourself up, just in case. I'll leave a few of Sergeant Saari's men behind as a safety precaution."

"Please make sure one of them isn't Vallin, Captain. I don't want to hear his complaints for however long you'll be ashore."

"That would be Sergeant Saari's decision."

"Wonderful." Knowles made a face. "Karlo still hasn't repaid me for the prank I pulled on him at the last noncoms' all-night card tournament."

Dunmoore raised a restraining hand, but smiled nonetheless.

"I don't want to hear about it. There are entirely too many games of chance going on in my ship."

She climbed out of her seat, crossed over into the passenger compartment, where several soldiers waited by the starboard airlock for permission to exit, and gave Saari the nod.

At his order, alpha section's point man pulled the door in and to one side with the ease of a veteran Marine, showing once again how well E Company of the Army's Scandia Regiment had adapted to its new role aboard a starship. The first pair cautiously entered the tube, looking for anything suspicious as they made their way to the far side.

While she waited for her escort's signal to exit the shuttle, Dunmoore finally noticed the less than one gee gravity imparted by the asteroid's spin. She felt just that much lighter which, after months in space living in a steady one gee environment, was a fresh, almost uplifting sensation.

The point men vanished into the station-side airlock and Saari sent out the next pair. A voice came over Dunmoore's earbug, set to the landing party's frequency.

"The airlock is clear. There's a droid waiting for Captain O'Donnell."

Saari sent through another pair, then gestured at Guthren and Vincenzo to follow, after which he allowed his captain off the shuttle.

Claustrophobes rarely lasted in the Navy, but even Dunmoore thought the tube was eerily confining. She wondered what a substantially larger Shrehari made of it. Perhaps they didn't suffer from such a thing as fear of small spaces. They certainly seemed fearless in many other ways, although she'd noticed they were becoming more cautious in battle as the war dragged on with no end in sight.

Dunmoore passed through an airlock barely large enough for four humans and stepped into a wide corridor lit by globes hanging at regular intervals. Its walls bore the marks of laser drills and the sheen of an atmospheric sealant blocking even the smallest pores that might let air escape.

However, it was so cold she could see her breath. Station management wasn't wasting much energy to heat the dockside spaces. Keeping them above the freezing point was enough.

The droid mentioned by the point man sat patiently across from the airlock's inner door. Short, round and built for functionality rather than esthetics, the little machine was covered in scratches, scars and dents, its once bright paint job dulled to a fading red. An upright display panel crowning the domed head showed her privateer name.

"I'm Shannon O'Donnell."

The droid chirped as her name vanished, replaced by the words 'please follow me.' For a second or two, Dunmoore wondered why the droid didn't speak. Then she realized that even among her own species, accents, pronunciations, and such could vary enough to make an artificial intelligence using the most basic form of spoken Anglic difficult to understand by some. Written Anglic, however, was the same no matter where.

The corridor seemed as endless as it was cold, and they met no other visitors or station personnel along the way. Finally, the droid led them through an airlock spacious enough for forty humans, or perhaps thirty Shrehari if they were close friends, and out into the main habitat cavern.

Almost as one, Dunmoore and her party checked their step, heads swiveling from side to side, eyes wide as they tried to absorb the strangeness of their surroundings.

Whatever the cavern beneath Kilia's surface looked like when the first entrepreneurs discovered it, decades of improvements created what was, in effect, a small city of two and three-story building clusters separated by broad streets crossing each other at ninety-degree angles.

High above, an artificial sun, probably fed by its own fusion reactor, provided both light and heat. But the short and narrow horizon on either side curved upward as it crept along the asteroid's inner diameter, and gave the scene a faintly surreal look, while both ends, the one they'd emerged from and the other, across town were abruptly vertical.

"Not something you see every day," one of Saari's soldiers muttered. "Real estate prices here must be out of this universe."

The sergeant glanced at Dunmoore.

"Haralson was in the property business before the war, sir. Even now, he can't stop appraising every bit of real estate he sees."

"Professional deformation, Captain," Haralson replied with an unapologetic grin. "Maybe after the war, I can set up shop here. Imagine what a four percent commission could bring in this place."

The droid tooted discretely, its display flashing for attention. Dunmoore gestured toward it.

"I think our guide wants us to stop rubbernecking and get a move on."

She took a deep breath of the rather odd tasting air and wondered about its oxygen content.

As most outposts on airless worlds do, this one would draw its water, its oxygen, the hydrogen for fusion reactors, and any other necessary gases from ice deposits. And that meant many boasted an atmosphere richer in oxygen than Earth. Perhaps the Kilia cavern itself had been at one time filled with ice, like the early Moon colonies, humanity's first extra-planetary settlements.

In contrast to the docking ring's main corridor, the habitat teemed with life. Most of it was human, of all shapes, sizes, and descriptions, but there were many non-humans as well, from species endemic to the hinterlands neither the Commonwealth nor the Empire had as yet bothered taking for their own.

Most were what the Navy called techno-barbarians, beings belonging to non-human civilizations that bought interstellar travel technology from unscrupulous merchants centuries if not millennia before they were ready, with the inevitable results.

One of the soldiers growled something unintelligible and nodded at a side street. There, three Shrehari enjoying drinks at an outdoor table were talking in loud voices, and roaring with what was probably laughter. But the sound put Dunmoore in mind of a wounded beast spitting out its last defiance.

"Ignore them, Knuth," Saari muttered. "We're mercenaries. We recognize no enemies but those we're paid to fight. And their employers could become ours the next day if the price is right."

"I was merely pointing out a place that serves Shrehari ale, Sergeant." Knuth sounded unrepentant. "It's something I haven't tasted since we kicked the boneheads off Scandia."

"And you won't today either."

"You're a hard man, Sergeant."

"But I'm good to find. Now can it."

Saari's quip drew the expected chuckles and smoothed over any anger caused his soldiers' first sighting in years of an enemy that tried to despoil their world.

They emerged in a central plaza dominated by a structure that resembled nothing so much as an old Earth step pyramid. A sign above its door, in Anglic and several other languages, none of them intelligible to Dunmoore because of their alien origin, announced it as the Kilia Station Principal Management Office.

A new message appeared on the droid's display. 'Shannon O'Donnell: your guards will wait outside; you will enter and turn left, into the harbormaster's office.'

"My two attendants," she pointed at Guthren and Vincenzo in turn, "must come with me. They carry the fee I am to pay."

The display went blank as if the droid was thinking or asking for fresh orders. Then it showed, 'Your attendants may go with you. Goodbye.' And with that, the stubby little machine silently trundled off on its next mission.

"We'll still be on the landing party network, Sergeant," Dunmoore said when Saari looked about to argue. "Besides, the cox'n and Vincenzo have been known to cause havoc. Enjoy the sights, but don't stare at any passing Shrehari. They consider an inferior, meaning anyone other than a member of the Imperial race doing so to be an insult."

"We'll just sneer behind their backs, Captain," Vallin tossed back with a good-natured grin.

"Not even," Guthren growled before Saari could intervene. "As far as you're concerned, there are no boneheads here."

Then, without waiting for an acknowledgment, he turned and led the way to the pyramid's ground level door, which slid aside at his approach. Dunmoore took one last glance at their surroundings, then followed suit, Vincenzo hard on her heels.

— Fifteen —

The door closed behind them, cutting off the habitat's insistent background buzz, a sound that seemed almost as if it was a living creature in its own right. A huge sign, again in many languages, dominated a lobby that reached right to the top of the structure like a broad chimney surrounded by walkways on each level. Here, silence reigned supreme even though Dunmoore sensed it was a hub of activity. As per the droid's instructions, they turned left where a sign advertised the harbormaster's office.

More doors slid aside at their approach. These opened on a large square area lined with booths. It possessed all the charm of a starship's engineering section and none of the energy. Dunmoore expected an AI projection to materialize, but a human in a cheap business suit stepped out of a side door and waved at them. He was cadaverously thin, with pinched, pale features and a shiny, receding hairline.

"Captain O'Donnell and party. Welcome."

His insincere, oily smile was faintly nauseating, but Siobhan replied in kind.

"I'm Shannon O'Donnell."

"Loris Horgan, assistant harbormaster. We prefer to greet first-time visitors personally rather than let our AIs take care of the various transactions." He bestowed a puzzled gaze on Dunmoore's companions. "And these are?"

"Ser Guthren and Ser Vincenzo, my business managers. I never go ashore, nor do I engage in business transactions without them."

"I see."

Horgan's expression betrayed disbelief, but he didn't seem inclined to protest. She was unlikely to be the first visitor insistent on keeping a pair of bodyguards nearby. After a moment's hesitation, Horgan waved toward the open door.

"If you'll come with me, we can register your ship, take care of the fees, and let you enjoy Kilia's amenities in no time."

Dunmoore tilted her head to one side in acknowledgment.

"Certainly."

They entered a corridor decorated in subdued pastels. Closed doors lined one side while poorly executed art, the sort beloved by those with more money and pretensions than taste, lined the other.

"I understand you're here looking for a private military contract."

"That's the case."

"We never heard of a mercenary ship by the name *Persephone* in these parts."

"That's because we used to operate in the Shield Sector area. But work dried up, so we came here at the recommendation of old acquaintances."

A knowing smirk creased Horgan's face as he ushered them into his office.

"Work dried up? Or is it more a matter of having crossed the wrong people?"

Dunmoore gave him a lazy smile in return and shrugged.

"Does it matter? No contract means no income. And that means changing your area of operations, right?"

"As you say." He slipped behind a metal desk and gestured at the only other chair. "Please sit, Captain."

"You're most gracious."

"A good first impression is important. Without paying visitors, Kilia isn't much of a business proposition, although we keep a low profile for obvious reasons. Which leads me to ask about the old acquaintances you mentioned. If the wrong people discovered our location, things might turn unpleasant."

"Who are the wrong people, Ser Horgan?"

He waved his hand dismissively.

"Surely you can guess. In this part of the galaxy, it would mean both Commonwealth and Shrehari naval forces."

Dunmoore repressed a smile. Did Horgan honestly believe those Shrehari corsairs drinking ale in his habitat were utterly unconnected to Imperial authorities? And surely *Iolanthe* wasn't the first Fleet ship to come this far even though the navigation database made no mention of Kilia.

"Of course. I certainly understand your concern. Our own dealings with the Navy aren't always pleasant though I try to operate beyond their remit."

"And the old acquaintances?"

"One of them is Aurelia Fennon, of *Kattegat Maru*."

Horgan's expression didn't change, though Dunmoore fancied she caught something in his shifty stare.

"Aurelia Fennon. Yes, she's a regular visitor. A fine starship captain and businesswoman. Pays in full every time and causes no problems. As a matter of fact, she came through here recently."

"Did she now? A shame I didn't get here sooner. It would have been grand to meet her again."

Horgan's head dipped.

"No doubt. Captain Fennon is well regarded. She'll be back, and if you make Kilia your newest base of operations, I'm sure you'll cross paths. You said she was one of the acquaintances. How about the others?"

"Why does that concern you, Ser Horgan?"

"We wish to know with whom we're dealing. I'm sure you understand."

"The other one who recommended Kilia was Kotto Piris."

Horgan's expression briefly froze, but he didn't miss a beat.

"Another regular. He was here recently as well. Now how long did you intend to stay, and what amenities do you want to purchase for your business needs and your crew?"

"Perhaps three days would be a good start, enough time to assess the market for my services. I not only own a ship able to support a full range of military operations, but I also carry an infantry unit, the Varangian Company. They're as well trained as any Commonwealth Marines and have seen more combat than most. I wasn't considering shore leave, but that might not be a bad idea."

"We offer a wide range of recreational possibilities, Captain O'Donnell. Your outlay would merely be for the shuttle docking costs and a per head fee to cover the expense of running Kilia's environmental systems. Said fee is charged in twelve-hour increments. I can assure you we track arrivals and departures with complete accuracy and provide detailed invoices."

"That sounds acceptable. So I'll pay for three days of orbit fees in advance, along with today's shuttle docking and the rest later?"

"Three days in orbit, plus a deposit to cover the fees for one hundred visitors times one twelve-hour increment each. Should the deposit not be fully spent, we will refund the balance."

"Why one hundred visitors, Ser Horgan?"

"You mentioned *Persephone* carries a full infantry company. Thus I can only assume your entire complement is at least three hundred, if not more, considering her size. It being the case, a thirty percent deposit is reasonable, wouldn't you say?"

Dunmoore noted Horgan had not yet broached the subject of actual sums, and thirty percent of a fortune might strain her reserves, but if Kilia kept its costs too high, visitors would stop coming.

"That sounds reasonable."

"I'm glad you agree. Some captains can be rather difficult, and we're not in the habit of dickering."

"Bottom line, Ser Horgan?"

He named a sum in Commonwealth creds that Dunmoore mentally converted to the value of the precious metals Guthren and Vincenzo carried. They had more than enough to cover the deposit, although Joelle would blanch at the expenditure.

Dunmoore waved over her shoulder with the imperiousness she thought would fit a Shannon O'Donnell, mercenary and privateer.

"Ser Guthren?"

"Captain." He stepped forward and handed her the small black pack with half of the precious metals they'd brought ashore. "This should cover Ser Horgan's bottom line."

"Thank you." Dunmoore opened the bag and produced a dozen small packages one after the other, each bearing a smelter's seal, and placed them on Horgan's desk in a neat row. "If you want to assay the contents, please do so, but I can assure you of their purity. This should cover the sum we discussed."

"In our business, we live by a motto, Captain. Trust but verify. If you'll excuse me."

He picked up the first package, opened it, and place the contents, rare precious alloy bars, under the scanner sitting on a sideboard. After a few seconds, he put them aside and subjected the remaining packages, one by one, to the same treatment. Finally, he turned back toward Dunmoore and gave her another helping of his oily smile.

"Your payment's purity is confirmed. Thank you."

"I don't cheat prospective business partners, Ser Horgan, nor do I play games with port authorities when I'm looking for a fresh base of operations."

"Not everyone thinks as you do, Captain O'Donnell, sadly. The stories I could tell... But a show of honesty during your first visit will stand you in good stead." He gestured at the office door. "I'll show you out. Now that your presence here has been regularized, I suggest you visit my colleague across the hall and register your business so you can advertise."

"For a fee, no doubt?"

"Nothing here is free, Captain, and without registering, no one can solicit business on Kilia."

Horgan ushered Dunmoore and her companions back into the lobby, still oozing insincerity and left them in front of the business registration office. She glanced at Guthren.

"Good?"

He turned to Vincenzo who nodded once.

"We're in business, Captain."

It was his way of saying that between them, Guthren and Vincenzo seeded the assistant harbormaster's office with tiny sound-activated pickups.

If her mention of Aurelia Fennon and *Kattegat Maru* touched a raw nerve, they should get a reaction sooner rather than later.

Dunmoore tapped the receiver in her pocket, linking her earbug with the listening devices and almost immediately heard Horgan's voice say, "I need to see Enoc Tarrant right now."

— Sixteen —

After dropping half of their remaining precious metals on an assistant business development manager's desk, Dunmoore, Guthren, and Vincenzo rejoined Saari's troopers on the plaza.

"I see no dead Shrehari littering the grounds. Congratulations on your restraint."

"There's no merit in it for us, Captain. None of the buggers came within sight. Where to now?"

With the hook set, returning to *Iolanthe* would be the sensible thing, but Dunmoore's instinct told her to loiter in Kilia for a while longer. Perhaps Horgan's urgent meeting with the mysterious Enoc Tarrant who'd commissioned Kotto Piris to salvage *Kattegat Maru* might shake things loose.

"Let's take in the sights. Enjoy a drink. Non-alcoholic, of course."

A few of the soldiers gave her mock disappointed looks, but Saari merely nodded.

"The sights it is. And in keeping with protocol, you, the cox'n and Vince can enjoy a drink. We'll do what gorillas are supposed to do. Intimidate anyone who gets too nosy."

They slowly meandered around the plaza, stopping by various storefronts where everything imaginable was on offer, including undecipherable items of non-human origin.

Dunmoore felt a bit like a celebrity accompanied by her entourage, or maybe an organized crime boss surrounded by hired muscle. But they attracted so little attention she decided it wasn't an unusual sight here in the depths of the wild frontier.

She eventually chose a table at an open-air cafe that gave them sight lines across the plaza and more importantly, a clear view of the administration building's main entrance. Guthren and Vincenzo remained standing behind her, hands joined, eyes always on the move. They projected the menace of tough, deadly bodyguards from a piece of popular fiction. Saari dispersed his half-platoon in pairs around the area, creating a secure perimeter.

Moments after Dunmoore sat, a hologram materialized over the table's center and took her order for an outrageously priced cup of coffee. When a droid trundled up with it a few minutes later, Guthren paid using another bit of their rapidly dwindling precious metal stash. Like any good supply officer, Joelle Biros would go through private conniptions at seeing the secret fund dwindle so quickly, for so little tangible results. But it was in a good cause.

They heard nothing more from the listening devices in Horgan's office and what little came from the assistant business development manager was thoroughly innocuous, though she listed *Persephone* as a private military corporation looking for work.

Dunmoore idly wondered whether someone would call her, offering a contract. And if so, whether she might take it on for appearances' sake. A trio of Shrehari crossed the plaza's far end, and she could almost feel her soldiers stiffen, though superficially, none seemed to react.

She felt equally strange at seeing humanity's enemy sharing a habitat with members of her own species, but wondered how they perceived the spin-induced gravity and the atmosphere's rich oxygen content. Dunmoore even gave her old foe Brakal a thought. Did he return from Miranda as safely as she did? Or was his ship overwhelmed by the more primitive but more numerous Mirandans?

She was halfway through her coffee when Horgan appeared from one of the side streets and crossed the plaza with a long, energetic stride. He gave no sign of spotting Dunmoore and her posse and vanished inside the pyramidal administration building.

More time passed in idle contemplation while she savored a brew rich in more ways than one. But they couldn't stay much longer. Ordering a second cup would cross from indulgence into fiscal irresponsibility. A mercenary looking for work couldn't afford profligacy. At least not in public.

"Look sharp," Guthren unexpectedly growled. "Bald male, built like a brick wall just came around a corner on my two o'clock. He's staring at the captain as if she's made of precious stones." A pause. "And coming here."

Saari's voice came through her earbug.

"Roger. Vallin, he's yours."

"Roger that," the corporal replied.

Dunmoore watched Vallin and his wingman peel off to the right, toward the swarthy, muscular man in a well-cut black suit who had her in his sights. An obvious pair of gorillas drifted into view behind him, and Dunmoore briefly raised her hand.

"Let them come. This might be business."

Vallin and his wingman checked their step though they kept watching the man and his escort with cold, hard eyes. The two gorillas halted just beyond Dunmoore's inner guard ring, their postures showing respect for the armed mercenaries, but the bald man kept coming until he stopped a few paces from her table. His massive, shiny head dipped in a polite nod

"Captain Shannon O'Donnell?"

He had a rough voice that sounded as if it came from the depths of a gravel pit. Up close he seemed much older than she first assumed. Faint lines radiated from the corners of his icy blue eyes and thin-lipped mouth. Small diamond studs sparkled in both earlobes while a few lines of body art peeked over his tunic's stiff, high collar.

"My name is Enoc Tarrant. May I join you with the offer of another coffee, or perhaps something else?"

Dunmoore waved at the chair across from her.

"Certainly, Ser Tarrant. The coffee on offer is of high quality and I'll gladly enjoy more."

Tarrant gestured over his shoulder and within moments, the droid returned, this time with two full cups. It left after carefully depositing them on the table. Dunmoore noticed Tarrant was neither asked for payment nor offered any.

She raised her cup in salute.

"And to what do I owe your largesse, Ser Tarrant?"

"Consider it a welcome, and payment for your time. As you might have noticed, everything on Kilia has a price, even the air we're breathing. We consider assuming someone will give you their time or anything else for free to be insulting."

"How practical." She took a sip and let it warm her insides. "What can I do for you, Ser Tarrant?"

"Answer a few questions, Captain." His cold eyes studied her as if she was a precious metal sample to be assayed, or a strange creature from the galaxy's edge, and she immediately sensed he was adept at spotting falsehood or equivocation.

"Ask away."

"Why has no one in this part of the galaxy ever come across the private military ship *Persephone* and the Varangian Company who I assume provides your guard detail? I know what you told Loris Horgan, but I want to hear it from your own lips."

"Ser Horgan must be a close friend if he's already made you aware of us."

Tarrant shrugged. "A business associate who has Kilia's best interests at heart."

"As I told him, we were operating on the other side of the Commonwealth until late last year, when an incident with the authorities caused contracts to dry up. We've been in this area for several months, but pickings are becoming rather slim."

It wasn't the whole truth but accurate enough to fool most human lie detectors. Special Operations Command had ordered *Iolanthe* to a new area of operations after the Toboso incident that saw Dunmoore become a temporary colonial governor and gave her ship too much local notoriety for continued undercover missions.

"What sort of incident?"

"We found ourselves on the losing side of a colonial tiff. Not because of anything we did, but our employers overplayed their hand and were forced to fold. The Commonwealth Navy encouraged us to find another playground."

"Mind telling me where?"

"The Cervantes system."

Tarrant nodded, although his soulless stare never left Dunmoore. "We caught a few faint echoes of that affair. Next question. You claim acquaintanceship with both Aurelia Fennon and Kotto Piris."

"I do."

"Funny. They don't gravitate in the same circles."

She cocked a sardonic eyebrow at him.

"No kidding. But then the circles we gravitate in overlap many others. You might say we're at the center of our own Venn diagram."

Her quip didn't raise so much as a twitch.

"I find it interesting that two acquaintances mentioned Kilia. We're not precisely a secret, but those we welcome understand the need to keep our existence, let alone our coordinates closely held, lest Imperial and Commonwealth authorities take exception to our business practices."

"Then I'm puzzled by the Shrehari corsair in orbit, Ser Tarrant. It's a well-known fact that half, if not more of them are actually undercover Deep Space Fleet or *Tai Kan* intelligence-gathering units."

Tarrant's face tightened briefly, the first sign of emotion he'd shown so far.

"One of the many rules governing Kilia is that one visitor never asks questions about another visitor."

She dipped her head in contrition.

"Of course, Ser Tarrant. My apologies."

"How did you come to first meet Fennon and Piris?"

"Ships passing in the night of interstellar space, Ser Tarrant. The people I count as acquaintances expect me to keep them out of my business affairs. I'm sure you understand."

"Nevertheless, I wish to know." His tone brooked no refusal.

Dunmoore held his gaze in silence for a long count, then said, "I saved *Kattegat Maru* from an attempted act of piracy."

"Did you now? And where was that?"

She waved a hand over her shoulder.

"On the fringes of the Commonwealth a few weeks ago."

"And Kotto Piris?"

"I helped him out of a tight spot with Commonwealth authorities. Mind you, his social circle and mine overlap more than you might think."

"So as thanks, both pointed you toward Kilia."

"I always ask for referrals. It's the best way to find my next contract." She gave him a knowing smile. "No doubt you're familiar with the method."

Tarrant's stare didn't soften, but Dunmoore fancied she saw an internal debate reflected in his eyes. Was her arrival here on the strength of claiming acquaintanceship with two of the actors involved in the *Kattegat Maru* affair a mere coincidence? Or did this glib mercenary with the menacing entourage represent trouble? If he already knew Piris vanished instead of bringing *Kattegat Maru* to Scandia, would he be acting any differently right now?

The man's jaw muscles worked for a moment.

"Why are you really here, O'Donnell? If that's your name."

"To find work, Ser Tarrant, nothing more."

"Unfortunately, I don't believe you. Everything you said is plausible, but I think it's based on a lie." He slipped a thin tablet from his pocket and held it up. The three-dimensional hologram of a lean, middle-aged woman's face appeared. "Who is this?"

"Aurelia Fennon." Another face appeared. "Kotto Piris."

"And this?"

Carrie Fennon's youthful features replaced the hardened spacer's ugly mug. The image wasn't recent, leading Dunmoore to wonder whether it came from a Kilia surveillance video dating back to one of *Kattegat Maru*'s earlier visits.

Acting on sheer instinct, Dunmoore shrugged.

"I don't know. A child. We don't come across many in our line of business."

The skin around Tarrant's eyes tightened.

"This is Aurelia Fennon's daughter. Surely you met her when you became acquainted with Fennon. She is part of *Kattegat Maru*'s crew."

Dunmoore shook her head.

"I wasn't aware Aurelia had a child, let alone raised her on a starship. How old is she? Fourteen? Fifteen? Since the Rules of War don't allow private military corporations to carry minors aboard our vessels, meeting the girl would have surprised me."

"Now I know you're lying. Fennon is rather proud of her offspring although a tad overprotective." Tarrant put away the tablet and climbed to his feet. "I'm afraid I must ask you to leave Kilia now and never return. There's nothing here for you. We will reimburse the fees you paid. Precious metals, was it? They'll be waiting by the docks."

"What gives you the power to throw us out, Ser Tarrant? I wasn't aware you belong to Kilia's administration."

"I am Kilia, and my word is law. Farewell, Captain O'Donnell. We won't meet again."

Tarrant turned and walked away, trailed by his guards.

"Wasn't that special," Dunmoore murmured, mildly stunned by his unexpected eviction order. She gulped down the dregs of her coffee and stood in turn. "Back to the docks, people. We're no longer welcome."

— Seventeen —

As promised, a runner from the station's administration was waiting by their assigned airlock with a bag containing precious metal ingots. Guthren and Vincenzo carried out a quick check, then the coxswain dismissed the runner with a nod.

Moments later, the landing party was back aboard and, at Dunmoore's order, Petty Officer Knowles sealed the hatches. The gangway tube broke free from their shuttle's hull and pulled back into the wall.

Knowles gently turned her craft around and found a traffic control droid, perhaps the same one as before, waiting to guide them. When Saari opened his mouth to speak, Dunmoore raised a hand and pointed at her ear, the universal sign for 'someone might be listening.' After that, no one said a word while Knowles threaded them back through the cavern and out into space where *Iolanthe*, patiently orbiting Kilia, waited for their return.

As soon as they were aboard and the Q-ship's hangar deck once more secure, Dunmoore motioned at Guthren and Vincenzo to abandon their bags in the shuttle and follow her. Then, she dismissed Sergeant Saari with a promise to talk later.

Once in the hangar deck control room, she said, "Quarantine what that runner gave us and see it's analyzed, Chief."

"Aye, sir. Vincenzo can bring the lot to Harry Simms right away." Simms was the supply department's chief petty officer and Lieutenant Biros' right hand. Guthren nodded at the leading spacer who immediately jogged off. "Do you expect foul play?"

"Tarrant was rather eager to refund everything we paid." She turned to Petty Officer Harkon, the man in charge of *Iolanthe*'s shuttles. "Scan our craft for subspace trackers or anything else suspicious. We might well have brought home hitchhikers, which is how the bad guys tracked *Kattegat Maru*. If you find something, leave it and tell Mister Holt or me right away."

"Will do, sir."

She found her first officer on the bridge, lounging in the command chair and chatting with Carrie Fennon. He jumped to his feet at her arrival.

"The thunderous expression on your face does not augur well, Skipper."

"We were tossed out on our ear, Zeke. Leave and don't let the doorknob hit you in the ass. I'd rather not repeat myself several times, so round up the department heads and see if we can open an untraceable tight-beam link with *Kattegat Maru*."

"In say, ten minutes? That'll give you time for a cup of coffee."

"I'm swimming in caffeine already, but ten minutes is good." She finally noticed the anxious expression on Carrie's face. "I'm afraid I didn't make much progress, but our eviction might set things in motion. Why don't you attend the department heads' meeting too?"

Dunmoore glanced at Holt who nodded in agreement.

"Excellent idea, Skipper."

**

"Commander?"

"What?"

Brakal's angular head snapped up to shoot an angry stare at the officer standing by his open door. The thrice-damned Strike Group Khorsan chief of staff, Gra'k, was still inundating him with barely decipherable reports, no doubt hoping to drown his acting commander in a sea of minutiae. As a result, Brakal was as irritable as a venomous serpent denied the opportunity to bite.

For once, Regar's habitual air of cynical disdain at the universe didn't relieve Brakal's vexation.

"I heard from *Chorlak*. A human starship calling itself *Persephone* and bearing a superficial resemblance to our ghost showed up at Kilia Station." Regar's Shrehari vocal chords struggled with the unfamiliar name. "Its captain is a female by the name Shannon O'Donnell." Dunmoore's cover name also came out as a set of mangled syllables. "She claims to be the human version of our corsairs — a privateer." The *Tai Kan* officer fought human sounds and lost again.

"Kilia, hmm?" Brakal rubbed his massive jaw with a hand powerful enough to break bones. "Perhaps the Admiralty's insistence we use it as a spot to gather intelligence instead of seizing the place or destroying it was one of the better decisions to come from those diseased cretins in robes. Even if they gave responsibility for oversight to the *Tai Kan*. Better yet, although it's not within our formally assigned area of operations, that filthy nest of putrefying vermin is within a short otherspace leap of our current position. I suddenly feel the urge to offer our brave *Tai Kan* pretend-corsair comradely assistance and at the same time see if we can spot our ghost."

"Violating our boundaries without being in pursuit of the enemy? That would give Gra'k a justification for knifing you in the back, bureaucratically speaking. Not that he has the courage to use a real blade." Regar's sardonic grin grew wide enough to expose his fangs. "Yet his sort can commit every manner of injury."

"Commit?" Brakal's massive fist slammed down on the metal desktop. "Gra'k can barely defecate on his own because he's scared of violating a general order or regulation. The worst he will do is sit on anything coming from the Admiralty and wait until it's too late before showing me. Not that it matters. Nothing worthwhile comes from Shrehari Prime anymore. Our betters no longer see their way to victory and meanwhile, indecision paralyzes half of the fleet. That's what we've come to, Regar. An Imperial Deep Space Fleet where inaction is deemed a lesser sin than independent action which might displease the leadership. I can think of worse things to do than annoy Gra'k and his vipers while I consort with rogues and outlaws. And find that damned ghost. A female captain, you said? Any description?"

"Flame-haired. That's the only thing *Chorlak*'s commander said."

A slow smile transformed Brakal's face into that of a gargoyle.

A flame-haired female commander? What are the odds there's more than one in the human fleet? The color is said to be rare among that ridiculously persistent species."

Regar frowned, lost in thought, then he grunted.

"Dunmoore. The one who gave us a merry chase to the star system of the lost humans. We were fortunate to return unscathed. That branch of the species wasn't just persistent, it was vicious beyond reckoning. A bit like our Arkanna neighbors."

"It's a good thing they don't know the secrets of otherspace travel or we might find them nipping at our heels. But back to what concerns us, you miserable spy. Kilia, the spacecraft *Chorlak* saw, and its flame-haired captain." Brakal stabbed his communicator with a thick, bony finger. "Urag."

"Lord?"

Tol Vehar's acting captain responded with commendable alacrity.

"It's still commander, not lord, you miscreant. Prepare a course for Kilia Station, best speed and when all ships are ready, leap into otherspace."

Urag made a strangled noise Brakal recognized as a subtle expression of doubt.

"It's not in our area of operations. Orders reserve it for the *Tai Kan*."

"Indeed, but I decided the *Tai Kan* requires friendly forces, namely us, to help it. Regar tells me his colleagues might have spotted the human ghost who's been devastating our shipping."

"Ah. In that case, I hear and obey, Lord. Shall I tell Khorsan Base of our new plans?"

"Under no circumstances. Those useless, flatulent whoresons would tell the Admiralty, and then where will we be? In a jurisdictional dispute between the Deep Space Fleet and the disease called *Tai Kan*? May every demon of the Underworld have its way with the poxed insects. Just take us to Kilia as fast as our tired engines can manage."

"Done."

Brakal cut the link, then, after waving Regar out of his office, turned around to stare through the thick porthole. Dunmoore. Could it be after all this time?

And yet the ghost's tactics, its ruthless success in decimating Imperial shipping in this sector, spoke of a bold enemy commander. The flame-haired she-wolf was one of the few humans with the mix of skill and luck necessary to prosper and win.

But what was she doing at Kilia? Didn't the Commonwealth leave it alone for the same reasons as the Empire — because it was a valuable conduit for intelligence and underhanded activities? Yet the ship reported by *Chorlak*'s commander might not be the ghost and its captain might not be Dunmoore.

Best to keep one's anticipation on a tight leash. Time would tell. Time and the forge of battle. Nevertheless, Brakal felt a tremor of excitement at the possibility of meeting his old foe once more, the female who destroyed *Tol Vakash* and his chances of becoming someone able to influence the course of a war he feared the Empire was slowly losing. Losing to the likes of Dunmoore and her peers.

— Eighteen —

"That's the fastest anyone's ever told us to leave," Cullop said when Dunmoore finished recounting her brief stint ashore. "Fast enough to make anyone suspicious."

"Oh, I'm suspicious all right, Emma, yet we still don't know whether the people taken off *Kattegat Maru* are here or elsewhere. But this is far from over. I attracted Tarrant's attention and aroused his suspicions. He won't leave matters as they are. Tarrant might well suspect his *Mary Celeste* gambit went awry."

"Hence the possibility of the precious metals refund being tainted, or a tracker planted on the shuttle."

She nodded at the first officer.

"It's something I would do."

"And if Petty Officer Harkon or the cox'n find something?" Sirico asked.

"We exploit it to our advantage. If Tarrant's people attached a subspace tracker to the shuttle, we'll leave it in working condition and turn the tables on anyone following us. It wouldn't surprise me to discover he ordered our elimination, perhaps even by the same ships responsible for *Kattegat Maru*, since they've already committed an act of piracy deserving summary execution."

Renny Halfen snorted.

"We can't hang them twice for the same offense. But since no one knows we're a battlecruiser under the skin, good luck to them."

"Good luck indeed."

The call waiting icon blinked in the lower corner of the conference room's main display.

"Here we go." She touched the controls embedded in the table and Petty Officer Harkon's face replace the Furious Faerie emblem.

"You called it, Captain. I found a subspace tracker cunningly affixed to the shuttle's keel. If no one thought to check, it would have stayed there until the next routine inspection. As ordered, I didn't touch the thing, but it's live and transmitting."

"So now we know how they might have tagged *Kattegat Maru* if it wasn't through an adulterated cargo container." Dunmoore glanced at Carrie Fennon, sitting quietly against the wall. "Comments?"

"Either is possible, sir, but if my mother feels paranoid, and she often does out in the Zone, she'll scan any cargo before taking it in. A hitchhiker on the shuttle, however, would escape notice."

"Since the pirates took both shuttles and cargo, we might never find out. But this is actually a good development. Kilia might have turned into a dead end for us if Tarrant accepted my story at face value. However, since he acted, we can be reasonably sure he's involved, even if the abductees aren't in Kilia. Once we're done..." The call waiting icon came up again. "Yes?"

"Vincenzo, sir. Those metal ingots they returned aren't the ones we gave them. They're nothing more than iron and lead with a thin veneer on the outside. Chief Simms says they're next to worthless."

Though Lieutenant Biros' face darkened with an angry frown, Dunmoore chuckled.

"No honor among thieves. That petty trickery makes striking back at Tarrant and Kilia an even more delightful proposition. If there's nothing else, let's break out of orbit and rejoin *Kattegat Maru*. Then, we'll make an FTL jump to the system's outer edge, where I hope the bastards try to screw us over like they did *Katie*. Try and fail, naturally."

Holt's piratical grin made a brief appearance. "Naturally."

**

"How long do you intend to loiter?" Holt asked after pouring himself a cup from the day cabin's urn. "Any normal vessel wouldn't spend more than a few hours sub-light to recalibrate once it's crossed the heliopause and can go FTL at interstellar speeds."

Dunmoore gave him a dubious grimace.

"I'll drag *Iolanthe*'s skirts until someone steps on them, Zeke. It's the best place to ambush anyone Tarrant put on our tail. Besides, a ship our size taking time to transition from in-system to interstellar wouldn't seem particularly strange."

"Let's hope it'll be the same pirates that attacked *Kattegat Maru*. Or part of the same confederation."

"Oh, no doubt they'll be related, if not the same, although I'm still puzzled by Tarrant's intentions. Are we to be terminated with extreme prejudice because we represent a threat? Or pirated in a time-honored manner because we represent an opportunity?"

"Or discretely tailed to see if we represent Commonwealth authorities?" Holt dropped into a chair across from Dunmoore. "Someone might have picked up a whiff of Navy blue from our emissions."

Dunmoore's right eyebrow crept up to her copper hairline.

"You mean that supposed Shrehari corsair, who could either be a spy or our counterpart, a Deep Space Fleet Q-ship instead of an ordinary marauder? Perhaps. If so, that would mean Kilia is playing footsie with the enemy."

"Not necessarily to the degree we might think, Skipper. If Tarrant and company think the Shrehari captain is one of their sort, an illicit profit-seeker, rather than a servant of the emperor, then it becomes chumminess between fellow crooks. For them, patriotism is a dirty word if there's money to be made. We were probably the most honest spacers to visit in living memory."

She raised her cup in salute.

"And the only ones capable of forcing Kilia to its knees. Thorin and his crew mapped out every weapons emplacement and shield generator. A few dozen stealth missiles fired from a standoff position, programmed to go live on final approach, and we can force Tarrant into cooperating. He can't risk even one Mark Five nuclear-tipped anti-ship bird striking hard enough to crack the asteroid and cause massive decompression."

"Why do I get a mental image of the Furious Faerie trying to kill a gnat with a sledgehammer?"

"Because you'd rather we be discreet instead of going in fully unmasked and telling the universe we're not a big, oafish privateer with delusions of grandeur."

Holt inclined his head in agreement.

"Discretion is my middle name. If we reveal *Persephone* is really the Commonwealth Starship *Iolanthe*, we'll need new hunting grounds once we finish this mission."

"Or the bad guys, human, Shrehari, whatever, will feel that sweet sense of doom every time they see a big, oafish freighter and steer clear, which would be good for honest civilian shipping."

"But not for our tactic of luring them in until we see the whites of their sub-light drives."

"So we change tactics, Zeke. Playing the weak little thing hasn't worked that well in recent weeks anyhow. Time for more aggressive tactics."

A mischievous smile appeared on Holt's lips.

"As a great general once said, when in doubt, find something and kill it."

"I think he said *in the absence of orders*, go find something and kill it, but your mangled version fits better."

"As I intended."

This time Holt raised his mug in salute.

Before Dunmoore could call him on it, her day cabin's communicator pinged.

"CIC to the captain."

Both recognized Sirico's voice.

"Yes, Thorin."

"Long-range sensors picked up three hyperspace trails. If they're our quarry, Chief Yens figures thirty minutes."

"Excellent." She glanced at her first officer. "So much for dragging our skirts until the end of days. Tell *Kattegat Maru* to make a hole in space and stay clear of any action. Put us at battle stations in fifteen minutes and prepare to unmask the Furious Faerie."

"*Avec plaisir, mon capitaine.* CIC, out."

"Since when does Thorin speak French with you, Skipper?"

She shrugged.

"It's a new affectation, something that appears whenever his bloodlust comes out to play."

Holt drained his mug and stood.

"I worry about Thorin sometimes. A combat systems officer should enjoy his job, but he positively revels in it. That can't be good for his sanity."

"Are any of us truly sane?" She asked with an impish twinkle in her eyes.

"In *Iolanthe*? I doubt it, considering everyone not only volunteered to serve the Commonwealth aboard starships but volunteered a second time to serve in Special Operations Command."

"Everyone? I seem to recall Tatiana's company was dragooned into joining this crew, never mind that Admiral Nagira didn't bother asking me whether I wanted this ship in preference to a shore billet."

His one good eye winked at her.

"Only because he already knew the answer. And every single Scandia Regiment soldier aboard is proud as punch to serve in *Iolanthe*, so there."

— Nineteen —

"I'm still not used to sounding battle stations aboard a civilian freighter," Lieutenant Theo Kremm, *Kattegat Maru*'s relief first officer remarked as he activated the klaxon Cullop designated as their siren. "Considering we'd be better off sounding 'run like hell' stations instead."

"Or in this case, 'make a hole in space' stations," Command Sergeant Aase Jennsen said as she took her seat on the small bridge.

"Don't worry," Cullop replied over her shoulder. "If things go sideways, we'll be rabbiting out in a matter of seconds. But since the three contacts *Iolanthe* picked up probably came from Kilia, they won't live long enough to dent the Furious Faerie's hull, let alone find us. We can just sit back and watch the mightiest Q-ship in the known galaxy unmask, which will be a new experience for us."

"Perhaps for you wonderful people," Kremm replied. "But I was privileged to witness her frightening transformation from *Herja*'s bridge a few months ago, remember?"

"In that case, no spoilers. I would love to get a taste for what our prey feels when it realizes she's not a defenseless civilian tub."

**

Apprentice Officer Carrie Fennon was already in her assigned seat at the back of the CIC when Dunmoore entered and took the command chair from Thorin Sirico. Because of it being an armored cube at the Q-ship's heart, the CIC was the safest compartment during battle and therefore the best place for a teenaged civilian.

Besides, Dunmoore figured Carrie would learn things that could be useful for her watch-keeping ticket examinations. It might even make her consider a hitch in the Navy, or at least think about joining the naval reserve. The look of intense concentration on her youthful face as she studied the tactical projection and each of the displays spoke of a mind absorbing everything as if it were a microfiber sponge.

Dunmoore exchanged an amused glance with Major Salminen, who'd been answering Carrie Fennon's whispered questions, then asked, "Status?"

"Hyperspace traces still heading in our direction. Estimated emergence, if they're after us, will be in under ten minutes," Sirico replied. "The ship is at battle stations and ready to unmask on command. *Kattegat Maru* is also at battle stations and running silent. If Chief Yens didn't know where she was, our sensors would struggle to spot her. Those dumb pirates are in for a lovely surprise."

"May I ask a question, Captain? Or would that be inappropriate while we're at battle stations?"

Siobhan swiveled her chair around to face Carrie.

"Please do. Until the enemy appears, there's little else to do. Once they're here, however..."

A grave nod greeted her response.

"Understood, sir. Are you assuming they're hostile? Lieutenant Commander Sirico explained what unmasking means, in that it gives *Iolanthe*'s true identity away."

"I intend to wait until I'm sure of their intentions. My working assumption is they want to seize what they believe is the privateer *Persephone*, much in the same way they took *Kattegat Maru*. Failing that, their orders might be to wreck us."

"Why is Kilia sending these pirates after *Iolanthe*?"

"Probably because I raised Tarrant's suspicions by claiming acquaintanceship with both your mother and Captain Piris. Alternatively, the Shrehari corsair we saw is an Imperial spy ship and its crew made *Iolanthe* for a Fleet unit, something they shared with Tarrant."

"Or both," Sirico said.

"True. As for the matter of unmasking, so far everyone who saw *Iolanthe* in battlecruiser mode didn't live long enough to spread the word. If Tarrant sent a trio of his pirates after us, they might well suffer the same fate. But if their mission is non-lethal, such as intimidation, we may just partially unmask and present the aspect of a privateer rather than that of a warship."

"Oh." Fennon slowly nodded as she digested this new tidbit. "That makes sense. A privateer would be better armed than a freighter, but not as heavily as a Navy vessel."

"However, if those three ships are coming for us, I doubt they'll stop at giving us a scare or making sure we leave this area. No. They'll be aiming to repeat what they pulled with *Kattegat Maru*. And that's not going to happen."

"There's another option," Ezekiel Holt, or rather his hologram floating by Dunmoore's right arm, said. "We could let a boarding party come into our lair and pounce. Do what Emma did with Piris' folks."

"Tarrant knows we carry an infantry company. They won't even try. It will be surrender under threat of destruction. If they bother with the niceties and don't just open fire the moment they're within range."

"Shame. I'm sure Tatiana's folks would enjoy a good live-fire repel boarders exercise."

"And mar our otherwise pristine interior? Pass, Zeke. I'm surprised a first officer known for running a tight ship would even think of such a thing."

The small hologram shrugged although Dunmoore fancied she could see a twinkle of devilry in its eye.

"It was an idea. Something different from our usual lure 'em into range and blow 'em away with nuclear missiles shtick."

"Shtick? Is that what you call how we wage war?"

"Yes, it is. When you do the same thing every time, it becomes a shtick. And nice alliteration, Skipper. I'd say Apprentice Officer Fennon is learning the wrong lessons from us right now. Lord knows what she'll tell her mother about the Navy. Probably enough to see us barred from ever hosting an honest Guild member again."

A strangled sound reached Dunmoore's ears. She turned to glance over her shoulder and winked at the round-eyed young woman. No need for explanations. Tatiana Salminen was already whispering something into her ear about how borderline crazy Dunmoore and her crew became in the face of an impending battle.

The next few minutes passed in silence, then Chief Yens held up a hand.

"Three emergence signatures approximately two hundred and fifty thousand kilometers aft."

Sirico let out a low whistle.

"Nice precision work."

"I'll wager Kilia partially vectored them in," Holt's hologram said. "Then dropped out of FTL just before entering our hyperspace scanner's range and triangulated with home base to get our most recent position courtesy of the subspace tracker stuck to the captain's pinnace."

Dunmoore gave her first officer a tight smile.

"Sounds plausible. The Navy should do something about Kilia when the opportunity presents itself. Vectoring pirates onto honest merchant ships is a capital offense."

"You'd attack Kilia?" Fennon blurted out.

Dunmoore glanced over her shoulder again.

"Tarrant obviously need to be taught a lesson. How that lesson will unfold depends on him although it won't be taught by *Iolanthe* alone. We're not quite that powerful. But first things first. Do you have an ID, Chief?"

"Aye. One of the three is the Shrehari corsair we saw at Kilia. The other pair are two of the human-built hulls that orbited alongside the bonehead."

"Sir?" The signals petty officer raised a hand. "We're being hailed. Audio only."

"Here we go. Put it on." When the petty officer gave her thumbs up, she said, "This is Captain Shannon O'Donnell of the private military vessel *Persephone*. I understand you wish to speak with me."

"Cooperate, and you'll live," a rough, but human voice replied.

"Oh? Care to explain?" Dunmoore's tone took on that honeyed texture her crew knew presaged a storm.

"We're targeting you with our weapons. Spool up your hyperdrives, and we open fire. You may or may not survive the opening salvo. But if you do cooperate, your chances of survival will be better. And at three against one, it's a given we out-gun you by a wide margin."

"Is it?" A feral smile twisted her lips. "How should we cooperate?"

"Heave to and surrender your ship. You'll be well treated as our prisoners and set free in a neutral port. Alive. Resist and die."

"So it's to be an act of piracy? How amusingly bold."

"You're still within an area of space claimed by Kilia, and we represent the station's management, so I'd call this a legitimate police action."

"In what way did we violate Kilia's laws, pray tell?"

"Not my concern, O'Donnell. I simply obey the orders we're given."

"Claiming to obey orders hasn't saved criminals from the noose since the mid-twentieth century. And the bonehead corsair with whom you're keeping company? You are aware humanity is at war with the Shrehari, right? Consorting with them makes you a traitor."

A pause, punctuated by a derisive snort.

"To hell with your damned Commonwealth. Kilia is a sovereign entity that has no quarrel with the Empire. We enforce our own laws, not those of the Commonwealth. And by the way, that insulting name you used for our Shrehari friends will be costly. It's an affront to their sense of honor, something they don't countenance."

"Sensitive souls, are they? Do they shrivel under the onslaught of put-downs?" Dunmoore's mocking intonations drew a muffled guffaw from Chief Yens. "Maybe the Navy would do better to fire disrespectful nicknames at them instead of anti-ship missiles. It might save the long-suffering taxpayers a fortune."

Though her tone was light, her eyes held a deadly glint as they studied the tactical display. Sirico, like everyone else in the CIC and on the bridge, knew she was talking with their prey to let them close the distance so *Iolanthe*'s opening salvo would prove as devastating as possible.

Her fingers tapped the controls in the command chair's arm, and the icon marking the Shrehari corsair pulsed a deeper red than the others, a sign she was designating him Tango One, the target for that first salvo. If the corsair was an undercover Imperial vessel, it would be the most dangerous of the three.

"I'm sure they'll treat you with the sensitivity you deserve, O'Donnell," the unnamed pirate replied. "Now what is it to be? Surrender and live? Or resist and die? Our superiors would prefer the former but will be content with the latter. It would be a shame to destroy your ship. Bulk haulers are useful in these parts."

"How about neither? How about you let us leave, and no one gets hurt? Enough sentient beings died in the last few years to make everyone sick of killing."

An ugly chuckle erupted from the CIC's speakers.

"You don't understand, do you? Kilia's management has ordered your arrest. Now make your choice."

Sirico raised a hand and pointed at the main weapons display. All three interlopers were entering optimum range.

"Unfortunately, the misapprehension is yours, not mine. A shame, but please tell the Almighty when you see him that I gave you a fair warning."

Dunmoore made a cutting motion, and when the signals petty officer indicated the link was severed, she said, "Unmask and open fire. Shoot to destroy."

**

"Holy shit."

Command Sergeant Aase Jennsen added something in one of the Scandian dialects, though to Cullop's ears it sounded very much like the Anglic equivalent, a swear word with a centuries-old pedigree. What was, seconds earlier, a large bulk carrier, its armament hidden behind moving plates, was now one of the most potent battlecruisers in the Commonwealth Navy, a mass of plasma gun turrets and anti-ship missile launchers.

"I second the sentiment," *Kattegat Maru*'s relief captain said, eyes glued to the main display as a smile slowly spread across her face. "The Furious Faerie coming to life is a thing of beauty when Captain Dunmoore gets annoyed. I knew it was coming, yet the sight still gives me the chills. I'd pay good money to see the face of that Shrehari corsair's captain right now, knowing his human buddies just led him to a premature death at the hands of the despised human Fleet."

Cullop and the rest of her tiny bridge crew had listened in on the conversation between Dunmoore and the pirate chieftain via a tight-beam link with *Iolanthe*, but seeing the Q-ship unmask struck them with awe nonetheless. Then, *Iolanthe*'s flanks, topside, and keel erupted with brilliant light as guns and launchers came online simultaneously.

And though they wouldn't see it until the pirates returned fire, Cullop knew the Furious Faerie was now encased in a cocoon of military-grade shielding, capable of deflecting anything the enemy could throw at her.

The corsair might be a different story, but it quickly became clear Dunmoore designated him as the primary, and therefore the most dangerous target, the one destined to die first.

— Twenty —

"We are at full power and maximum shielding; the subspace radio jammer is active, and the first missile flight is away, heading for Tango One," Lieutenant Commander Thorin Sirico reported in a matter-of-fact tone. He could have been announcing the opening strokes of the All-Commonwealth ProAm Golf Tournament.

"Guns are firing on Tango Two and Three." A pause. "Second missile flight is away, heading for Tango Two." Soft vibrations from launch tubes reloading coursed through the deck again. Then, "Third missile flight is away, heading for Tango Three."

Three clouds, each made up of tiny blue icons, filled the void aft of *Iolanthe* in the tactical projection. Propelled by small but powerful sub-light drives, the missiles were accelerating toward their designated targets at a rate starships couldn't match.

The three pirates were themselves accelerating toward the Q-ship and thereby her missiles, and the gap between weapons and targets shrank with terrifying speed. Too much so for defensive calliopes that were not quite up to the task of dealing with saturation salvos.

At this range, not even the Shrehari, though he probably carried Imperial Fleet ordnance, could prevent a dozen nuclear warheads from exploding against his shields —

warheads capable of producing enough energy to overload generators via massive feedback pulses.

A bright purple aurora flared, encasing the corsair in a cocoon of light. Then it collapsed with stunning suddenness, leaving the alien vessel's armored hull exposed to streams of plasma from *Iolanthe*'s guns.

"Bonehead's firing back and veering off," Chief Yens announced. "Hyperdrives are spooling up. He's about to try a Crazy Ivan jump."

"No one leaves this battle without my say so," Dunmoore growled. "Concentrate fire on the Shrehari, Mister Sirico."

"Concentrating fire, aye."

A foreshortened, light blue aurora briefly flared around *Iolanthe*'s aft quarter as the Shrehari's guns struck home.

"Tangos Two and Three kicked out half a dozen birds each."

Red dots separated from the icons representing two of the three pirates.

"Finally woke up, did they?" Sirico asked through clenched teeth as he watched thick plasma streams eat through the corsair's hull. The alien ship wavered as its drives tried to form a hyperspace bubble, but it was too late. "The bastard's not leaving. One of our rounds probably struck part of his power system because he's venting radiation through that hole like a damn geyser."

"Eight missiles struck Tango Two. His shields are wavering. Seven on Tango Three. Same result." Deep purple auroras enveloped both human-built hulls as competing energies fought for dominance.

Then, a tiny yet incredibly bright star flared up for a few seconds.

"Scratch the bonehead," Chief Yens said in a tone suffused with visceral satisfaction.

"Engaging enemy birds." Concentrated small-bore plasma rounds, pumped out by the belt of multi-barrel calliopes encircling *Iolanthe*'s hull and hyperdrive nacelles gave life to a curtain of destruction. Tiny red icons winked out of existence one by one in the tactical projection.

A second purple aurora encircled one of the remaining pirates as *Iolanthe*'s main batteries struck hard but it also vanished without warning. "Tango Two lost his shields. Tango Three is also spooling up drives for a Crazy Ivan. Concentrating fire on Tango Three."

But the latter didn't make it into FTL either. His shields collapsed just as he tried to form a hyperspace bubble, and the rest of the salvo struck his starboard side nacelle, cutting through the antimatter feed line. Tango Three vanished in a silent explosion that created a short-lived miniature nova.

"Hold your fire on the last survivor unless he spools up his drives. Signals, open a channel."

"Aye, aye, Captain." No more than a few seconds passed. "Channel open."

"Unknown ship," Dunmoore said, "I'm giving you one chance to live. Cooperate, and you won't join your two mates in the fires of hell, or wherever Shrehari end up when we kill them. Further aggressive action on your part or any attempt to flee will be seen as trying for suicide by privateer. One which I will help along without hesitation. There is no way out of this."

With neither response nor return fire forthcoming after almost a minute, Sirico chuckled softly.

"Stunned into a catatonic state, I'd say. One moment, cock of the walk, the next a bare step removed from becoming another deep space wreck. I do so love my job."

Finally, "What do you motherfucking assholes want?" A rough voice barely recognizable as female demanded.

"Your surrender, and answers to my questions."

"So you can hang us as pirates?" Contempt oozed from every word. "Not a chance, darling."

"Surrender, and I will spare your lives. Don't surrender, or worse, pretend to surrender and play me false, you die. Instantly. Your ship is forfeit that goes without saying, but I'll release you in a suitable port at my first opportunity."

"And what the hell does suitable mean?" The woman sneered.

"One with a breathable atmosphere. Which is more than you'll get if I fire another salvo." Dunmoore paused. "Sixty seconds. I have business elsewhere. I'll take you with me as detainees or leave you behind as corpses. And I'm not particularly fussed about my options. But perhaps you should be. Or if you don't care, maybe your crew does."

The unknown woman snorted.

"If you think they'll mutiny, it's a bit late. I already shot the dumb jackass who dragged us into this mess."

"So you *are* looking for a way out." Dunmoore ran a gloved finger down the faint scar decorating her jawline. "Otherwise, you'd have gladly died alongside your heroically stupid comrades. I'll bet Kilia isn't paying you enough to make the ultimate sacrifice and Tarrant doesn't strike me as the type who'd so much as pay for a miserly flag to cover your caskets."

Another pause, then, "What are your terms."

"Load every living being into your shuttles and run them out a hundred kilometers. We'll scan those shuttles and your ship to make sure you're not screwing around. If both are clear, the ship becomes my prize, I recover your shuttles, and you live in my brig until I put you ashore. If you mess with me, you die. Understood?"

"Yeah? How many have swallowed your brand of bullshit so far and lived to tell the tale?"

"More crews than you might think. Someone fires on me, I shoot back. But once you stop fighting and surrender, you're entitled to the full Aldebaran Conventions treatment."

A sound reminiscent of someone spitting on the deck came over the comlink.

"Are you telling me you're *Fleet*? Did that idiot Tarrant send us after the fucking *Navy*?"

"No. We're privateers, but a letter of marque comes with an obligation to respect the Conventions, just like regular Navy ships. Now tell me this. Why do I think you're not one of Enoc Tarrant's fans?"

That spitting sound came through the CIC speakers again.

"No one else ever drove me to shoot my captain so I could live. And definitely no one else ever sent me after a fucking Q-ship, regular or privateer."

"Did Enoc Tarrant send you after a freighter by the name *Kattegat Maru*?"

A long silence followed Dunmoore's question.

"What's it to you?"

"I want to know what happened with the crew and passengers."

A note of challenge crept into the woman's voice, but it sounded false to Dunmoore's ears.

"What makes you think anything happened with them?"

"Call it a hunch. We found *Kattegat Maru* abandoned but otherwise fully functional close to here. She was outbound from Kilia, meaning Tarrant might well have planted a subspace tracker on her. He certainly didn't hesitate to plant one on us."

"How do you know she was outbound from Kilia?"

"We checked her logs." A half-choked inhalation greeted Dunmoore's assertion, proof the unnamed woman and her crew took part in seizing *Kattegat Maru*. "Is something wrong? Or are you wondering how we reconstructed the logs her attackers wiped, thereby finding enough evidence to connect the piracy to both Kilia and your ship? And the other two we destroyed."

"No comment."

"Where are *Kattegat Maru*'s crew and her passengers? Remember, what I said about cooperating? I want your surrender and answers to my questions or I open fire one last time."

"If I talk out of turn, we're dead anyway."

"Tarrant isn't the forgiving sort, is he?"

The woman cackled.

"He doesn't know what forgiveness is. But he knows how to uphold *omerta*. I'll surrender my ship and crew, but none of us will say a word."

"You know there are interrogation techniques no one can resist."

"Yeah, and they're illegal as fuck, even for Special Security Bureau assholes."

"Inside the Commonwealth perhaps, but as Tarrant seems to believe, this area is beyond the accepted Commonwealth sphere. What about that Shrehari corsair, or whatever he was? Is information about him also covered by *omerta*?"

"Tarrant is good friends with the boneheads. Apparently, it dates back to well before the war. They're always welcome in Kilia so long they're not Imperial military."

"Does Tarrant always send a corsair out on raids along with his human-crewed ships?"

"No. This is new crap. Last couple of sorties. But don't ask me why. We're told what to do, no explanations given."

"I suppose the Shrehari helped you seize *Kattegat Maru*?"

She cackled again.

"Nice try — O'Donnell, is it? I know nothing about this *Kattegat Maru*. Now do you intend to sit around all day talking smack, or will you accept our surrender?"

"Evacuate your ship, fly at least one hundred kilometers out, and wait for orders. We will scan you, so forget about playing dirty tricks."

"Give me fifteen minutes."

"By the way, what's your name and that of your ship? And how many are aboard?"

A snort.

"Skelly Kursu at your service. This useless tub goes by the name *Bukavac,* and there are thirty-five of us still breathing. Forty when we started out. You'll find the bodies on the hangar deck. Toss 'em out into space, burn 'em in the plasma tubes, or sell 'em to resurrectionists. I don't care."

"How the hell did Tarrant intend your wolf pack to take my ship if your crew numbered only forty, presuming the others didn't carry much more?"

"Boneheads. There was over a hundred of them, warriors who could do the boarding party dance really well. Some jobs, we bring extra. This one, there was no time to round up more muscle. It meant Shrehari shock and awe again, just like — well..." Kursu's voice trailed away.

Dunmoore glanced over her shoulder at Carrie Fennon and gave her a significant look. That explained the alien scent Fennon picked up when she came out of her cubbyhole after the attack on *Kattegat Maru.* An icy mask froze the young woman's features, and she nodded wordlessly.

"Leave your ship and remember, there's only one punishment for misbehavior. Death."

"Yeah, yeah. I hear you, O'Donnell."

Dunmoore made a cutting motion, and when the signals petty officer gave her the nod, she said, "Zeke, ask Chief Trane to prepare the brig for our guests. Tatiana, the usual brig chasers to the hangar deck when we pick up those shuttles. Chief Yens, do your magic on them and *Bukavac* once they've launched."

After three almost simultaneous "Aye, ayes," Holt asked, "What about a prize crew?"

"I thought *Bukavac* might serve us better as part Trojan horse and part guided missile."

— Twenty-One —

Dunmoore, ensconced once more in the hangar deck control room with Petty Officer Harkon, watched *Bukavac*'s former crew walk off the pirate ship's two shuttles with hands on top of their heads. Most carried a small pack of some sort containing their worldly possessions and resembled typical star lane rogues: rough, mean-faced, widely individualistic in their dress and appearance, and of every human phenotype.

As a precaution, she'd ordered the two craft brought aboard under control of the hangar deck tractor beams after Chief Yens' sensors gave the all-clear. Skelly Kursu and her people seemed more interested in survival than making a grand gesture for Enoc Tarrant's sake now that the brief, violent battle was over.

They obeyed Major Salminen's soldiers, armed and menacingly anonymous in their powered armor, without demur as the troopers directed them into three evenly spaced ranks. There, they subjected the prisoners to an extensive search, looking for weapons, drugs and other proscribed items. Chief Petty Officer Third Class Marko Trane, *Iolanthe*'s master-at-arms and non-commissioned officer in charge of the brig, looked on from the open door leading aft to his domain.

One of the pirates, a rangy woman in worn leathers caught her eye. Dark complexioned, with a hatchet face framed by thick black hair plaited into a queue at the nape of her neck, the woman was almost an exact match for Dunmoore's mental image of Skelly Kursu and her raspy voice. She was about to leave the control room and make her way across the hangar deck when her communicator buzzed for attention.

"Dunmoore."

"It's Holt, Captain. Renny and his crew finished their survey of *Bukavac,* and he figures we can turn her into a drone without too many difficulties. She shows no hull integrity problems and her drives are undamaged. Astrid still needs to commune with the ship's AI and confirm that it will not only accept the necessary navigation instructions but carry them out in the absence of a human supervisor. Fixing the shield generators is another matter altogether. That will take time. We gave them a massive overload."

Dunmoore frowned in frustration.

"Without shields, she'll be too easy a target and not much good as a Trojan drone, and we dare not delay too much. Tarrant will expect his wolf pack's victorious return. The longer that takes, the more he'll smell a rat."

"No doubt. Renny is preparing an estimate of the time required to bring the forward shields back online. They should be enough for our purposes. He also suggested we reconfigure a flight of missiles as penetrators and load them aboard *Bukavac.* If they don't fit in the pirate's own tubes, we can attach a pack to the hull."

"Penetrators?" A faint smile replaced Dunmoore's earlier frown. "Now there's an idea. If even one or two make it through, Tarrant will find himself contending with improvised nuclear mines under our control embedded into the asteroid's surface. His shields only cover the habitat cavern and its immediate surroundings, but our mines need not be anywhere near there to cause him sleepless nights."

"Advantage *Iolanthe*, or rather *Persephone*."

"It's even better than my original idea of using *Bukavac* to degrade Kilia's defenses ahead of our arrival. While I think about it, any luck finding the Shrehari's black box? If he's Imperial Fleet or *Tai Kan*, he might be equipped with one of the newer recording beacons, and I'd rather not leave an image of the Furious Faerie for his pals to find."

"And avoid eroding *Iolanthe*'s mystique as the ghost that makes starships vanish. I couldn't agree more. We've enjoyed an almost perfect run so far. Chief Yens is still looking, but I could send a Growler for a run through the debris field."

The Growler, a shuttle configured for electronic warfare, was capable of intense short-range scanning and jamming.

"Launch one as soon as our prisoners clear the hangar deck." She thought for a moment. "Then, once Chief Trane finishes processing them, have him bring Skelly Kursu to the conference room."

**

The door chime pulled Dunmoore from her study of *Bukavac*'s image on the main display. Part of her thought it a shame the sleek, menacing starship would die in a day or two. Never mind HQ's reaction to her sacrificing a potential undercover unit in a war ruse designed to recover seventy-odd civilians of no great importance.

"Come."

Chief Petty Officer Third Class Marko Trane stepped in and came to attention. His first few weeks in *Iolanthe* were not happy ones, and he came with a lot of baggage, not least for his role in the Toboso affair. But he surprised everyone by asking to stay as part of the ship's company when the

Admiralty shifted her to the Shrehari front. And so Trane quickly became Bosun Dwyn's invaluable right hand in addition to his duties as the Q-ship's master-at-arms, responsible for the brig and prisoners of war.

"Skelly Kursu is in the conference room, Captain. I checked her for weapons, and she's guarded by two E Company soldiers."

"Thank you, Chief. You may return to your duties. I intend to let the prisoner stew for a while."

"Aye, aye, sir."

Trane pivoted on his heels in a movement crisp enough to please *Iolanthe*'s coxswain and left her cabin.

Dunmoore switched her main display feed from *Bukavac*'s image to a view of the adjacent compartment. Skelly Kursu was indeed the dark, rangy woman she'd spotted from the hangar deck control room.

She sat in one of the chairs, arms crossed, a look of infinite patience on her sharp, angular face, though her deep-set eyes kept moving as she scanned the room without being obvious.

A lance corporal and a private from the Scandia Regiment, both carrying slung scatterguns, stood against the bulkhead behind her. The soldiers wore the Army's rifle green battledress and brimmed field cap, but without their regiment's loping timber wolf on a snowflake insignia. *Iolanthe* was still, as far as the prisoners were concerned, the privateer *Persephone* and they, members of the Varangian Company.

Dunmoore poured herself another cup of coffee, then zoomed in on her involuntary guest's face. A network of small lines radiated out from the corners of Kursu's eyes while deeper ones etched the skin around her nostrils and lips. Her features seemed roughened by years of hard life in hostile environments, but Siobhan guessed Kursu was about her age. Perhaps a few years older.

Brown, mobile eyes beneath arched brows revealed nothing, not even curiosity, and her breathing appeared regular, relaxed, as if she was resigned to the change in her circumstances. Only a slight tightening of her full lips betrayed what might be annoyance.

After waiting for what she figured was an appropriate amount of time, Dunmoore drained her mug and tugged at the hem of her half-open black privateer's jacket before running a gloved hand through short, copper-colored hair. A last glance in the mirror confirmed no one would mistake Shannon O'Donnell for a straight-laced Navy officer.

It was time to see if she could convince Skelly Kursu to break the law of *omerta*.

**

The pirate's head pivoted toward Dunmoore when she entered the conference room through the door connecting it with her day cabin. Two cold, expressionless eyes examined *Iolanthe*'s captain in silence.

"Skelly Kursu, I presume? I'm Shannon O'Donnell, *Persephone*'s owner and by the same token president and chief executive officer of the Persephone Private Military Corporation."

Kursu's head dipped in a curt nod though her gaze never left Dunmoore as she walked around the oval table and took her accustomed seat.

"I trust my people treated you and your crew with due respect for the Aldebaran Conventions?"

"So far everyone has been suspiciously correct," Kursu replied in her rough voice. "A girl might think your PMC is a front for the damned Navy."

Dunmoore cocked an ironic eyebrow at the woman.

"I gather you've run across PMCs that weren't quite as professionally run as mine. It's a sad statement on our industry, but the sketchiest characters can get licensed and bonded by the Commonwealth government, and the only way that license can be revoked is if someone complains loudly enough. Which never happens because there's usually no one left to complain. Fortunately, the government is more particular in issuing letters of marque. Officially recognized privateers are held to a higher standard. As you can see," she waved an arm as if to encompass the entire ship, "that higher standard gets us backers with deeper pockets than your Enoc Tarrant. And deeper pockets means better ordnance, among other things."

"Sounds fascinating. Where do I sign up?" But Kursu's disdainful sneer fell flat under Dunmoore's withering stare.

"I recruit by invitation only, and I prefer crew who aren't bound by the rules of *omerta*. It keeps things honest, and contrary to your employer, I strive to stay in the good graces of our Commonwealth overlords since they can easily put me out of business."

"Something they might find more difficult with Enoc Tarrant. He acknowledges no overlord."

"That'll work only until he does something stupid and attracts reprisals. Such as sponsoring acts of piracy which result in the kidnapping of Commonwealth citizens. Not to mention fraternizing with the enemy."

"So we're back to this *Kattegat Maru*, eh? I still have nothing to say."

Dunmoore gave her a cruel smile.

"I said I'd drop you off at the next suitable port. Kilia is suitable, from my point of view."

A look of alarm widened Kursu's eyes.

"You wouldn't. Tarrant will kill us for losing him a ship."

"Not my problem."

"I should have fought you until the end." The pirate sneered.

"If you want to take a swim through the main airlock without a pressure suit, be my guest. It'll be the same death as fighting me."

"Weren't you the one making a big deal about respecting the Aldebaran Conventions? And now we're your prisoners, you want to see us die?"

"What I want is to recover *Kattegat Maru*'s crew and passengers. You were in on the kidnapping. Where are they?"

Kursu stared at Dunmoore in silence for almost a minute, then the defiance in her eyes died away.

"I couldn't tell you even if I wanted and that's the truth. The only thing I know for sure is Tarrant will kill us. Both for failing to take your ship and for surrendering. I'd rather you toss me out the airlock than to subject myself to his tender mercies. It would be quicker and less painful. Rumor says he's good at making a body suffer without letting you die."

"Tell me what happened that day, and I'll set you free far from Tarrant's grasping hands. In fact, by the time I'm done, there might not be a Tarrant to grasp anything. Not if he's behind the abduction."

"You'll never be able to prove his involvement, and since he's operating outside the Commonwealth's recognized sphere, good luck proving jurisdiction, let alone finding a willing prosecutor."

"You seem remarkably well versed in legal matters. But I don't intend to haul him or anyone else before a judge. Not while I command the most powerful warship in this part of space."

Kursu's eyes widened.

"You intend to attack Kilia?"

"Using *Bukavac* as a Trojan starship, yes. And once I do, Tarrant's fascination with the ancient rules of *omerta* will be irrelevant. Now tell me what happened that day."

"You know how many people live in Kilia? Thousands. You don't strike me as the type who'd murder that many just to kill one unpleasant mob boss, and I doubt you have the troops for a successful seizure. If you even make it close enough. Those guns of his are an order of magnitude bigger than yours."

"How I do it is my business. Now tell me what happened. Tell me, and I'll make sure you live long enough to find a new and hopefully more honest employer."

"I suppose you'll keep being this fucking annoying until I do." When Dunmoore nodded, Kursu sighed. "It was just another job for us. Tarrant, as he sometimes does, ordered his goons to plant a tracker on *Kattegat Maru*'s shuttle, exactly like they did on yours. He sent us to wait for her in interstellar space, on the course she would take to her next destination. Us being *Bukavac, Baba Yaga,* and the bonehead corsair, *Chorlak.*"

"Tarrant sent you ahead of time?"

Kursu nodded.

"Yeah. You were a last minute job. The *Kattegat Maru* business was planned in advance. Why Tarrant made us do what we did, no one knows. But that's how he operates. He compartmentalizes information. Anyway, *Kattegat Maru* dropped out of FTL some distance from the Kilia system's outer edge, we picked up the subspace tracker's signal and made a quick jump from where we were waiting.

"Under the guns of three ships, her captain surrendered and allowed us to board. The boneheads did the job, shackled everyone, and brought them over to *Baba Yaga.* Our orders were to abandon *Kattegat Maru* and make sure no one would find a trace of what happened or figure out she carried passengers. You know, leave a mystery. The boneheads were to wipe the logs and everything, but since you tracked her back to Kilia, I guess they missed a spot. Bastards are better at cutting throats than sanitizing databases. Then, *Baba Yaga* left for an unknown destination while we and the corsair returned to Kilia."

"*Baba Yaga* and *Chorlak* were the ships we destroyed a few hours ago?"

"*Chorlak*, yes. But the other one was *Chernobog*. *Baba Yaga* hasn't returned to Kilia yet."

"You don't know where she went?"

The pirate shook her head.

"Not a clue. We were ordered to forget the attack on *Kattegat Maru* ever happened on pain of punishment. That's all I can tell you."

"A last question, then. We saw evidence one of the cargo holds was plundered. Why?"

Kursu raised her shoulders in a weary shrug. "Damn boneheads enjoy taking their payment in kind, no matter what Tarrant says."

— Twenty-Two —

"Life would be too easy if Kursu knew anything concrete," Holt said in a philosophical tone after Dunmoore showed him a recording of her conversation with their captive. "And Lord knows we should only encounter almost insurmountable challenges, lest we prove ourselves unworthy of crewing the Furious Faerie. We'd better hope the plan to blackmail Tarrant by threatening Kilia's atmospheric integrity works. Otherwise, we're not only fresh out of leads, but the local crime syndicate will be seeking revenge. And that could interfere with our real job."

Dunmoore made a dismissive hand gesture.

"They can try to seek us all they want. Touching us is another thing altogether."

"Speaking of which, what do you want to do with the subspace tracker?"

"It'll stay as is until we go FTL and head back. Once we're in hyperspace, off and into the metal crusher it goes. No sense in advertising our return if we intend to screw Tarrant. How's Renny doing with *Bukavac*?"

"A few more hours until she's ready. That includes getting the forward shields up again. The missiles turned burrowing mines are good to go. A full dozen, their targets pre-programmed based on our scans of Kilia's defenses.

The only thing left is mounting the launch pack onto *Bukavac*'s hull. The bosun is going out with a crew and a shuttle as soon as Renny clears them. I figure we can be on our way in under twelve hours."

"And another ten to Kilia's hyperlimit." Dunmoore frowned. "Tarrant might wonder if his wolf pack hit a snag by then. Oh well, there's no helping that now. We'll have to rely on him being human and seeing what he wants to see — a ship coming back to announce success, with the rest a few hours behind her."

"One whose crew won't answer."

"By the time Tarrant works up the nerve to open fire on his own ship, it'll be in perfect range to launch our nuclear mines."

"So long as his sensors don't pick them up during their acceleration phase."

Dunmoore smiled cruelly.

"Hence the Trojan starship to keep everyone's attention occupied while *Iolanthe* skulks in the background and makes sure our little gifts land where they will cause Tarrant the most heartache."

"Let's hope it works." Holt stood and tugged his tunic into place. "By the way, I'm making Carrie Fennon shadow the officer of the watch since we stood down from battle stations. I thought we might continue her education when she's not confined to the CIC under your gimlet eye and treat her as if she was an Academy cadet on a familiarization cruise."

"Except we don't take cadets into an active war zone, but an excellent idea nonetheless. Perhaps also let her shadow one of Renny's people, so she gets an idea of how engineering on a man-o-war compares to *Kattegat Maru*."

"In fact, Renny volunteered to take Carrie himself the moment he's done with *Bukavac*. Believe or not, the old grouch told me this morning she reminds him of a favorite niece who's an ensign in one of the new Voivode class frigates." Holt paused and grinned. *"Jan Sobieski."*

A look of pure pleasure lit up Dunmoore's face.

"For its vast wartime size, I suppose our Navy is still something of an extended family. The niece of my chief engineer serving under my former first officer. What are the odds?"

"Last Renny heard, his niece considered Gregor Pushkin an exacting but fair taskmaster, well respected. And apparently, he has a certain tactical flair that makes him a frequent winner against the Shrehari. I wonder where Pushkin learned that."

"She'd hardly say anything critical about her captain to a man of Renny's integrity, but that sounds like Gregor."

Holt's communicator buzzed softly. He glanced at it and nodded.

"Speak of the devil. Renny just cleared the bosun to bring her missile pack over. We may be able to leave a lot sooner than in twelve hours."

"Good." She stood as well. "My subconscious is trying to sell me on the idea that time is of the essence."

"Dwyn and her crew are boarding the shuttle. Care to watch the maneuver on a bigger screen than the one in your day cabin?"

Dunmoore nodded.

"Sure, but let's use the conference room instead of the bridge or the CIC. That way we can let our folks bask in the notion we're allowing them to work without supervision."

"While spying on them."

Holt went to the urn and held up two mugs inscribed with the image of the Q-ship's namesake.

"Sure."

Once seated at one end of the oval table, Holt switched on the main display and called up an outside view of *Iolanthe*, fed by a camera forward of her hangar deck doors. They

were in time to see one of the large unmarked transport
shuttles, used to ferry supplies, cut through the force field
keeping the deck pressurized. The moment it was clear, the
space doors closed, reinstating hull integrity.

Their view changed to one of the lower cameras as the
shuttle carefully dropped beneath *Iolanthe*, its pilot aiming
for the missile launcher loading hatch. The shuttle flipped
one hundred and eighty degrees on its long axis, presenting
its belly to the Q-ship's keel and hovered a few meters over
the broad, square opening. A flat, rectangular container,
also unmarked, slowly emerged from the hatch and mated
with the shuttle's underside. The craft then gently
increased its distance from the Q-ship's hull before veering
off toward *Bukavac*.

"Nicely done. Who's at the controls?"

"Petty Officer Knowles, Skipper. Who else has that sort
of touch?"

Holt tapped the controls embedded in the conference
table, and their view shifted to *Bukavac*. It, along with
Iolanthe and *Kattegat Maru*, was now aimed back at Kilia's
sun, a small, faint dot, almost indistinguishable from the
background stars at this distance.

"I certainly don't."

"And you a former fighter pilot."

A devilish gleam lit up Holt's single eye.

"Youthful conceit. I never said I was any good at it."

As the shuttle crept toward *Bukavac*, carefully matching
velocities, a pair of pressure-suited figures came through
one of the lower airlocks. They made their way around the
hull's curvature until they stood on the pirate ship's flat
keel, where Commander Halfen intended to mount the
missile pack.

Petty Officer Knowles adjusted the shuttle's attitude until
it was lined up belly to keel and less than two meters over
the designated spot. Four pressure-suited spacers carrying

large tool bags emerged from the shuttle and joined the waiting duo.

At an unheard command, hand-held grapples snagged the missile pack and it separated from the shuttle. Careful, measured, and coordinated movements took the ten-meter long container away from the small spacecraft. It settled on *Bukavac*'s hull, where the six spacers, tools in hand, busied themselves for almost fifteen minutes, attaching the pack solidly in place. Then, four kicked away toward the waiting shuttle and the remaining pair returned to the airlock.

"Bridge to the captain."

"Dunmoore."

"From *Bukavac*, sir. The missile pack is installed to Commander Halfen's satisfaction. He says another four hours to repair the forward shield generators."

"Thank you."

"Bridge, out."

Dunmoore and Holt exchanged an amused glance.

"Renny is still padding his estimates, I see," the former said. "From just under twelve hours to just over four. How much do you want to bet we'll be accelerating in three?"

"No bets, Skipper. Like every other chief engineer in the Fleet, he can't help making a job seem harder than it is to keep his reputation for working miracles."

Siobhan laughed.

"Ain't that the truth? It must be a union rule with them. Keep up the mystique that naval engineers practice wizardry."

"Maybe I should check the engine room for evidence of ritual sacrifices, pentagrams, or a demonic summoning." Holt drained his coffee and stood. "If we'll be underway in three hours or less, I'd best make sure everything is ready."

"Leaving me once again with nothing to do but fret."

Holt gave her a wink.

"Or figure out what you'll do if this plan and the five contingencies stewing in your brain fail one after the other."

"That's what I mean by fret, Zeke." She pointed an imperious finger at the door. "Go annoy someone else. Better yet, find the Shrehari corsair's beacon."

— Twenty-Three —

"*Bukavac* and *Kattegat Maru* came out of FTL in formation," Chief Yens reported once both humans and artificial intelligences shook off the emergence disorientation that always accompanied a return to normal space. "*Kattegat Maru* is silent as the grave, but *Bukavac* is emitting a normal signature."

"We are silent as well. Kilia should only see *Bukavac*, especially at this range," Commander Ezekiel Holt's hologram at Dunmoore's elbow said.

"Command link with the missiles is live," Thorin Sirico added. "*Bukavac* appears to be on course for Kilia as per programming."

"Thank you." Dunmoore exhaled silently. So far, so good. "How's the navigation link, Zeke?"

"Solid. We can override the prize's AI on command and take remote control of her helm."

"So long as we didn't miss a backdoor allowing Kilia to override us."

"Not a chance. Renny physically disconnected her subspace and radio receivers. The only way she'll accept outside commands is via laser, and then solely from *Iolanthe*. It's an unexpected advantage of *Bukavac*'s shield generator problems. With her bow shields up and aft shields down, only laser comlinks coming from something behind her can make contact."

"Good."

With nothing left to say, silence blanketed both the bridge and the CIC while *Bukavac* and *Iolanthe* hurtled toward Kilia. As ordered, *Kattegat Maru* remained at the hyperlimit, safely out of range and by running under dampened emissions, invisible to Kilia's sensors. Dunmoore, who'd taken up meditation to deal with her fidgeting during a time such as this one, when she could neither relax nor influence events, fell into a light trance.

She remained conscious of everything and everyone around her but was at the same time detached from herself, almost floating above the command chair. If anyone noticed that an eerie serenity replaced their captain's habit of drumming her fingers on the command chair's arm, or against her thigh, they didn't care to comment. Not even Ezekiel Holt knew of Dunmoore's latest efforts to stamp out tics and unconscious behaviors that betrayed her state of mind — and annoyed the people around her.

"*Bukavac* is firing forward thrusters to decelerate." Chief Yens' voice called Dunmoore's spirit back into her body, and she blinked twice to chase away her idle contemplation of *Chorlak*'s missing beacon. Either the corsair didn't carry one, which seemed hard to believe, or the Shrehari made their beacons invisible to the most modern of Growlers. "Kilia is bound to notice her now."

Dunmoore glanced at the countdown timer, then at the tactical display. Right on time as per programming. They were entering the most critical phase of Operation Trojan Starship as she privately called it.

The more *Bukavac* neared Kilia before launching her improvised nuclear mines, the less chance they would be intercepted and destroyed. Everything depended on the station's traffic control personnel and their level of paranoia.

She recited her private mantra a few times while taking deep breaths as the urge to drum her fingers returned in full force. The old dictum about war being long periods of boredom punctuated by moments of sheer terror, suitably updated for the twenty-fifth century to read combat in space was long periods of waiting for a few moments of intense action, never seemed apter.

More time passed in silence. Even Carrie Fennon, seated beside Major Salminen, seemed transfixed by the tactical projection. Apart from the odd whispered exchange between them, the loudest sounds in the CIC came from crewmembers breathing and *Iolanthe*'s almost subliminal hum.

Lieutenant Commander Sirico finally broke the spell.

"Entering maximum effective missile range."

As if on cue, the signals petty officer raised a hand.

"Kilia is hailing *Bukavac*. They're asking where everyone else is and what happened to *Persephone*."

Dunmoore exhaled quietly.

"That took long enough."

"But they were nice to wait until we came into range," Sirico replied. "Though allowing us a little closer before launching would be even nicer."

"Kilia Control is getting a little insistent on a reply, sir."

"Zeke, do we still have a clear link with *Bukavac*?"

"Yep. You want her to send the decoy message now?"

"I would."

The decoy message, a last bit of bluff, was a text-only transmission telling Kilia control of *Bukavac*'s battle damage and that *Persephone* was a few hours behind her, escorted by *Chernobog* and *Chorlak*. Because of the damage, *Bukavac* was coming home early while the others took control of the privateer.

The lie wouldn't stop Kilia from firing for long. Perhaps no longer than it took to inform Tarrant. Kilia's master struck Dunmoore as someone with a sixth sense for trouble, judging by how successfully his operation was threading its way through the long war without incurring either side's wrath. But every kilometer the prize ship with its poisoned cargo gained gave the station less reaction time.

"Transmitted," Holt said a few moments later.

The CIC signals petty officer nodded, "I can confirm."

"Keep in mind we need to maneuver soon if we want *Iolanthe* to stay out of Kilia's own effective weapons range, Skipper, and then they might well notice *Bukavac* isn't alone."

Timing was key. And the closer she came to the decision point, the more impossible a perfect solution seemed. Dunmoore almost bit the inside of her lip, then remembered to recite her mantra. It sufficed. A wave of calm flooded her veins, and it was as if she saw the tactical projection with more clarity than ever.

At its center, Kilia and four visiting starships in orbit, the station's defensive emplacements marked by red triangles, its projected shields a red shimmer which would harden once they came online. Then, sailing in as if everything was normal, *Bukavac* in blue.

Iolanthe and *Kattegat Maru* were too far away and didn't appear in the projection at the current scale. If things went well, neither would. With any luck, Kilia's management would never find out the latter visited their system twice since the piratical abduction of her crew and passengers.

"They're not buying the decoy message," the signals petty officer said. "Kilia Control is demanding *Bukavac* reply to a coded challenge. The word is 'eternity' for what that's worth."

Dunmoore, reactions faster than her thoughts, stabbed the control screen embedded in her command chair's arm.

"Captain to the brig."

Chief Trane replied with remarkable alacrity.

"Sir?"

"Prisoner Skelly Kursu. Ask her for the answer to the word 'eternity.' Quickly."

"Wait one." A minute passed, during which Dunmoore pushed away an aching desire to fidget. Then, "The answer is 'sentience,' sir."

"Thank you, Chief. Did you hear that, Zeke?"

"Yes. I'm having *Bukavac* send 'sentience' now."

Dunmoore sat back, conscious her shoulder and neck muscles had bunched without permission.

"Chief Trane."

"Sir?"

"You obtained that answer pretty damned fast. How?"

A rumbling chuckle came over the intercom.

"I gave Kursu the idea we would die in the next few minutes under Kilia's guns if we didn't give the countersign, sir."

"Nicely done. CIC, out."

Dunmoore made a mental note to discuss Trane with Chief Petty Officer First Class Guthren. He was showing real potential, but the coxswain needed to ensure it was channeled in the right direction. Trane had a history of questionable decision making during his time on Toboso, although nothing as serious as his then commanding officer, whose misconduct opened the way for the infamous incident.

"Kilia turned on its defenses," Yens said. "Shields are up, and guns are deploying."

"They either didn't like the answer or thought it took too long."

"Perhaps, Thorin," Dunmoore replied, "or they work on the principle you can never be too paranoid out here. If I were Tarrant, I'd think something about the situation feels just a tad off."

"I'm not picking up the power surge characteristic of charging gun capacitors, sir."

Dunmoore nibbled at her lower lip as a fresh idea swam into focus, driven by gut instinct. Tarrant *wasn't* buying *Bukavac* as the battle-damaged advance party returning from a successful starship capture operation. He just didn't know yet what was really happening. Fortunately, Renny Halfen removed most of the prize ship's built-in limitations, at least the ones designed to keep humans alive and happy.

"Zeke, order *Bukavac* to accelerate as hard as she can without shaking her frames apart and aim for Kilia's center of mass."

"You're giving up guile and stealth?"

"In favor of spooking Kilia into opening fire earlier than they might otherwise be planning. Thorin, as soon as sensors register Kilia's guns powering up, cold launch the missiles, but eject them out the back end of the pack, so they're masked by the prize. Once Kilia engages *Bukavac*, light the missile drives. With any luck, Tarrant's minions won't see them accelerate if their sensors are being blanked by their own guns. Especially if they think our Trojan starship is the main threat and not a diversion."

"Aye, aye, sir," Holt and Sirico replied almost simultaneously. The former added, in a tone half-teasing, half-admiring, "Sneaky. I knew there was a reason Admiral Nagira picked you to command the Furious Faerie."

"You mean other than my sterling combat record?"

Holt gave her a broad grin.

"No comments, Skipper." A pause, "*Bukavac* accepted the commands. Her sub-light drives are up and pushing."

"Confirmed," Chief Yens said.

"Let's see how long it'll take Kilia to notice she's accelerating at a rate that would make her inertial dampeners howl in terror before they die and turn the ship into a human jam-making factory."

"You have a way with words, Mister Holt," Yens said over her shoulder at the first officer's hologram.

"I have a way with many things, Chief."

Dunmoore heard a suppressed if youthful sounding giggle behind her. *Kattegat Maru*'s captain probably didn't allow much banter on her bridge — not when they were about to fire weapons in earnest.

"What I'd love to see," she said, "is the expression on the Kilia controllers' faces as they realize one of their own ships has turned into a kinetic weapon aimed straight at them."

"They seem slow on the uptake," Sirico said after several minutes passed in silence.

"Would you want to open fire on a starship belonging to the local mob boss without obtaining his express consent?"

The combat systems officer gave her a rueful shrug.

"I guess not, Captain."

"Kilia is pinging *Bukavac* with growing urgency," Holt said. "They want to know what in blazes is happening. Shall I make her send a reply to the effect that battle damage is playing havoc with her drives?"

"Sure. There's always room for added confusion."

"Done."

Yens raised a hand. "I'm reading a power spike on Kilia. They're charging capacitors."

"Cold-launching the missiles."

"*Bukavac*'s threat detectors are screaming bloody murder, Skipper."

A faint smile appeared on Dunmoore's lips even as her shoulder muscles bunched again. The die was cast.

"Kilia is firing."

— Twenty-Four —

The front half of *Bukavac*'s image on the main display was suddenly awash in a blue-green aurora as the forward shields fought off Kilia's opening salvo. Tendrils of energy resembling miniature lightning bolts bled off halfway where the shields ended. They gently caressed her hull leaving black streaks in their wake.

"The missile drives are lit," Sirico announced. "One-minute burn."

Twelve tiny blue icons in the tactical projection began to move and quickly overhauled the slightly larger symbol representing *Bukavac*.

"And now we pray they don't spot our birds behind the radiation set loose by their guns."

"It's a time-limited proposition," Sirico said as he watched the next salvo from Kilia's massive guns strike home. "Her aurora is turning a deep purple. Those shields will live through one more volley, no more. Then it's farewell *Bukavac*."

"Been nice knowing you," Holt murmured. "Our sacrificing her will thrill HQ."

Dunmoore glanced down at the first officer's hologram.

"Let's leave those considerations for afterward, Zeke."

He nodded once, but his expression didn't show the slightest hint of contrition.

"Shall I use the occasion to change course unseen before we witness the royal purple of large bore plasma battling shields up close?"

"Do it."

Dunmoore's command was timely. Another violent flare encapsulated the prize ship's front half. This time the aurora collapsed with finality.

"Firing thrusters," Holt said. A pause, then, "Kilia is calling *Bukavac* again. A final summons to decelerate and change course."

"No reply."

"They didn't notice our missiles yet," Sirico said. "The birds' threat detectors are quiet."

Another salvo bloomed like bright flowers of death on Kilia's rocky surface.

"And we're done."

"I can't believe Tarrant would destroy one of his own ships," Carrie Fennon said, macabre awe tinging her words.

Dunmoore glanced over her shoulder at the girl and smiled sadly.

"Tarrant understands she's no longer his ship. Not when she's coming at Kilia with a rate of acceleration no human could survive. He can't afford the slightest mistake. Too much rides on the station maintaining a reputation for invincibility and its masters a reputation for ruthlessness. And that's how we'll squeeze answers from him."

"If at least one of our missiles makes it through the defenses and burrows into Kilia's surface," Holt said.

Sirico jerked a thumb at the tactical projection which still showed twelve tiny blue icons speeding toward their target.

"So far so good."

Kilia's latest salvo connected with *Bukavac*'s unprotected hull and ate through the metal as if it were butter. Superheated air vented through the resulting holes and crystallized at once. Secondary explosions erupted on both sides and the keel as gun capacitors fully charged by Renny Halfen before releasing the ship exploded under the onslaught. Though Dunmoore and her crew expected the conflagration, *Bukavac*'s transformation into a tiny nova took them by surprise nonetheless.

Chief Yens let out a low whistle.

"That never gets old."

Sirico nodded in agreement.

"It sure doesn't."

Dunmoore forced her shoulder muscles to relax while mentally reciting her mantra lest she start drumming her fingers again. The entire scheme depended on those missiles burrowing into the moonlet's surface and presenting Tarrant with an existential threat that could only be removed by answering her questions. Minutes ticked by without further reaction from Kilia and the twelve blue icons in the tactical projection kept nearing their target unhindered.

"They're scanning so hard we might appear on their sensors at this rate, though as nothing more than a ghost."

Holt chuckled.

"Which would be appropriate since our intelligence intercepts of Shrehari communications seem to indicate they consider us a phantom, Chief."

"Kilia's calliopes are opening fire. They spotted our missiles." A few moments later, "they scored one hit — sorry make that two."

"And now they're wondering who else is here since they figure those missiles couldn't possibly come from *Bukavac*," Sirico said.

"They nailed two more of our birds." Then, "Shit." Chief Yen's muffled curse drew everyone's attention. "Four emergence signatures at the hyperlimit. Shrehari. I make two *Tol* class cruisers and two *Ptar* class corvettes. They dampened their emissions, at least by normal Shrehari standards, meaning Kilia might not see them yet. Probably older ships which haven't undergone the refit that makes them harder for us to detect."

"The boneheads are transmitting on an Imperial Deep Space Fleet channel in code," the signal's petty officer said.

"Trying to raise their spy ship *Chorlak*, I suppose."

Dunmoore nodded. "Probably, Thorin."

Though her voice remained calm Dunmoore mentally cursed the fates that put a Shrehari task force across her path. Though *Iolanthe* was a battlecruiser under the skin, taking on four Shrehari starships when two of them were *Tol* class cruisers would be foolhardy and could even be fatal.

The trick she pulled on Brakal several years earlier with *Stingray* wouldn't work against them. Not now that Shrehari commanders such as Brakal were improving their game.

"It'll take them time to enter firing range," she continued. "Long enough to squeeze Tarrant dry and make our escape."

"You intend to pass on such a target-rich environment?" Holt asked with an air of amusement. "That you didn't consider him worthy of a good fight will crush your opposite number."

"He can drown his sorrows in a vat of that disgusting ale they so enjoy. I'm not inclined to flatter his vanity by sticking around when we have people to rescue."

"Two more birds down, sir. That's half of them."

Dunmoore raised a finger to acknowledge Sirico's report. Not long now. Eyes locked on the tactical projection she mentally willed the remaining missiles to slip under Kilia's defenses so they could bury themselves into the asteroid's crust. Another small blue icon winked out of existence. Five left.

**

"Well?" Brakal gave Regar an irritable stare.

"*Chorlak* is no longer answering calls. It last reported being in orbit around Kilia."

"Is anything there?"

"The sensor officer reports three non-military human ships. He also reports gunfire."

"Someone is attacking the station?"

Regar big hands flipped outward in a gesture conveying uncertainty.

"The fire is one-way only, originating from Kilia's surface. We cannot yet make out the nature of the target."

Brakal stroked his massive chin, black within black eyes studying Regar.

"Could they be shooting at the ghost? Maybe it is here."

"And maybe your spectre has destroyed *Chorlak*."

"I should not weep for any *Tai Kan*, but even they might have proved useful in our hunt. We must listen for its beacon."

A bark of laughter rang out. "Our pretend corsairs don't carry beacons, Commander. My superiors would rather the Deep Space Fleet find no traces of *Tai Kan* operations that fail. Better we ask the scum who own Kilia about *Chorlak* and your ghost."

"In good time, Regar. In good time. If Kilia is battling one or more human warships we cannot detect, then it is best no one finds out yet we are here."

Regar inclined his head.

"I bow to your greater tactical instincts, Commander."

"And so you should, miscreant."

Yet even as he spoke, Brakal wondered whether his ships would indeed be invisible to a human Navy vessel commanded by a peer of the flame-haired she-wolf. On the other hand, Dunmoore was a brilliant tactician, as brave as any Shrehari commander. She would not be foolish enough to engage in open battle with four foes at once, not while enduring Kilia's gunfire.

"Let us wait, Regar. Wait, watch, and discover what is occurring before we leap in."

"As you say. And if you wish me to deal with the humans on Kilia, I shall do so. I may not be able to pronounce their barbaric names, but I have enough knowledge of their tongue to permit basic communication. And if my *Tai Kan* brothers use this place as a base of operations, surely I will find a creature capable of speaking the Imperial language. Perhaps even a *Tai Kan* officer whose duty station is Kilia itself. After all, this thrice-damned place is considered a reasonably useful intelligence-gathering hub."

"Why thrice-damned?"

"Once for being infested by humans. Once for being beyond Imperial authority."

"By orders of the Admiralty," Brakal interrupted.

"Indeed. But that doesn't change the fact there's a den of villainy operating in our rear area."

"Which is also the humans' rear area."

"And the third damnation is because of the government giving responsibility for intelligence gathering here to the *Tai Kan* rather than the fleet."

Brakal made a noise of agreement.

"If ever I am able to do so, I would create an intelligence-gathering organization separate from our beloved secret police."

Regar rumbled with laughter.

"Only a *kho'sahra* could wield sufficient power. Anything less would meet with obstruction from everyone including the Admiralty."

"Then perhaps it is time to re-establish the ancient office of military dictator, so we might end this war with a modicum of honor instead of letting those idiots around the child-emperor and his whorish regent drag us further into the abyss."

A sly look crept into Regar's eyes. "I daresay you might find many in the Deep Space Fleet ready to support that idea, especially among the Warrior caste."

"Bah." Brakal made a dismissive hand gesture. "Who would be mad enough to rally the disaffected around his banner and challenge the lords of the Four Hundred as well as the Admiralty?"

"Obviously another lord and admiral."

**

"Yes."

Sirico's exultant yet subdued cheer pulled Dunmoore from her contemplation of what she might do if none of the missiles reached Kilia's surface. So far, the alternatives seemed bleak. Subterfuge was the only tool at her disposal since Kilia was impervious to direct attack by anything less than a full task force.

"Three hits," the combat systems officer said. "Their warheads report penetration to a depth of five meters. The payloads are undamaged and ready to accept arming instructions."

Dunmoore felt her taut nerves relax just an iota. Three out of twelve would suffice.

"And the rest?"

"They went dark on impact. Either they struck the surface at the wrong angle, or they didn't survive penetration."

"Hopefully Kilia control picked up the impact vibrations and are wondering what just happened."

Dunmoore's fingers almost escaped her control, but she stopped them before they could start dancing while she decided how long to wait until calling Tarrant. However, a glance at the tactical projection, which now showed four red icons representing the Shrehari vessels, helped make up her mind.

"We will stay silent but open a tight-beam link with Kilia. Signals, please call them and tell whoever answers that Shannon O'Donnell wishes to speak with Enoc Tarrant."

Several minutes passed before a querulous voice Dunmoore recognized as belonging to the mob boss came over the CIC speakers.

"I suppose you're to thank for *Bukavac*'s destruction, O'Donnell?"

"Technically, your guns were responsible, but I'll gladly admit wrecking the other pirates you sent after me, *Chernobog,* and the bonehead corsair *Chorlak*. I'll also claim ownership of the five nuclear warheads I planted in Kilia's crust. They're not armed yet, but one command from me and they will be live, ready to detonate. I'm sure you can imagine what that might do to your oh so fragile little domain. They might not cause your asteroid to break up outright, but can you afford thousands of microfractures letting your precious air escape? Even the best sealant has a limit to how well it can resist the shock of nuclear explosions."

"You're dead, O'Donnell, and so is every single member of your organization. You can't hide, you can't run, you can't escape the fate you bought for yourselves."

An amused smile twisted Dunmoore's lips.

"Are you going to quote Herman Melville at me now?"

"What?"

She considered reciting the famous passage from *Moby Dick* but figured it would pass right over Tarrant's head. He didn't seem the sort to read much, least of all classics dating to a time well before the human diaspora into the wider galaxy.

"Never mind. Let's stick to business. Do I have your full attention? Or do you want to look at the mines I planted before discussing my demands? Or should I trigger a warhead to prove I'm not the one who can't run, can't hide, and can't escape her fate? And don't bother looking for me. I'm well out of your guns' range. By the way, you still owe me a stack of precious metals to replace the fakes your minions palmed off on us. Careless, that. Terrible for the reputation, especially if you want to be the boss of bosses in this sector."

Tarrant didn't immediately reply, and Dunmoore could almost visualize him chewing on his anger, jaw muscles working while a vein throbbed in his temple.

"Oh, and sticking subspace trackers to visiting shuttles is also considered a no-no in polite society. Once word gets around, you might find the more skittish among your visitors deciding to take their wealth elsewhere. You're not the only shady operator in this sector, and I daresay the competition would be more than happy to clip Kilia's wings."

When Tarrant finally answered, his voice resonated with barely suppressed rage.

"What the hell do you want from me, O'Donnell?"

— Twenty-Five —

"Where are the crew and passengers of *Kattegat Maru*?"

"That's what you want?" The mob boss sounded incredulous. "You set up this elaborate scheme to find out about a bunch of sketchy spacers and their low-rent customers? Are you fucking insane, O'Donnell? Besides, how do you even know about *Kattegat Maru*?"

"We found her abandoned in interstellar space. After I advised the authorities, people interested in the crew's welfare hired us to retrieve the people your pirates kidnapped."

"You *found* the damned ship? And were hired in what? The space of a few days? How is that even possible?"

"Yet here I am, as are those nuclear warheads stuck up your backside. Both should be enough proof we're not people you should annoy. I want Fennon, her crew, and her passengers, alive and well. Otherwise, Kilia won't stay alive and well. You and the fine people breathing that expensive, yet somewhat stale air will join the crews of your three ships in whatever hell the Almighty uses to dispose of subhuman scum and boneheaded vermin."

"You are so finished, O'Donnell," Tarrant snarled. "Finished. Dead. And it won't be an easy death."

"Neither will yours if I don't hear answers. Shall I order my gunner to arm and detonate the first device, so we can test the sealant your people slathered on the inner cavern walls? We might find out whether hiring the lowest bidder was a good idea."

"Using a nuclear device on an inhabited colony is a war crime, O'Donnell."

Dunmoore's laughter sounded unearthly.

"Only within the Commonwealth sphere and as you've pointed out with great satisfaction, Kilia isn't part of it. That makes the Aldebaran Convention clauses concerning the use of nuclear weapons on human settlements a moot point. Good luck finding a prosecutor willing to take on the case. But enough of this persiflage. I don't want to waste more time watching your inadequate intellect deal with the notion there's no way out but through cooperation. Tell me where I can find Kattegat Maru's crew and passengers, and I will leave you and the rest of your space rats free to die another day. If I don't hear you talking within the next sixty seconds, I will arm and detonate the first nuclear device. The ball is in your court, Tarrant.

"I'd suggest you choose wisely, but wisdom does not seem to be your forte. Otherwise, you'd be tripping over yourself to cooperate with someone who has the absolute power of life and death over you and the thousands living inside your rock. Especially since all I want is information. I'm not even going to ask you to reimburse me for the precious metals you replace with dross, let alone give you the punishment a pirate commodore deserves. Destroying three of your ships was enough satisfaction even if, technically, Kilia's guns destroyed *Bukavac*."

"I don't have a fucking clue where they are." Tarrant sounded as if he was speaking through clenched teeth.

"Want to try again, before I unleash my gunner and let him play with his toys?"

"I swear. Someone hired my organization. We were to seize *Kattegat Maru*, take everyone off, and let her drift in interstellar space to be found by another hireling. What happened to the damn ship was supposed to be a complete mystery."

"And the people your goons kidnapped?"

"Hand them over to those who hired us, unharmed, and in good health, at a specific set of interstellar coordinates. My ship *Baba Yaga* is still carrying out that part of the contract."

"Funnily enough you're not telling me much I didn't already know. But I want you to tell me who hired you and where *Baba Yaga* took the abductees. Care to do so before my trigger finger gets twitchy?"

There was a moment of silence. Then, Tarrant said, "I don't know who hired me, but they pay well, extremely well even by my standards, and communicate through half a dozen cut-outs. Before you ask, I did not try to trace those cut-outs. That's not how I work. Otherwise, clients would quickly become hard to find."

"And the delivery coordinates?" When Tarrant didn't immediately reply Dunmoore said, "This isn't the time to be shy."

"Yeah, yeah, don't go ballistic. I need to call them up. It's not something I memorize." Another pause, then, Tarrant rattled off a set of numbers — three groupings separated by commas.

Dunmoore trusted Astrid Drost to check those coordinates without waiting for orders.

"What's supposed to happen when *Baba Yaga* gets there?"

"Her captain will receive instructions upon arrival."

This time it was Dunmoore's turn to be silent for a few moments. Did she dare trust Tarrant? The man was, without a doubt, a born liar, cheat, and irredeemable crook.

"You understand what will happen if you're lying, right? Those mines I planted are active and ready to ruin your day whenever I feel the urge. Trying to remove or deactivate them will merely cause their warheads to arm and detonate so I would suggest you stay away. I will pursue *Baba Yaga* and find *Kattegat Maru*'s crew and passengers. If at any point I discover you've fed me a load of bullshit, I will come back and make sure Kilia's existence comes to an abrupt and irrevocable end."

"I get it, O'Donnell. Those who hired me didn't pay enough to ensure my complete silence, not when my station's future is at stake thanks to sociopathic privateers. The profit versus risk balance doesn't make misplaced loyalty a winning proposition. Is there anything else you want from me or can I wish you happy travels?"

"Why was a Shrehari corsair working for you? Most of them are undercover military or *Tai Kan* ships and therefore agents of the Imperial Government."

"They can be useful, undercover or not. I do business in the Empire, as is my right. Kilia is neutral in this stupid war between the Commonwealth and the Shrehari. Money knows no boundaries and recognizes no existential enemies, only opportunities, and I'm in this business purely for money. If it's patriotism you're after, check the bottom of a black hole."

"Commendable," Dunmoore replied, her words dripping with sarcasm. "The values and ethics you espouse do the freelancer community proud."

"And yours are better, O'Donnell? Threatening a space habitat with nuclear weapons just so you can pull off what is no doubt a profitable job on behalf of someone with deep pockets? There's no real difference between the two of us, other than size, as you will soon find out. My organization is powerful enough to make this job your last. Unless you wish to hand your ship over as reparation and submit."

"If fantasizing about getting revenge helps you sleep at night, Tarrant, feel free. Since I already destroyed three of your ships, including one bonehead, I dare say you may not find many takers if you put a price on my head. Besides, there's still the matter of my nuclear warheads adorning your precious Kilia."

"Whatever."

The abrupt silence that followed his last word proved Tarrant had cut the link. One glance at the signals petty officer gave Dunmoore instant confirmation.

"I believe he left in a huff." She glanced down at Holt's hologram. "Where are those coordinates, Zeke?"

Her first officer's lean features took on a mystified air.

"Less than two parsecs away, on the edge of the acknowledged Commonwealth sphere in the opposite direction from Imperial space. But they are relatively close to a star system called Hecate. The database lists no colonies, outposts, or habitable planets orbiting Hecate, though the gas giant Raijin has a moon by the name Temar that's marginally suitable for human life."

Dunmoore, ever alert to her first officer's moods, asked, "Then what's the problem, Zeke? That counterintelligence officer's 'I smell a rat' expression is plastered across your face."

"Entry into the Hecate system is proscribed by order of the Commonwealth government."

Her eyebrows shot up.

"What? If Hecate is on the edge of our sphere today, there's no way it could be one of the systems contaminated during the Second Migration War and therefore permanently off-limits. The Commonwealth was a lot smaller back then."

"Indeed, Skipper. And what would you make of Raijin's nickname, Satan's Eye, in such a context?"

"That we need a Fleet-approved exorcist if you intend to pay a visit, sir?" Sirico suggested with a sly grin.

Dunmoore gave him the stink-eye, though she meant it in jest.

"You usually try harder, Thorin."

The combat systems officer gave her an unapologetic shrug.

"I'm only as good as the material you throw my way."

"Then how about an update on the Shrehari task force?"

A disconsolate frown wiped the mirth from Sirico's face.

"There's no humor to be found among boneheads, sir. But I will try. What are your intentions concerning our nuclear mines?"

"Make sure they self-destruct without exploding if someone tries to tamper with them, in case we can't pass through this system again for a while. Or if the Shrehari decide to help Tarrant by sampling human technology."

"Aye, sir. Not that the bastards will learn much from our sanitized version of the Navy's standard-issue anti-ship missiles. They've seen millions over the years."

"Shall I ask Astrid to plot a course for Hecate?"

Dunmoore nodded at her first officer.

"Please. It's time to scram before the Shrehari gets a whiff of us and decides *Iolanthe* is the ship that's been raiding their convoys in recent weeks. The last thing we need is four of them chasing us across this sector while we're looking for the abductees. And update Emma on the situation. We have no choice but to take *Kattegat Maru* with us to this proscribed star system."

"You think that's where my mother and the rest are, sir?" Carrie Fennon, who'd been quiet as a mouse until now, asked in a tone that mixed excitement and fear.

Dunmoore swiveled her command chair to face her and smiled.

"I doubt the kidnappers abandoned them in interstellar space. And since Hecate is not only the closest star system to the rendezvous point but also inexplicably out of bounds by government fiat, it seems a natural place to start looking."

"Can you simply ignore the proscription, sir?"

Holt's hologram chuckled.

"Who's to find out we violated the order if no one sees us sneak in? Navigation logs can be altered."

"Don't go teaching Apprentice Officer Fennon any wrong-headed lessons, Number One," Dunmoore growled. "If lives are at stake, I prefer to act first and ask for permission later. If required."

This time, Holt laughed outright.

"Mere semantics, Skipper."

**

"Lord?"

Brakal snarled silently as he looked up from another indecipherable report foisted on him by the ineffectual Gra'k. Would that he was on *Tol Vehar*'s bridge, in the chair now occupied by the one calling him. Brakal stabbed a thick, bony finger at the communications unit.

"What is it, Urag? And don't call me lord, you unredeemable villain."

"A human ship, previously undetected, appeared on our sensors as it powered up drives. The ship is large, Commander, but appears to be a non-combatant, since it matches no warship listed in our databanks. The vessel was at a certain distance from Kilia, beyond the station's effective weapons range, and not in orbit like the others we detected earlier."

Brakal ran his hand through the ruff of fur crowning his angular skull and grunted. "That ship maintained silence until now, and Kilia was engaged in a battle with something unseen. Perhaps this non-combatant is the equivalent of our *Tai Kan* corsair vessels, a *kroorath* masquerading as a *yatakan*."

"The ghost." Urag's flat tone made his reply a statement rather than a question.

"And if he is here, we might know what happened to *Chorlak*."

"He suffered the same fate as the others who encountered that dishonorable phantom." Another statement.

"Dishonorable?" Brakal's throat gave birth to a disparaging growl. "Because he does as *Tai Kan* corsairs and hides in plain sight? I think this human's successes against us has bought him plenty of honor. Dishonor comes from a failure to use every legitimate ruse of war in pursuit of victory."

Urag, long inured to his commander's unorthodox views, merely made a noncommittal sound.

"Do not let your fascination with the flame-haired she-wolf blind you to our ways, Commander."

"Our ways? The ones that see us unable to win against a weaker species?"

This time Urag didn't even clear his throat. It was an argument almost as old as the war itself, one that was partially responsible for Brakal's assignment to a sector where little happened. Or to be more precise, where little happened until the ghost showed up and played havoc with Shrehari shipping, which led to Hralk's relief and Brakal's unexpected appointment. But it meant Strike Force Khorsan's failures were now his. And being higher up the command ladder, his fall would be harder and could even prove fatal.

"Have you fresh orders, Commander?" Urag asked instead of continuing the discussion.

"Yes. Open a link with Kilia and let Regar find out what he might about recent events, *Chorlak*, and your so-called non-combatant. Keep observing him and prepare a course to pursue."

Urag knew from bitter experience nothing would stand between Brakal and his goals but felt honor-bound to try anyhow.

"We are already beyond our sphere of responsibility, Commander. Should the enemy act while we're away from our patrol routes, the blame will fall on you."

"I won't tell the robed fools at the Admiralty we went looking for the enemy in his lair instead of waiting for him to nip at our heels if you won't Urag."

"As you wish, Commander. I hear and obey."

— Twenty-Six —

"May I return to my ship when we recalibrate after crossing the heliopause, sir?"

Dunmoore, who'd led Carrie Fennon to her day cabin for a cup of coffee after *Iolanthe* went FTL, gave the young woman a searching look.

"Bored of life with us?"

"No, sir." Fennon accepted the proffered mug with a gracious tilt of the head by way of thanks. "I've learned a lot since coming aboard, and I know I'll still learn much from Lieutenant Commander Cullop. But my place is in *Kattegat Maru*."

A warm smile softened Dunmoore's sharp features.

"I understand, Apprentice Officer, and I share your sentiments when it comes to the starships in which we serve. Perhaps Major Salminen will want to rotate her platoons on the same occasion. Permission granted."

"Thank you, sir." Fennon took a sip. "May I ask a question?"

"Always. It's the best way to learn. Ask away."

Dunmoore dropped into her chair behind the desk.

"Why would Hecate be out of bounds?"

"Perhaps the survey ship that charted it found a grave peril for humans and the Admiralty wasn't inclined to share the nature of said peril? Or the government established a top-secret facility of some sort in the system, maybe for research and development? It could be any number of reasons."

Fennon studied Dunmoore with her expressive gaze, then asked, "What do you think, sir?"

A grim expression hardened Siobhan's face again.

"There are branches of the Commonwealth government known for doing things that wouldn't withstand public scrutiny. I've encountered one of them a few times. Perhaps they established an outpost in the Hecate system."

"To do things requiring the secrecy afforded by distance and isolation?"

Dunmoore raised her cup in salute.

"Very perceptive of you. These aren't nice people even if they work for the government."

Worry clouded Carrie's eyes.

"And these not nice people might hold my mother?"

"Let's not borrow trouble ahead of time."

"But you think it's a possibility, Captain. I can see it in your expression."

"It is. Yet whoever kidnapped your crew and passengers did it in such an elaborate manner I'm convinced they're at pains to ensure everyone's safety and continued survival."

Fennon slowly nodded.

"True. But trying to figure out why worries me, sir."

"It worries me as well. Yet the only way to find answers is to go there, and we shall, proscription or not."

**

"What news do you bring?" Brakal sat back in his chair and stared at Regar with his black in black eyes.

"There is indeed a *Tai Kan* colleague stationed on Kilia, and he was most accommodating. Almost strangely so. But perhaps it stems from speaking to a fresh Imperial voice after living for such a long time among lesser beings. The shooting we saw was the tail end of a battle between Kilia and the human corsair ship *Persephone* previously identified by *Chorlak*."

As was his habit Regar mangled the unfamiliar human name almost beyond recognition.

"Apparently the human corsair destroyed *Chorlak* and a ship belonging to Kilia's ruler, and turned another of the ruler's ships into a crewless attack craft, forcing him to wreck it."

Brakal's face twisted into something that might frighten even an Arkanna alpha female at the height of bloodlust.

"For what reason?"

"It gets better, Commander. The human corsair also planted nuclear demolition devices in Kilia's crust, and all to blackmail the station's ruler, a human called Tarrant, who claims to be the sector's biggest purveyor of illegal acts."

"Your colleague must live in this Tarrant's pocket to be so well informed."

A predatory smile split Regar's rough-hewn features.

"Or perhaps Tarrant lives in the *Tai Kan*'s pocket, Commander."

"What does Kilia's brave *Tai Kan* operative say about *Persephone*'s true nature or that of its flame-haired captain?"

"Nothing. Other than the ship's greater than usual size, this human corsair appears no different from any who visit Kilia, and its captain the usual fortune hunter intent on profit. Although Tarrant apparently has many other names for her, none of them flattering in his crude language."

Brakal's snort echoed off his cabin's unadorned metal bulkheads.

"I can imagine. If this is the Dunmoore who bested me a few years ago and all but annihilated *Tol Vakash*, then perhaps I could teach Tarrant names for her he's never dreamed of." When he saw Regar's sly expression, Brakal growled, "Are you holding something out on me, you whelp of a sand serpent?"

"Tarrant gave the human corsair captain coordinates where his people supposedly took the imprisoned crew and passengers of a human freighter, people she is trying to find."

"You were going to share this information with me when?" Brakal asked in a tone oozing with peril.

"No later than the moment your navigator finishes translating those human coordinates into something we of the one true race can understand."

A meaty fist slammed on the scarred tabletop.

"Hah. One day you will overstep your bounds, Regar. No one can dance so close to the line without eventually finding himself on the wrong end of a warrior's blade. But for this once, well done. Strike Force Khorsan will hunt the corsair because I am ever more convinced it is the ghost that has destroyed so many of our ships. What its captain did to Kilia seems familiar. I would wager the same mind is responsible for that delightfully underhanded stratagem."

Unlike *Tol Vehar*'s temporary commander, Urag, the *Tai Kan* political officer didn't bother arguing about assigned areas of operation or the displeasure of Brakal's superiors.

He knew words of caution would do nothing more than needlessly rouse Brakal's ire. Besides, if this *Persephone* was the ship that plagued them, chasing it would be in the Imperial Deep Space Fleet's best interests and bugger anyone who said otherwise.

**

"How did you enjoy *Iolanthe* and Captain Dunmoore?" Lieutenant Commander Emma Cullop returned Carrie Fennon's crisp, almost military salute.

"It was, um, interesting to say the least, sir."

Cullop led her off the hanger deck so that the soldiers from Command Sergeant Jennsen's number four platoon could finish their handover with Command Sergeant Alekseev's number two platoon and head back to *Iolanthe*. Cullop knew Dunmoore wanted to be on her way the moment both ships finished cycling their hyperdrives to prepare for interstellar space.

"What was so, um, interesting?" Cullop asked with a wry grin, suspecting she already knew what the young woman would answer.

Fennon seemed to hesitate as if unsure her observations would find a receptive audience, then she shrugged.

"It's the endless banter, sir. My mother would never allow that much levity on her bridge. Yet Captain Dunmoore and the others were joking before and during the attack. It was quite extraordinary."

This time, Cullop laughed outright. Tatiana Salminen made the same observation shortly after her company joined *Iolanthe*'s crew and she began to frequent the CIC on a regular basis.

"Not all commanding officers have Captain Dunmoore's tolerance for levity on duty. But it helps pull the crew together when things become tense. We enjoy it that way."

"Yes, sir. I noticed." A pause. "*Iolanthe* is an amazing ship. I stood a few watches with Commander Halfen, and he showed me around. The idea something so powerful can seem so innocuous is awe-inspiring."

"I don't think awe is what our enemies feel when they see *Iolanthe* unmask."

"That's what Chief Guthren said. He recommended I buy toilet paper futures in whatever sector she operates."

"Trust our cox'n to find just the right words for every occasion. And what did you think of Captain Dunmoore herself?" When Cullop saw the hesitant expression on Fennon's face, she said, "I withdraw the question. One should never ask someone's opinion of one's commanding officer."

"I don't mind. I like her. She treated me as if I was an adult rather than a child wearing a borrowed uniform. In fact everyone I met treated me as a grownup."

"Would I be wrong in guessing that's not always the case with *Katie*'s regular crew?"

They reached Fennon's cabin, but before Carrie entered to drop off her gear, she said over her shoulder, "You wouldn't be wrong, sir. *Katie* is a family business. It's hard for my mother and my other relatives to forget I'm the youngest of the Fennons and still legally a minor. Even if the Merchant Guild carries me on the rolls as an apprentice officer."

"That makes sense, I suppose. Get yourself squared away and join me on the bridge. I'm happy to have another watchkeeper during our crossing to Hecate. We'll go over the navigation plot while we wait for Captain Dunmoore's signal to jump."

"Were heading straight there?"

"Not exactly. Even though we could reach the system's edge in one jump, Captain Dunmoore wants to do this in at least three. When we go over the plot, I'll explain why."

— Twenty-Seven —

"You know, I was thinking it's a shame we can't put kill marks on the Furious Faerie's hull. With the two we bagged near Kilia, especially the bonehead intelligence ship, we're getting quite a collection. If we're not the record holder by now, we must be within single digits."

Commander Ezekiel Holt dropped into the seat across from Siobhan Dunmoore with a lunch tray in his hands. *Iolanthe*'s wardroom was empty save for them. Both had remained at their posts, Holt on the bridge and Dunmoore in the CIC, while the respective officers of the watch took their midday meals. They used the time for an informal after-action review, ahead of the formal one scheduled at four bells in the afternoon watch, or fourteen hundred hours in Army parlance.

Dunmoore, as was her habit, kept the crew on its toes by running drills at every occasion. She'd called one when they dropped out of FTL on the run to Hecate so they could query the nearest subspace array for data packets addressed to *Iolanthe*.

"Advertising our true nature would defeat the purpose, Zeke," Dunmoore replied around a bite of her sandwich.

"I know, but it's a given the bony devils will eventually catch on, sir. They might be slow in some areas, but they're not stupid. One of these times, perhaps even the next time, someone will get off a message fingering us for a wolf in sheep's clothing before we send them to the netherworld. Remember, we never found *Chorlak*'s beacon."

Dunmoore shrugged.

"When that happens, I'll ask Renny and his merry engineers to change our emissions signature and mask our lupine aura so we may exude sheepishness once more. And if the Shrehari become suspicious of every large freighter they detect, so much the better. They might lose their enthusiasm for raiding our shipping."

"You'll ask me to do what, Captain?"

"Speak of the devil, and he appears." Holt glanced at the wardroom door and grinned. "Paint the warp nacelles bright pink, Renny, so we look less warlike and ferocious."

"That'll be the day," Commander Halfen growled. He went to the sideboard, poured himself a cup of coffee, and joined them. "You'll be glad to know everything is well. The shield generator that wobbled after taking a bonehead broadside when we wiped out the convoy a few weeks ago is as good as new again."

Holt grimaced.

"Perhaps, but we should plan on swapping it out for one fresh from the shipyards during the next overhaul cycle. It's taken more hits than the rest combined."

"And whose fault is that? If we didn't spend so much time shaking our tail to entice boneheads looking for quick plunder, we might not take so many shots on the aft shield."

"Don't blame me," Holt replied, then nodded at Dunmoore. "I take my maneuvering orders from the CIC."

"And fine maneuvering orders they are, to be sure. Now, what's this idea of looking less ferocious?"

"Zeke figures it's just a matter of time before the Shrehari peg us as a warship in disguise."

The chief engineer nodded.

"Probably. They're smarter than the assorted riffraff we put away during the Toboso cleanup. But a coat of pink paint won't do it. If I could find any. Speaking of the enemy, here's a question for you, Mister First Officer — how do we figure out they've decided we're not a big, cuddly target?"

"When three or more *Tol* class cruisers come after our shaking tail instead of the usual patrol ships. Intelligence tells us the enemy strike force operating in this sector normally operates *Tols* in pairs, escorted by two or three corvettes. I'd say a force larger than that stalking *Iolanthe* will be a sign from God."

"Which would exclude the four we spotted approaching Kilia." Halfen swallowed the rest of his coffee. "Well, that's me. I just came for a taste of the good stuff. Try as I might, my crew still can't understand why what they brew isn't proper."

At that moment, Dunmoore's communicator pinged.

"Captain, this is the bridge."

"Dunmoore."

"We snagged a subspace signal packet from the Octavius Array."

"Excellent. Place the *Iolanthe* at jump stations and pipe the packet to my day cabin. You may take us FTL to the rendezvous coordinates when both ships are ready."

"Aye, aye, sir," Lieutenant Astrid Drost, currently sitting in the Q-ship's bridge command chair replied. "Place the ship at jump stations and go FTL when *Iolanthe* and *Kattegat Maru* are ready."

"Dunmoore, out."

"Are we expecting fresh orders?" Holt asked before scarfing down the rest of his sandwich. "Something that might bugger up our quest for Captain Fennon and company?"

"I hope not."

"We might regret making a detour to query the array, Skipper."

"I can get away with only so much, Zeke. Ignoring the order to ping subspace arrays at regular intervals would raise more questions than snooping around a forbidden system. HQ hates it when you don't give their summonses the right degree of reverence."

Holt chuckled.

"Ain't that the truth? But consider this. With our success raiding Shrehari commerce and convoys deep inside their space, I keep expecting HQ to broaden the effort. Maybe even place a task force of Q-ships under the command of Acting Commodore Dunmoore."

Her lips twitched with a suppressed smile.

"I suppose I probably have the most experience of any Q-ship captain, after running my own mercenary flotilla for a few weeks."

"And twice as acting commodore, if you count the convoy command when you were in *Stingray*."

"That wasn't official, Zeke. It didn't come with a broad pennant, and everything involving Lucius Corwin never happened."

A loud chime swallowed Holt's reply.

"Now hear this, prepare for transition to FTL in one minute. I repeat, prepare for transition to FTL in one minute."

"I guess Astrid was ready and waiting," Dunmoore said. "We might as well stay here until our stomachs catch up. I doubt there's anything in the packet requiring an immediate reply."

"And if there is, too bad."

"Rebel."

The jump klaxon sounded three times. Ten seconds later, Dunmoore wished she'd waited to eat her lunch, but the sensation passed as quickly as it appeared.

"If you have no pressing engagements, why don't you come read the mail with me," she suggested, climbing to her feet.

"Don't mind if I do. In fact, I'll take your spare terminal and reroute any personal stuff."

Holt let her lead them out of the wardroom and up the spiral stairs.

"Expecting a missive from an admirer you neglected to mention?" Dunmoore asked over her shoulder.

"Please, Captain. You know *Iolanthe* is the only one for me."

"I thought that was my line, you know, captains being wedded to their ships and all that ancient rot."

"You're into faeries now?" He asked with a straight face. "I thought you were more of a dragon lady."

"Which would work if this ship were named *Abraxas* or *Fafnir*. But she's named after one of the Fae..."

The door to Dunmoore's day cabin opened at their approach.

"Another coffee?" She asked waving at the urn.

"Thanks, but no. My nerves are taut enough."

Holt slid in behind the spare terminal while Dunmoore took her desk.

"HQ was generous," he said after a minute of silent reading. "Half the packet is personal messages for everyone, including most of our Scandian Marines. It seems the Army finally figured out how to route mail through Special Operations Command. They took long enough."

"E Company, 3rd Scandia is the only Army unit serving aboard a warship, so I'm not surprised," Dunmoore replied in an absent tone. "And we're not on anyone's order of battle, just to make things even more obscure."

Holt noticed a catch in her voice and looked up.

"Something in the orders giving you heartburn, Skipper?"

"Our independence may be at an end, Zeke, and it's in part my own damned fault." She touched her screen. "Contrary to expectations, HQ has been listening. Why don't you read the orders yourself?"

Holt obeyed, then raised his eyes again.

"Task Force Luckner? They may have been listening, but didn't come to the right conclusions. Will we be able to keep looking for *Kattegat Maru*'s missing crew and passengers?"

"I intend to take the time required. The task force won't assemble overnight and if we show up after everyone else, so be it. Rear Admiral Kell Petras can either crap all over me or think of the bad publicity that would ensue from orders ending our hot pursuit of pirates who abducted Commonwealth citizens."

"Risky. Petras, whatever faults Fleet gossip might hang on him, has a reputation for being both competent and demanding."

She shrugged dismissively.

"Tough."

"Losing our status as a free runner really rankles you, doesn't it, Skipper?"

Dunmoore gave Holt a cold stare, then relented under his unchanging good humor.

"I'm annoyed at myself for suggesting SOCOM expand Q-ship operations to build on our success, and that's giving me a bad case of cognitive dissonance. Broadening special operations' reach is the right thing to do, even if it means I'm no longer exclusively in charge of *Iolanthe*'s fate."

"I understand your meaning. But on the bright side, you'll see Gregor Pushkin again, maybe invite him over for a meal, and show him around. Didn't you say he thought they posted you to a desk job?"

"I was ordered not to discuss *Iolanthe* when our new assignments came in after *Stingray*'s decommissioning."

"Some folks are about to discover the truth."

"Aye, and that's the rub. I hoped HQ would enhance our efforts with more Q-ships or perhaps use one or two of the new *Reconquista* class cruisers to act as commerce raiders. I didn't expect them to create a task force of conventional warships with us as a designated lure."

"Luckner includes *Jan Sobieski*. She may not be a cruiser, but as frigates go, she's a beast, and she's fresh out of dry dock with a captain you trust."

"Always looking at the positives, aren't you?" She gave her first officer a fond smile. "Unfortunately, we'll be under the command of Rear Admiral Petras."

"He's known as a fighting admiral."

"One who sat behind a desk at Special Operations Command on Earth for the last three years. The war has changed since his most recent command in space. Carrying out deep raids is a new phase, one Fleet Command is only starting to appreciate. Besides, he's never actually run special ops. His experience is on the planning and staff side, meaning theoretical."

"Do I sense a fear he'll override our hard-won practical experience, potentially putting him and you at odds?"

"Only a fool would think otherwise." Dunmoore's voice took on a thoughtful cast. "And a rear admiral commanding a task force comes with his own flag captain, a four-striper with more time in rank than I do and stars in her eyes. In this case, one Lena Corto. I'm not personally acquainted with her, but she also has a reputation — for ambition."

Holt chuckled.

"And now we reach the nub of the issue. I recall you don't play nice with flag captains."

"Only those who labor under the mistaken belief they're second in command rather than chief planners. And since this new task force won't operate from a starbase, the admiral won't be alone in riding herd on us. We'll also spend quality time with his flag captain."

"At least neither will be in *Iolanthe*. They've given Petras a Type 260 destroyer configured as a flagship."

"Indeed — *Hawkwood*. I think they call that variant a Type 261. But she's much smaller than *Iolanthe*. Our CIC is twice that of a destroyer's, enough to accommodate a task force commander along with our own needs, and we have more cabin space as well as better amenities."

"Then I'll see to making *Iolanthe* as grubby and inadequate as possible."

Dunmoore chuckled.

"There you go rebelling again. Admiral Petras well knows our capabilities and configuration. If he hoists his flag over *Iolanthe*, we can do nothing more than smile and make his every wish happen." Dunmoore paused for a moment, then sighed. "I suppose I've become overly used to operating well away from a flag officer's gimlet eyes. A task force commander reining me in doesn't sit well."

"I doubt Petras will chain you to his flagship's starboard flank like a mere corvette, demanding we conform to every signal he makes. Even if he's been riding a desk at Special Operations Command, he'll know it's not the way to use a Q-ship."

She smiled at him again.

"I'll be an optimist and believe he intends to practice mission command — tell me what he wants and let me do it my way. Otherwise, the next few months won't be to my liking. But first, we must finish this job. Petras can wait until we're done. Not only will we be the last to join Task Force Luckner but I suspect we won't make it within the required time window either. Not from where we are now, let alone after chasing our kidnappers to Hecate the Mysterious."

The first officer gave Siobhan a wry look.

"That's what happens when you go on wild hunts behind enemy lines. HQ can't keep up with your position anymore."

"Wild hunts? I heard no bugles." She glanced down at the screen embedded in her desk. "But let's look at this task force's name as a good omen."

"Why?"

"According to the historical database, Captain Felix von Luckner could be called our spiritual ancestor. He was one of the most famous and successful commerce raiders in pre-diaspora times. Funnily enough, his crew were nicknamed the Emperor's Pirates."

"If Admiral Petras came up with the name, I hope it was because he understands the exigencies of unconventional warfare and not out of affection for ancient naval lore."

— Twenty-Eight —

"So that's Satan's Eye." Dunmoore studied the gas giant in the main display with appreciative eyes. "Aptly named. The polar vortices, as seen from this angle, do resemble the pupil and iris of something sinister. It reminds me of a tale about an evil entity which existed only as an all-seeing and all-knowing virtual eyeball."

Iolanthe had crossed Hecate's heliopause a few hours earlier, after a single jump from the rendezvous which, as expected, was devoid of clues, not even a recent ion trail from a starship. The Q-ship was still a few light hours away from Raijin, her sensors looking for signs of sentient life before Dunmoore ordered that last, short jump to the gas giant's hyperlimit.

An automated buoy, one of several orbiting the distant star, was broadcasting a warning on a loop. It told anyone coming within range of Hecate that entry into the system was forbidden by order of the Commonwealth government, on pain of dire penalties. After listening to the message once and recording it for posterity, Dunmoore ignored its baleful words in favor of approaching the moon Temar unseen.

If Tarrant's unnamed employers took the captives to this system after receiving them from *Baba Yaga*, that moon seemed the most logical destination. It was the only body capable of sustaining human life with no need for artificial habitats.

But if they found nothing, Dunmoore would be forced to decide between continuing her hunt and reporting to Task Force Luckner's assembly point as ordered. Abandoning Carrie Fennon's people to their fate would be gut-wrenching, yet she couldn't survive Admiral Petras' wrath unscathed if she continued with no new evidence to guide them.

The task force's entire premise depended on *Iolanthe* serving as designated bait to lure the Shrehari. Without her, Petras commanded only a light battle group, good for nothing more than quick hit-and-run raids on the fringes of Shrehari-held space. He wouldn't consider seventy-odd civilians sufficient justification to delay assembling his first command after years ashore. Especially not with Admiral Nagira's eyes on him.

Who knew what Petras promised the head of SOCOM or even Admiral Nagira himself? What innovative tactics he proposed to prove in the crucible of battle and not coincidentally improve his chances of promotion to vice admiral?

Moments after the thought crossed her mind Dunmoore felt a stab of shame. Accusing someone with an honorable record of seeking glory to earn another star was unworthy. Yet, the Fleet's upper echelons used to be rife with careerists and many of them stayed on after most of their sort wilted away under the pressures of war.

Raijin's image wavered, then shifted with a jerk and a small, bluish dot floating above the planet's colorful, orange-hued outer atmosphere swam into focus at the center of the CIC's main display.

"Temar," Chief Yens said. "At this range, the sensors can't detect anything useful, other than to confirm the moon is within the expanded parameters for habitability, albeit barely. And that's pretty much everything I can see in this system other than the damn buoys."

"Thank you, Chief." Dunmoore rubbed her jawline.

"What are you thinking, Skipper?" Holt was present in person for a change, rather than via hologram from the bridge, and recognized the gesture. "If someone's hiding on Temar, I'd bet they seeded Raijin's high orbitals with surveillance satellites. There's no point in proscribing a star system if you can't pick up intruders and make good on your threats."

"Detection? Sure," she replied in a thoughtful tone. "Making good on threats, now that's another question altogether. I've not heard of any naval units stationed in the Hecate system, and it would take at least a task force if not a full battle group to chase down and apprehend trespassers. If they're serious about dire penalties. And the Fleet has precious few ships to spare for guard duty in a star system whose only remarkable feature is a habitable moon orbiting a gas giant."

Dunmoore fell silent, eyes still on Temar's small blue disk. After a moment, she slowly shook her head.

"I doubt there's anything in this system capable of threatening *Iolanthe*. At least in the physical sense."

"Agreed, to a point." Holt's dubious tone belied his words. "But if we disobey orders keeping everyone out of the system and a report makes its way to Fleet HQ, *Iolanthe* or to be more precise you will face a disciplinary threat."

"True. But finding *Kattegat Maru*'s crew and passengers in this system could be our trump card. If whoever ordered their abduction has set up shop here, they aren't about to complain once we confront them."

"What if we draw a blank? What if we don't find the abductees and you're charged with disobeying a government order?"

Dunmoore gave her first officer a wry grin.

"What's life without a little risk?"

"Something that might allow you to end the war with an admiral's stars on your collar?"

She laughed with delight.

"You expect the war to last another decade? Because Q-ship captains, especially those with only a few years in rank, aren't on the fast track to flag officer. If you were hoping to ride my coattails into a starbase's executive suite, sorry. Not going to happen. I'm having too much fun as a starship captain. I'll take my lumps if necessary. At worst Admiral Petras or perhaps even Admiral Nagira will give me a sharp rap on the knuckles and a downgrade on my efficiency report. I don't think the Navy will send one of its own to a penal colony on Parth for the crime of trying to save innocent civilian lives."

"You underestimate the viciousness of a bureaucracy thwarted."

"The bureaucracy does not understand how vicious I can be when *I'm* thwarted. We will approach Raijin with due caution and try to stay off their sensors. But if they notice us, we will flex our muscles shamelessly. I want to know whether Fennon and company are on Temar."

Holt recognized the steel in Dunmoore's voice and knew any further argument was futile. He climbed to his feet.

"Astrid will prepare a navigation plot to get us there. Will you leave *Kattegat Maru* here or take her with us?"

Dunmoore tilted her head to one side as she considered the question.

"No. She'll make a hole in space again and wait. That way if I annoy the tinpot gods of the bureaucracy into showering reprisals on us, at least they won't find any justification to confiscate *Katie* and take away the Fennon family's livelihood. Besides Carrie is a civilian and while the Navy might shield us from the consequences of trying to do our duty, she has no such protection."

"Agreed, although Emma might be disgruntled by missing out on exploring a proscribed star system."

"Life is full of little disappointments, Zeke. We can take plenty of visuals and send them over so she has something to occupy her time when she's not standing watch."

"Knowing Emma, that blessed event will be the third Sunday of never."

Thorin Sirico guffawed.

"I'm sure I've seen her enjoy the odd five-minute break in the wardroom, sir. Although perhaps she was inspecting it instead, looking for something that might keep the boatswain and her mates occupied."

Dunmoore stood.

"Okay, you comedians. I'll be in my day cabin. Send me the navigation plot once Astrid has worked her magic. And keep watching Raijin while we're waiting."

"I kind of prefer the name Satan's Eye," Sirico replied. "It has a certain *je ne sais quoi*."

"If we're going to use colorful imagery instead of proper names, what does that make Temar?" Holt asked with a cocked eyebrow.

Sirico turned a perfectly innocent gaze on him.

"The Stye on Satan's Eye?"

**

Brakal, unwilling to breathe down Urag's neck on *Tol Vehar*'s bridge, fought his impatience in private while the cruiser's sensors, linked to those of *Tol Vach* and the corvettes, scanned the coordinates provided by Kilia's resident *Tai Kan* spy.

Though they had pledged him their loyalty when Hralk left, he knew his starship commanders were nervous at penetrating this deep into human-held space. They were now well beyond their assigned area of operations and out of range from the nearest Imperial subspace radio relay, let alone reinforcements. But Brakal was chasing this *Persephone* on a hunch, one he felt would pay off, if only by unmasking the damned ghost, so his ships might know in future whence the gravest peril came.

With Brakal's temper more ferocious than usual, Regar was the acting strike force commander's only regular companion and even now watched him from across the compartment, cup in hand, a sardonic twist to his features. Fortunately, the *Tai Kan* officer knew when to hold his tongue even if he exercised little control over his facial expression.

"What?" Brakal snarled after finally noticing Regar's sly look.

"Nothing of importance."

"I order you to speak, excrescence."

"What if we find no traces here? Will you pursue deeper into human territory? Or return to where your formal responsibilities lie?" Before Brakal could reply, Regar continued. "Your internal debate on the matter is far from concluded. You do not wish to join Hralk on the home planet explaining to those fools wearing an admiral's robes why you disregarded their commands and left our sector open to enemy attacks."

A feral growl escaped Brakal's throat.

"Their commands? What commands? I saw nothing that resembled a useful order in months. Since before we traveled to the world of the lost humans, even. They issue no plans, develop no strategies, and yet demand we win a war that was unwinnable before it even started."

"Ah, yes. Our pursuit of the flame-haired she-wolf. Another mission without orders and wasn't Hralk pleased with you, Commander. The only reason he didn't relieve you of your duties then was because we discovered the fate of *Ziq Tar* and its crew."

Brakal slapped the tabletop with an open hand.

"And we made those humans fear us for eternity. Glorious days, Regar, glorious days."

"This time you hope identifying the ghost and perhaps stopping it will buy you the same forgiveness from admirals sitting in judgment on matters they can only understand with difficulty?"

"Forgiveness means failure. I intend to succeed. Then, perhaps, we shall never see Hralk's diseased face again, and I will be given command of the strike force permanently."

"That would please your chief of staff to no end."

"Bah. Gra'k is wiser than he might appear." When Regar gave him a questioning look Brakal burst out with laughter. "He was wise enough to not overtly challenge my taking control in Hralk's absence."

Regar raised his hand in a gesture of submission.

"Agreed. Gra'k showed wisdom in accepting his life would be foreshortened if he tried to assume Hralk's mantle." Regar raised the mug he was holding to his mouth. "I salute your success in advance. May an admiral's robes adorn your uniform even as you plant your foot on the neck of the human ghost ship's captain."

"Stifle your impertinence, *Tai Kan* creature." Brakal's outburst merely served to feed Regar's obvious amusement. But an insistent bugling from the intercom cut the latter's reply short. "What is it?"

Urag's voice came from the hidden speaker.

"Sensors have detected nothing of use. The human creature in charge of Kilia lied."

Brakal rubbed his chin with the back of his paw-like hand.

"Perhaps. And if so he will pay for his impertinence. But I am not ready to turn back. What is the nearest star system?"

"One the humans call Hecate." Urag mangled the name to the point where even Brakal understood only with difficulty. "It is but a short other space transit from here, yet our records show no usable worlds or artificial habitats."

"Our records?" Brakal sneered. "The day I find an accurate entry about a human-held star system I will offer a magnificent feast of thanksgiving to the gods. Take us to this Hecate. We will at least study it from the star's outer boundary."

"And penetrate deeper into enemy space, thereby roaming further from our assigned sector," Urag said in an unapologetic tone. "Be glad we choose to follow you nonetheless."

"That is what I like about the commander of my flagship. His uncanny ability to state the obvious with absolute conviction." But Brakal's playful tone took the sting out of his words. Besides, Urag became inured to Brakal's moods and sharp humor long ago.

"I hear and obey, Lord."

— Twenty-Nine —

"We're running silent," Ezekiel Holt confirmed from the bridge moments after the emergence nausea dissipated, "and are just shy of Raijin's hyperlimit."

"Thank you." Temar's blue disk against the gas giant's riotous colors drew Dunmoore's eyes the moment the image stabilized on the CIC's main display. "Let's hope no one over there was looking at this part of space when we dropped out of FTL."

"How long do you want to wait before initiating the burn that'll put us into Raijin orbit?" Holt asked. "Astrid calculates we have up to four hours before we need course adjustments that might betray us to military-grade sensors."

"I don't intend to wait that long, Zeke. If our sudden appearance drew anyone's attention, we'll find out soon enough."

Memories of the apparent ease with which Admiral Corwin detected her previous command as she tried to approach Arietis without being detected years earlier resurfaced. But *Iolanthe* was not a tired Type 203 frigate. Her emissions signature while running silent was a fraction of *Stingray*'s, especially after the old girl took a few bad hits from Brakal's cruiser in the Cimmeria system, even though *Tol Vakash* suffered a far worse fate.

"The sensors detect no threats," Chief Yens announced shortly afterward. "But I make at least a dozen artificial satellites orbiting Raijin and another eight orbiting Temar."

Dunmoore's gloved hand slapped the command chair's arm with glee.

"Someone is living on that moon, protected by our government placing this star system out of bounds."

"That means defenses as well sir," Sirico said, "something to give surveillance satellites a few sharp teeth."

Yens grunted. "We'll only detect them once they power up and prepare to enforce the ban."

Dunmoore nodded.

"And they'll have something capable of scratching our paint job. Zeke, make sure the *Iolanthe* beacon is hot and ready. If the locals turn out to have a hostile disposition, I want to give them pause so they might reconsider shooting on a Navy ship."

"And what if they do anyway?"

"How long do you think it will take us to sweep Temar's orbit clear of any satellites?"

"A few minutes after you say the word 'fire' sir," Sirico offered.

"Pretty much."

Holt knew it was useless to argue with Dunmoore once she decided on a course of action. His hologram at her right elbow inclined its head.

"Shall I stand the ship down from battle stations and give the crew time for a meal before we come within range of whatever Temar might throw at us?"

Dunmoore's stomach made its opinion heard at that moment, and she replied, "Yes." Then she gestured at Sirico. "Why don't you go eat now, Thorin? I'll take the CIC watch. No need to hurry."

Sirico sprang to his feet with alacrity.

"Yes, sir. Thank you, sir." He gave Salminen a nod, and both left the CIC together.

Alone with the duty watch, Dunmoore settled back into the command chair and steepled her fingers below her chin. She studied both Temar's growing disk on the main display and the tactical projection now showing small purple icons to represent the satellites orbiting planet and moon. Chief Yens deliberately chose the color as a blend of friendly blue and hostile red since no one would know what the beings occupying Temar were until *Iolanthe* made contact.

"Who are you?" She murmured. "And what are you doing there?"

Was another Corwin living out his fantasies on that moon? Or was it the Special Security Bureau this time? Perhaps doing something to support a reprehensible scheme cooked up by its director general to increase the Bureau's reach and power over Commonwealth affairs? Or was it even more nefarious?

Though she couldn't fathom what or who might hide on Temar, Dunmoore's instincts told her this was the final destination for the folks taken from *Kattegat Maru*.

She was startled to find a smiling Thorin Sirico standing by her chair half an hour later.

"I'm ready to relieve you, sir. The wardroom is serving the usual post-battle stations sandwich bar, but there's also a nice Scandian asparagus soup."

Ever since Major Salminen and her company became permanent members of the ship's complement, the menu in the various messes often featured offerings culled from their icy home world's traditional cuisine.

She climbed to her feet.

"I stand relieved. The CIC is yours, Mister Sirico."

**

"Nothing's stirring around Raijin, sir," Sirico announced moment Dunmoore entered the CIC several hours later. "If it weren't for the satellites orbiting it and Temar, I might almost believe the system uninhabited. Whoever is there exercises commendable emissions discipline. No radio waves, and no subspace carrier wave. The satellites must talk to their control station via tight-beam links or possibly lasers."

He slipped out of the command chair and stepped aside.

"Thank you, Thorin." Dunmoore study the tactical projection and the now more distinct image of a blue orb passing in front of Raijin's colorful swirls. "Bridge."

"Drost here, sir."

"Initiate thruster burn to reorient us for an orbital trajectory."

"Aye, aye, sir."

"Dunmoore, out."

Though she could neither hear nor feel the thrusters pushing *Iolanthe* on a new vector, one that would allow the gas giant to capture her, the data on one of the CIC's side displays showing course and speed began to change.

That change was nevertheless so small it didn't seem to affect the ship's relative position in the three-dimensional holographic tactical projection. Nor did Temar's image waver on the main screen thanks to the optical sensor array's smooth tracking.

Several minutes passed in silence before Astrid Drost's voice came through the speakers.

"CIC, this is the bridge. Course correction completed."

"Acknowledged," Dunmoore replied. "And now we wait to see if someone spotted *Iolanthe*."

"They would have to look straight at us with sharp sensors, sir," Yens said. "The emissions that little thruster nudge gave off barely register."

Dunmoore nodded in agreement. Over the last six months, Renny Halfen and his crew had done a miraculous job making the already stealthy Q-ship even harder to detect by the best military-grade sensors.

The fact he broke several engineering regulations in the process didn't matter. Halfen did whatever was necessary to improve *Iolanthe*'s most important asset: her ability to appear out of nowhere and turn from an innocuous freighter into a starship captain's biggest nightmare.

At this range, Temar's surface features were taking on a more distinct edge. Wispy clouds of brilliant white half covered a dun-colored landscape slashed by dark blue, almost black seas and lakes.

About two-thirds the size of humanity's original home and of a similar appearance, its status as a moon orbiting a gas giant struck Dunmoore as slightly incongruous. But it wasn't the only moon known to nurture life.

At least two orbited similar gas giants in the Sol system, where unmanned exploration droids found the first evidence of primitive alien beings, though both were uninhabitable by humans.

Even those such as Temar, marginally able to support sentient, oxygen-breathing species, were hardly unique, although few attracted anything more than small resource extraction settlements. There was something about living under the looming presence of a gas giant that disturbed the human psyche.

Dunmoore knew Yens, her sensor crew, and the ship's AI were subjecting every visible part of Temar's surface to intense scrutiny, but she did not expect them to find anything. At least not without active scans which would most assuredly betray their presence to functioning threat detectors.

If someone was there, they would likely try to keep their existence and location well hidden.

Or not.

By now, both *Iolanthe*'s new course and Temar's orbital motion around Raijin were revealing parts of the surface facing the tidally locked moon's primary.

The image on the main display wavered before vanishing, replaced by the close-up view of a slash in the dull native vegetation. It looked entirely like a landing strip big enough to accommodate the most massive starships capable of maneuvering in an atmosphere.

"That's at the bottom of an equatorial valley on the Satan's Eye side," Yens said. A smaller view of Temar appeared on a secondary display, with the location marked in glowing red.

Sirico studied the data scrolling by on his own console and nodded.

"Makes sense. The atmosphere at sea level appears to be a tad thin, and the bottom of that valley is below sea level. That must be why it's richer in flora than the rest of the surrounding landmass. Interesting they settled in the hemisphere always facing Raijin rather than the other one. They would only get a true night when Raijin is blocking Hecate completely."

"Maybe because there's no suitable location in the hemisphere facing outward," Yens said, "if the criterion is ground lower than sea level."

"Imagine Satan's Eye constantly staring at you." Sirico shook his head. "Not a recipe for keeping one's mind intact."

"I doubt you can see the polar vortices from Temar's surface, Thorin, so it's not as if you'd live under Raijin's evil gaze."

"Sure, but still. Those psychedelic color bands, each with its own set of boundary vortices? Damn thing must cover a big chunk of Temar's sky. Drive me mad after a few days, it would."

"I'd stop looking up," Chief Yens said, practical as always. "And there's evidence of aboveground structures by the strip."

A new image appeared on the main display, it was that of low rectangular structures camouflaged among the native vegetation. One of them boasted the unmistakable dome of a ground control unit on the roof.

"I guess we found the owner of those satellite constellations."

Dunmoore nibbled on her lower lip, eyes half-closed as she studied the tactical projection again. *Iolanthe*'s planned orbit around Raijin was further out than Temar's, meaning they wouldn't get more than a short glimpse of the installation each time they passed each other.

Yet changing the Q-ship's course so she could assume an orbit lower than Temar's and study the surface would involve another thruster burn, this one closer to the satellite constellations and therefore more readily detectable. Never mind that a lower orbit would betray *Iolanthe*'s silhouette against Raijin's bright atmosphere every time she passed between it and the moon.

The same thought must have struck Ezekiel Holt. His holographic image appeared at her right elbow.

"What do you figure, Skipper? I can't think of an easy solution that'll leave us undetectable."

"I don't know why I thought any possible settlement would be in the hemisphere facing away from Raijin, Zeke. Shows you how my personal quirks can interfere with clear tactical thinking."

"Quirks?"

"I'm with Thorin. Spending my days basking in the glare of Satan's Eye wouldn't do my remaining wits any favors. Clearly, the folks who cut that landing strip into the valley floor were of a different opinion."

"Or there was no other choice. Don't sell human instincts short. That being said, what's the plan?"

She exhaled noisily.

"Send Tatiana and her company down in full battle order—"

"Minus one platoon."

"Minus one platoon — to seize the place. Or maybe the bosun can form a landing party to replace the soldiers currently in *Kattegat Maru*. Chief Guthren would be an ideal leader."

"She could and he would. It's an idea, but perhaps not a good idea. Judging by the hardware we've seen floating around this system so far, that's a Commonwealth government installation, folks supposedly on our side."

"Not always on our side," she growled in reply. "As you might remember. But I was joking, Zeke. When did I last charge headlong into a situation?" Upon hearing her first officer's strangled exhalation, Dunmoore said, "Never mind. Forget I asked the question."

A soft laugh prefaced Holt's reply.

"Probably for the best. If you want my opinion, since we must go live at some point, it's best to do it from a position of superiority. Forget orbiting Raijin until we build a full picture of the situation. Slip into Temar orbit right away and see what happens.

"We're hardened enough to absorb ground-based fire until we can evade it and if Chief Yens' sensors didn't up orbital gun platforms so far, it's because they're dormant. And that means we'll have time to either target or evade them when they power up. This far from the Empire, the only hostile forces that might disregard the warning buoys and come sniffing around wouldn't be much of a challenge for standard aerospace defense pods."

Dunmoore considered Holt's advice for a few heartbeats before answering in measured tones.

"Agreed. Make it so. But I don't mind taking whatever time necessary if it means we can hide our thruster burns from surveillance satellites just that much longer."

"Consider it done. Next stop, Temar orbit."

— Thirty —

"Up close, Temar exudes all the chill of Scandia and none of the charm." Dunmoore glanced over her shoulder at Major Salminen.

The soldier's eyes broke away from the main display, and she nodded.

"Agreed, sir. As habitable worlds go, I doubt it'll make the top one hundred destinations for desperate colonists fleeing persecution, even though it doesn't boast my home's continental icecaps."

This close to the moon, even Iolanthe's passive sensor suite painted a reasonably accurate picture of conditions on the ground, and they were harsh. The question of how habitable it was outside that broad valley slicing through the heart of the largest landmass, one of four covering well over half of the surface, remained up for debate. Without deep oceans to temper its climate, cold winds scoured the entire moon save for a handful of oases protected by high mountain chains.

"We're almost in orbit," Sirico said. "I wonder when they're going to wake up."

"Wonder no more, sir," Chief Yens replied. "Something came to life. Scratch that. Several things came to life. Active scans signals are emanating from the satellite constellation around Temar." A pause. "And now those around Raijin."

Dunmoore shrugged. "I suppose it was too good to last. Even though our emissions control ranks among the best in the Fleet, *Iolanthe* isn't exactly small."

"They're not locked on yet. Our threat detectors are still quiet. Whoever's standing sensor watch probably saw our ghost."

A grin split Sirico's bearded face. "Or maybe they sensed a disturbance in Raijin's aura. As if a million Shrehari voices called out in rage and were silenced — by the hottest Q-ship ever launched."

"Time to dial back on the coffee, sir," Yens said, rolling her eyes.

"Entering orbit," Holt's hologram announced at Dunmoore's right elbow. "Chief Guthren is at the helm, in case you're wondering, Skipper. That means no unnecessary thruster burns."

"Good."

The coxswain was known as the best ship handler aboard and one of the best anywhere. But he didn't steer *Iolanthe* quite as often as *Stingray*, not even in battle, preferring to give the younger quartermasters — superbly trained spacers, like the rest of the crew — a chance to perfect their craft. That he took the Q-ship now showed a keen understanding of what might betray her to unseen watchers.

"It means we'll finally see every square kilometer of the Raijin-facing hemisphere."

When the installation finally came into view, Sirico let out a low whistle.

"There's more than a landing strip and some structures. It's a whole damned town nicely camouflaged by native vegetation."

"Town, sir? Examine it closely," Yens suggested. "What does it remind you of?"

Sirico scratched his beard while Dunmoore, eyes narrowed, tried to see what the sensor chief noticed. Tatiana Salminen was the first to understand.

"It's a prison. Or at least part of it is a prison, Captain."

The combat systems officer turned to her with a questioning frown.

"What makes you say that, Tatiana?"

"The remote weapon stations in the corners and along the outer berm. They're facing inward. Plus, there's an inner berm, meaning a double enclosure. If you're defending against an external threat, you'd set a buffer zone beyond the perimeter — mines, sensors and such. You wouldn't bother with a double fence."

She squinted at the high-resolution video feed on the main display.

"And then we can see what appear to be police or guard droids patrolling inside the fence — those cylinders on articulated tracks. Useless in combat, but highly effective at intimidating unprotected humans."

Yens tapped an extended index finger against the side of her nose.

"The major's figured it out. That's a stockade, or I'll send my chief's starbursts back to HQ and swallow the anchor."

"Why would anyone set up a stockade on a marginally habitable moon at the far edge of the Commonwealth? And forbid entry into the system with dire warnings? We're on the damned threshold of nowhere here. Isn't Parth the designated prison planet?"

Holt's hologram cleared its throat.

"I can think of a few reasons based on my time working in counterintelligence while I was beached, none of them good."

Dunmoore glanced down, eyebrow cocked.

"And they are?"

"Unsavory. If that's a stockade, it might well be for prisoners who can't be housed in any facility on Parth, folks whose status and whereabouts can't be made public knowledge." He grimaced. "And if it belongs to a certain branch of our government, we might be stepping into a nuclear minefield."

Dunmoore exhaled, eyes half-closed. "A rendition site. Please tell me that's not a damned rendition site. I've heard rumors about them for years, but the Commonwealth doesn't simply disappear people. It would violate every law in existence."

"Not every law, Skipper. The SecGen has a bit of leeway when faced with existential threats to humanity's survival. It's how the Special Security Bureau gets away with things that might sink other agencies."

"Why would the government want to abduct the crew and passengers of an innocuous merchant ship, using Tarrant's pirates no less, and make them vanish into a black site that doesn't officially exist?"

"I can speculate as much as you want, but it won't get us closer to the truth. You face a decision, Captain. We can tiptoe out of this system, wipe our logs, and pretend we never heard of Temar, and thereby avoid becoming a target for our own government."

"Or?"

"We flip this rock over, expose whatever's underneath, and take the risk of becoming inmates on Temar, should the Navy be displeased enough with your actions. Which it will be if the folks we're looking for aren't there and we exposed a covert site for no good reason."

Dunmoore's bitter laugh echoed off the bulkheads.

"That's no choice, Zeke. Morally, rendition sites shouldn't even exist. If the government wants to remove people from circulation, they should do so under strict oversight."

"Who says there's no oversight," he replied in a gentle tone. "What I'm saying is we might have stumbled onto something we can't handle. For the sake of the crew and this ship, it might be best to withdraw."

"And my promise to Carrie Fennon?"

"We go through official channels. Ask Admiral Nagira to use his connections in the SecGen's Office and find out whether *Kattegat Maru*'s people are being held here, and why."

Dunmoore knew her first officer was merely doing his job by pointing out the pitfalls ahead of time, so she didn't charge to the rescue without fully understanding the risks involved. Except this time, the risks were not tactical, but political. Nevertheless, she swallowed a surge of irritation.

"That could take months, Zeke. And in the meantime? We can't drag *Kattegat Maru* around for much longer. The moment we join Task Force Luckner, Admiral Petras will claim her as a Navy prize and too bad Fennon family. Here's payment for what we think she's worth. Thank you for supporting the war effort and enjoy the rest of your life. No."

She shook her head.

"I'm not leaving this system without finding out whether Carrie's family is here. And I will take sole responsibility for this ship's intrusion. Besides, anyone who hires a piece of shit such as Tarrant to kidnap Commonwealth citizens needs serious examination. Guess what. I'm the examiner. And for everyone's sake, I will log my actions so that any blowback is directed at me alone."

"So it's to be damn the torpedoes, full speed ahead."

"Quoting Admiral Farragut won't change a thing, Zeke."

This time, it was his turn to chuckle.

"I figured not, but I've always wanted to use that line. So, what's the plan?"

"We unmask fully, switch on the official beacon, and reveal ourselves as the Commonwealth battlecruiser *Iolanthe*, hot in pursuit of pirates who abducted innocent civilians. Then, we see how the nice people running a black site in a quarantined star system react."

"*L'audace* and all that?"

A wry smile twisted her lips.

"*Encore et toujours l'audace*, Number One. I should go with my strengths, right?"

Holt's throat gave birth to a heartfelt sigh.

"Sure. Why not? I suppose we should change into proper uniform before this blessed event occurs. It wouldn't do for privateer ruffians to crew one of the Commonwealth Navy's premier battlecruisers."

"That's how I prefer my first officers. Always on top of the fine details." She stood with renewed energy. "Pass the word we're rejoining the Navy. Or for Major Salminen's troops, the Army."

**

"What fresh devilment is this?" Brakal's rumbling tone spilled over *Tol Vehar*'s bridge like so much molten rock.

"It is a message in the human tongue emanating from one of several buoys dispersed around the star system, Commander," *Tol Vehar*'s communications officer replied.

Brakal scratched the ruff of fur crowning his skull.

"I can see that. Since we are in human space, the message would hardly be in the Imperial tongue. What does it say?"

"My automated translator believes the message to be an order forbidding entry into this system on pain of automatic and cruel punishment. The order appears to come from the human government."

A ferocious rictus twisted the Shrehari commander's face.

"Did we stumble on a secret base? A place where the poxed humans are preparing dire weapons to use against us?" He thumped Urag's shoulder with a meaty fist. "Think how pleased the robed idiots on the homeworld will be once we bring proof of further human perfidy. And we can thank the demonic ghost for this fortuitous discovery."

"Perhaps it would be wise to avoid selling the *yatakan* hide before you've killed it, Lord," Urag growled.

"If those gormless worms aren't doing something sinister, something that could threaten the Empire, why quarantine an entire star system from their own species?"

"Yet we can see no world suitable for human habitation."

"In that case, an artificial habitat," Brakal replied. "What do you say we find out?"

Regar made a sound eerily reminiscent of a herdbeast choking to death.

"A quarantine without enough force of arms to back it up is worthless, Commander. Though you lead four ships, I would counsel caution lest we enter a trap from which we cannot escape. *Tol Vehar* and *Tol Vach* are older and easier to detect even with our chief engineers' best efforts to dampen emissions. We already know the ghost is more capable in that respect and therefore the humans will operate sensors capable of surpassing our ability to confound them."

"And where would you suggest we go first, Lord?" Urag asked.

Brakal studied the combined data from their navigation records and the most recent sensor imagery in silence before pointing at the gas giant closest to the Hecate system's sun.

"That planet, Raijin, is within what the humans and we consider the habitable zone. It has many moons. Some might even support life. The Empire rules over such worlds, no? That being the case where better to hide nefarious doings? Take us there, Urag. We shall come out of otherspace before the limit, dampen our emissions, and observe."

"Might I suggest you leave a *Ptar* here?" Regar asked. "In case things go awry, someone should be able to warn the Empire of this place."

Brakal clapped him on the shoulder and smiled, exposing cracked yellowed fangs.

"We shall make a proper naval strategist of you yet, Regar."

"Since the *Tai Kan* didn't make me an appropriately treacherous spy, perhaps I should master other skills."

"You should indeed, Regar. A mind such as yours must not be sullied by working as a political officer on an honest warship. Prepare the navigation plan for my approval, Urag. We visit Raijin."

— Thirty-One —

When Dunmoore returned to the CIC thirty minutes later, it was staffed by watchkeepers in midnight blue Navy battledress complete with gold rank and qualification insignia, save for Major Salminen. She wore the Army's rifle green as always, but this time with the proper blackened silver Scandia Regiment badges instead of Varangian Company regalia.

"They're still scanning," Chief Yens reported the moment she caught sight of Siobhan, "but didn't stumble over us yet." Her rough hand patted the sensor console with affection. "Our old girl is still the stealthiest starship anywhere."

"They might not," Holt's hologram said, "but our Shrehari friends seem to have stumbled into the Hecate system. Emma broke radio silence to send us an encrypted microburst message on the emergency subspace channel. That Shrehari flotilla we saw near Kilia followed us. Enoc Tarrant probably gave them the rendezvous coordinates, treasonous weasel that he is."

"Why would they..." Dunmoore's voice trailed away, and she grimaced. "Let me guess. Their commander pegged us for the raider who's been playing havoc with Imperial shipping, and he's looking for payback."

"Without a doubt," Holt replied. "I can't think of any other reason for them to stray this far from the Empire's usual hunting grounds. And finding the rendezvous deserted, the Shrehari commander deduced our most probable destination - Hecate. In any case, two *Tol* class cruisers and two *Ptar* class corvettes dropped out of FTL just short of the heliopause, loitered for a few hours. Then all but one *Ptar* went FTL again, headed inward. Emma waited until they were in hyperspace before transmitting. The *Ptar* that stayed behind is trying to hide its emissions, but Emma can still spot him."

Dunmoore cursed softly in at least three different languages.

"That strike force commander must be insane to operate so far from home."

"More to the point, what will he do to this system once he figures out it's quarantined and occupied by the Commonwealth government? I can't see your average Shrehari simply turning back after translating the warning buoys' message. He'll probably think we're developing and testing doomsday weapons to be used against the Empire and make the eradication of every single surface and orbital installation his paramount duty."

Dunmoore bit back another surge of irritation.

"In other words what you're telling me is our presence here might condemn whoever is on Temar."

"Unless we make it obvious the cost of attacking would be too great for someone so far from home. Shrehari are aggressive, but they are not known for throwing away lives needlessly. Even the dimmest of them understands the notion that discretion is sometimes the better part of valor and therefore not dishonorable."

"Then it's just as well we're about to make a rare appearance as the battlecruiser *Iolanthe*. Perhaps I can use the upcoming arrival of a Shrehari strike force as a bargaining chip when I speak to whoever's in charge."

"Just don't tell anyone the Shrehari intrusion is our fault, Skipper."

Dunmoore gave her first officer's hologram the evil eye.

"Just confirm the ship is ready, Zeke."

"*Iolanthe* is ready to go up systems and reveal herself as one of the Navy's newest battlecruisers."

"And not coincidentally give the local inhabitants a heart attack," Sirico added in a droll tone. "It will be nice to do so under our true colors."

"In that case, Mister Sirico, unmask. Number One, once she's become the Furious Faerie, please bring her systems to full military power and switch on our official beacon."

"Aye, aye, sir," both replied in unison.

Save for the distant rumbling of camouflage plates moving out of the way and gun turrets deploying, little seemed to change — until Chief Yens raised a hand.

"They see us now, sir. Military-grade orbital sensors are ogling us as if *Iolanthe* was a nautch dancer performing at Sunday mass."

"I didn't peg you for a churchgoer, Chief," Sirico said.

"I'm not," Yens replied, deadpan. "There aren't enough nautch dancers in most churches for my taste. Plenty of weapon systems around here though. Ten orbital defense platforms within sensor range just powered up as did the aerospace defense pods on the surface. They might not see us until we want them to, but there's nothing wrong with their reflexes now we appeared out of nowhere. Mind you, this ordnance might make our shields scream, but not long enough to cause harm before we return fire."

"And right on cue, a message from the surface," Holt said. "Temar control urgently wants to speak with the Commonwealth Star Ship *Iolanthe*'s commanding officer. It's audio only."

"Please, pipe it to the CIC." When the signals petty officer gave her thumbs up, she said, "This is Captain Siobhan Dunmoore. I command the battlecruiser *Iolanthe*."

"What the hell are you doing here, Dunmoore? I'm sure you're aware Hecate is a quarantined system. There are enough damn warning buoys scattered around to make even the dumbest starship commander understand no one is allowed in."

"And who might you be?" She asked in a reasonable tone.

"That's none of your business. Now leave this system. Tell your admiral he or she can expect a message from Fleet HQ ordering you be disciplined for violating the quarantine."

"I'm sure it will thrill my admiral. He'll be equally pleased with the fact I'm the only thing standing between you and four Shrehari warships, three of which are inbound as we speak. Two *Tol* class cruisers and one *Ptar* class corvette, with a further *Ptar* standing guard at the system's heliopause. And that I'm in hot pursuit of pirates who abducted over seventy Commonwealth civilians."

Silence. Then an incredulous, "What? Shrehari? Are you insane, Dunmoore? This system is well out of range from their operating bases."

"And yet, they're presently FTL somewhere between Hecate's heliopause and Raijin's hyperlimit. I'll ask again nicely. Who are you? This isn't an idle question. Unless I'm convinced you're friendlies, I see no reason to help you fight off the Shrehari. Better yet, unless you convince me you're friendlies, I'll assume you're in league with the pirates who handed you the crew and passengers of a freighter by the name *Kattegat Maru*. And treat you like outlaws guilty of a capital crime. One kinetic strike from orbit and your control center won't ever control anything again. The same goes for your entire satellite constellation."

"Are you threatening me? I'm an official of the Commonwealth government, and this is a federal installation. Threats made against either are a federal crime. Your admiral won't just be ordered to discipline you, he'll be ordered to remove you from command and put in front of a court-martial. I'm giving you one last chance to leave. Otherwise, your career and life as you know it are over."

"Earth and Fleet HQ are far away. I'm here, and I hold the high orbitals. The Shrehari will be here in half a standard day at most. Therefore, I doubt you'll have a chance to make good on your threats. Let's try this again. Who are you, and which government agency is operating in this system? You're not Fleet. That's for sure. Otherwise, you'd be more than happy to discuss our fighting off the Shrehari together. Besides, no one in the Fleet would deal in human flesh with a gangster like Enoc Tarrant."

Dunmoore thought she heard a sharp intake of breath at the other end of the comlink.

"You seem remarkably well informed for a battlecruiser captain, Dunmoore. These are matters of national security and classified beyond anything you've ever imagined. Take care you don't overstep your bounds any further. The consequences could go well beyond the end of your naval career."

"Such as ending up in your stockade after an extraordinary rendition under the Navy's nose? Perhaps I'll finally meet the folks taken off *Kattegat Maru* so it wouldn't be a total loss."

"All right," the man responded in a voice tinged by repressed fury. "I think you and I need to speak, privately and face-to-face before this spirals totally out of control and does immeasurable harm to the Commonwealth's interests."

"I agree. And for the last time, who are you?"

"My name is Blayne Hersom. I'm a senior director, the civilian equivalent of a Navy flag officer, in a classified agency reporting directly to the Secretary-General's Office on Earth. The Hecate system is my responsibility."

"Shall I come down, or would you prefer a tour of *Iolanthe*?" Dunmoore asked, though she already knew what Hersom's answer would be.

"You're coming here, Dunmoore. Within the hour. I'm sure you can see our landing strip. Try not to make things worse in the meantime. Temar, out."

No one spoke for almost a minute, then Holt said, "Might I see you in your day cabin, Skipper?"

"If you intend to remind me that captains should stay in their ships and send proper landing parties into dangerous situations, Zeke, you can spare your breath. Prepare enough shuttles and gunships to land Major Salminen's company, augmented by a platoon of Chief Dwyn's boarding party-qualified ratings. I won't be alone."

"In full battle armor?"

"Of course. If Chief Guthren feels the urge to stretch his legs, he can lead the spacer platoon and be my shadow. And Zeke..."

"Sir?"

"I won't invoke General Order Eighty-One this time. Blayne Hersom's classified agency is the damned Special Security Bureau. There is no question about it unless the SecGen created another unsupervised secret police monster to circumvent the Senate and the Fleet. The fact they're not only running a covert rendition site but hiring pirates to abduct innocent civilians offends me to my core. If he tries anything hostile while we're there, he and his become the enemy. You and I will act accordingly."

"He won't expect you to land with a company of armored infantry. He might react in unpredictable ways."

"I doubt Hersom has any troops capable of standing up to Major Salminen's soldiers. His sort is only good at intimidating people already in their power." She climbed to her feet. "Thorin, make sure you register every satellite within line of sight as a target, along with the aerospace defense pods around the stockade."

"And the ground control center?"

"That too." She glanced at Salminen. "Shall we?"

"I've already put my company on alert, sir. They'll be ready and waiting on the hangar deck in fifteen minutes, with a full load of live ammunition and our portable crew-served weapons, in case the guard droids turn on us. I've yet to meet one capable of withstanding a twenty-millimeter automatic cannon."

Dunmoore gave the soldier a knowing grin.

"That's the spirit, Major."

"I just have one question," Lieutenant Commander Sirico said in a mournful tone. "Why is no one ever happy to see us when we suddenly show up on their sensors?"

— Thirty-Two —

Eight gunships, each flown by one of *Iolanthe*'s pilot qualified petty officers and carrying half a platoon of armored soldiers, surrounded Dunmoore's shuttle as her flight swooped down to land on the empty strip fronting the mysterious base's ground control center. It relieved her to note the aerospace defense pods were not tracking the craft over open sights and understood Hersom was providing further proof of his apparent goodwill in attempting to resolve the situation.

They touched down to the whine of thrusters, each seeming light as a feather under the deft touch of its pilot. Within seconds, aft ramps opened to disgorge the soldiers of E Company wearing full battle order, minus Command Sergeant Courtlyn Alekseev's platoon which was still in *Kattegat Maru*.

The troopers silently dispersed to form a protective perimeter around the grounded spacecraft while Major Salminen and her company HQ remained near her command gunship. At an unheard signal, Dunmoore's shuttle dropped its aft ramp and a naval landing party, as well armored, and armed as the soldiers, marched off in two files, scatterguns, and plasma rifles at the high port. They were led by a hulking, barrel-shaped figure wearing a chief petty officer first class' starburst and anchors on his battlesuit's chest plate.

The spacers came to a synchronized, crashing halt and Chief Petty Officer Guthren raised his gauntleted fist in the air telling Dunmoore's it was safe to disembark. She appeared at the top of the ramp and paused for a few moments. Unlike her escort, she wore only battle dress, though a large bore blaster sat in an open holster at her hip.

Dunmoore did not, however, wear the Armed Services' sky-blue beret. Instead, a naval version of the Army's brimmed field cap covered her short copper locks. The cap gave her a more sinister, hard-edged appearance, an effect she deliberately cultivated for this meeting.

Eyes moving from side to side, Dunmoore studied her surroundings. The air temperature was above freezing, but she felt a chill nonetheless, both from the cold breeze and from the dull alien landscape bathed in the equally dull sunlight reflected by Satan's Eye. Then, with deliberate steps, she walked down the ramp to where her escort waited in an orderly assemblage of faceless war machines.

Though she could sense life beyond the low, elongated control center separating the main installation from the strip, Dunmoore saw no welcoming committee. Perhaps Blayne Hersom was playing the usual, petty bureaucratic games by making her wait to show he outranked a mere Navy captain on the greasy pole of the Commonwealth government hierarchy. Dunmoore knew any uninvited attempt to enter the installation proper via the double doors facing the landing strip would meet with failure.

And so she assumed the parade rest between Guthren and Leading Spacer Vincenzo, hands clasped in the small of her back and composed herself to wait until Hersom decided he'd drawn the game out long enough to make his point

Tatiana Salminen's voice in her earbug broke a silence punctuated only by the sounds of the endless, chilly breeze.

"Fourteen guard droids are moving to encircle us, sir. We're also picking up signs of armed humans accompanying them. Neither presents a threat as yet."

Hersom making another point? Or a belated reaction to the unexpected arrival of a combat-ready infantry company?

Dunmoore nodded once, knowing Salminen was watching her, waiting for an acknowledgment.

Nothing else moved for almost ten more minutes. That they were under intense scrutiny by Hersom and his people was beyond question.

Finally, the control center doors opened, and a lone figure emerged. Lean, tall, his craggy features topped by luxuriant gray hair, the man moved with the athletic vigor of someone half his age. The confidence in his stride and his posture gave Dunmoore enough cause to conclude this could only be Blayne Hersom.

He wore an expensive, tan-colored safari suit, the kind favored by wealthy individuals who enjoyed spending astronomical fortunes hunting alien creatures on distant worlds. A tooled, brown leather gun belt and holster heightened the effect.

The man stopped a few paces in front of Dunmoore and studied her with dark, expressionless eyes. She forcibly repressed a shiver at their cold, dispassionate emptiness. Here was someone who wouldn't know the meaning of pity, much less how to spell empathy.

"Captain Dunmoore, I presume. I'm Blayne Hersom, the senior Commonwealth government official in the Hecate system, which makes me the de facto governor." Instead of offering his hand, as Dunmoore half-expected, he indicated the soldiers and spacers surrounding her. "A bit overwrought, wouldn't you say? There's no call for a display of force. We are on the same side."

Dunmoore gave him a dismissive half shrug.

"My Marines need regular exercise, and this seemed a good occasion. The same goes for my naval landing party."

Hersom's expression made it clear he knew she was lying.

"Apologies for making you wait. I needed to deal with a few urgent matters before I could give you and your dire news about a Shrehari strike force my full attention. I hope my tardiness didn't try your patience."

"Patience isn't thought of as a virtue in my world, Mister Hersom, or as something innate. We consider it a skill to be trained and nurtured, and I take advantage of every opportunity to better myself."

"Commendable, I'm sure. Hopefully, your people are just as well trained in the art of exercising patience, Captain. I would prefer we don't experience a sudden outbreak of accidental gunfire. My guard droids possess better reflexes than your best Marine and an almost unlimited supply of ammunition."

"I trust your droids and the humans accompanying them are just as patient and equally well trained in differentiating between friend and foe. Or programmed, I suppose."

Hersom nodded over his shoulder at the ground control building.

"I suggest we hold our discussion in my office rather than out here under the gaze of Satan's Eye, but your escort will stay behind. We can't countenance a hundred troopers wandering around unescorted. However, rest assured that your safety is guaranteed on Temar."

"I never thought any differently, Mister Hersom. Of course, as is our custom, my Marines, the naval landing party, and I became expendable in the eyes of my first officer the moment we left *Iolanthe*, should the ship's safety become an issue. But I will insist on bringing at least my bodyguard along with me." She indicated Vincenzo with her thumb. "I'm sure you understand."

Hersom's eyes briefly slipped to the right, but the only thing he saw was the spacer's blank visor.

"You may certainly bring your bodyguard on the condition he stays in the corridor while we talk in my office."

She inclined her head.

"Naturally."

"If you'll follow me."

Hersom turned on his heels and walked away without waiting for her acknowledgment.

After a moment's hesitation at his abruptness, she complied, trailed by the ever faithful Vincenzo.

The building's innards were as bland and utilitarian as those of every prefabricated outpost Dunmoore had ever visited. Closed doors with numbered plates affixed to the panels lined both sides of the broad passage.

Hersom led them up a metallic spiral staircase and along a second story corridor almost identical to the one below. He stopped by a door at the far end of the passageway.

"You may leave your escort here, Captain."

She gave Vincenzo a nod and then preceded Hersom into a spacious and well-appointed office. He motioned toward the chair in front of a bare metallic desk.

"Can I offer you a cup of coffee?"

Dunmoore shook her head.

"Thank you, but no. I drank my quota for the day."

Hersom served himself then took a seat and studied her over the rim of his mug with those unnerving, almost reptilian eyes.

"Your presence here is problematic on so many levels I don't quite know where to start, Captain."

"Why? You and I work for the same government and toward the same goals, don't we?"

"True," Hersom replied in a thoughtful tone. "To a certain extent. But you and I are charged with reaching those goals in very different ways. The difference is such that our paths should never have crossed and therein lies my dilemma. Why don't you explain how you came to enter the Hecate system despite the warning buoys?"

Dunmoore expected the question and figured telling the truth about most things, save for the Shrehari, would be best when dealing with one of the Secretary-General's secret police thugs.

"We responded to a distress signal from a freighter by the name *Kattegat Maru*, which was intercepted by pirates while outbound from Kilia. Unfortunately, we found only one remaining crewmember aboard, someone who escaped detection by hiding in a shielded compartment. But that individual gave us enough clues to trace the piracy and kidnapping back to one Enoc Tarrant, a mob boss who seems to own a profitable and illegal free port beyond the Commonwealth frontier. I convinced this Tarrant to tell me where his people were taking *Kattegat Maru*'s crew and passengers."

Hersom's face tightened at her words and Dunmoore thought she could see the first flicker of emotion in his eyes. Anger. Good. If she could provoke a falling out among thieves between Hersom and Tarrant, so much the better.

"From there it wasn't difficult to deduce the Hecate system was their final destination. Imagine my surprise at discovering it was occupied by the very government that pays my salary. Tell me Mister Hersom, since when does your agency engage in kidnapping and piracy?"

"None of this concerns you, Dunmoore. Our work here is of the highest importance to national security, and I assure you everything we do is in pursuit of a single overriding aim — the survival of the Commonwealth and through it, that of humanity. You would be well advised to forget about *Kattegat Maru*, wipe every reference to her from your logs, and return to your patrol route forthwith. The ship's fate and that of those who were aboard will enter history as an unexplained puzzle, and soon they will be forgotten. Any claims made by this survivor you found will be deemed pure fantasy and dismissed. Now tell me about these Shrehari. How did they get here?"

Dunmoore made a dismissive gesture.

"I don't know. Perhaps they heard about your highly important work and figured it would be best for the Empire if you were put out of business. I dropped a surveillance buoy at the edge of the Hecate system, in accordance with standard operating procedures, and it warned me about the Shrehari's arrival shortly before we made ourselves visible to your sensors. Because they're the furthest thing from stupid, I can only assume the boneheads will soon discover not only the satellite constellations orbiting Raijin and Temar, but that your little home away from home is both habitable and occupied. Since this system is quarantined, they will conclude we hairless apes are cooking up something nefarious and try to destroy your installation. But your little settlement isn't a research and development center, is it? The Special Security Bureau doesn't dabble in weapons development. Even the Secretary-General knows enough to leave such matters in the Fleet's hands."

She allowed herself a sardonic smile.

"It would be a shame if the Shrehari mistakenly massacred your prisoners." Though Hersom's bored expression didn't change, there was a distinct flicker of irritation in his eyes. "This is an extraordinary rendition site, isn't it? A place to warehouse and interrogate humans deemed enemies of the Commonwealth without going through the niceties of an arrest warrant let alone a trial. Last I checked, what you're doing isn't legal, even if the SecGen personally ordered it."

"You just crossed the line into perilous territory, Dunmoore." His tone was carefully neutral, yet it carried a dangerous edge. "Desist, walk it back, and we can both forget this happened."

Dunmoore raised her hands, palms outward, in surrender.

"I'm not about to argue there aren't plenty of people in the Commonwealth who imperil humanity's future by merely existing. And as a warship captain with plenty of human and alien blood on her hands, I'm probably not one to discuss morality with you, even if I've never given the Special Security Bureau a warm thought. But I draw the line at abducting and detaining innocent civilians. *Kattegat Maru*'s crew and passengers can't all be enemies of the Commonwealth and that being the case you have no business with them. I'll tell you how we can walk this back and forget *Iolanthe* ever came near the Hecate system. Hand them over. I will restore them to their ship, and we could treat this as a piracy operation thwarted by the Navy. Your agency's name need never come up. And if you want to help me assuage my conscience, so I can also forget any of this happened, tell me why."

"What makes you think you can bargain with me, Dunmoore?"

She turned a perilously sweet smile on Hersom.

"I hold the power of life and death over you, Blayne. She who owns the high orbitals dictates the terms. And before you mention those defense satellites, *Iolanthe*'s targeting sensors are already tracking them. At the merest sign of hostile action, my first officer will open fire and destroy your ability to deal with anything bigger than an unarmed merchant ship. If I leave you to deal with the Shrehari after I shred everything that can shoot... Well, you get the picture, right?"

"You wouldn't dare." This time, his growing anger was unmistakable.

"I would. And once I'm done, who will complain? Officially, your little colony doesn't exist. The Commonwealth government doesn't run black sites, and the Hecate system is quarantined for scientific reasons. I wipe my logs and return to my patrol route. You'd be surprised how easily I can live with myself after doing things most civilians would consider highly questionable."

"I'll see you in my stockade for this, Dunmoore."

"No, you won't. We both know that. You don't want your superiors on Earth to find out a bullheaded battlecruiser captain compromised this operation so easily. It might put the brakes on what I'm sure is a stellar career with the Bureau."

Dunmoore watched Hersom's jaw muscles work as he chewed on his alternatives.

"Reveal anything of what I'm about to say, and you *will* become the subject of an extraordinary rendition, Dunmoore."

"Make it worth my while. Give me the *Kattegat Maru* folks and satisfy my curiosity, and I'll help fight off the Shrehari before forgetting about this place."

Hersom took a deep breath, then let it out in a controlled exhalation.

"Since you and I are both professionals dedicated to preserving humanity, I suppose we can find common ground."

— Thirty-Three —

"You are correct in assuming this is a Special Security Bureau detention facility," Hersom said after swallowing a healthy sip of his coffee. "For future reference, no one uses the terms rendition site or black site outside of bad fiction, so I'd appreciate it if you dropped the term. My job is to detain and interrogate those deemed a clear and present danger to the Commonwealth. Once we obtain the information we need, we transfer most prisoners to regular facilities, where they await trial or prepare for release. Some, those who will always represent a danger to the Commonwealth, spend the rest of their lives here."

He paused to study her reaction. When he saw nothing, Hersom continued.

"My agency received word one of those dangerous individuals was traveling along the frontier, aboard a tramp freighter called *Kattegat Maru*. I was ordered to arrange the person's capture and detention by any means necessary, without regard for collateral damage. There was just one problem. No one knew our target's identity, only that he or she was on that freighter. We've used Tarrant before this. His people are not really pirates in the purest sense but unregistered mercenaries. Crime syndicate soldiers if you wish. They don't hunt for fun and profit but only on orders. Their main job is enforcing Tarrant's will in the Kilia system and on those who deal with him in the Zone. You'd be amazed at how many hidden human colonies are out there, beyond the Commonwealth sphere."

Hersom took another sip of coffee.

"In any case, we paid Tarrant to seize *Kattegat Maru* and bring the passengers to a rendezvous point where we would take them into custody. Once here, the plan was to find our person of interest and eventually release the others on one of the unregistered colonies. The contract with Tarrant included creating a mystery for our target's employers by making him, or her vanish without a trace. But it didn't go quite as expected and I'll take some blame for not being specific enough."

"What do you mean?"

"They weren't supposed to kidnap the crew and abandon the ship to be found by salvagers. *Baba Yaga*'s captain blamed the Shrehari corsairs when he met us at the rendezvous point. Apparently, they were in charge of the actual seizure and improvised."

"Considering those Shrehari were probably *Tai Kan* and not real freelancers, I'm unsurprised. The Imperial secret police enjoys doing things its own way and to hell with orders or legality." She smirked. "They resemble the SSB in that respect."

Hersom's eyes narrowed just enough for Siobhan to notice.

"Careful, Dunmoore. We're nothing like those thugs. But I agree with your assessment about the corsair being undercover *Tai Kan*."

"So you admit everyone taken off *Katie* is here? Did you discover who your suspect might be?"

The SSB officer shook his head.

"Not yet. Despite your low opinion of my agency, I can assure you we don't use illegal interrogation methods on people who might be innocent. It means identifying the target will take time."

"But you'll use illegal methods on the guilty."

An air of exasperation twisted Hersom's face.

"Let me guess. You were a barracks lawyer at the Academy, right? I'll take care to choose my words more carefully from now on. We won't use coercive methods with people who have a one in fifty chance of being our target."

Dunmoore gave him an ironic smile.

"Glad to hear it. And the crew? I mean there's a zero chance your target is among them, so why are they detained?"

"They're not. We didn't take them from *Baba Yaga*. I gave its captain strict instructions to release the crew at a safe port inside the Commonwealth, on the assumption that their damned salvage scheme was already in motion."

Siobhan's heart sank. The sort of enforcers who worked for a boss such as Tarrant were just as likely to find a slave market and earn extra coin on the side. But she took care not to show her dismay.

"I temporarily designated *Kattegat Maru* a naval auxiliary, assigned a relief crew, and took her with me. She's not in Temar orbit but hidden nearby. I want to put her crew back on board. Her passengers as well, minus your arch-criminal, of course. It's a shame you didn't accept the crew. That means I'm forced to continue my chase, and I can't keep going back and forth between Kilia and here. There's a war on, as you might remember, and *Iolanthe* is a warship."

She was pleased with her cool, even tone. Part of her wanted to grab Hersom by the throat and ask how he could be so callous as to let known criminals decide the fate of innocents. Something must have shown in her eyes because his exasperated look returned.

"They'll carry out my orders and land the crew at a safe location. Tarrant knows he can't afford to alienate my agency, and not only because we pay well."

"Since Tarrant showed no qualms at giving me the rendezvous coordinates, I doubt he cares about your agency. He probably gave or sold those same coordinates to the Shrehari, considering he employed a *Tai Kan* spy ship pretending to be a corsair."

That should help precipitate a permanent break between the SSB and their tame mobsters, if not worse, she thought.

"Should anything happen to Captain Fennon and her people, I will hold you personally responsible."

Hersom waved away her threat.

"Please spare me the moral posturing. Considering how many died in this war so far, what are another two dozen? Especially when your own actions are probably responsible for taking ten, twenty, or even a hundred times more lives."

"*Kattegat Maru*'s crew didn't sign up to fight in this or any other war. They signed up knowing about the dangers of traveling through the galaxy's more perilous sectors, that's a given. But they damned well did not accept the risk of getting fucked over by an agency of the government that's supposed to ensure their safety."

This time, a quiver of righteous anger colored her voice, and she immediately felt annoyed with herself at showing emotions in front of this automaton made of soulless flesh.

"I understand, but what's done is done. All we can do now is hope for the best. Feel free to pursue *Baba Yaga* or squeeze Tarrant for more information. I don't care. And if that was it, perhaps we can discuss the inbound Shrehari strike force."

"We're not done yet. You need to find your suspect among the passengers between now and when I've chased off those Shrehari because I'm taking the rest back with me."

Hersom sat back and crossed his legs in a gesture that convey both weariness and disdain.

"Shall we discuss your options for early retirement on Parth again, Captain? I'm sorry, the detainees leave this place when I'm good and ready to let them go, not before."

"If you can't figure out who the target is by now, don't you think he or she might not even be among *Kattegat Maru*'s passengers? What if your information was wrong and you hold forty-five innocents? Or is the SSB's fearsome reputation for always getting a confession vastly overblown? If you don't know the person's identity yet, I doubt you ever will. Mainly because he or she isn't on this moon."

"Perhaps. But our sources are usually accurate and trustworthy."

"Does that include Enoc Tarrant?"

"Could we stop harping on about him? My agency will talk to Tarrant about his failures in due course."

"Hopefully your colleagues will do more than just talk, but you're the one facing an unpleasant Shrehari infestation, and I hold the key to saving your rendition — pardon me, detention site from orbital bombardment."

Hersom, elbows on the chair's arms, fingers steepled, stared at her in silence for a moment. Then he said, "Tell you what. While you deal with the Shrehari, I'll urge my people to redouble their efforts. Once you've chased them off, we can see how things stand and talk again."

Dunmoore held his gaze for an equal amount of time before replying.

"Agreed. On one condition."

He cocked an eyebrow, inviting her to continue.

"I want to visit the *Kattegat Maru* passengers before I rejoin my ship. Perhaps a new pair of eyes can spot someone who doesn't seem to belong."

"And it'll allow you to see where and how they're housed, in case you decide to send those fearsome Marines on a daring raid."

She gave him a thin, mocking smile.

"Whoever said SSB officers were as thick as two short planks obviously never met you."

He uncrossed his legs and stood with slow deliberation.

"It might be interesting to see you try. We've not run a real test of our security measures against armed intruders. My guard droids do okay against detainees, but I suspect your Marines aren't particularly impressed by them."

"They're not." Dunmoore climbed to her feet as well. "The passengers?"

"We'll go see them right away. You may even bring your tin man along with us."

— Thirty-Four —

As Hersom led Dunmoore and Vincenzo down the spiral staircase and through the main corridor, she said, "I never thought to ask, but where's the ship that carried the detainees from the rendezvous?"

"On another errand. I'm afraid my agency has only so many to go around, and beyond a handful of sub-light shuttles, I'm bereft of long-range transport. Before you ask, my craft are in a hangar next to this building. And no, they're not sufficiently armed to be of use against a Shrehari strike force, nor are my pilots capable of flying combat against anything other than run-of-the-mill marauders."

They stopped at a double door similar to the one on the tarmac side, and Hersom touched a control panel. The panes slid aside with a soft groan, allowing the chilly outside air to wash over them.

Dunmoore stepped through, then stopped as her eyes took in a deceptively large installation. The tall, flat-topped native trees didn't just hide one stockade but several square compounds surrounded by high, opaque fencing and separated by broad, rammed earth paths.

"We keep detainees separated into small groups, depending on their reason for being here. It reduces the risk of cross contaminating information. The *Kattegat Maru* passengers are in their own enclosure. They don't know where they are or suspect who we are. Other than the target, I suppose."

"If that individual is among them."

Hersom didn't reply. Instead, he walked off without looking back. After a moment's hesitation, Dunmoore and Vincenzo followed.

She spotted guard droids in most of the side passages, near what seemed like openings in the slick, pearly gray fencing, but no living beings. Nor did she hear any sounds betraying a human presence. It was as if a dampening field further isolating the inmates from their surroundings smothered each compound.

The camouflage nets strung overhead to cover gaps between the treetops let through a surprising amount of light reflected by Satan's Eye, keeping the stockade in a partial twilight.

Finally, after passing several enclosures on each side of the main path, Hersom turned left and approached a silent guard droid standing by a closed gate. The setup was in all respects identical to those she'd seen along the way, with nothing to show this part of the stockade housed the SSB's latest batch of detainees.

Hersom made a few quick hand gestures, and the droid backed away. A minute passed, then the gate opened to something that resembled an airlock except the inside walls and doorway were transparent, allowing for a clear view of the compound within.

Four buildings, each made from shipping containers fused together and pierced with openings for windows and doors occupied the center of a surprisingly spacious and clean open space.

"Three are barracks for fifteen apiece, though they could easily accommodate thirty, and the fourth is the mess hall and recreation facility. The inmates don't lack for space." The outer gate slid shut behind them. "A few armed officers would normally come with me, but I expect your bodyguard's presence will suffice to discourage any foolhardiness. Besides the detainees wear bracelets that not only allows us to check their status and communicate with them but also to shock anyone attempting violence into submission. And of course, my control center has eyes on every cubic centimeter of every compound."

"Charming," Dunmoore muttered. Then, in a louder voice, "Where is everyone?"

"The guard droid ordered them to go into their respective barracks via the bracelets. One of the first things we teach detainees is the importance of obeying orders."

When he noticed the expression on Dunmoore's face, Hersom chuckled.

"No, not via shock therapy. Disobedience entails loss of privileges and may even result in reduced rations if it persists. Our procedures are very much in line with the Commonwealth Correctional Service's methods. One last thing before we enter. Could you and your bodyguard please remove all naval insignia? It wouldn't do to let the detainees think they're being visited by members of the Armed Services. It's better for everyone if they return to their regular lives not knowing the government detained them. We prefer to avoid the need for memory wipes. Not everyone can handle those without suffering side effects."

She indicated the transparent walls.

"Shouldn't we have done that already?"

"No. We can see in, but anyone on the other side can't see us."

"Ah."

Dunmoore gestured at Vincenzo to peel the leading spacer's rank insignia, Navy badge, and ship's crest from his armor, while she did the same to her battledress and field cap. Hersom gave both a once-over, then nodded his approval.

"That should do."

They entered the compound proper, and the sound of wind rustling through the high canopy vanished, confirming Dunmoore's suspicion that a dampening field covered the enclosures.

The detainees in the first of the three dormitories variously sat or were lying on their cots. Fifteen pairs of eyes anxiously examined her and the formidable looking Vincenzo as they passed through. Dunmoore met each gaze with as much warmth as she could muster, silently promising to arrange for their release. But none triggered the slightest bit of suspicion he or she might be Hersom's elusive target.

The adjoining dormitory also resembled nothing so much as a platoon barracks in an Armed Services primary training center. None of the men and women in this one caught Dunmoore's attention either.

They seemed equally bewildered, frightened, and lost. But they appeared healthy and well fed, and none bore visible signs of abuse, which was primarily what she wanted to see. Though Hersom might not realize it, Vincenzo was the one recording every detail with the help of his sophisticated battlesuit in case a raid became necessary.

She was preparing for the same disappointment in the third dormitory, thereby dashing her hopes of helping Hersom find his suspect so she could retrieve the other forty-four abductees. But when she walked down the center of the barracks, meeting each set of eyes in turn, a middle-aged man caught her attention.

Silver-haired, with a vaguely aristocratic profile, his face was not one she knew or might even have seen in passing, but it triggered an eerie sense of familiarity nonetheless. Cognizant of the video pickups watching her every move, she took care to keep a blank expression as she continued her quick inspection of the last fifteen detainees. Once back in the chilly air Dunmoore shook her head.

"Sorry. No one seemed out of place. I still think whoever told you the suspect was traveling in *Kattegat Maru* lied or knew nothing. Otherwise, you'd have noticed by now that one of those sad sacks in there wasn't quite as sad as the rest. I may not be fond of your lot, but you are good at this sort of thing."

"Pity." Hersom gestured toward the gate. "Can we now discuss how you intend to deal with the Shrehari?"

"Certainly. It's simple. I will take *Iolanthe* to Temar's trailing Lagrangian point and go silent. If your sensors didn't detect me until I went up systems, the boneheads won't see my ship until moments before I open fire. You will act as if nothing was happening and wait for my signal to activate your own defensive platforms. Make sure your gunners don't shoot before I tell them and make damn sure they don't aim at my ship."

"Sweet and simple. It shall be as you say."

"Impress on your folks it's essential we take the Shrehari by surprise. We will get one chance to smack them hard and convince their commander this isn't a battle he can win and still make it home. That means they must not know I've alerted you, let alone that my ship is lying in wait for them. Nothing goes live, nothing shoots, and no shields go up until I give the signal."

"Understood. I'll take you back to the tarmac and let you return topside so you may prepare. Once you've chased away the Shrehari, please feel free to come back so we can conclude our discussion about the fate of the *Kattegat Maru* detainees."

"Make sure you either find that person of interest or conclude he or she isn't among them. I'm not leaving the Hecate system without at least forty-four of those people."

As she expected, Hersom didn't respond. They spent the rest of the walk back to the landing strip in silence. After passing once more through the control center, he ushered them out, then turned away without a word of goodbye.

Dunmoore caught sight of both Salminen and Guthren's helmeted heads turning toward her, and she made the 'mount up' signal. Within minutes, the eight gunships and the single armed shuttle were loaded and ready to lift. Dunmoore, sitting in the gunner's seat beside Petty Officer Purdy, mentally replayed her visit of the *Kattegat Maru* detainee barracks.

Why did that one man stir a vague memory? Coincidence? Or something more sinister? She barely noticed the thrusters lighting, or the craft lifting as she rummaged through the dark corners of her mind for something, anything that might fit.

It wasn't until she saw *Iolanthe* framed by the shuttle cockpit's window that a vision of Toboso bubbled up unbidden. Dunmoore knew who he was, or at least who she suspected he could be.

If she was right, his presence raised more questions than it answered, and posed a moral dilemma. But it would need to wait. In a few hours, Shrehari warships would appear at Raijin's hyperlimit, looking for *Iolanthe* and whatever the dastardly humans were doing in this remote, quarantined system.

— Thirty-Five —

Ezekiel Holt, standing beside Petty Officer Harkon in the hangar deck control room, watched the shuttles settle into their assigned positions while the space doors closed. Once they disgorged E Company and Chief Guthren's landing party, he gave Harkon a friendly nod and went through the now open airlock to greet his captain and ask her about Hersom.

But the moment she saw him, Dunmoore pointed at the door and mouthed the words 'day cabin.' Holt immediately spun around and retraced his steps although he cut his long stride in half so she could catch up.

"And?" He asked once Dunmoore fell in beside him.

"It is indeed an SSB rendition site, although Hersom prefers we use the term detention instead of rendition. They hold the *Kattegat Maru* passengers, but not Fennon and company. One of the passengers is supposedly a threat to the Commonwealth, but they don't know who."

"Where's the crew?"

"Still in the clutches of Tarrant's pirates. Or at least, I hope they are." She related the rest of her conversation with Hersom, and her visit to the stockade.

"Son of a bitch," Holt said with genuine anger once she finished speaking. "I can't believe this sort of shit is actually happening. What the hell are they thinking on Earth to allow extra-judicial kidnappings?"

Dunmoore led them into her day cabin and tossed the field cap on her desk.

"I don't know that anyone is thinking clearly, period. But I wouldn't be surprised if the SSB is exploiting wartime hysteria to extend its reach and power. It's possible no one outside the Bureau has a clue this place exists."

"It won't end well."

Holt automatically drew two cups of coffee from the urn and handed one to Dunmoore.

"That depends on your point of view." She sat with a sigh. "If you're a SecGen who believes in centralizing power on Earth rather than respecting the rights of sovereign star systems, a more powerful SSB is a feature, not a bug."

"I wish they would leave political games for after the war."

A bitter laugh escaped Dunmoore's lips.

"What? Let a crisis go to waste? The politicians and their minions could no more do that than tell the truth."

"Speaking of crisis games, wasn't poking at a senior SSB officer a tad risky? His sort holds grudges beyond the grave and has the wherewithal to reach out and hurt you."

Though she could hear the reproach in Holt's tone, Dunmoore shrugged off his comment with an unrepentant grimace.

"It's a bit too late for regrets or recriminations, Zeke. However, I doubt he'll bother reaching out so long as I don't spoil his reputation by telling the universe I snuck up on him unnoticed and forced myself into his detention site. That wouldn't help him earn a promotion and reassignment to the centers of power. Plus he'll owe us for helping chase off those Shrehari."

"And their person of interest? If they don't find him or her among the *Kattegat Maru* passengers by the time we're ready to leave, what'll you do?"

Dunmoore made a wry face.

"I may know who it is."

Holt sat up with a start.

"What?"

"Unfortunately, I'm not sure if it's something I can share with Hersom. Speaking from a moral and ethical point of view rather than a utilitarian one. Hang on." Dunmoore touched her communicator. "Captain to the cox'n."

A few moments passed, then, "Guthren here, sir."

"Has Vincenzo uploaded his battlesuit recordings yet?"

"If he hasn't, I'll make sure he does within the next few minutes. Standby for a notification."

The first officer tilted his head to one side and gave her a curious glance.

"Hersom didn't object at your taking visual evidence of his operation?"

"I doubt it occurred to him that our battlesuits can log everything around them. It's not something I advertised, and Vincenzo took care to appear concerned merely with my welfare." A soft ping interrupted her. "Ah. Here we go. I'll run the sequence where we visit the detainees. Tell me if anyone strikes your former spook catcher's fancy."

Holt turned to face the day cabin's main display and nodded once.

"Go for it."

They sat through the first and second dormitory inspection video in silence. But upon seeing the third, Holt suddenly leaned forward and raised a hand.

"Can you please pause the playback?"

A frown creased his forehead as he stood and approached the display to study the image. Then, he tapped a face with his index finger. It was the same silver-haired aristocratic profile that raised her own suspicions.

"This man's features ring a very faint bell. He vaguely reminds me of someone I've met." Holt turned toward

Dunmoore. "The memory is fairly recent, not from my days in counterintelligence."

"Do you want a hint?"

"Sure. I love charades."

"Think back to the Toboso incident."

Holt swung around to face the display again and nodded.

"Of course. My recognition skills must be rusty."

"You'd have twigged right away had you been with me. Thinking back at the moment, I swear I saw a brief flicker of recognition when our eyes met. I think it's what kicked my subconscious into high gear."

"If that is Mikhail Forenza in disguise, why are the SecGen's goons after him? Back on Toboso, I nurtured a sneaking suspicion he might work for the Bureau and not the Colonial Office like he told us. Is the SSB at war with other government branches? And more importantly why are they unable to identify him?"

"I've been asking myself those questions for the last half hour without finding an answer."

"So that's why you're in a moral quandary."

She grimaced.

"I can't simply point him out to Hersom and say that guy bears a resemblance to a Colonial Office agent I once met, someone who I suspect makes his living cleaning up political messes with extreme prejudice. What if I'm wrong and the resemblance is innocent? What if it really is Forenza? I still owe him a debt of gratitude for coming in on my side when I took control of Toboso and ended the Devine gang's conspiracy."

"He murdered Anton Gerber, and no doubt many more."

"We're not exactly wide-eyed naïfs when it comes to killing, Zeke. Besides, we merely have suspicions, not proof."

"Only because Forenza is a professional."

Holt dropped into his chair and crossed his legs.

"I wish Carrie Fennon was here instead of back in her ship. She might enlighten us about this man, and I don't want to risk another subspace burst before we engage the Shrehari."

"A wise precaution, Skipper. What are your immediate intentions?"

She made a dubious face. "Hope Hersom's people will find their target before we finish with the boneheads, so they'll hand the others over to us for repatriation."

"And if not? Since they're still in the dark after scrutinizing their prisoners for days on end with every means at the SSB's disposal, I don't think counting on a sudden breakthrough is realistic. And we can't stick around. Not if we want to track *Baba Yaga* before the bastards do something unpleasant with Captain Fennon and her crew. By the way, did you ask whether anyone knows what heading *Baba Yaga* took after transferring the detainees? It might give us a hint about where to look."

An air of disgust briefly twisted her features.

"No, but it should have occurred to me once I found out Tarrant's pirates still held Carrie's family. I'll remedy that before shifting to Temar's L5 point."

Holt jumped to his feet.

"On that note, we should get underway. If this ambush is to work, *Iolanthe* must be a hole in space at L5 before the Shrehari drop out of FTL."

**

Brakal, unable to stay away from *Tol Vehar*'s bridge for the drop out of otherspace, gripped the arms of the spare command chair. Urag had it installed during the crossing for just such an occasion, lest Strike Force Khorsan's acting commander evict him from his own.

The unpleasantness of transition faded though Brakal suspected the sensation was worsening as he aged. Fortunately for his temper, humans and subject species suffered from something similar. Otherwise, he might curse the gods for afflicting only the Imperial race.

Knowing it would take the sensor operators time to complete a full scan of Raijin and its many moons, he settled back and drew on his shallow reserves of patience while simultaneously fending off a sense of worry. What if this system was genuinely beset by something evil and deadly, something that might gobble up his ships and crews so that no one could return home and warn the fleet?

As he waited for the first report, Brakal studied the colorful gas giant on the main display. Shrehari intelligence records said the humans called it Satan's Eye in jest but didn't specify who this Satan might be and why a gas giant should resemble his eye.

Brakal was about to stand and take his impatience to the mess hall for a cup of hot *tvass* when the senior sensor operator turned around to face Urag.

"One of the gas giant's moons falls within our and the human's habitability parameters, Commander. There is also evidence of artificial satellites orbiting both the giant and this moon. But we cannot detect any starships or any transmissions on the bands used by the hairless apes."

Urag acknowledged the report with a curt nod, then glanced at Brakal.

"Your orders, Lord?"

"We make ready for battle and approach this habitable moon. I want to know what the humans are doing and find out if our ghost is hiding here."

Tol Vehar's acting commander gave Brakal a doubtful glare, but said, "I hear and obey."

"Keep your cheer, Urag. At least we're not as far from home as the last time we chased the flame-haired she-wolf. That was a hunt for the ages."

"From which we barely returned alive."

"As we will from this expedition. The human capable of killing Strike Force Khorsan's valiant crews has not yet been whelped."

"The ghost has killed Shrehari and subject races aplenty in recent times, Lord. And if he's the one we pursue..."

"Bah." Brakal made a dismissive hand gesture conveying disdain. "He's a commerce raider, Urag. One fit only to chase transport ships and their escorts. But against *Vehar* and *Vach*? That will be a different hell altogether — for him."

— Thirty-Six —

"Two *Tol* and one *Ptar* dropped out of FTL at Raijin's hyperlimit a few minutes ago." Lieutenant Commander Sirico climbed to his feet and stepped away from the command chair as Siobhan Dunmoore entered the CIC, summoned by news of the enemy's arrival. "Our link with Temar ground control remains active, and I've warned them. The orbital defense platforms are still dormant and almost impossible to detect, even at this distance. Their duty officer says the surveillance satellites can't see us and he's a little weirded out by speaking with a phantom."

"Then everything is as it should be."

"Damn boneheads think they're running silent, but I can see them all right," Chief Yens added. "I hope they never figure out how to make themselves invisible to sensors like we do."

Sirico pointed at the tactical projection.

"On their current heading and speed, I figure they'll come up our rear unless the Shrehari commander decides he'd rather swing around Raijin on an opposite heading to Temar's orbit."

"Doubtful." Dunmoore dropped into the command chair and studied Sirico's estimate. "He'll want to creep up on the only habitable world in this system and close with it on his own terms. It's what I would do. Our aft guns will be able to work their usual magic."

"And we won't lose any time by having to unmask either." Sirico rubbed his hands with glee. "It'll be up systems and fire at will."

"Has anyone ever mentioned you take entirely too much pleasure in your job, Thorin?" Tatiana Salminen, who'd entered the CIC on Dunmoore's heels, asked with a knowing smirk.

"A true craftsman takes pride in everything he does, even if it's destroying the Commonwealth's enemies."

"Whether they be alien or domestic, right?"

Sirico gave the soldier an exaggerated bow.

"I aim to please."

Dunmoore rolled her eyes at the pun.

"Just make sure that aim is true, Mister Craftsman. We'll get off one clean salvo, so it has to count."

"For that precise reason, Chief Yens and I will spend our time profitably between now and then by trying to identify the Shrehari command ship so we may gift it with that one clean salvo."

But an hour later, Sirico admitted defeat.

"The boneheads are being cannier than usual. Even though their emissions dampening isn't up to our standards, their communications discipline seems to be. I can't tell which of them is the command ship. For all we know, it could be the *Ptar*. Intelligence reports are hinting at them learning a few tricks from us."

"So long as they don't pick up our scent before they're within optimum firing range, it's not a big issue, Thorin. Choose the *Tol* with the best target profile for our first salvo, then direct the orbital platforms on the second one. We can leave the *Ptar* for last. I suspect its captain will veer off the moment we engage the *Tols*."

"Funny how I'm still not used to seeing them while they don't see us," Salminen said, eyes on the visual feed now dominating the main display.

"Knowing where to look is the real trick," Sirico replied. "If they bothered to check Temar's L5 point, I daresay they might notice our hull occluding the background stars, or making a smudge on the moon's lovely blue orb."

"Surely they know about Lagrangian points."

Dunmoore nodded.

"They do. I can't recall the Shrehari name for the phenomenon, but their grasp of orbital mechanics is easily as good as ours. The reason they're not searching the L5 with passive means is that their doctrine doesn't involve using a Lagrangian as springboard for an ambush. Neither does ours for that matter, outside the small Q-ship community. So they're concentrating on picking up emissions and giving more likely places the benefit of visual scans."

A satisfied smile softened Salminen's serious features.

"I guess we're about to show them the errors of their ways."

Sirico turned a wolfish smile on the soldier.

"And if we can nail all three, that lesson won't be passed on to their fellow boneheads, which is how I want my enemies to not learn."

"I'll settle for driving them out of the system and back toward their own sphere. They can't afford heavy damage so far from home. Contrary to myth, the Shrehari propensity for aggression doesn't mean they're suicidally brave."

The conversation flowed with its usual ease, yet Dunmoore could sense the underlying tension of an approaching battle as if it were a physical presence in their midst. *Iolanthe* could effortlessly outfight a *Tol* class cruiser since it wasn't much more than a heavy frigate by

Commonwealth standards. But two of them plus a corvette almost evened the odds. It also reduced her margin for error.

Temar's orbital platforms would help. However, she didn't know how powerful they were, or how skilled Hersom's operators might be, and he'd resisted putting them under Dunmoore's tactical control for the duration of the battle.

When her fingers tried to break free and dance on the command chair's arm, she took a deep breath and mentally recited her mantra. Waiting silently for the enemy to come within range was always a test of her patience, and this one seemed to know a thing or two about making a cautious, unhurried approach.

**

"Where are you hiding, demon spawn from the Seven Hells?" Brakal's rough voice was a soft murmur, almost entirely subsumed by *Tol Vehar*'s ambient noise, but Urag heard nonetheless.

"Either the ghost is not here or hiding well enough to escape detection. One pass of the inhabited moon, Lord, to find what the humans are doing, then we turn back?"

Brakal's dark lips split apart to show his cracked fangs.

"Nervous, Urag? What is there to fear but fear itself?"

"Something is not right. By my ancestors' bones, I can feel it."

"Your ancestors can't feel anything, my friend. They *are* ghosts!"

He laughed uproariously at his own joke. But behind his jovial facade, Brakal felt the first hints of worry nibbling at his self-confidence. He had traveled immeasurably farther from Imperial space than this, and with *Vehar* alone.

But Urag's ancestors might not be entirely demented, even though they've been dead for generations. The flame-haired female was a trickster and a deadly one at that.

Yet if she hid in this system, then where? Logically, it would be near the habitable world. Those artificial satellites were an obvious clue of human activity. His black within black eyes alternated between the planet Raijin and its moons on the main screen, and the data collected by *Tol Vehar*'s passive sensors on a secondary.

Not a hint of activity.

Even the artificial satellites were at low power and could carry out any function — communications, weather, surveillance, scientific observation. None so far betrayed the telltales of an orbital defense platform, but he knew humans kept them silent until it was time to strike, a protocol he wholeheartedly approved.

Brakal sifted through his half-digested knowledge of human doctrine and tactics and tried to picture them in the light of immutable facts such as orbital mechanics. The complexities of a large moon, one of dozens, orbiting a gas giant which orbited a star almost undid him.

"Where are you?" He muttered again. "You're here. I can feel it."

This time it was Urag's turn to peel back his lips and show his fangs.

"It pleases me to hear you agree something is not right. Perhaps we should give that moon a wide berth, Lord. Scan it from a distance, then use the gas giant as a slingshot back to where we can enter otherspace."

Brakal rubbed the side of his face as he considered Urag's suggestion. No one would blame him for avoiding battle so far from home, especially if the payoff was news of nefarious human doings in this isolated system. But the ghost? If he could eliminate that thorn in Strike Force Khorsan's side...

"We will make one pass of the moon, Urag. *Vehar* to navigate between it and Raijin, and *Vach* on the far side, so we can scan its entire surface. *Ptar Qilm* to follow *Vach*. Inform them via a low power, narrow beam radio pulse. If we find something requiring immediate action, we will complete a full orbit around Raijin and attack. Otherwise, we leave."

"I hear and obey."

It might be Brakal's imagination, but Urag sounded relieved.

**

"I'd swear..." Chief Yens' growl betrayed a hint of frustration born from the long wait as they watched the Shrehari creep up on Temar. "Nope, there it is again. Bastards tried to hide it well, but they're firing attitudinal thrusters."

Dunmoore leaned forward in her chair, placed her right elbow on her knee, and leaned her chin on her fist. She studied the tactical projection even though any course change wouldn't become apparent for a while. How they'd fired thrusters showed *Iolanthe* was still invisible to the Shrehari who were trying to stay undetected themselves.

"What are you up to?" She murmured. "You wouldn't increase the risk of detection without a good reason, and I doubt it's because you saw us."

Sirico was the first to figure it out even though it took almost fifteen minutes.

"I bet they intend to scan Temar, one ship covering the hemisphere facing Raijin and the other the far side. For some reason, the *Ptar* is following the *Tol* on the outside."

"Having the corvette swing around Raijin at a greater distance than the cruisers allows it to see further and spot threats earlier," Dunmoore said.

"Of course, Sir." Sirico nodded. "I should have thought of that myself."

He winked at Salminen over his shoulder.

The tactical projection, fed by *Iolanthe*'s sensor data, now showed each ship's new estimated course past Temar, confirming Sirico's conclusions.

"Unless this is a clever ploy to take us from both sides at once, they still don't know we're here. That means they probably plan on doing one reconnaissance pass, then if nothing of immediate concern shows up, slingshot back to the hyperlimit."

Dunmoore nodded her approval.

"It's what I would do if I were far from home and on what might be a wild goose chase, Thorin." She studied the projection again. "We will engage both *Tols* simultaneously when they're almost past us rather than concentrate on one and leave the other to the orbitals as they're approaching. That way the boneheads will have less time to react and respond before we're no longer within their weapons' optimal arcs of fire. And it might convince them to leave Hecate on the rebound. Dependent on their not spotting us before we light up, of course."

"Understood. I'll prepare a message for Temar control, to go out the moment we're up systems, telling them about the change in tactics. Our SSB friends can strafe them with the orbitals as they swing past and give them another reason to find the exit." He paused, then said, "Both *Tols* are entering effective range."

— Thirty-Seven —

"All ships are on the new course, Commander," *Tol Vehar*'s navigation officer announced.

Urag grunted his acknowledgment. Though happier with Brakal's plan to make a single reconnaissance pass of the habitable moon before leaving — unless they found a clear and present danger to the Empire — he still felt uneasy but didn't know why. Urag glanced sideways at the acting commander of Strike Force Khorsan. Brakal seemed lost in his contemplation of the three-dimensional schematic dominating *Tol Vehar*'s command center, almost as if he was communing with the gods, or perhaps even demons of the Underworld, beseeching them for answers.

Suddenly, he reared up with a start and cursed volubly, startling everyone within earshot.

"The co-orbital points," he roared. "Search the damned moon's leading and trailing co-orbital points. The diseased ghost is hiding at one of them, waiting for us. I can feel it by *my* ancestor's bones."

"With your indulgence," the navigation officer turned to face Brakal, "the co-orbital points of a moon orbiting a gas giant are not considered particularly stable."

"Are they stable enough so a ship may keep station on the moon for a few days or even a few hours without using its drives?"

"Perhaps."

"Then they will suffice for our enemy's purpose."

"How did you make such a deduction?" Urag asked.

"We are chasing a phantom. A human who may or may not be Dunmoore, the trickster, but someone who knows how to hide in preparation for an ambush. What better method to lie in wait without being seen than use orbital mechanics?"

"Shall I go active, Lord?" Menak, *Tol Vehar*'s sensor officer asked.

"No. Look for emissions and a visual signature. If he's not seen us, I don't want to give anything away. He may not think I've figured him out yet. Best it stay that way until we see him and are ready to open fire. Inform *Vach* and *Qilm* so they may search as well."

"We and *Vach* are about to pull level with the trailing co-orbital point," the navigation officer warned. "If the enemy hides there..."

Brakal's face split into a fierce rictus.

"If the enemy hides there, battle will be upon us shortly. Are you ready to power up so we might fight, Urag?"

"You need to ask, Lord?"

"In this ship? Never."

Urag gave him a long-suffering stare.

"Then speak the word. As always, I shall hear and obey."

Brakal glared at his erstwhile first officer, then settled back to wait for the sensor operator's findings, though it tried his exceedingly thin reserves of patience. Answers were not long in coming.

"Lord, there appears to be something occluding the background stars at the moon's trailing co-orbital."

"Hah." Brakal's fist pounded the command chair's arm with such force even Regar, sitting silently at the back of the bridge, felt the vibration run up his spine. "What did I tell you? Our ghost is hiding."

"Or waiting in ambush," Urag warned. "Menak, resolve the image and put it on the main screen."

"At once, Commander."

A blurry shape replaced Temar's image. The shadow appeared to be no more than a blot of darkness against the myriad pinpricks of light, each a blazing star or perhaps even a galaxy distant enough a thousand lifetimes would not suffice to reach it.

Its lines sharpened and solidified as *Tol Vehar*'s computer analyzed the image and turned it into that of a starship. But not one fitting the human fleet's standard combat hulls.

"Can we determine the size and class?" Brakal asked.

"Not without going active, Lord," Menak replied. "But my instincts tell me it is large. A capital ship."

"We are within effective engagement range," the cruiser's gun master offered.

Brakal turned his chair toward Urag's.

"What do you say, strike force flagship commander?"

"Perhaps we should avoid tempting the dark gods and leave this one by the wayside so we might study the moon unhindered before leaving."

"Two *Tols* aren't enough in your opinion?"

Urag studied the unknown starship's image.

"Menak has the right of it. That *thing* is large. Larger than a *Tol*, perhaps even larger than *Vehar* and *Vach* put together. Larger and more powerful."

"But the ghost is reputed to be an armed freighter whose success depends on underhanded tactics and the element of surprise. If so, size does not confer power. It merely means bulk and therefore a bigger target, easier to hit. Pass the order to power systems. The moment gun masters acquire their target, they may fire missiles without delay."

**

"The Shrehari are lighting up," Chief Yens announced.

"Meaning whoever's in command over there thought of checking the L5 point and saw us lying doggo. Mister Holt, up systems.   Mister Sirico, engage when ready, all launchers, both *Tols*."

Though nothing seemed to change in the CIC, one of the side displays lit up with data showing *Iolanthe*'s shields raised and ready to repel enemy fire, her gun capacitors charging and her reactors delivering full military power.

Soft vibrations coursed through Dunmoore's soles as the launchers began pumping out missile after missile, fed by magazines beneath the shuttle hangar.   The tactical projection shimmering at the CIC's center narrowed its three-dimensional image down to the sphere of space containing *Iolanthe* and her foes.

Two clouds each of tiny red and blue dots winked into existence as the AI added human and Shrehari anti-ship missiles to the mix.   The blues, half headed for each Shrehari cruiser, numbered almost as many as the reds, a testament to *Iolanthe*'s higher number of tubes and larger magazine.

"Temar ground control is activating the orbital defense platforms.   That should increase the boneheads' pucker factor."

The Q-ship's ring of close-in defense guns — fifteen four-barreled calliopes on each flank — opened fire at extreme range to decimate the first Shrehari missile salvo before it could reach the ship and weaken her shields.   Moments later, tiny blossoms of light erupted along both *Tols*' hulls as their own defensive fire came into play.

A second salvo of missiles left *Iolanthe*'s launchers, crowding the tactical projection even further with blue icons.

"Do you think the Shrehari commander is wondering whether he blundered?" Sirico asked no one in particular while red and blue icons vanished, only to be replaced by newly launched missiles.

"I certainly hope so," Dunmoore replied, fascinated as always by the silent clash of deadly ordnance beyond her ship's hull.

⁎⁎

"That's no armed freighter, Lord," the sensor officer whirled around to face Brakal. "It has the missile launcher capacity, defensive guns, and power curve of a battleship. I also picked up the presence of large bore plasma cannon, bigger than anything a *Tol* carries. So far, I can make out four mounts with two each of those massive tubes, along with at least six mounts bearing triple tubes of smaller caliber and thirty multi-barrel defensive guns."

Brakal fixed Menak with his black in black eyes, momentarily unable to process the information. He expected to find a commerce raider, a converted merchant ship capable of overwhelming unsuspecting convoys and single patrol vessels through guile and surprise, not this behemoth.

Then the first human missiles, those who passed through *Tol Vehar*'s curtain of plasma, exploded against his flagship's shields. A blue-green aurora briefly enveloped the cruiser as competing energies fought for supremacy, but it would take more than a handful of nuclear explosions to overwhelm a *Tol*.

"His main cannon are opening fire, Lord. Four barrels on us, four on *Vach*."

Brakal watched with growing dismay as plasma from guns the likes of which few Imperial ships carried blotted out the battleship's flanks. Moments later, smaller ones joined them, and the aurora enveloping *Vehar* lost what little green remained as it took on a bluer hue, one that would soon shift to purple.

"*Vach* and *Vehar* are registering hits on the human's shields. Not many, but some."

"Open fire with guns."

Brakal rubbed the crest of fur on his skull, thinking furiously about his options. Overwhelming the battleship with his strike force's weight of ordnance wouldn't work. He was engaging both *Tols* simultaneously and forcing a more significant strain on *Vach* and *Vehar*'s shields than both were putting on him. This was not a ghost, but a *bahnshia*, one of the Underworld's terrifying demon warriors.

"Lord. Orbital defenses are coming to life around the moon."

That news helped Brakal decide. His ships could not scan the moon's surface, let alone use the gas giant as a slingshot without incurring damage they could ill afford this far from home.

"We will disengage. Order everyone to accelerate at maximum rate and break away from the gas giant at a perpendicular from our present heading. But keep firing on the human."

"I hear and obey," Urag said.

How? Brakal wondered. How is it we followed what I thought was our ghost to this system and found a battleship instead? His eyes tracked a fresh missile volley erupting from the human's launchers, half again aimed at *Vehar*, the other half at *Vach*, while massive cannon kept striking both ships' shields with metronomic regularity.

Withdrawing in the face of such firepower entailed no dishonor. Not when orbital defenses of unknown strength waited to break him as his ships passed the moon.

The war was surely tipping in the humans' favor if they could build powerful battleships capable of hiding so well and others, such as the ghost, able to vanish without a trace.

For a brief moment, Brakal wondered whether this latest example of the humans' growing power and his phantom raider were the same, but he quickly dismissed the thought. Even the technologically savvy hairless apes couldn't mask a battleship so well it might seem no more than a corsair.

Or could they?

**

Dunmoore watched the ammunition inventory tally on a side display change with each missile salvo and gun volley. Her ship carried healthy stocks, but a shock and awe rate of fire was unsustainable. And the boneheads were getting in licks of their own.

The aurora surrounding *Iolanthe* where her shields met enemy missile explosions, and plasma gunfire was taking on a deep blue hue. Not as fast as the two *Tols* or the *Ptar* now fending off shots from Hersom's orbitals. But three smaller ships against a battlecruiser was still three against one as proved by the growing strain on *Iolanthe*'s shield generators.

That devil Brakal almost destroyed the massive battleship *Victoria Regina*, last of her kind, years earlier with smaller vessels before Dunmoore bluffed and convinced the Shrehari commander to withdraw.

"The boneheads are firing attitudinal thrusters and accelerating."

A purple aurora briefly enveloped the Q-ship as fresh Shrehari gunfire struck home. Dunmoore thought she could almost hear the generators howling in protest.

"It looks as if they're trying to break away from Raijin orbit. Maybe they're running."

"I'm sure they consider this a withdrawal in the face of something more powerful than they're willing to handle, Thorin. Running is dishonorable. Retreating to fight another day, not so much."

"Smart move," Holt's hologram at Dunmoore's elbow said with grudging approval. "I was afraid we might face one of the true fight-to-the-death boneheads. The way we're going through our ammo reserves worries me. The Shrehari aren't the only ones far from home. After this, we must choose our battles carefully until we can meet up with a replenishment ship."

"Agreed. Reduce our rate of fire by fifty percent, Thorin." She examined the projected Shrehari course. "Make that by two-thirds. Just enough for a final push since I didn't intend to destroy them. Best they return to their own lines thinking the ghost who's been ravaging their convoys slipped away once more. I doubt anyone will connect it with the Furious Faerie in her battlecruiser incarnation."

"Not chasing them will keep Renny happy. He's already worrying about the strain on our shield generators. You might have noticed us climb into the purple, Skipper."

"The boneheads are seeing even deeper purple," Sirico said. "Their generators must be screaming now that the orbitals are joining the fight."

"Hence a withdrawal at full acceleration." She glanced at the tactical projection again. "You might as well cease fire now. They won't come back to haunt us any time soon after a course change this drastic."

"Do you think they'll leave?" Holt asked.

"Probably. Our unexpected presence must be thoroughly painful in light of what I figure was an attempt to track a notorious commerce raider. Besides, this isn't the first time I convinced a Shrehari to back away and live to fight again."

Holt chuckled.

"I remember reading the after-action report. Wouldn't it be something if Brakal commanded that strike force?"

"What are the chances? We don't even know whether he returned from beyond the black, let alone whether he's operating in this sector. But I'm not about to call the enemy for a chat. Not this time. If Tarrant described Shannon O'Donnell of the privateer *Persephone* to the Shrehari and word spread through the Deep Space Fleet's frontline units, it might allow Brakal or anyone who served with him back in the day, to connect our cover identity with this battlecruiser. Let's see them off and leave the matter of their ultimate fate for another encounter."

"So no impassioned discussion in Shrehari between the redoubtable Siobhan Dunmoore and whoever represents the Empire's finest in the Hecate system?"

"I see you read the classified part of my after-action report on *Victoria Regina*'s final battle as well."

"Every last word, Skipper. If I were you, I'd be itching to open a link and find out if their commander is an old acquaintance or the friend of a foe. Maybe someone who survived *Tol Vakash*'s quasi-destruction in the Cimmeria system."

"No." The sharp edge to her tone told Holt their conversation was over.

"Orders?"

"We wait here until we're sure the Shrehari are heading to the hyperlimit and not coming around for a rematch. Then I want to speak with Carrie Fennon over a secure subspace channel."

— Thirty-Eight —

"Why aren't you pursuing?" Blayne Hersom asked in a faintly supercilious tone once Dunmoore gave him a thumbnail sketch of the brief, inconclusive battle. "Isn't the Navy under permanent orders to close with and destroy the enemy?"

"Where possible. But they have the edge on us in terms of acceleration and top speed — our size has its drawbacks. And a stern chase is a long one, with no guarantee of ever coming into effective range. By the time we reach Hecate's heliopause, they'll be crossing interstellar space on a course we can only guess at."

"Surely they're headed back to the Empire."

"Of course. If they burned through their ammo at the same rate as we did, the Shrehari commander will look to replenish sooner rather than later. But that doesn't mean I can draw a straight line between Hecate and the nearest Shrehari outpost, and hope to stumble over them by sheer luck."

Dunmoore fought to hide her impatience. She would have preferred to speak with Carrie Fennon first, but Hersom called while they waited for the Shrehari to reach Raijin's hyperlimit and go FTL. Giving them the idea another ship might be waiting at the system's edge was too much of a risk. *Kattegat Maru* could probably outrun a *Tol* and perhaps even a smaller *Ptar,* but she would never outfight either, not even with a battle-hardened Emma Cullop at the controls.

"Won't the Shrehari come back, now they know we're running something covert here?"

"Doubtful. That bunch was probably following us and not engaged in a reconnaissance mission. After being smacked on the nose by your orbital defenses and my ship, their senior commanders won't be in a hurry to let anyone return. This system is too far from their sphere of control for comfort."

Hersom nodded but nonetheless seemed unconvinced.

"I see. And what are your intentions?"

"I'll stay near Temar until we're sure the Shrehari crossed into interstellar space and won't be back. Then, I need to find *Baba Yaga* and recover *Kattegat Maru*'s crew."

The SSB man's eyes narrowed in question for a moment, as if he was wondering why she had not yet mentioned the ill-fated freighter's passengers. But the next words out of his mouth were, "How will you report this incident to your flag officer?"

"By stating the facts, so I can account for the generous ammunition expenditure. But I won't go into details about your operation if that's what worries you. I will pass off your stockade as a classified government installation we helped in a crisis, nothing more."

**

"A damn shame we missed the fireworks," Emma Cullop said after listening to Dunmoore's description of the brief battle that sent the Shrehari packing. "Sounds like it was missile heaven for a few minutes. As a wise man once said, hit 'em hard and hit 'em often, right?"

"To the tune of almost half our missile reserves. Theirs too, no doubt. But I didn't call you only to gloat over another inconclusive fight. The Almighty knows we've seen our share of those."

As Dunmoore explained what hid on Temar and why Cullop's face hardened until repressed fury blazed in her eyes.

"How can they do that?"

"I wish I knew, Emma. My immediate concern is finding a way of liberating *Kattegat Maru*'s former passengers before we leave this system, and then find her crew. However, until Blayne Hersom gets his target, he won't let anyone go. Unfortunately, one of them reminds me of an old acquaintance from the Toboso incident, someone who might fit the profile of a fugitive from the SSB. Mikhail Forenza."

"The Colonial Office cleaner? Why would the Bureau want him?"

"Your guess is as good as mine. Zeke agrees on the resemblance. But that leaves me in a quandary. If I finger that man as Hersom's target so we can recover the others, I might condemn an innocent to suffer. And even if he is Forenza, how can I, in good conscience, leave him to the SSB's tender mercies? Not to mention that perhaps whatever he's been up to might benefit the Fleet along with his own department. The enemy of my enemy, that sort of thing."

A commiserating look extinguished the embers in Cullop's eyes.

"Understood. How can I help?"

"I want Carrie Fennon to look at the image we took of this man and tell us everything she knows."

"Certainly. I'll put her on at once."

"I'm sending the picture now."

The young woman's thoughtful mien replaced Cullop's face shortly after that.

"Sir. I overheard your conversation. I hope that was all right."

"Absolutely, Carrie. Your stake in this is as big as ours. Bigger, even. And yes, I will do my best to find your mother and her crew once we're done here."

"Yes, sir. I know." Her eyes shifted to one side. "I see the man's face now. He calls himself Mostar Quantrill, or at least that's the name he gave for the manifest."

"Where did he come aboard?"

Fennon's cheeks suddenly took on the rosy hue of embarrassment. It made her appear even younger.

"We're not supposed to speak of the ports we touch in the Unclaimed Zone, sir. Mother keeps those off the books, so we don't get hassled by the Navy, or the Bureau or anyone else."

"A man's life is at stake, Carrie. I promise this will never make it into any official report."

Fennon chewed on her lower lip while an air of indecision replaced her earlier embarrassment. Dunmoore knew better than to push and waited patiently until Carrie came to a decision.

"We picked Mister Quantrill up at an unregistered human colony two parsecs from Kilia," she finally said. "A planet the inhabitants call Cullan. It's a rough place, settled by folks who fled the Commonwealth. But they pay with high-grade precious metals and gems, and we're one of the few merchants willing to travel inside the Unclaimed Zone. Mother says we often make most of our real profit there on any trip, the kind of profit that doesn't go straight back into the ship's operating account."

Cullop chuckled.

"Or show up as taxable income either, I'll bet. Most, if not all independent merchant captains engage in deals that stay off the ledgers."

Fennon gave her ship's relief captain a pained glance.

"What's the expression I learned from the Scandian soldiers? No names, no pack drill?"

"Indeed, Apprentice Officer," Cullop replied with a delighted grin. "You'll go far in this business."

"Did you pick up any other passengers on Cullan?"

"Yes, sir, almost two dozen. But Mister Quantrill was the only one without a booking. He showed up at the landing strip unannounced, asking for a berth. But since he offered to pay handsomely, mother took him aboard."

"Luggage?"

"As I recall, one bag, medium sized. I led him to his cabin."

"Any other unplanned or unusual passengers during that entire run?"

Fennon shook her head.

"No, sir."

Dunmoore sat back in her day cabin chair with a frown. Fennon's revelations proved nothing beyond the fact that a man resembling a Colonial Office agent with deadly duties boarded *Kattegat Maru* on an unregistered human colony, one beyond the reach and authority of Forenza's employer.

Perhaps the Colonial Office kept tabs on human worlds beyond the Commonwealth's acknowledged sphere. Maybe it even interfered in their affairs. As Toboso proved, it certainly didn't hesitate to do so on regular, registered, and completely legal self-governing worlds.

Now what?

"Was there anything else, Captain?"

"Not for the moment. Thank you, Carrie. Emma, take care you stay hidden while the Shrehari retreat, but see if you can make out their heading when they go FTL."

"Will do, sir."

"*Iolanthe*, out."

— Thirty-Nine —

"What choice do I have?" Dunmoore spun around to face her first officer. "We can't leave forty-four, if not forty-five innocents in the SSB's hands. Be content I'm merely thinking of them and not the other detainees held on Temar despite a wee little legal doctrine you may remember as *habeas corpus*, which has existed for over a thousand years. I could shutter Blayne Hersom's operation altogether and challenge the SSB to complain."

A bitter laugh escaped her throat.

"Complain to the Admiralty that we fucked up an illegal rendition site? Good luck. I know flag officers who'd leak the SSB's misdeeds to the media in a microsecond, and so does the Bureau's senior leadership. The last thing they want is a public feud with the Armed Services."

Holt, used to his captain's moods, merely nodded. He'd voiced his objections in the usual way and now waited for them to temper her first ruthless, and some would say reckless impulse to right a wrong. It was a dance hearkening back to their days as captain and first officer of the corvette *Shenzen*.

"I'm just saying giving Hersom an ultimatum might not be the best idea if it's your way of covering for a midnight raid by our favorite Scandian troopers."

"That Shrehari incursion taught my friend Blayne he can't afford to lose those orbital platforms. Yet we can destroy them at will. The trade-off is easy. If he refuses to hand over the detainees we want, I'll send Tatiana to fetch them, covered by the Furious Faerie's guns."

"And once he reports back to his own HQ on Earth?"

"Then the Admiralty can decide whether it favors saving Commonwealth citizens from illegal imprisonment over placating a security service guilty of massive overreach."

When she saw his mouth open to reply, Dunmoore raised a restraining hand.

"I'll take that risk, Zeke. Otherwise, I won't be able to live with myself. Besides, we don't enjoy the luxury of time. Who knows what the idiot commanding *Baba Yaga* might do with Captain Fennon and her people. I don't trust him — or her — to carry out Hersom's instructions. There's too much profit waiting for the unscrupulous out in the badlands, as Carrie so cogently pointed out."

"Or you could give your conscience time off and point Forenza out to Hersom. What concern is it of ours if the Colonial Office and the SSB are playing games so long as it doesn't affect the war effort? And if Forenza's not their man, then we'll still rescue forty-four souls from the Bureau's clutches."

Dunmoore gave him an unpleasant smile.

"The needs of the many, Zeke? You want to play that card with me?"

"It is a valid, if utilitarian outlook, Skipper."

"You? A believer in utilitarianism?"

"After serving as your first officer in two different ships?" His mouth twisted into a rueful grin. "No. I learned better. When Doña Quixote is tilting at windmills, I'm better off making a credible Sancho Panza imitation. But despite your ill temper, my job is to challenge assumptions and plans. Remember — your first duty is to the mission; mine is to the ship and its crew. I daresay you were just as annoying a first officer in your day."

"Probably even worse." Dunmoore reached over to touch her desktop. "Bridge this is the captain. Open a link with Temar. I wish to speak privately with Blayne Hersom. His people shouldn't overhear what I intend to say."

"Aye, aye, sir," Lieutenant Magnus Protti, the officer of the watch, replied. "Wait one."

"Do you want me to leave, Skipper?" Holt made as if to stand.

She waved him down again.

"Just stay quiet and out of the video pickup's arc. I may need a witness for the defense at my court-martial."

Hersom's face appeared on her day cabin's screen shortly afterward.

"Are you calling to say goodbye? With the Shrehari gone, there's no reason for you to stay."

"Not without *Kattegat Maru*'s passengers. Did you figure out who, if anyone, might be this dangerous individual your agency is so keen on detaining?"

Hersom hesitated for a fraction of a second before shaking his head.

"No."

"Then it's clear you never will. The SSB may be many things, but I've never taken your lot for incompetents. Whoever sold you the information about a person of interest aboard *Kattegat Maru* was lying. And you know what? I think your source is none other than Enoc Tarrant himself. It's a great plan. Make money by selling you false information, then arrange to get his hands on an abandoned ship and its cargo, both worth a lot of creds, with no danger of government reprisals. After all, he acted on SSB orders. How am I doing so far?"

Hersom's smile, though not quite dismissive, nevertheless didn't reach his eyes.

"Interesting theory, Captain. I confess some of our sources in the frontier regions are sketchy, and Tarrant has already shown himself to be less than reliable. But my colleagues will surely have vetted the information about our person of interest before tasking me with the abduction and detention."

Dunmoore's right eyebrow crept up to her hairline.

"Oh? Are your colleagues somehow blessed with infallibility? Of always separating fact from fancy, especially when the intelligence originates with outside informants? If they were, I daresay the SSB would run the Commonwealth by now. But you don't."

The first glimmers of uncertainty tinged Hersom's expression.

"Face it. Your mythical target isn't one of those forty-five, or you'd know. This is what you and your people do best, yet you've failed, and it wasn't because of incompetence. The target wasn't aboard *Kattegat Maru* when Tarrant's pirates seized her. Maybe he left at Kilia and boarded a different ship. That being the case, hand everyone over and I'll repatriate them, no questions asked or answered. I'll make sure your cover and your reputation stay intact. Just as I made sure your installation didn't suffer from Shrehari depredations."

Hersom's lips compressed into a thin line, annoyance writ large on his face.

"You won't let go, will you?"

"No. We're each responsible for the protection of Commonwealth citizens. You in the aggregate and I in the particular. This case is about the latter." When Hersom didn't immediately answer, she said, "I'll repatriate them with or without your cooperation, Mister Hersom. My Marines will make short work of your ground defenses and guard contingent while my ship wipes out your orbitals. And before you threaten retaliation, I'm sure the Bureau won't be keen on publicizing such an incident by pushing for my removal from command and court-martial. Besides, the Fleet would probably tell your bosses to go pound sand. But I can propose a way of getting them out of your stockade and aboard my ship without shooting or betraying the fact an agency of their own government held them illegally."

Hersom locked eyes with Dunmoore and held her gaze for what seemed like hours. It felt as if he was searching her soul for a lie.

"Good God, I believe you're dead serious."

"I'm as serious as an extinction level asteroid strike."

"You realize you're basically asking for my surrender."

She shrugged.

"Semantics. I'm suggesting you declare the targeted individual isn't among the forty-five. Let your agency find the informant and ask hard questions. I'd recommend starting with Enoc Tarrant if there's anything of his operation left after I pay Kilia a return visit. Let me land my Marines and pretend to rescue *Kattegat Maru*'s passengers. No one gets hurt, nothing is destroyed, and you can tell your bosses about successfully ending an operation gone wrong because of bad intelligence."

When she paused, Hersom asked, "Or?"

"Or I raid your stockade with live ammunition and take whoever I want, which might well include every single Commonwealth citizen in unlawful detention. Call it enforcing a writ of *habeas corpus*."

**

"Let me see if I understand," Command Sergeant Karlo Saari said after Major Salminen opened the floor for questions. "We're to carry out a pretend raid on that stockade, grab the folks taken off *Kattegat Maru*, but no one else, and make it look real to them but not to the guards. Sounds kind of crazy, sir."

"Why are you expecting sanity after all this time in *Iolanthe*?" Sergeant Major Haataja asked. "Didn't you notice what we do starts at crazy and goes up from there? Be thankful this isn't a shooting mission."

Saari grinned.

"I am, Talo. I most assuredly am. And doing the SSB a dirty trick is always amusing."

"Except this won't be a dirty trick," Salminen cautioned. "The operation will happen with the full concurrence of the stockade's commanding officer. You could say our captain is doing him a favor of sorts by removing a potential source of embarrassment."

"And why would we be doing favors for the SSB, Major?"

"Would you rather shoot them, Karlo?"

"Well..."

"Maybe Karlo's platoon should stay at the landing strip," Haataja suggested. "He sounds a little trigger happy this morning. If we weren't already down to three platoons, I might even propose he stay here."

"You're a cruel man, Talo."

"It comes with the starbursts." Haataja pointed at the rank insignia on his collar. "But keep going, and you'll never find out."

"Why? Are you recommending me for a direct commission?"

Salminen raised both hands.

"Okay. Enough. Does anyone have real questions and not editorial comments disguised as such? The captain is anxious to wrap this up so we can find *Kattegat Maru*'s crew."

Command Sergeant Jennsen raised her hand.

"I do, sir. If this is a sham raid why are we taking three platoons?"

"In case the sham turns into a cock up. It's improbable but not impossible. The SSB goons will think twice before doing anything stupid against most of an armored infantry company, whereas a mere platoon might tempt them."

"If the captain wants to remind the SSB that stupid hurts, she should send Chief Guthren with us."

Haataja gave Saari a mock scowl.

"I think we can handle it without the Navy, Karlo, despite your itchy trigger finger."

"Just looking out for the mission."

"Anything else?" Salminen asked. When no one answered, she clapped her hands once. "Brief your platoons. We leave in sixty minutes. And make sure everyone is in Varangian Company getup. The SSB might know we're Fleet, but the captain wants the rescuees to believe we're a PMC hired by *Kattegat Maru*'s owners. The moment we break out of Temar orbit, the Furious Faerie turns back into *Persephone*."

**

Brakal, alone in his office, a cup of *tvass* in hand, was staring sightlessly at the bulkhead when Regar stuck his head through the door.

"Not our most glorious hours," the *Tai Kan* officer said, "but you'll be pleased to know we still obtained decent readings of the moon's surface and a good accounting of their satellite dispositions."

After swallowing a healthy mouthful of *tvass*, Brakal turned his massive head and scowled.

"Not our most glorious hours? Take care you don't overstep the generous boundaries I granted you, spy. Would we have found glory in slugging it out with that battleship?"

He gestured at Regar to enter and sit.

"No. Not once the orbital defenses joined in. The mood aboard is somber, as you might expect, but most are privately relieved we came through with our ship able to return home, especially Urag. That human vessel was a nasty surprise."

"You spoke of sensor readings."

Brakal's question and his tone put an end to any discussion of the abortive, inconclusive, and ultimately unsatisfying battle.

"There appears to be only one set of artificial constructs on that moon, in the hemisphere facing Raijin. Although it has a good landing strip, the adjoining building cluster, well hidden, by the way, is relatively small. The rest of the surface seems untouched. Whatever the humans are doing there, it does not bear the hallmarks of a major research and development facility."

"Perhaps the installation is mostly underground."

"Possible, to be sure, but not probable."

"A spy's opinion?"

"A spy's instinct."

"Then you're saying whatever the humans are up to doesn't present an immediate peril to the Empire?"

Regar raised his hands in a gesture of uncertainty.

"No one can know for sure. The moon's defenses show the humans consider it important, but not everything they do is related to the war. Their version of the *Tai Kan* also struggles with internal security issues."

"Should I recommend a return visit with a full strike force?"

"How would I know, Commander? I'm an execrable *Tai Kan* insect assigned as *Tol Vehar*'s political officer to ensure your loyalty." A disingenuous look crossed Regar's angular features. "But the former Imperial Deep Space Fleet officer in me doesn't think another mission to this system is worth anyone's while. At least not until human phantoms cease bedeviling our sector and leave your ships idle."

Brakal finished his *tvass* and said, "A surprisingly sensible conclusion from someone who underwent *Tai Kan* initiation rituals."

"New members aren't actually subjected to a lobotomy even if it sometimes appears that way. What will you do now?"

A grunt.

"Return to Kilia and see if we might find better information about the human raider. Perhaps your colleagues finally removed their heads from their nether regions."

"Doubtful, but since there's nothing else to go on, I suppose it's a sensible destination. Our path home cuts through the general area anyway."

Brakal's reply dripped with sarcasm.

"I am gratified by your agreement, spy. It means so much to one such as me."

But Regar, as usual, let Brakal's ill humor slide off his back.

"Another serving of *tvass*? Or something stronger?"

"*Tvass* now. Ale once we're in otherspace."

— Forty —

Dunmoore, once again wearing her privateer's quasi-uniform, watched from the hangar deck control room as Major Salminen's soldiers gently led forty-five blindfolded men and women to the forward cargo hold. There, Chief Dwyn and her mates had set up cots, chairs, tables, sanitary and entertainment units, transforming the cavernous space into an improvised barracks. Once the last of them vanished, Dunmoore entered the hangar and waved Salminen over.

"Anything of note we didn't see on the live feed from your battlesuits?" She asked once the soldier was within earshot.

"No, sir. Hersom's guards and droids stayed well clear, though they gave us dirty looks. The guards, not the droids. I didn't see Hersom himself, but he probably observed the whole thing from his command center."

"No one let on we were Fleet?"

The soldier shook her head.

"They're confused, understandably, but I think everyone believes the private military corporation story."

"Thank you for speaking with them. I'd have done it myself up here, but showing my face again after they saw me in their compound wouldn't do our cover story any favors."

"My pleasure, sir. I rarely get the chance to playact as a mercenary in front of a non-hostile civilian crowd. It makes for a nice change. When did you wish to speak with Mostar Quantrill and see if he's the Forenza we remember from Toboso? The general resemblance is rather striking up close."

"Once we're FTL. Just in case. I'll ask the officer of the watch to let your sergeant major know."

"Yes, sir." Salminen came to attention. "With your permission?"

"Dismissed and give your folks a Bravo Zulu from me."

"I will. Thank you."

She saluted and turned on her heels.

Dunmoore's communicator buzzed for attention a moment later.

"Yes?"

"Holt here, Skipper. We're ready to break out of orbit and leave this benighted place. Did you want to exchange parting words with Mister Hersom?"

"No. We've said everything we wanted to each other. Besides, he's probably still sore from my forcing him to give up the *Kattegat Maru* passengers."

Holt chuckled.

"As he should, the SSB sonofabitch."

"Take us out, Zeke. Make for the hyperlimit at best rate of acceleration and warn Emma we're coming. Speaking of which, has she seen the Shrehari pass by yet?"

"Yes, they crossed the heliopause while you were watching Tatiana's gunships land. We should hear about them going FTL at interstellar speeds within the hour and good riddance. For Astrid's planning purposes, do you wish to pass by the Octavius Array and see if there's mail?"

A sinking feeling filled her gut with lead. Admiral Petras would expect her to join his task force as soon as possible. If she followed protocol and interrogated the array, new orders might compel her to abandon the chase and leave *Kattegat Maru*'s crew to their fate. If she disobeyed them and Petras found out, things would surely become unpleasant. Best to commit a minor sin by skipping the array than a mortal one through insubordination.

"Ask Astrid to plot the most direct route for Kilia. We'll skip the dogleg to Octavius this once under the doctrine of hot pursuit."

And hope Petras would either understand or fail to notice, she silently added.

**

The silver-haired man who entered *Iolanthe*'s conference room took in his new surroundings with an expression of keen interest before his gaze rested on Dunmoore, sitting at the head of the table.

"Ser Quantrill, I believe? Please take a seat." Dunmoore pointed at the nearest chair. "I'm Shannon O'Donnell, captain of the privateer *Persephone*."

He complied, eyes never leaving her face. Eyes that held an undisguised glimmer of recognition.

"O'Donnell? Did we ever meet, Captain? But where are my manners?" His voice vibrated with the same educated, almost refined rhythms as Forenza's. "Thank you for rescuing us from that place of perdition."

"As my infantry commander told you, we were hired to do so. Therefore thanks are superfluous."

He inclined his head.

"As you wish. May I ask why I was singled out to speak with you? Or am I merely the first of forty-five?"

She heard a hint of mockery in his tone.

"You may ask. Or we could cut the bullshit, Ser Forenza. Your disguise is good, but I'm skilled at recognizing faces, especially those of people who helped me through tough spots.   Besides, I spent years with your sister at the Academy, and you share the same family traits, especially the eyes."

A broad smile relaxed his aristocratic features.

"I suppose we should, as you say, cut the bullshit, Captain Dunmoore.   I've never been a fan of dissembling for appearances' sake.   And this time I insist you accept my thanks for pulling us from the SSB's clutches."

"You knew who was detaining you."

"I can recognize the signs. They're not particularly subtle. I suppose the Bureau was after me."

"What makes you think that?"

"Please, Captain, you're no dissembler. If you thought I was nothing more than bycatch in an SSB operation, we wouldn't be speaking. This ship's cover as a privateer is more valuable than satisfying your curiosity."

"How about we make a deal? I'll go over the events that led to us speaking in my ship's conference room today and in return you tell me why the Bureau went through a complex piracy rigmarole to capture you — without having the slightest clue about your identity?"

"What makes you think they're keen on me?"

She gave him a knowing smile.

"Instinct.   The SSB hired mercenaries to seize *Kattegat Maru* and detain her passengers on the strength of information that a person of interest presenting a peril to Commonwealth security was among them. Or at least what the Bureau defines as a peril. It would be too much of a coincidence if there was someone of interest aboard besides an agent of the Colonial Office with wide-ranging, let's call them duties, and avoid more questionable euphemisms. Your joining the ship on an unregistered colony beyond Commonwealth control at the last minute simply adds to the equation."

"So you recovered the crew, then?"

Dunmoore shook her head.

"Not yet, but Carrie Fennon hid during the attack and sent out a distress call once your abductors were gone. We answered her signal and have been looking for both passengers and crew ever since. The mercenaries' employer helpfully gave me the coordinates of the general area where I might find you and your fellow detainees, which in turn let me here. Although when we arrived, I found the SSB declined to take the crew. It's still out there somewhere, at the mercy of Enoc Tarrant's people."

Forenza grimaced.

"Not good. I assume your next move is to rectify that situation?"

"It is. We are on our way to the Hecate system's heliopause, where *Kattegat Maru* is waiting under a prize crew from my ship. From there, I intend to head for Kilia — again."

"I see. May I ask how you convinced the SSB to release us? I assume you recognized me during your walk-through and thought I might be the object of their search."

"By a combination of persuasion and strength. I planted the idea they'd been misinformed by a source looking to make money off this operation since their interrogators couldn't figure out who the target was. And let it slip I wouldn't be averse to conducting an armed raid."

"Which you carried out anyway."

"A sham, for the benefit of your fellow passengers."

"Why tell me this?"

"For a quid pro quo, Ser Forenza. What does the SSB want from you? Is it to do with Colonial Office interest in Cullan? Or was this elaborate abduction scheme part of a greater interagency war between the SSB and your lot?"

He didn't immediately answer though his gaze never left Dunmoore. She could almost visualize his internal debate on how much to reveal as a sign of gratitude for not betraying him.

"Our relation with the Bureau is about as problematic as the Fleet's. Perhaps worse, since we operate in the same environment while you're focused on keeping the Shrehari at bay and hopefully one day ejecting them from our star systems. As part of my duties — call me a fixer if you wish — I often come into conflict with SSB operatives. But things usually end with one side or the other withdrawing to avoid bloodshed. It's part of a tacit understanding between us."

"I'd say kidnapping a shipload of innocent civilians just to capture one man is the moral equivalent of drawing blood between covert services, wouldn't you agree, Ser Forenza?"

"Kidnapping me was a way of avoiding bloodshed, in a sense. I would vanish in a supposed pirate attack, just one victim among many and no one would know the SSB held me in their dungeon. Thus, no risk of retaliation by my agency. Rather brilliant, if heavy on collateral damage."

Dunmoore made a face.

"I'm not sure brilliant is the right word. Callous, perhaps. What I don't understand is how an informant might figure someone the SSB wants was aboard *Kattegat Maru* yet didn't know either the target's identity or appearance."

Forenza's lips twisted into a dismissive moue.

"Easily explained, Captain."

"Try me."

— Forty-One —

Forenza settled back in his chair, elbows on the armrests and steepled his fingers.

"I've been active in the Unclaimed Zone for months, changing names and faces at will. My current identity dates back to an hour before I boarded the freighter. And this most recent trip wasn't my first in Captain Fennon's ship. I've used her to shift between unregistered colonies ever since I started my mission in these parts. The SSB is quite able to assemble a partial picture and act on it. They also run a network of agents and informants in the badlands. Perhaps Enoc Tarrant was already under contract to the Bureau and merely waiting for a signal that on a given run out of the Zone, a person of interest traveled in *Kattegat Maru*. Or perhaps it would be more accurate to say the informant believed a man wanted by the Bureau was aboard. Half the passengers joined her on Cullan, and I daresay the credentials they — we — carried at the time of our capture didn't match those recorded during departure, hence the difficulty in identifying me. Truth is rather fluid out there."

He waved at the bulkhead as if to indicate the Unclaimed Zone.

Dunmoore studied Forenza with cold eyes, wondering whether his smooth explanation was the truth or a false story spun by a born liar. Did it matter? Probably not.

Whatever games the Colonial Office or the SSB or any other government agency was playing in a part of the galaxy almost untouched by the war didn't concern her. Retrieving Captain Fennon and her people did.

"I suppose it's useless to ask what you were doing on Cullan and elsewhere, or why the SSB might not want your office meddling in affairs there. Or whether your explanation of how this mess happened even bears a minute resemblance to the truth."

Forenza inclined his head. A faint smile tugged at his lips though she couldn't tell if it was mocking or appreciative.

"Just so, Captain. Now I'm no longer in the SSB's hands, this incident will be forgotten by everyone involved and better luck next time."

"Your fellow passengers or the crew won't forget it. If we even find the latter before something worse happens."

"You know what I mean, Captain. Forgotten in the bureaucratic universe which often bears no relationship to reality. And I would suggest your after-action report is written in a way that shows you know nothing about the abductors' identity or motives. It will avoid any heartache that might come from your superiors asking the Bureau's leadership awkward questions."

"Or your superiors for that matter."

"I knew you'd understand the situation."

"Understand, yes. Like, no. But since I don't get a vote..." She shrugged dismissively.

A sympathetic, and Dunmoore suspected wholly false smile relaxed Forenza's expression.

"Indeed, you do not. The same goes for me if that makes you feel better. Our sort exists to carry out orders, not make policy decisions."

"What I still don't understand is how the SSB set up the attack on *Kattegat Maru* so handily. I doubt Cullan has a subspace radio connection with Kilia, let alone Temar. Yet someone told Enoc Tarrant a person the SSB wanted was traveling in her."

"I've been wondering the same." His face hardened.

"Perhaps the Colonial Office has a double or triple agent on Kilia? Everyone else in the known galaxy seems to think that benighted station is spy central, the place where every dirty deed can happen so long as Tarrant gets his cut. He or she sold you out somehow without either knowing or betraying the cover you assumed upon leaving Cullan."

He nodded.

"A fair presumption, Captain. My agency will find out in due course and deal with the problem. But congratulations. Operating as a false privateer seems to have sharpened your instincts for treachery."

Dunmoore didn't know whether to take Forenza's words as a compliment or a subtle insult. Either could be just as likely.

"So where does that leave us? Tarrant's pirates are in my brig; your fellow passengers are in one of my cargo holds turned accommodations pod; part of my crew is operating *Kattegat Maru,* and that ship's real crew is still in the wind. Not to mention my earning the SSB and Tarrant's undying enmity."

"An impressive list, Captain." His mouth twitched with amusement. "At least you can count on the Colonial Office's gratitude once again."

Her cocked right eyebrow expressed a world of skepticism.

"Your superiors were pleased with my handling of the Toboso incident?"

"Delighted would be a more apt word to describe their reaction at the outcome, something I'm sure they passed on to the Admiralty. But if you can keep both brig and passenger accommodations filled for a while longer, finding Captain Fennon and her people should be priority number one. Tarrant is a vile piece of work who won't blink an eye at seeing them sold off into slavery, or simply tossed out an airlock. He doesn't enjoy leaving witnesses."

"I daresay he'll enjoy me even less once I'm done."

Forenza gave her an ironic salute.

"Bravo, Captain. That's the spirit. Kilia's management has been a thorn in the Colonial Office's side for years, but since Tarrant operates under SSB protection, we've not been able to assert even a modicum of control so far. My superiors would surely be grateful if the Navy helps change that state of affairs."

"*If* the Navy changes that state of affairs it will be for the greater good, not to give the Colonial Office a leg up on its war with the SSB." She waited for him to acknowledge with a polite nod before continuing. "Not that I can solve the Kilia problem by myself, but small steps, right? How do you wish to proceed, Ser Forenza? Keep this cover identity and return to your fellow *Kattegat Maru* passengers until I land them at a safe port?"

"I would prefer to avoid that course of action, now you've singled me out with this interview. Besides, I might be useful in dealing with Tarrant. Could you possibly allow me some sort of status aboard as an officer of the Commonwealth government? Something like a supercargo as I believe you naval types call it? I will subject myself to the Universal Code of Military Discipline until I leave *Iolanthe*, of course."

Dunmoore studied Forenza, wondering whether he knew the full meaning of the term supercargo and if so, whether he mentioned the term intentionally as a way of showing he controlled the government's interests for the rest of this operation. She quickly decided that he did.

"So long as we're clear I will see to the interests of the civilians involved and those of the Navy before considering the interests of the Colonial Office or your own mission."

Forenza inclined his head.

"I would not wish it any other way, Captain."

"In that case, welcome aboard."

**

"Forgive me, Skipper, but did you lose your ever-loving mind?"

Holt's incredulous stare matched his tone once Dunmoore told him about her truce with Forenza and his temporary status as an officer of the Commonwealth government in *Iolanthe* until they were done.

"The man's a bloody serial killer in the service of the Colonial Office, not one of the most illustriously patriotic and law-abiding departments from what I noted in my days with naval counterintelligence."

"I can't put him back with the other abductees. Who knows what mischief he might cause? Besides, Forenza might be useful when it comes to Enoc Tarrant or, God forbid if we're forced to go deeper into the Unclaimed Zone."

She paused to let Holt digest her words. When he gave her a grudging nod, she continued.

"But I won't go so far as trusting him. Or rather, I will trust him to pursue the Colonial Office's interests as well as his own, and they seem to coincide with ours at the moment, especially where the SSB is concerned."

"The enemy of our enemy is not necessarily our friend, Skipper. However, I get your meaning. Just keep in mind gratitude isn't a big thing in his universe, nor is interagency cooperation. I'll make sure he doesn't stray into areas off-limits to anyone not part of the ship's company."

"Thank you, Zeke."

"You can thank me by making sure we're not unwittingly pulled into whatever power games the Colonial Office and the SSB are playing in this sector. And by sending a confidential report on the matter to Admiral Nagira, so he can decide whether it's a matter for my erstwhile counterintelligence colleagues."

"Going over Admiral Petras' head will put his nose out of joint, since technically we already belong to Task Force Luckner, but yes to both."

Holt winked at her.

"Only if Petras finds out, and Nagira will make sure he doesn't after reading your report."

"You think the Colonial Office being at odds with the SSB could threaten the Fleet?"

He shook his head.

"Not directly, but since the Shrehari seem to be operating in these parts as well, who knows how this internecine warfare between branches of the Commonwealth government could affect the war effort?"

"I doubt it'll help." She exhaled softly, suppressing a sigh of irritation. "I'd love to know what Forenza and his lot are doing in the Unclaimed Zone, and what everyone is up to on Kilia. It's telling that we were probably the most honest people there during our last visit, even if we were masquerading as a privateer."

"True, sadly. Not to change the subject, but what are your intentions concerning our rescuees, *Kattegat Maru,* and Skelly Kursu's pirates. We're not an accommodation ship, and chances are we'll find ourselves in battle again before this operation winds down."

Her lips twisted with indecision.

"There are no ideal options. I can't risk dropping anyone off in a civilian port, no matter how safe. We need to dock *Kattegat Maru* at the nearest starbase and see our guests registered and processed by the Navy before their release. That should reduce the risk of Tarrant, the SSB, or anyone else trying to make them vanish so they can re-establish the mystery that would have enshrouded the freighter fate, were it not for Carrie Fennon. It means *Kattegat Maru* and everyone involved stays under *Iolanthe*'s wing until the end."

"Good thinking. Forenza was right in complimenting you on your heightened instinct for treachery. Should we even transfer the abductees to *Kattegat Maru* before leaving Hecate?"

"If we can make them reasonably comfortable, they might as well stay put for now, assuming we carry enough supplies to feed another forty-five people on top of Kursu's crew for a few more weeks."

"We do."

Knowing Holt had even the minutest details on *Iolanthe*'s condition at his fingertips, she didn't bother asking for more information.

Instead, she said, "Then it's settled. The risk of being aboard *Iolanthe* if we go into battle is no greater than traveling in a soft target such as *Katie*."

"Even less risky this way, and I'm sure Emma will concur. Although she has a platoon of Tatiana's finest to back up her relief crew, hauling almost four dozen unknown individuals around while maintaining both our cover and her ship's safety might be a bit much." Holt climbed to his feet. "I'll see that the bosun starts improving our improvised passenger pod."

"And make sure we stay in character as the privateer *Persephone* if our guests draw Chief Dwyn's mates into conversation, or worse yet, one of them escapes the pod for an impromptu tour."

— Forty-Two —

"We are just under half a million kilometers short of Kilia's hyperlimit and running silent," Holt announced once the transition nausea wore off after a twelve-hour jump from the system's heliopause. "If they're watching the limit, I doubt they saw us."

"*Kattegat Maru* is running silent too," Chief Yens added. "She's as tight as any Navy unit."

Dunmoore had debated leaving the freighter at the system's edge to make her now habitual hole in space during the interstellar crossing from Hecate. That crossing included a dogleg to approach the Octavius subspace array so she could send a classified report to Nagira via the SOCOM priority channel. *Iolanthe*'s signals chief, however, took great care to avoid picking up any messages.

But when they emerged at Kilia's heliopause, she decided it would be safer if *Katie* remained under the Q-ship's direct protection, to Lieutenant Commander Cullop's relief. The latter made no bones about her feelings at watching a small Shrehari strike force pass within detection range while she loitered near the Hecate system's edge, alone and vulnerable in the dark.

"Are the warheads we planted in Kilia's crust still transmitting?"

Yens didn't immediately respond. Then she glanced over her shoulder at Dunmoore with a look of disgust.

"Nothing, sir. Either those goons are jamming the signal, or they deactivated them." One of the sensor techs nudged her, pointing at his console. "Or perhaps the boneheads helped. There are four of them trying unsuccessfully to replicate our trick by trailing Kilia's approximate L5 position with systems dampened. Two *Ptar* and two *Tol*. Their emissions signature, what little we're getting, is consistent with those we encountered in the Hecate system."

Dunmoore stroked the scar on her jawline, eyes narrowed.

"Why did they come here instead of returning to Shrehari-controlled space? And why wait in ambush rather than orbit the station openly like any other visitor?"

"A better question would be why is this entire mess centered on Kilia?" Holt, or rather his holographic projection at her elbow asked.

Mikhail Forenza, present in the CIC for their approach to Kilia at Dunmoore's behest in case he might prove useful, albeit over her first officer's objections, broke his silence.

"Commander Holt is right, Captain. Kilia appears to be a locus of sorts. Perhaps not a major one, but of some importance nonetheless."

Dunmoore swiveled her command chair around to face the Colonial Office agent, sitting next to Major Salminen, whom she'd appointed Forenza's keeper during his time in the CIC.

"Would you care to enlighten us?"

"If I had answers, I'd share them with you, Captain."

"In that case, would you care to speculate?"

A thin smile tugged at his mouth.

"I'm a field operative, not an analyst."

"Field operative?" Her sardonic smile dripped with skepticism. "Is that what they call your job nowadays? Never mind, I don't want to know, but I'd still appreciate hearing your views since we appear to be intruding on Colonial Office interests."

"SSB interests as well, don't forget." Forenza turned his eyes upward to stare at the deckhead as if parsing his memories and steepled his fingertips beneath his chin, a gesture Dunmoore recognized as an unconscious tic.

"Let's see if I can find sense in this, leaving aside the Shrehari which are your area of expertise."

For a second or two, Dunmoore fancied she could actually hear Holt roll his one eye, and she forcefully repressed the urge to grin.

"I let the Shrehari hunt *Iolanthe* instead of the other way around. It saves on fuel although the end result is always the same. That's the beauty of commanding a Q-ship."

Thorin Sirico wasn't entirely successful in swallowing a guffaw.

"Sir?"

Dunmoore turned back toward Yens.

"What's up, Chief?"

"None of the ships orbiting Kilia match the specs for *Baba Yaga* we recovered from *Bukavac,* and I can't detect anyone else trying to hide other than the boneheads. There are a few interesting hulls in orbit, however. The sort preferred by spacers who value speed and firepower over carrying capacity if you know what I mean."

Dunmoore swallowed a curse. Her fingers began their accustomed dance on her thigh while she scrolled through the available options. Opening a comlink with Tarrant would pinpoint their position and if he was cozying up to the Shrehari, betray *Iolanthe* to a superior force as well. Yet he was probably the only one who knew where *Baba Yaga* and therefore Fennon and her crew might be headed.

And if the warheads they'd planted in Kilia's crust no longer transmitted a signal, she'd lost her sole means of pressuring Tarrant into cooperating. Or did she?

"Zeke, how hard would it be to rig the Growlers so they appear as rated warships to anyone more than a few hundred thousand kilometers away? I want Tarrant and the boneheads to consider the wisdom of not fighting."

A moment of silence punctuated her question before the first officer replied.

"You're plotting a bluff, Skipper? Pretend we're Task Force Luckner by ourselves? Once every bastard in this system picks up the emissions, they'll lock on with visual sensors and see that our Growlers aren't heavy frigates. Maybe we can make *Kattegat Maru* look like one, but that's about the extent of it."

"I was thinking holographic projections on top of a jury-rigged emissions generator, Zeke. It only has to work until Tarrant gives us answers."

"That would mean unmasking *Iolanthe*. No one will buy a privateer escorted by a couple of smaller privateers, all of whom can ruin any marauder's day. Otherwise, their fame would have spread throughout the sector already."

"So we go in as a Navy battlecruiser, and you talk with Tarrant as *Iolanthe*'s commanding officer. That way the secret of *Persephone* and Captain Shannon O'Donnell stay intact. The Shrehari already saw our true form and know how savage we can be. Add in a pair of Growlers projecting the image of Voivode class frigates — Gregor Pushkin's *Jan Sobieski* and whichever was next off the slipways..."

"*Charles Martel*," Sirico helpfully offered.

"Those two. Make *Katie* up to appear as if she were a corvette and that'll convince anyone we're a task force with teeth."

"I'll ask Renny."

Holt's tone was less than enthusiastic, and she knew he would voice his objections in private shortly.

"Please do."

"Aye, aye, sir. By the way, we could disguise your appearance for the comlink and pass you off as Captain Corto, for example, or even Admiral Petras. I've always wondered how you'd come across as someone of his sort."

"No. For one thing, I wouldn't be able to mimic a flag officer in speech and mannerisms as well as you. Besides, it would be best if *Iolanthe*, in her battlecruiser incarnation, was ostensibly commanded by someone other than a woman, red-haired, icy blond or otherwise. The fewer similarities between the Furious Faerie and her privateer alter ego, the better. Besides, you're a more talented actor than I am."

"You mean talented bullshit artist. Do I get a temporary promotion to commodore?"

"No, but you can borrow a set of my captain's stripes."

"Shame." Holt grinned. "Wearing a star on the collar is one of my lifetime goals."

"Stow your ambitions and speak with Renny."

"I hear and obey."

The first officer's hologram faded out of existence.

Behind her, Forenza chuckled softly.

"I like your style, Captain Dunmoore. Funnily enough, many appear to believe you're a reckless damn the torpedoes officer who prefers charging at the enemy headlong. Your reputation is sadly off the mark." When she glared at him, his mirth grew. "Oh yes, I sounded out my contacts in the Fleet when the Colonial Office ordered me to Toboso. This was right after Anton Gerber sent a distress signal about your interference in Colonial Office business."

"Reputations in the Navy are often off the mark, Ser Forenza, as you might remember. Having a reputation at odds with reality can be helpful. Unexpected tactical choices can confuse an opponent and give a ruthless warship captain the chance to land a fatal blow."

Forenza inclined his head in acknowledgment.

"I could say the same about successful operatives in my line of business."

Holt's hologram reappeared at her elbow.

"I spoke with Renny, Skipper. He figures it can be done, but won't vouch for the quality of the results. Faking a starship's emissions is one thing. Wrapping a Growler in a believable hologram to make its appearance match a fake power curve is another altogether."

"How long?"

"Up to a day."

"Which means eight hours in Renny-speak. Let's do this."

"Consider it done."

Holt's hologram vanished once more.

"Renny-speak?" Forenza asked, amused curiosity dancing in his hooded eyes.

"There are rumors Fleet engineers always multiply their time estimates by a factor of three, so they might pass for miracle workers."

"Ah. The Colonial Office bureaucracy has something similar, except it's not to pass for miracle workers by delivering faster than predicted. They enjoy dragging things out in the hope a problem might disappear."

"That's true of any large headquarters, even in the Navy. Changing the subject ever so slightly, did you come up with any fresh insights on Kilia?"

"Other than it serves as the hub for Enoc Tarrant's criminal and quasi-criminal activities? A hub with spokes reaching into the Unclaimed Zone as well as the Commonwealth and I daresay the Empire's outskirts, one used by many other interests so long as Tarrant gets a taste? No. Places such as this exist on the margins of the law, often beyond government control, choosing no favorites among warring parties, and profiting from all sides. I don't believe you'll find the solution here. It's only a waypoint in these parts, not a destination."

"I'd already figured that out, Ser Forenza."

He noticed the sarcastic undertone in her reply, and his thin smile returned.

"Then you'll agree the trick is determining which of the spokes radiating from Kilia will lead to answers."

"Now there's a shocker. And that brings us back to your mission. Perhaps it's time you stopped being coy and shared with us, Ser Forenza. Human lives may depend on it." When he didn't respond, Dunmoore stood. "How about we repair to my day cabin for a cup of coffee? If you can, please join us, Zeke. Mister Sirico, the CIC is yours."

— Forty-Three —

Brakal woke with a start and sat up, wondering what could rouse him from an uneasy rest. He reached for the cup of now cold *tvass* by the side of his bunk and drained it in one gulp. The liquid tasted worse than *yatakan* droppings, but it helped drive away the last wisps of sleep along with the lingering memory of a dream that could only come from gods seeking to punish him. He took a deep breath and listened intently, wondering whether an unexpected noise was responsible for this interruption. But *Tol Vehar* sounded as it always did. Brakal's fist smashed into the control panel above his head.

"Bridge."

"Yes, Lord," Urag replied with commendable swiftness.

"Did anything unusual happen?"

"No. Everything is as it should be. Strike Force Khorsan is still trailing Kilia with systems dampened, the *Tai Kan* rats on that damned station haven't said a word since Regar last spoke with them, and no new ship has appeared on our sensors."

A disconsolate grunt erupted from Brakal's throat unbidden. He had elected to stay near Kilia instead of returning to his patrol route despite the objections of his ship captains. Escaping virtually unscathed from what many were now calling the Great Hecate Missile Shoot seemed to them a sign from the gods they should withdraw and cease overstepping their bounds.

Brakal couldn't tell whether this uncharacteristic caution stemmed from eroding morale, thanks to years of inconclusive warfare. Or whether newfound fear at human ships able to hide in plain sight until they opened fire without warning, such as the ghost decimating Shrehari shipping or the battleship that ambushed them in the Hecate system, was to blame. But sure as black holes devoured stars, the Imperial Deep Space Fleet's fighting edge was fading, worn away by a lack of decisive victories.

Even members of the Warrior caste didn't want to die for a cause that seemed less and less likely to end with the humans' abject defeat. They understood there was no honor in a senseless death.

Perhaps Regar was right when he said many within the Fleet would rally around the banner of an admiral and hereditary lord striving to claim the *kho'sahra*'s robes and end this war before the Empire's strength dwindled further.

Brakal already held his family's seat in the Four Hundred and owned the wealth of its estates. If he could formally claim Hralk's command and obtain promotion...

But for that, he needed a victory. Something to show the Admiralty he surpassed Hralk in tactical skill and acumen. The destruction of the human ghost who was devastating Imperial shipping would do nicely.

And his instincts told him the hunt for that damned phantom was far from over. It would come to Kilia again because this *Persephone* who'd bedeviled Enoc Tarrant could be no other, just as its commander must be the flame-haired she-wolf.

And this time, *he* would wait in ambush at one of Kilia's co-orbital points, using a human tactic against them. He gazed at the outer bulkhead, wondering whether her arrival, as yet undetected, was the cause for his sudden restlessness and growing irritation. A pox on the hairless apes and their refusal to submit. If it were not for the *Tai Kan* using Kilia as a base of operations in this sector, Brakal might be tempted to vent his spleen on its mostly human inhabitants.

**

Commander Holt passed out coffee mugs and took a chair next to Forenza, facing Dunmoore's desk.

"Tell us about your mission."

Her tone was soft yet demanding.

"With the understanding that anything you hear from me doesn't make its way into official reports or idle wardroom discussions. If your superiors insist on details, feel free to take credit for tracking down the relevant information with no help from anyone else."

Forenza held Dunmoore's eyes, and when she nodded, he turned his gaze on Holt until he too signified his agreement.

"But I would prefer if as little as possible of this matter became general knowledge. It might affect more than just a few innocent lives."

"I can promise that after hearing you out, I'll avoid using your or the Colonial Office's name. But if it's something the Fleet needs to know, I will pass any relevant information to Admiral Nagira directly."

Dunmoore conveniently omitted any mention of the report already in Nagira's hands, courtesy of the Octavius subspace array.

"That's right. I almost forgot — you're one of his protégées. Evidently, you still have a direct line."

"Which I take care to not abuse. He personally arranged for me to get this command."

"Fair enough. Even our lot thinks highly of Nagira."

Holt snorted.

"Will wonders never cease."

"In an infinite universe, Commander, everything eventually comes to pass."

"An assassin and a philosopher." The first officer smirked at his captain. "We are truly blessed to be in the presence of such greatness."

Forenza graced him with an ironic, albeit seated bow.

"I'm a man of many talents, Commander. Solving the Office's intractable problems and regaling an audience with profound remarks are only a small part. Now if we're done with the persiflage, perhaps I might tell you something about my mission."

Dunmoore threw Holt a warning glance before saying, "Please do."

"As you've no doubt surmised, the Colonial Office doesn't merely administer colonies under a federal charter. It also keeps an eye on, and sometimes even a hand in the affairs of colonies established by the Commonwealth's various sovereign star systems. What you might not know is that in addition, we monitor unofficial settlements, both within and beyond the Commonwealth sphere. You'd be amazed at how many and in what variety of extreme environments. To do so, the Office developed its own intelligence service decades ago since neither the SSB nor the Fleet is prone to share. My branch doesn't officially exist. Ostensibly, we work for the Colonial Office's Assistant Secretary, Governance and Oversight."

"The oversight part kind of went sideways on Toboso, didn't it?" Holt asked. "Considering we solved your agency's problem by the time you showed up."

Forenza dismissed the first officer's words with a half shrug.

"Politics interfered with a prompt response, Commander, as they often do. I don't decide when and where to act. Only how."

"Pray continue." Dunmoore gave Holt another quick glance to forestall a reply.

"Naturally, we've been watching human colonies emerge in the badlands, settled by people fleeing the Commonwealth government's reach for any number of reasons. Politics, trouble with the law, wanderlust, or a sense of adventure — name the cause and you'll find someone willing to own it. Unfortunately, settlements of this sort are vulnerable to every predator with an FTL-capable starship, and the current war simply makes matters worse. A few colonies arm themselves, others are forced to accept so-called protection, and some are wiped out. Oh, we try to help where possible, but since these are folks with an ingrained distaste for Commonwealth authorities, it can be painful. In most cases, the Office uses more or less unwitting intermediaries to supply aid."

"Such as *Kattegat Maru*?" Holt asked.

Forenza tapped the side of his nose with an extended forefinger.

"Most perceptive of you, Commander. *Kattegat Maru* and other traders brave enough to sail the badlands route. They mostly deliver medical supplies, spare parts for essential tech and so forth. Untraceable stuff donated anonymously."

"Weapons and ammunition?"

"That too, Captain. And yes, I know shipping ordnance without a permit is against the law. But then so is the Colonial Office operating its own in-house intelligence service, or if not against the law, then not sanctioned by it. Anyway, that was a bit of context to help you understand the situation. In recent times, things have changed out there."

He waved at the far bulkhead.

"And not for the better. Marginal settlements are vanishing; others display open hostility to outsiders; a few turned into downright nasty places ruled by violence and fear, and several colonies suddenly sprouted no-go areas that were inhabited, yet out of bounds to visitors such as me. Before you ask, I don't hold the Shrehari responsible. They've never shown much interest in this part of space other than for trade and the occasional bit of piracy. Conquering it outright would create an open flank with a space-faring species living deep within the Unclaimed Zone known as the Arkanna. Did you hear of them?"

Dunmoore nodded.

"Independent-minded, aggressive, unable to tolerate any form of subjugation, and from a Shrehari point of view, not worth the price of conquest, which says a lot about how dangerous these Arkanna are."

"Just so, with one more caveat. They're not expansionists. On the contrary. The Arkanna may be the first example of a multi-system autarky we've ever encountered. Therefore, if we accept the Shrehari aren't to blame for recent events in the Zone, this leaves only one set of possible actors."

"Other humans."

"Just so, Commander. With the Navy busy fending off Shrehari advances into our sphere, various interests are using the opportunity to impose their will on outlaw colonies."

"Tarrant?" Dunmoore asked.

"Not directly. He's a facilitator, preferring to skim a percentage or offer carefully circumscribed services via his mercenaries rather than meddle in the affairs of frontier systems living in a bizarre mixture of pre-industrial and high-tech conditions. The human version of techno-barbarism, I suppose you might call it, minus the desire to engage in rapine and plunder."

"Is the Colonial Office expecting a future expansion of the Commonwealth that will return these lost souls to the bosom of humanity and place them under your direct and benevolent authority?"

Forenza didn't seem to hear the sarcasm in Holt's tone.

"Of course. Expansion is inevitable."

"That's what the Shrehari thought," the first officer replied. "A lot of good it's done them."

Dunmoore raised a hand.

"So someone's been messing with outlaw colonies since shortly after the start of the war, someone from our side. And your job is to find out what's happening."

"Find out and if possible end it."

"Except someone betrayed you to the SSB. Does that mean it's to blame for events?"

"Until I found myself in the Temar rendition site, the Bureau's involvement was merely one of several possibilities. Now I'm convinced that if the Bureau isn't acting alone, then it at least controls some of the actors."

"Such as Enoc Tarrant."

"I wouldn't say anyone controls Tarrant, Captain, but as you've seen, he is cooperating with them."

"Why is the SSB operating in the badlands? I can't see how that helps increase its power inside the Commonwealth."

The ghost of a smile creased Forenza's face.

"That, my dear Commander, became the question. Finding out was my mission this time around, hence my planet-hopping along the trade route."

"And did you?"

The Colonial Office agent nodded.

"I did, and they somehow noticed, either through a slip-up on my part or as you suggested via betrayal by a traitorous colleague."

"Care to discuss what you found?"

— Forty-Four —

"How will we turn *Katie* into a Navy corvette?" Carrie Fennon's earnest face wore a frown of incomprehension. "Don't the bad guys know what she looks like?"

"They do, but if we confound their long-range visuals with contradictory data, it will fool the bad guys long enough." Lieutenant Commander Emma Cullop nodded toward Lieutenant Zhukov who was studying a readout on the bridge's engineering console. "Yulia is about to mess up *Katie*'s systems to make her power emissions appear as if they come from an older, less well-shielded warship. And since *Katie* is of almost the same tonnage as a corvette, she'll make those emissions consistent with a ship of that type. Then, Yulia will tweak our naval beacon, so when we go up systems, it'll broadcast the identity of a corvette by the name *Eyvind*."

"Does this *Eyvind* exist?" Fennon asked.

"Aye, but she's assigned to the Shield Sector, so no one around here has seen her in recent memory, if ever," Zhukov replied without turning around. "Transforming *Katie* into something more fearsome is the easy part. I shall be interested to see how Commander Halfen rigs *Iolanthe*'s Growlers so they can project credible holographic images of Voivode class frigates."

"Do you think he can do it?"

Zhukov responded with a fatalistic shrug.

"Growlers are stuffed full of high-end electronics, Skipper. That ought to give the boss a good basis. But I'm not sure their power plants can generate enough juice to create holograms of that size and keep them stable long enough against all the radiation out there. Making shuttles seem like warships beyond increasing their emissions signature isn't exactly something they teach at the Academy. But if anyone can figure out how it would be Commander Halfen."

Cullop nodded.

"True. He's a remarkably capable sideways thinker — for an engineer."

"Careful, Lieutenant Commander Cullop, sir," Zhukov rumbled with mock ferocity. "Or I'll have a sideways thought you won't enjoy."

Kattegat Maru's temporary captain gave Carrie Fennon an exaggerated wink and said, "A thousand pardons, Yulia. I wouldn't want you to reverse the vacuum flow in my cabin's toilet."

A wide-eyed Fennon, uncertainty writ large on her fine features, glanced at the two naval officers in turn.

"Has that ever happened?"

"Yep. We once took a mercenary ship as a prize after the crew surrendered and a joker reversed the vacuum flow for the toilets aboard as revenge. A good thing the asshole fessed up before shit literally hit the fan."

Zhukov grunted.

"Never a dull day in our part of the Navy. There, the first step is complete. The fusion reactors will seem as if they're putting out fifty percent more power. Now comes the fun part."

"Which would be?"

The engineer stood and turned a sardonic grin on her commanding officer.

"Make the capacitors feeding *Katie*'s pop guns come across as those of a warship but without destroying them. It's a bit touchier." When she saw Fennon's alarmed expression, Zhukov shook her head. "Don't worry, young lady. The worst that could happen is the Navy buys you a couple of brand new units which, considering how old your capacitors are, would be an improvement."

With that, Zhukov left Cullop and Fennon to stand watch on the bridge by themselves.

"Do you think Captain Dunmoore's bluff will make Enoc Tarrant tell us where *Baba Yaga* took my family, sir?"

"There are no guarantees, Carrie. But if anyone can talk her way out of a tight situation, it's the skipper. She has a reputation for bamboozling the enemy."

"How so?"

Cullop sat back in her command chair and glanced at the main display.

"I guess there's time for a few war stories. Mind you, some of them happened when she was captain of the frigate *Stingray* so what I know about those days comes from Chief Guthren."

**

"I'm sure you know before the war, many of the Commonwealth's core star systems exercised a policy of deporting dissidents. They shipped members of banned political movements, habitual criminals, what they call social parasites and anyone else the regimes didn't like, to colonies they owned along the Commonwealth frontier. It removed undesirables from society, kept political dynasties in power and seeded newly opened worlds with workers, albeit involuntary ones."

"So I heard," Dunmoore said. "It's a tradition that goes back long before the first spaceship left Earth's surface."

"When the war broke out, involuntary colonization dwindled thanks to many of the target worlds coming under Shrehari rule. Not long afterward, the Senate ordered deportations stopped altogether, ostensibly to support the war effort. But it was mostly an attempt by a slim majority of senators hoping to end involuntary colonization for good."

"Which means those worlds experienced an increase in what their governments consider undesirables with no way of getting them off-planet."

"Just so, Commander. But several star system governments refused to acknowledge the Senate's authority and searched for alternatives."

Dunmoore's chuckle held a grim edge.

"Let me guess. They found those alternatives out in the Unclaimed Zone."

"Excellent, Captain. Well deduced. The Colonial Office heard about a whole new category of people appearing on planets such as Cullan, folks dumped into settlements segregated from the rest. Word filtered out that these were deportees from star systems who had previously used their own colonies as dumping grounds for unwanted citizens."

"So they sent you to investigate."

"I and many others, Captain, though I fear few of my colleagues are still alive."

"Did you find proof that Commonwealth star systems are illegally deporting people into the Unclaimed Zone?"

Forenza nodded.

"Yes, on Cullan, but it's not the only destination. What I found was disturbing. Tossing folks out of the Commonwealth sphere against their will and in defiance of the law is bad enough. Unfortunately, deportee settlements need administrators, security, and what not, to make sure there's no commingling with voluntary colonists, lest the secret gets out, and to create economic activity capable of feeding people and producing enough profit to keep the enterprise worthwhile.

"Because it's illegal, the cadres are perforce hired from less than savory sources, such as through Enoc Tarrant's web of interests, and they operate virtually unsupervised. Thugs, mercenaries, mobsters, if not worse. As you might imagine, the conditions in those settlements are not far removed from penal or slave colonies. The law is whatever the local boss says. Even worse, this has affected the existing settlements. Not content to just run their open-air prisons, several deportee camp managers are forcing their rule on free communities with the help of well-armed mercenary troops. And, of course, the original colonists can't compete with an indentured labor force, and that means precarious economies are becoming even further impoverished."

"Hang on for a moment," Holt said. "Are you telling me humans are actively practicing slavery in the Zone, or the closest thing to it? With the connivance of Commonwealth star system governments desirous to be rid of their inconvenient citizens? How is that even possible?"

A sad smile crossed Forenza's lips.

"I should imagine some senators and highly placed federal officials are either closing their eyes or actively helping. Then there's the SSB, a law unto itself, which seems involved, and that means persons in the Secretary-General's office itself have given their sanction to this scheme." He noticed the barely repressed rage in Dunmoore's gray eyes and gave her a sympathetic nod. "That was my reaction as well when I figured it out, Captain. And I almost took my knowledge to the grave."

Silence descended on Dunmoore's day cabin as she and Holt digested Forenza's revelations. Finally, the first officer asked, "What can the Colonial Office do about this, if highly placed federal officials and the damned SSB are involved?"

"My superiors have several options, Commander. You understand that making the matter public in a time of interstellar war might not be advisable if only for civilian morale." When he saw Holt open his mouth to voice an angry retort, Forenza added, "We will eventually put an end to the deportations, and it wouldn't surprise me if my superiors asked for the Navy's help."

"Send in the Marines," Holt growled. "They'll make short work of the slave-running thugs."

"A possibility, yes. But keep in mind the most effective remedy is one that won't force those high-placed federal officials to act against us in a fit of self-preservation. And that means no public trials, let alone executions."

"Why wait for a face-saving remedy? How about drumhead courts-martial for the bad actors in the Zone, followed by a quick visit from the friendly neighborhood firing squad after we liberate the camps?" Holt gestured at Dunmoore. "I'm sure we can find a set of drums for the captain and form a dozen volunteer firing squads from our embarked Scandian soldiers. Then your lot can concentrate on ending the deportations and not worry about the bureaucratic infighting that would accompany any hint of the Colonial Office becoming officially responsible for a bunch of outlaw settlements."

"How about we don't get ahead of ourselves?" Dunmoore replied. "Our immediate mission is to recover *Kattegat Maru*'s crew and deliver them, along with the passengers, Ser Forenza, and Skelly Kursu's bunch to the nearest starbase. Then, as you might recall, Zeke, we received orders to join our new task force. I've stretched my excuse of hot pursuit to the limit as it is. Cleaning up the Unclaimed Zone, even under the aegis of anti-slavery, won't happen just yet. Let the Colonial Office do its job while we do ours, which is to kick the boneheads out of our space."

"You forget something, Skipper."

Dunmoore cocked a skeptical eyebrow at Holt.

"Oh? What?"

"If *Baba Yaga* isn't here, then she must be on her way to a place where the captain can profitably dispose of two dozen embarrassing, albeit technically trained humans. Somewhere either operated by Enoc Tarrant or by someone who gives him a taste of the profits."

"The commander has a point, Captain. Those involuntary colonist settlements would find experienced people such as a starship crew invaluable compared to most of the deportees, a wide swath of whom are functionally illiterate and only marginally employable. I'm sorry. I should have thought of it before."

"You figure we'll find them on Cullan?"

"Perhaps, but it's not the only destination within a reasonable distance."

"Then we still need Tarrant to tell us where his ship went."

"And if it's Cullan," Holt said with a piratical grin, "Ser Forenza can show us where we might do a little labor camp liberation along the way."

— Forty-Five —

"The Growlers are ready," Commander Renny Halfen announced in a matter-of-fact tone as he entered the wardroom, eyes on the coffee urn. Dunmoore and Holt were the only officers present, taking their meal well after everyone else as usual. "And I need a cup of java that doesn't reek of reactor fuel drippings."

"Gave up on teaching the engineering crew how to make a non-toxic brew?" Holt asked around a mouthful of chicken curry.

"It's not that they don't know." He filled his mug and took an appreciative sip. "It's that they don't want to. Not a working taste bud to spare among them. At least for coffee."

"Tell me about our Growlers?" Dunmoore asked, checking the time. Nine hours had elapsed since she gave the order. Renny Halfen was running true to form.

The engineer dropped into a chair at their table and sighed.

"I filled most of the aft compartments with spare batteries because their reactors can't produce enough power for holograms that'll fool anyone watching. And even then, they won't be full size, nor will you get much over thirty minutes before the solar wind blows them away. And that's optimistic. One heavy burst of radiation passing over us, and you'll be seeing two wee shuttles instead of Voivode class frigates. The holographic projectors we carry aren't designed to work out where it's nasty and definitely not while trying to keep a huge image stable. In any case, I made enough modifications to be censured by the Chief of Naval Engineering, if that worthy personage ever finds out."

"Thank you, Renny. I'm pretty sure thirty minutes will be more than enough. If we can't convince Enoc Tarrant to speak and the Shrehari to keep hiding in the first ten minutes, then we never will."

"That long?" A smirk twisted Holt's lips. "Remember who'll do the talking."

"Are you laying down a challenge, Ezekiel?" Halfen asked. "Shall we run a wager? Or a betting pool? I'm sure I could find plenty of takers."

"There is to be no gambling in my ship."

An impish expression replaced Holt's smirk.

"Aren't most of our operations a gamble, Skipper?"

"Aye." Halfen nodded enthusiastically. "And that makes you the biggest gambler of all, sir."

"Since we're on the subject," Holt continued, unrepentant, "when do you intend to roll the dice? Emma can turn Kattegat *Maru* into the Commonwealth Star Ship *Eyvind* at any time and now that the Growlers are ready, there's no point in waiting. Besides, we should run this gamble from beyond Kilia's effective weapons range, lest they land a salvo on our pretend Voivodes and collapse the illusion."

Dunmoore swallowed the last bit of her chicken, wiped her lips, and stood.

"We go to battle stations in fifteen minutes and launch the Growlers. Once they're in position, Mister Holt or should I say Captain Larkin, you may order our private iteration of

Task Force Luckner to go up systems and then prove your silver tongue hasn't tarnished through disuse."

**

"Wow." Lieutenant Commander Sirico let out an appreciative whistle. "If I didn't know they were holograms projected by a pair of standard-issue Growlers, I'd be wondering how those frigates snuck up on us undetected."

"The emissions are certainly convincing. *Kattegat Maru*'s not doing too shabby as a pretend corvette either," Chief Petty Officer Yens said. "Those three, plus the Furious Faerie in full battlecruiser mode ought to wake up the bonehead-loving scumbags on Kilia."

"And the boneheads we're pretending not to see at Kilia's trailing Lagrangian."

Well done, Renny and Yulia! Dunmoore mentally congratulated her chief engineer and his assistant, the latter having transformed *Kattegat Maru* into a convincing *Eyvind* as her beacon now proclaimed.

"How does it feel to command the better part of a modern task force?" Holt's hologram asked.

"Like a game of Eridani Hold'em where my two hole cards are brown dwarfs. Besides, you're in charge, remember?"

"I'm only the talking head, Skipper, but those captain's stripes on my collar sure feel nice." A pause. "And it looks as if I'm about to go on stage. Kilia is calling, and judging by the tone, they're feeling slightly alarmed."

"Now entering stage left, Captain Ezekiel Larkin, Commonwealth Navy. Knock 'em dead, Zeke."

A split view replaced the star field on the CIC's main display as the bridge signals petty officer established a link with Kilia. Her first officer, in Navy battledress with one of Dunmoore's spare rank insignia on the collar filled one side, while Enoc Tarrant swarthy face, twisted into a mask of displeasure, filled the other.

"I'm Captain Ezekiel Larkin of the battlecruiser *Iolanthe*, acting commodore of Task Force Luckner. And you are?"

Holt's languid tone verged on a patrician arrogance designed to irritate.

"Enoc Tarrant. I run Kilia Station. Why are you here, Captain? This sector isn't under Commonwealth jurisdiction. We're neutrals and generally don't permit warships from belligerent polities to enter our space."

"Don't permit?" Holt's derisive laughter echoed across the CIC. "And you enforce this rule with what, precisely? The only ships I see wouldn't survive more than a single salvo from mine."

"With my ground-based ordnance, Captain. I'm sure you're scanning Kilia's surface right now. We can make any attempt at attacking us prohibitively expensive."

"I suppose that's why four Shrehari warships are trying and failing to stay invisible near your L5 point? So much for not welcoming belligerents."

Tarrant's eyes narrowed, though his lids did little to mask the ire blazing in them.

"My dealings are none of your concern."

"But they are, my good man. I am commanded to hunt and destroy the enemies of the Commonwealth, and what do you know? I find four Shrehari ships and a nest of traitors to humanity. It's a target-rich environment if I've ever seen one. As to your ground-based ordnance, best not hide behind illusions. Sustained fire by my four ships will make quick work of your shields since you can't maneuver. After that?" Holt shrugged. "A few well-placed nuclear warheads slamming into Kilia's crust and that'll be the end of your criminal enterprise. I know, using nukes on populated places is technically forbidden, but since you claim independence from the rest of humanity, expecting me to care about such niceties would be futile."

He let his words sink in before continuing.

"However, today is your lucky day, Ser Tarrant. I'm on a mission that overrides my desire to destroy the filth arrayed before me. Cooperate, and I'll let your little den of thieves live. Otherwise..."

"What do you want?" Tarrant asked in a tight voice.

"You hold people I'm charged with recovering. Captain Aurelia Fennon and twenty-four of her crewmembers."

"I don't know who you're talking about."

"Come now, your ships attacked *Kattegat Maru* and took everyone off. A letter of marque who turned the matter over to the Navy recovered it. You might recall the privateer's captain, Shannon O'Donnell. A strange woman, remarkably ruthless on occasion and probably a bit of a sociopath in the bargain. Thanks to her information, we retrieved the passengers who traveled in *Kattegat Maru*, but our intelligence indicates one of your ships, *Baba Yaga*, is carrying Captain Fennon and her people."

"Still not following you, Captain. I hold shares in a ship by the name *Baba Yaga*. But she's not here right now. This Fennon however, is unknown to anyone in my employ."

"Shame." Holt's lips drooped in a display of disappointment.

"Why is it a shame?"

"Since you refuse to tell me where we can find *Kattegat Maru*'s crew, I shall end your tenancy of this star system." Holt's head turned to one side. "Gunnery officer, please tell the task force to lock on and prepare for the opening salvo."

"Wait just a moment, Captain. There are thousands of sentient beings in Kilia. You'd condemn them to death for the sake of two dozen space rats?"

Holt rolled his single eye.

"Not another damned utilitarian. The needs of the many and all that garbage? I don't give a flying fuck about your station or the soon-to-be crispy critters therein. You're a thug surrounded by thuglets and therefore no loss whatsoever to our species. I won't even mention how much better the universe will be without the boneheads you harbor. My sole mission is to recover Fennon and company, with no restrictions set on the level of collateral damage I can inflict out here, beyond the limits of the Commonwealth sphere. Now decide. Tell me where I can find Fennon and live, or prepare to die along with everyone else cowering in that rock you call home."

**

"By the dark gods, what is this fresh example of our damnation?" Brakal growled as he studied the four human warships that suddenly appeared on *Tol Vehar*'s sensors, just beyond weapons range. "How did they come so close with no one noticing?"

"Lord, the largest of the four, a battleship, is the same one we fought in the Hecate system. The next largest ships appear to be from what we believe are the newest cruisers of their warlord class, what they call *frigates*," he used the Anglic word. "The other is a corvette. According to the latest intelligence, the human warlord class cruisers are fresh off the slipways and more than a match for our *Tol* class." Menak pointed at a side display where human text shimmered brightly. "They broadcast their identities."

Brakal rubbed his chin with a leathery paw and grunted. Three capital ships and an escort, including the one that already drove him to withdraw. The odds were not in the Empire's favor. As much as it pained his warrior's soul, there would be no honor in attacking the human formation.

It outgunned him ship-for-ship, and that meant this was not a good day to die.

"Lord, the humans speak with Kilia."

"Can we intercept their communication?"

"They take no pains to hide it."

"Show me."

Perhaps he would finally see who ambushed him near the human-occupied moon named Temar.

The image of a pale human male with one eye materialized along with that of the vile, untrustworthy hairless ape ruling Kilia. Regar's *Tai Kan* colleagues had regaled the spy with many tales of doings within that hollowed-out rock, each worse than the other while Brakal waited for the ghost to reappear.

In turn, Regar recounted them to his commanding officer over many cups of freshly brewed *tvass*. Brakal no longer wondered why the *Tai Kan* considered Kilia such a fertile hunting ground for information and a superb base of operations for their pretend-corsair missions.

The human male was unknown to him, and he realized with a pang he had hoped to see the flame-haired she-wolf, Dunmoore. But then he believed his old foe to command the ghost, and this was a different ship. A real warship.

Though their speech remained unintelligible to his ears, a haphazard translation scrolled past on a nearby side display. The pale human was on a quest to find members of his species who disappeared and held the despicable serpent ruling Kilia responsible, something the latter denied. And now the human was threatening to destroy Kilia. How strange. No subject of the Shrehari Empire, even one living beyond its bounds, would dare refuse a senior officer of the Deep Space Fleet.

"Lord."

The sensor officer's voice drove away his thoughts.

"What is it, Menak?"

"Something about the two warlord class cruisers, *Jan Sobieski* and *Charles Martel*, appears disturbingly strange." He massacred the human names with the usual Shrehari gutturals.

"How so?"

Brakal's black in black eyes turned to the main display now showing one of the ships in question.

"We are detecting the expected emissions from something that size, but the visuals seem to blur here and there, in random blotches."

"Defective equipment? Solar wind interference?"

"Perhaps, but an uneasy feeling is eating at my guts, Lord. Might I suggest you contemplate allowing me to scan with active sensors? If the passive sensors are defective or experiencing interference from natural radiation, we would know."

"Suggestion noted. Not yet."

Brakal sat back in his chair, knowing Urag, quietly watching him from his own seat at the center of the bridge, would recommend caution in the face of superior enemy strength. As he studied the image, a sense of unease enveloped him too. What was wrong with those cruisers that tickled his instincts?

— Forty-Six —

Dunmoore, fascinated by the verbal standoff between her amusingly arrogant first officer and an increasingly irritated Tarrant almost missed the subtle flash of an incoming call on the screen embedded in her command chair's arm. She glanced down and frowned. Renny Halfen wouldn't call her in the middle of the action unless something was about to go wrong. Dunmoore touched the panel.

"Tell me it's good news, Renny."

Halfen grimaced.

"Sorry, Captain. You won't get the thirty minutes I promised. *Jan Sobieski*'s holographic projection is degrading fast. The emitter just isn't strong enough to keep fighting the solar wind."

Dunmoore's heart sank.

"How long?"

"Ten minutes. Maybe less."

A muffled curse almost escaped her lips.

"Let Zeke know."

"Already done. I flashed a priority message to the bridge. He acknowledged." Halfen's eyes slipped to one side. "The *Charles Martel* projection is beginning to degrade as well. Sorry."

"There's nothing to apologize for. You did the impossible in under a day, Renny. Besides, it only needs to work a few minutes longer. Zeke almost has Tarrant convinced he's a bloodthirsty career climber who eats babies for breakfast."

"I've been listening. He almost has *me* convinced. Mind you, that eye patch adds a lot to the aristocratic psychopath persona."

At that moment, Holt spoke again.

"All right, Tarrant, since you don't appear to possess the brains God granted a stalk of broccoli, I'll give the human gene pool a thorough cleansing." He waved at someone off-screen. "Gunnery officer, confirm target lock."

"Confirmed, sir," an invisible Lieutenant Protti replied. "The first flight of missiles is ready to launch. Forty-five warheads. The next one will follow half a minute later."

Holt tapped his chin with a gloved index finger.

"Ninety warheads. I wonder if that's not overkill. What do you think, Ser Tarrant? Is it too much? I hate wasting the taxpayer's money."

Dunmoore saw the color drain from Tarrant's face in the space of half a second. His jaw muscles rippled beneath the skin as he chewed on Ezekiel Holt's threat.

"Your superiors will hear of this gross intrusion into the affairs of an independent neutral. Threatening thousands of innocent civilian lives means the end of your career, Larkin. I'm connected to powerful people in the Commonwealth government. They will make sure you pay."

"Good. My after-action report will sound so much better with corroboration from the local asshole. Just make sure you spell my name correctly. That's L-A-R-K-I-N. Of course, that's assuming you're about to tell me where I can find Fennon and her people. Otherwise the only one you'll be complaining to is Beelzebub. And he'll commend me for sending him a fresh batch of blackened souls." Holt's fist struck the command chair with a loud thump. "For the last time, where are they?"

"Uh-oh." Thorin Sirico looked up from his console. "Pretend *Jan Sobieski* is flickering."

"Come on, Tarrant," Dunmoore murmured. "Give it up."

An ugly snarl replaced the languid expression on Holt's face.

"Gunnery officer, prepare to fire."

"Wait. *Baba Yaga* is taking them to the Hestia system."

Dunmoore glanced over her shoulder at Forenza who grimaced and said, "It's the next closest after Cullan, but with considerably less charm and more marginal conditions for our species. I wasn't able to pinpoint the deportee settlements there, but they exist. The place is known among smugglers for producing opaline-type gemstones of exceptional quality, unmatched anywhere else in the known galaxy, and such mines would need a workforce familiar with advanced machinery."

"Coordinates?" Holt demanded. "Keep in mind if I don't find Fennon and her people, or something happened to them, I will scour Kilia with my nuclear fire."

Tarrant glanced away and rattled off an alphanumeric sequence.

A heartfelt curse escaped Sirico's lips.

"We lost one hologram, sir. The Growler is still emitting as if it were a frigate, but *Jan Sobieski*'s image is gone."

Moments later, a text message appeared on one of the CIC's side screens. It was from Lieutenant Drost, confirming the coordinates matched that of a G class star with at least one known habitable planet called Hestia.

"Time to end this charade," Dunmoore said, "before the Shrehari figure out it's just us and one freighter, and decide on a rematch. As much as I want to finish the job we started in the Hecate system, this time we can't count on orbital defenses as a backup."

Eric Thomson

She tapped out a message for Holt and saw him glance down briefly. An acknowledgment flashed on her command chair's display.

"Many thanks, Ser Tarrant," Holt said, inclining his head in a polite bow. "Keep my warning in mind and do yourself a favor. Evict those Shrehari lying doggo at your L5 point before the Admiralty brands Kilia as a hostile system. I know several flag officers who'd love to transform your little station into a forward operating base. None of them are known to offer compensation, by the way. One last thing, don't be alarmed but my ships and I will vanish from your sensors in a few seconds. *Iolanthe*, out."

"And we're clear," the CIC signals petty officer said.

"Thorin, shut off the Growlers. PO, tell Commander Cullop to execute the planned course change then go silent. Zeke, put tractor beams on those shuttles, fire thrusters to conform with *Katie*'s movements and go silent as well."

**

"Lord, one of the human cruisers — I can still detect its emissions, but it vanished from the visual pickups."

Brakal turned his eyes on Menak.

"Show me." A brief recording of the purported *Jan Sobieski* flashed by on the main screen. For a few heartbeats, its image wavered, then disappeared without warning. "But the power signature remains unchanged?"

"Less intense, but yes, Lord."

"And the other cruiser?"

The now familiar form of the second Voivode class frigate replaced the recording of its mate dissolving into nothing.

"It flickers as well, though its emissions are stable."

An amused rumble sounded from the back of the bridge.

"Decoys, perhaps," Regar suggested. "To intimidate the ruler of that well-defended habitat? Judging by the last exchange between him and the human commander, it succeeded."

"But how is it possible to create such a convincing image of otherspace-capable ships?"

"Convincing but short-lived," the *Tai Kan* officer replied. He pointed at the screen. "Both are gone."

"As are their power emissions," Menak added. "And those of the corvette and the battleship, though both fired attitudinal thrusters to change course beforehand."

"Do you still have a visual fix on them?"

"No, Lord. Their unexpected course change threw the visual sensors off. I am trying to find them again."

Brakal's noisy exhalation sounded like that of an enraged fire dragon. Two decoys and two real ships? Or three decoys and one real battleship?

"We recorded the name and coordinates of the planet in question. It allows us to pursue."

Urag, who'd remained silent throughout, gave Regar a poisonous look.

"Chasing that battleship and whatever actual companions it might have won't allow us to find and destroy the ghost. Let the humans go on their quest since it seems unrelated to anything that might interest the Empire. Our duty is elsewhere."

Unbowed by Urag's outburst, Regar made a dismissive gesture.

Ignoring both his advisors, Brakal turned toward Lieutenant Tuku, *Tol Vehar*'s navigator.

"Show me the planet's location."

"The instant I finish translating those primitive human coordinates into proper ones, Lord."

Urag's suspicious gaze shifted to Brakal.

"We've neglected our patrol route long enough. Who knows what trouble the ghost has caused during our absence? Chasing a battleship that is not an immediate threat while failing to hunt the commerce raider we must eliminate will give a *yatakan* such as Strike Force Khorsan's chief of staff more knives to plant in your back. Hralk is already paying for his lack of success. Fail, and you will face the Admiralty's opprobrium so much faster."

"And yet..." Brakal murmured, "Something about that battleship still tugs at my instincts, Urag."

"You witnessed its commander. A human male, not the flame-haired female that has been haunting the most evil of your dreams since she nearly destroyed *Tol Vakash* many years ago. A female resembling her commands the human corsair we encountered in this system, the one you believe is our phantom. Two different commanders, two different ships. We must return to our assigned sector and resume our hunt there. Besides, we will need to resupply soon. Another engagement such as the one in the Hecate system and our missile launchers will be empty."

"Lord, I found the star system named by those coordinates," Tuku said. He indicated the three-dimensional navigation plot, where Hestia, Kilia, and Shrehari occupied space were clearly marked.

A sad rumble rose from Brakal's chest. Following the battleship would take them a fair distance from their assigned patrol route once again. One such occurrence might pass without notice, but not two. And Urag was right. He would fall harder and faster than Hralk if Gra'k and his minions decided they could produce enough evidence to see him permanently relieved by the Admiralty. Still, something bothered him about the behemoth with its one-eyed commander.

"Very well. We will wait here for a few more days and see if the phantom appears. Then, we head back to our demon-spawned base of operations so we may resupply. If a convoy finally made it through."

"With the ghost operating in these parts instead of raiding our shipping lanes?" Regar asked. "I'd say the warehouses will be full. And since our sector no longer suffers its depredations, you might even find your chief of staff sitting on a missive from the home world confirming you as the admiral in command of Strike Force Khorsan."

— Forty-Seven —

Iolanthe's wardroom erupted in applause when Ezekiel Holt, once more wearing a commander's three stripes on his collar, entered for the evening meal. He made a theatrical bow and said, "Thank you, thank you." He pointed at Lieutenant Protti. "I had a great supporting cast, and you were a wonderful audience."

"How did it feel playing the villain of the piece, sir?" Sirico asked with a grin. He dropped his voice by two octaves and said, "*I will scour Kilia with my nuclear fire.* Brilliant! I almost believed you would do it."

"It's the eye patch," Protti said. "You had to be on the bridge while it happened for the full effect. Chilling, just chilling."

Dunmoore made a face at her first officer.

"But calling Shannon O'Donnell a sociopath? Really, Zeke?"

"You wanted to put distance between *Persephone* and *Iolanthe.* I merely did my best to make the difference believable."

Holt piled food on a tray before joining her and Forenza at the captain's corner table.

"The Growlers are back in the hangar, Skipper, but Renny thinks they'll need a starbase-level overhaul. Some of the more delicate electronics are one power surge away from frying. I don't envy you explaining why when the inevitable questions arise. You know how Fleet engineers are when they find evidence of unauthorized modifications on anything under their purview." He sat and dipped his spoon into the thick stew. "*Kattegat Maru* is in fine fettle and keeping good station on our port quarter. Emma says young Carrie Fennon received quite an education in the fine art of winning without fighting. She'll make our apprentice officer read Sun Tzu during the crossing to Hestia."

"What about the Shrehari?"

"Still trailing Kilia with dampened systems. It looks as if they learned to avoid battle unless the odds are overwhelmingly in their favor."

"Years of getting nowhere will do that to the most aggressive species. I think they're as tired of this crap as we are and no longer inclined to die for the emperor without a damn good reason."

"Especially since their reasons for attacking us were spurious in the first place, Captain," Forenza said. "Using war with an external foe to mask or divert attention from internal problems will only take you so far. With no great racial, religious, or existential issues at play, there's a limit to how much sentient beings will endure."

"Do you think they'll get tired enough to seek an armistice?" Holt asked.

The Colonial Office agent made a so-so hand gesture.

"It depends on who's in charge over there. The only armistice we'll accept is their vacating the star systems they took from us, and that is the biggest stumbling block. No Shrehari leader wants to be reviled because he handed back hard-won conquests without a fight. It would take something like a military dictator to enforce an armistice based on the status quo ante, a *kho'sahra*."

"May I ask how you know so much about the boneheads?"

A faint smile creased Forenza's features.

338   *Eric Thomson*

"I devote many hours of personal study to the present situation, Commander, because I believe a well-rounded operative needs broad horizons. They help one better understand the second and third-order effects of one's actions."

"It would be nice if our politicians thought the same. Their horizons don't seem to extend beyond the next election, even in wartime."

Forenza raised a finger and said, with mock sententiousness, "It has ever been thus, Commander, since the first stirrings of democracy in ancient Greece. Sadly, I doubt most of them even know what second and third-order effects are, based on the short-sighted decisions emanating from our illustrious Senate, or our even more illustrious Secretary-General."

Dunmoore, coffee cup raised to her lips, watched the banter between her late nemesis' brother and Holt, wondering how two people, born of the same parents and presumably with a similar upbringing could become such different adults. Helen had been self-indulgent, possessed of an undisciplined intellect, and quick to pull family strings when the consequences of her actions came home to roost. Until she ruined a frigate's crew to the point where even the Forenza name meant nothing.

Mikhail, however, seemed to be the complete opposite. Self-possessed, thoughtful, and in his own way, meticulously professional. Dunmoore knew he would do her a bad turn if his mission called for it, and without the slightest compunction, but never out of sheer spite like his mercurial sibling, even though he was much deadlier.

So far, the Colonial Office agent was the soul of politeness, helpful to a fault, but still very much a man serving his own masters. Forenza gave Dunmoore a knowing glance as if he could divine her thoughts, but his conversation with Holt went on unabated. Finally, they ran out of pithy comments, and Holt scarfed down the rest of his meal.

"If you'll excuse me," he said, climbing to his feet. "A first officer's day never truly ends. When do you intend to discuss next steps, Skipper?"

"I want Emma in on the conversation, and that means when we drop out of FTL at the heliopause. Knowing Renny, he'll want a good two or three hours before our first interstellar leg, giving us plenty of time. Between now and then, perhaps Astrid and Ser Forenza can put their heads together and come up with what information is available on the Hestia system."

The latter inclined his head by way of acknowledgment.

"I shall do my best. Hestia was not my primary objective, but that of a colleague whom I suspect is no longer among the living."

"Shame we weren't able to reconstruct *Kattegat Maru*'s log. It would at least have given us basic navigational information, including landing areas."

"Chief Day hasn't given up, Skipper. But unless Carrie Fennon has something substantive to add, we're stuck playing this one as we go along. Astrid already checked the database, and there is little on Hestia besides information from the initial survey, now woefully out of date. The same appears true for most of the systems Ser Forenza's office is investigating."

Dunmoore exhaled softly.

"I suppose someone's making sure outlaw colonies stay unmentioned in official records. Nice to know corruption runs rife in the Survey Service as well."

"A hazard in any government agency, Captain. Organizations are only as good as the people running them. Statistically, half of all humans are below median intelligence and easily led astray by the ten percent who

combine above average intelligence with a defective sense
of ethics."

"Only ten percent?" Holt asked with a smirk.

"It depends on the agency, of course. If you think the SSB
has a higher percentage of ethically impaired employees, I
daresay you'd be right." Forenza drained his coffee and
stood as well. "Please ask Lieutenant Drost to contact me
when she's ready. I'll be at her disposal no matter the time
of day. Now if you'll excuse me, I wish to take advantage of
your fitness facility. Even though I grow older, my duties
remain as physically demanding as always."

**

"Hestia." Lieutenant Astrid Drost, *Iolanthe*'s sailing
master, nodded toward a dun orb dominating the
conference room's main display. "We found nothing more
than the basic survey data in our and *Kattegat Maru*'s
navigation library. Between them, Ser Forenza and
Apprentice Officer Fennon filled in a few blanks." She
nodded at the Colonial Office agent and Carrie's hologram.
"But it isn't much. We'll need to run our own survey upon
arrival."

"Assuming we don't stumble across *Baba Yaga* still
carrying Captain Fennon and crew," Dunmoore said.
"Though with their head start, the safest assumption is by
the time we arrive, they'll have landed our people and left."

"But since we'll already be there, we might wish to
liberate a few involuntary laborers and shut the operations
using them," Holt said to approving nods. Forenza had
briefed them extensively on the secret deportation scheme
before Drost took center stage. "Even if we can't bring any
deportees home ourselves."

"That will indeed be a job for the Colonial Office,"
Forenza said. "In due time."

Dunmoore gestured at Drost. "Please continue, Lieutenant."

"Yes, sir. Hestia has an oxygen-nitrogen atmosphere, even though it's a little lean on the former — approximately eighteen percent at sea level. Water covers just under half the surface. The land masses are largely desert, ranging from mostly ergs at the equator to arctic tundra near the poles, with a narrow band of what passes for temperate zones in each hemisphere. According to Ser Forenza and Apprentice Officer Fennon, the sole settlements and known mining operations are in this area, within a hundred kilometers of the water's edge."

She pointed at a ragged strip of color between the sandy beige circling Hestia's midriff and the extensive white polar region. A long, slender inland sea running almost from icecap to icecap cut across the surface.

"With an axial tilt of less than five percent, seasonal variations are minimal and mostly dependent on the planet's uneven orbit around its primary."

"Which makes the temperate zone rather chilly all year long," Forenza said.

"And makes the polar regions extremely cold," Drost continued. "The native flora and fauna are inimical to humans and there is no evidence Hestia was ever home to sentient beings. The chief town, called Arden by the settlers has the sole serviced spaceport. But the other settlements and the mining operations are served by rammed earth landing strips capable of taking a ship *Kattegat Maru*'s size, provided it required no ground support. Ser Forenza has kindly agreed to take over the rest of this briefing and discuss what he knows of conditions on the surface, and the probable locations of deportee labor camps."

— Forty-Eight —

"If it weren't for Ser Forenza and the young apprentice officer telling us there are human settlements on that dust ball, I'd figure this system was devoid of sentient activity," Chief Yens said after a tense fifteen minutes examining Hestia and its surroundings from the hyperlimit. "No orbital stations, platforms, or satellites, no ships, no antimatter fuel cracking stations and no artificial power emissions."

"But I am picking up radio waves coming from the planet," the CIC signals petty officer said, "proving someone's home, although I see no evidence they're operating subspace transmitters or relays."

"Outlaw colonies don't have the money for them," Forenza replied, "and the people operating illegal deportee camps don't want to attract attention."

"May we assume they're not equipped to detect active scans from passing starships?"

"You may, Captain. And even if they detect your ship once we're in orbit, what could they do with the information?"

"True. You may go active, Chief. Let's see if the orbitals are truly bare. Then we can find out what's on the surface."

"Aye, aye, sir. Switching to active scan." Shortly after that, Yens shook her head. "No trace of anything artificial in orbit. If *Baba Yaga* came here, she left already."

"There wouldn't be much point in her lingering after delivering *Kattegat Maru*'s crew," Sirico said. "With two of his ships destroyed alongside the Shrehari corsair, thanks to the dastardly privateer O'Donnell, part-time sociopath, and terror of the star lanes, Tarrant would want *Baba Yaga* to make a fast turnaround so she can take care of other business."

"Dastardly? Part-time sociopath? Unless your name is Larkin, those aren't things you should say about me." Dunmoore's tone made light of her words. "I believe the term cunning is more appropriate." When she saw the impish glint in Sirico's eyes, she raised a restraining hand. "Don't say it. Don't even think about it."

"I wasn't headed there, Captain, I swear."

"Bull," Salminen growled. "Everyone knows what goes on in the lump that passes for your brain, Thorin."

The combat systems officer put on a mock wounded air and raised his right hand to his heart.

"I'm deeply hurt by your insinuations. Besides the Captain forbade me to think."

Chief Yens, eyes fixed on the sensor readout, shook her head in despair at her department head's antics.

"Back to business, folks," Dunmoore said. "We can ditch silent running. Fire up the sub-light drives and take us into orbit, Mister Holt. *Kattegat Maru* is to follow suit."

"Aye, aye, Skipper. Hestia orbit it is."

"Captain?"

Dunmoore swiveled her chair to face Salminen.

"Yes, Major?"

"Would it be possible to recover the platoon in *Kattegat Maru* during our transit to Hestia? I'd rather bring my entire company on the raid, and with *Iolanthe* keeping a close eye on her, *Katie* shouldn't need extra bodies to repel boarders."

"Sure." Dunmoore paused for a moment, then added, "We'll shift Carrie Fennon back here at the same time. She can identify her people for us more easily than your troops might by working off the pictures we took from *Kattegat Maru's* crew roster."

**

"We'll need at least two recon patrols."

Salminen, standing close to the conference room's wall-sized main display, studied the high-resolution images of Hestia's settlement area, near the shores of the pole to pole inland sea.

"One per mining operation. Put each site under observation until we find our people. There's no point landing in company strength until then. A single platoon split in half will do."

She turned around to face E Company's command group surrounding the oval table — her four platoon leaders, Lieutenant Jon Puro, and Sergeant Major Haataja. Dunmoore sat at her accustomed place, with Guthren, Holt, Forenza and Carrie Fennon on either side, observing Salminen's planning session with great interest.

"Not much cover around the targets," Haataja said. "Setting up long-range observation posts instead of patrolling will reduce the chances of being spotted."

"True, but examine the security dispositions. Just like the rendition site on Temar. Everything's turned inward. They're not expecting an external threat."

"Huh." Command Sergeant Karlo Saari squinted at the image. "You'd figure the local population has its share of thieves, considering the value of the stuff extracted."

"If I may," Forenza raised a hand. "The free settlers appeared thoroughly cowed by the mining operations' management, or rather their enforcers when I briefly passed through a few months ago. Objectors are rumored to be either taken out into the wilderness and shot or pressed into unpaid work. Whatever happened to them, the most vocal opponents supposedly vanished without a trace."

Haataja nodded.

"So no big incentive to guard against external threats, but I'd still go with observation posts only until shortly before we insert."

"Fair enough." Salminen let her eyes roam around the table. "Which platoon gets the honor of being our recon force?"

Saari fished a deck of cards from his battledress tunic.

"How about we decide in the usual manner? Five-card stud? Eridani Hold'em? Old Maid?"

"Since when do we gamble in a Navy ship, Karlo?" Sergeant Major Haataja growled with pretend ferocity. "There are rules about these things."

An unapologetic grin split Saari's face.

"Especially when the captain, the first officer, *and* the coxswain are watching us, right, Talo? Tell you what. In that case, I volunteer my platoon for the recon."

Salminen and her sergeant major exchanged glances. When the latter nodded, she said, "If the enemy spots you, 1st Platoon pays for the post-mission vodka issue."

Saari's grin widened.

"Deal. And what's our reward if we run a perfect recon?"

"We'll worry about that blessed event if, by a miracle, it occurs."

"Challenge accepted, Major."

"Then you can start by working on your platoon's insertion." She looked up at Dunmoore. "With Emma in

Kattegat Maru, who should Karlo, and I for that matter, speak with about flight plans."

"Chief Dwyn."

"Thank you, sir. Karlo, I want to see your scheme of operations in three hours. Is that enough time?"

"Plenty, Major. Especially if I can get Gus Purdy and Eve Knowles as pilots. They're used to my ways by now."

"I'm sure that can be arranged. One last question, Captain. Do we go in as Varangian Company or Commonwealth Army?"

Dunmoore turned to the Colonial Office agent.

"What would you recommend, Ser Forenza, since this is your area of operations?"

He tapped his chin with an extended index finger, eyes narrowed in thought, then said, "I believe Major Salminen's unit should display their Army colors, so to speak. It would send a salutary message to others involved in this scheme that the Fleet's reach now extends deep into the Unclaimed Zone."

"Even if it's an unofficial, if not unsanctioned raid well beyond our sphere?" Holt asked.

"Especially because it's unofficial, Commander. Once word gets out, perhaps my office will have better luck persuading your admirals to extend their reach and ease some of the misery endemic in these parts."

"Ask not for permission beforehand, but for forgiveness afterward." The first officer nodded. "We're getting pretty good at that."

**

Dunmoore found Salminen and Haataja standing behind 1st Platoon on the hangar deck, listening to Command Sergeant Saari's mission briefing. The two gunships assigned to carry them, piloted by Saari's pals Purdy and

Knowles, served as a backdrop. Both petty officers stood to one side with Sergeant First Class Maki Mattis, whose half of the platoon would scout Ruby Two as the smaller of the mines was baptized. Saari was taking Ruby One, the larger and more likely target, for himself.

She joined E Company's leaders, exchanging wordless greetings, and studied the three-dimensional holographic projection of the target areas serving as the briefing's centerpiece. Though Saari had laid out his plan for Salminen and Dunmoore's approval a few hours earlier, she still found it interesting to hear how that translated into clear instructions for the troops.

"Questions?" He asked after concluding.

As everyone expected, Corporal Vallin, E Company's resident critic and barracks lawyer raised a fist.

"If we stumble across one of them motherfucking slavers and kill him without alerting anyone, does that still count as being spotted by the enemy? It would be a shame if that means you pay for the hooch."

An evil smile crept up Saari's face.

"What makes you figure I'll be the only one paying? This is a team effort. All for one, one for all and if one fucks up, everyone coughs up a few creds. But let's ask the Major. What's the verdict on Vallin's question, sir?"

"Knife 'em silently before they raise the alarm, and it's as if nothing ever happened."

"Thank you, sir. Any other matters bothering you Corporal Vallin?"

"It's about the rules of engagement once we raid the target."

"And what of them?"

"Will the major let us use bug hunt ROEs on account we can clean up this place?"

"Nope. Even slavers are entitled to a quick drumhead court-martial before we shove them through an open airlock without a pressure suit. Those that surrender, I mean. If they won't surrender, fill your boots, but don't waste ammo. Two taps to the chest and one to the head."

"Mozambique Drill it is, Sarge. And if they're not human?"

"Shoot until they stop twitching. Any more pertinent questions?" He let his eyes roam over the assembled soldiers, then glanced at his platoon sergeant and both pilots. When they shook their heads, Saari clapped his gauntleted hands. "Helmets on, button up and get into your assigned shuttles. It's almost midnight in the target area, and I want us settled into the observation posts before local first light."

As the soldiers of 1st Platoon dispersed, Saari turned his eyes on Salminen.

"Permission to execute, sir?"

She nodded once.

"Make the Scandia Regiment proud, Karlo."

"Yes, sir." Saari saluted, pivoted on his armored heels, and jogged toward the nearest gunship. He took a last glance around, listened to something over the platoon push, and then vanished up the aft ramp.

Dunmoore nudged Salminen and nodded toward the hangar's inner airlock.

"Time to clear the deck." When she saw the expression in Salminen's eyes as the soldier watched the gunships prepare to leave, she said, "Saari will do just fine. I've seen Marines with twenty years of starship duty less confident about a detached mission."

"I'm not worried about Karlo lacking confidence, Captain." She and Haataja fell into step beside Dunmoore. "My concern is him suffering from the contrary — overconfidence. Something tells me the moment Karlo spots our people, he'll be looking for a way to rescue them single-handed while we're still getting ready to launch."

"The major's concern is valid," Haataja said. "Karlo's taken to this lifestyle like no one else in the company, and that's a double-edged dagger. He fancies himself the equal of any Marine sergeant on starship duty, and he's not far off. But I'm sure his common sense will kick in before he tries to tackle the entire mission alone."

"And if not, Sergeant Mattis will find a way to kick his ass by remote control," Salminen added with a dry chuckle.

— Forty-Nine —

The two gunships flew nap of the earth for a long time, approaching their target areas from a considerable distance to minimize the chances of detection. With no moon, Hestia's cloud-flecked sky was dark enough to hide the stealth-coated aircraft from prying eyes, if any roamed the veld beneath their wings. At the prearranged waypoint, the gunships parted company, each reaching for its destination via a network of shallow glens and canyons carved out eons ago by long-gone rivers.

Shortly afterward, a faint glow outlining a distant hillock's crest alerted Sergeant Saari and Petty Officer Purdy their destination lay close by. The latter immediately cut his airspeed until they moved no faster than an autonomous urban transport pod while Saari searched for the designated landing zone using the visual component of the craft's targeting sensor. It turned the ground's inky black into an eerie greenish hell populated by strange plants and even stranger nocturnal creatures who froze in place rather than run at the approach of something they couldn't comprehend.

"There." Saari's gloved finger touched the controls, giving birth to a targeting pip on Purdy's navigation display. "Stick with a hover when we're over the spot. Not too high.

I'll send Vallin and his winger to make sure the ground will take your bird."

While the gunship slowed to a crawl, Saari climbed out of the gunner's seat and entered the aft compartment where half of his platoon waited, helmet visors closed, weapons stuck between the knees.

"Rurik, you and Andres get ready. Sensors show nothing but local life forms within visual range."

"Roger that, Sarge." Vallin and his fire team partner released the seat restraints and stood. Their dark, menacing armored shells seemed massive in the small enclosed space.

"Don't land on anything that bites. Damned critters around here look mean enough to chew through triple-laminate."

The red light bathing the aft compartment died away, leaving the soldiers in total darkness. Then, the aft ramp opened onto silent, scrub-covered hills, velvety dark beneath a partially star-speckled sky.

When the sensation of forward movement ceased altogether, Purdy said, "I'm one and a half meters above what my sensors say is the ground. You can hop off at any time."

Vallin gave him thumbs up, then he and Private Bergstrom vanished into the night. They landed with a faint rustle of crushed foliage but made no other sounds. A minute passed, then two before Saari heard a soft rapping against the ramp's underside. Three knocks to signal the surface was adequate for landing. Purdy settled on the ground so gently it took the soldiers a moment to realize they'd landed.

With a sweeping hand gesture, Saari sent the rest of his half-platoon to join the corporal, then turned to wave at Purdy before disappearing as well. The gunship's aft ramp closed seconds after Saari cleared it and the craft lifted off.

It was headed for a box canyon just over thirty kilometers away where it and the one flown by Petty Officer Knowles would be undetectable while they waited for the rest of E Company or to give 1st Platoon air support in case the recon went totally pear-shaped.

Saari knew the same scene would play out with Sergeant First Class Mattis' half of the platoon about twenty kilometers to the south. But since they were under tight emcon, he wouldn't know what was happening at Ruby Two until one of them broke radio silence and either sent confirmation of the Fennon family's location to *Iolanthe* or reported that the mission was compromised. Even then, it would be no more than a hard-to-trace microburst transmission.

Using only hand signals, Saari sent his soldiers toward a crest outlined by a faint orange glow. Anyone not equipped to see through the darkness wouldn't notice them creeping through the scrub in two section columns a few meters apart, weapons at the ready, heads swiveling ceaselessly from left to right.

The Hestia night was almost halfway over before Saari, flanked by a pair of troopers, crept up the hill's reverse slope, slithering between thorny bushes, looking for the perfect spot to place his observation post. After a few false tries, he found a natural depression surrounded by native vegetation that gave a decent and more importantly hidden view of Ruby One.

He left his soldiers to set themselves up for the first watch before reversing course to join the others in the low-lying thicket of trees they'd chosen as a hide. The night air, though chilly, didn't penetrate their armor but even if it had, the bite would remind Saari and his troopers of home, a place so far away Scandia's sun wasn't visible to the naked eye from this backwater planet.

**

Dunmoore found Tatiana Salminen and Jon Puro hunched over their tea cups, lost in quiet conversation, when she entered the otherwise empty wardroom at two bells in the morning watch, or oh-five-hundred as both soldiers would call it. They glanced up and said, in unison, "Good morning, sir."

"Good morning, Tatiana, Jon. Can't sleep either?" Dunmoore drew a cup of coffee from the urn and took a small, dainty pastry from the overnight tray.

Salminen grimaced.

"Fretting about my people when they're on the surface by themselves, and I'm up here while we're operating under full emcon, never gets easier. Please join us."

"Thanks." Dunmoore snagged a chair with her foot and sat. She took a healthy bite from the pastry and chased it with a swig of the strong, black brew. "We should hear something within the next few hours. Dawn broke over the target area not long ago, which means the mines should be stirring to life."

"Good morning, sirs," a tentative voice said from the wardroom door.

Dunmoore glanced over her shoulder and smiled at a bleary-eyed Carrie Fennon.

"Good morning, Apprentice Officer." Salminen and Puro nodded politely but remained silent. "Please, grab something from the buffet table and join us. We were discussing the joys of waiting for the first reconnaissance report."

"If you don't mind my presence."

"Of course not."

The young woman served herself then perched uncertainly on the edge of the chair facing Dunmoore.

"I was just noting," Siobhan said, "that we should hear something shortly since dawn just broke over the target area. They'll be rousing the workforce right about now. If Enoc Tarrant wasn't lying about *Baba Yaga*'s destination, chances are good we'll see your mother and other relatives among them."

"And if we don't?"

Fennon's large dark eyes, set in a grave face, met Dunmoore's gaze.

"Then we'll keep searching."

"Even if your admiral has recalled *Iolanthe*, sir?"

Dunmoore nodded. "Even then."

**

Command Sergeant Saari silently slipped into the observation post at daybreak. As he expected, one of the two soldiers occupying it had his eyes glued to the unpowered optical elements of the portable sensor suite. With the rest of the complex electronics shut off, it was virtually undetectable.

"How are they hanging?" Saari whispered.

"Side by side, Sarge," the man on close protection duty replied in the same tone.

"Want to look?" His winger backed away from the sensor. "They're stirring. Until a few minutes ago, it was just regular two-man patrols walking the perimeter. But now, there's a bunch of them coming out of the barracks, each uglier than the bastardized children of boneheads who mated with lizards, even if they're human. Damn mercenary fucks."

Saari crawled up and glued his helmet visor to the rectangular eyepiece. The mining camp, at the base of a rocky tor, swam into view. Even though it was several kilometers away, Saari felt as if he could reach out and touch the wicked-looking fence crowned by razor-sharp wire capable of amputating limbs.

Black-uniformed mercenaries carrying side arms and shock sticks milled about in the early morning light until they coalesced into six-person teams. Each team headed for the closed doors of large huts built from containers set end-to-end and pierced by square openings filled with dark, reflective plastic panes. Another dozen took position on three sides of the open space fronting the huts, shock sticks in hand and judging by their facial expressions, joking about something.

A siren, audible even at this distance, shattered the stillness. Four of each six-person team entered a hut and soon thereafter, men, women and even children streamed out to form up in orderly rows. They wore gray workers overalls and solid, calf-length boots, and though most seemed unkempt, the men with beards ranging from scraggly to luxurious, none appeared to be suffering from malnutrition. But Saari could see bruises on more than one squinty-eyed face.

The scene unfolding before him resembled nothing so much as convicts herded together for morning roll call in a military stockade on Parth, something Saari saw on video during the law and order portion of his basic training. A few of the mercenary guards seemed shock stick happy when it came to motivating laggards, but the involuntary labor force formed up with commendable alacrity and in what appeared to be total silence. Enough of them had probably suffered through painful punishment for tardiness and disobedience early on that everyone understood how the game was played.

Yet a few still needed encouragement. Saari saw a brief, but violent exchange between a pair of prisoners and the guards. It ended with the former writhing in agony at the feet of the latter, their nerve endings on fire. Habitual dissenters? Or...

Saari zoomed in on one of the two laborers as he painfully pulled himself up to avoid the guards' vicious kicks. The man bore the unmistakable markings of a severe beating on his face — split lip, black eye, bruised cheekbones. But he didn't sport the long, wild hair or beard common among his fellow sufferers. A newcomer.

He called up the images of *Kattegat Maru*'s crew, culled from the crew roster and loaded in his helmet's databank, and quickly scrolled through those of the males. He compared each to the man now leaning on his comrade's shoulder as both joined the formation until he hit a match.

Second engineer Gene Ross. There was no mistaking the resemblance. Even after a shit-kicking from the mercenaries.

A muffled curse must have escaped his lips because the soldier lying next to him asked, "What's up, Sarge?"

"I think I see one of them, Tuvi, a member of *Kattegat Maru*'s crew."

"Hot damn!"

— Fifty —

Dunmoore was recounting one of *Stingray's* less embarrassing misadventures, as much to distract the soldiers and help calm Carrie Fennon's nerves as to pass the time when her communicator chimed.

"CIC to the captain."

"Dunmoore."

"Sergeant Saari is calling on tight-beam, sir. He says he's spotted eleven of *Kattegat Maru's* crew inside Ruby One so far."

Salminen raised a clenched fist and grinned at Carrie. "Yes!"

"He sent up video so Apprentice Officer Fennon can confirm the identification."

"We're on our way."

Dunmoore drained her coffee and stood, but not without smiling at Carrie's wide-eyed impatience. The young woman was almost quivering with anticipation.

"And as luck would have it," Sirico continued, "Sergeant Mattis just reported seeing fourteen of the missing in Ruby Two, including a woman who looks very much like Captain Aurelia Fennon. That accounts for everyone. A word of warning, however, they bear signs of having been ill-treated by their captors."

"Acknowledged."

Once it the corridor, Dunmoore placed a restraining hand on Carrie's arm, lest she break into a sprint for the CIC.

"Remember what I said about the proper demeanor of a starship captain. No running, unless it's a life or death emergency. Otherwise, your crew will assume something's gone terribly wrong."

"Yes, sir."

Fennon, anxiousness oozing from every pore, checked her pace with visible reluctance.

When they entered the CIC, minus Lieutenant Puro, Salminen guided Fennon to an unoccupied seat next to her console while Dunmoore took the command chair.

Sirico, back at his own station, gestured toward the main display.

"Ready for the Ruby One video?"

"Run it."

When the first bruised and battered face swam into focus, Fennon gasped.

"That's Uncle Gene. He's the second engineer. What did they do to him?" A second face, less damaged but far from unmarred replaced that of Gene Ross. "Cousin Patty Fennon, our purser."

And so it went until they accounted for the eleven *Kattegat Maru* crewmembers Sergeant Saari saw in Ruby One.

"Ruby Two's coming up now," Sirico said.

A sob greeted the appearance of a hard-faced, middle-aged woman with a distinct resemblance to her younger version at the back of the CIC. She also bore signs of the mercenaries' brutality.

"That's my mother," Fennon said in a soft, almost mournful tone.

"Cheer up." Salminen patted her on the shoulder. "At least she and the rest are alive. Bruises and cuts will heal."

"What happens now?"

"Now?" The normally staid Scandian officer gave her a bloodthirsty smile. "E Company, 3rd Battalion, Scandia Regiment will raid both targets, retrieve your crew, free the remaining prisoners and put the assholes running those camps out of business permanently."

Dunmoore turned to face Salminen.

"When do you intend to strike?"

"After dark. Say in eighteen standard hours. Jon, Talo, and the command post crew will shortly begin to analyze the video we received from Karlo and Maki. They'll give 1st Platoon a list of what other essential elements of information we need and let them continue the recon while we draw up our plans."

"How difficult do your rate the targets?"

Salminen made a non-committal gesture.

"The targets themselves are easy. Dump one and a half platoons in the middle of each at oh-dark-thirty while the recon teams make a lot of noise to distract the enemy; take out their guard detail; smoke the mercenaries' barracks and seize control. The trick will be to do so while avoiding casualties among the detainees, either from our fire or if we don't take out the guards cleanly, from theirs. Those huts don't appear able to withstand an angry glare from Talo Haataja, let alone twenty-millimeter plasma from a squad automatic weapon." She climbed to her feet. "With your permission, Captain, I'll join my command team and start planning the raid. If everything goes well, I should be able to brief you before the end of the afternoon watch."

**

"I wonder how deep that shaft runs," Corporal Vallin said, eyes glued to the sensor.

"You can always check with the sergeant major after we're done taking the place," Private Bergstrom replied. "I'm sure Talo will love the idea of a sightseeing tour, and it's not as if we need to be somewhere else right away. I mean other than this new task force the brass is putting together."

Vallin made an obscene gesture at his winger.

"It was a rhetorical question, asshole."

"So is this." Bergstrom returned the gesture with unfeigned glee.

"Bored, boys?" Saari's unexpected presence startled both soldiers.

"Shit, Sarge. We didn't hear you."

"That's because you're too busy kibitzing and I'm the king of stealth. What's happening?"

"Nothing. Damned guards aren't even patrolling the perimeter. So far none of the prisoners came back from wherever they went. Not even for lunch." He indicated Hestia's sun, hanging low on the far horizon, its bottom half partially hidden by a distant dust storm. "And it's getting close to supper time."

"Maybe they don't eat lunch."

Saari, remembering the deportees' decently fed look, shook his head.

"They're eating. Must be ration bars stocked at the work sites. Otherwise, they'd waste time coming up to eat halfway through the shift."

"Makes sense. I guess that's why you're the sarge."

"That and many other reasons, Rurik. But I didn't visit you just to shoot off my mouth. We received orders from the boss."

"Tell me there's a bug hunt coming."

"I'm about to break your heart. You and Andres will stay in the OP until it's over. I'm taking the rest on a close-in recon a few hours before the raid which the boss scheduled for oh-one-hundred. That means I need someone with brains to watch our backs, in case the mercs get antsy at the wrong time. Once we're in control, Gus will pick you up on the way to Ruby One."

"Crap. You're a real bastard, Sarge."

"How often do I need to tell you my parents were married?"

"But not to each other."

Saari thumped Vallin on the shoulder.

"I'll send up relief in a short while so you two can eat, piss, and take a nap. And I'll brief you on the operation while you're eating. The rest already know everything they need."

"You're a prince among men. A prince of darkness, but still..."

"Cheer up, son. I'm giving you a front-row seat to the sweetest little raid anyone in our regiment's ever carried out. In forty years from now, you'll be able to tell your grandchildren about it. And mightily bored they'll be."

Bergstrom guffawed.

"That's only if Rurik finds someone crazy enough to reproduce with him, and Scandia was plum out of crazy the last time I checked."

Saari chuckled.

"You obviously never met my ex."

"Good point. Anyone marrying you has to be fucking nuts, Sarge."

**

At seven bells in the evening watch, ninety minutes before H-Hour, Dunmoore with Carrie Fennon at her side, stood by the hangar deck door. They looked on as Major Salminen, armored, and armed like the rest of E Company, led her troops through their final preparations before boarding the waiting gunships. At an unheard signal, they came to attention as one, armored boots crashing on the deck loud enough to wake the dead five parsecs away, and broke up, each half-platoon jogging to its assigned shuttle.

Salminen turned to face Dunmoore and raised her hand in salute.

"Permission to begin Operation Ruby Rage?"

"Granted, Major. *Hakkaa päälle.*"

A big grin spread across Salminen's face at hearing Dunmoore use her battalion's ancient war cry. And pronounce it correctly.

"*Hakkaa päälle!*"

She pivoted on her heels and, after a last glance around the hangar deck, to make sure everyone was loaded, Salminen vanished into the rear of her command gunship.

Dunmoore nudged Fennon, and they withdrew to the control room where Petty Officer Harkon was waiting for the signal to open *Iolanthe*'s space doors once the airlocks leading to the hangar deck were shut.

"May I ask a question, sir?"

"Certainly, Carrie."

"What does *Hakkaa päälle* mean?"

Fennon's pronunciation would have made everyone in E Company cringe.

"It's commonly held to mean something along the lines of 'cut them down' in a language called Suomi, the ancestral tongue of most in the 3rd Scandia."

"Oh." Fennon seemed both puzzled and impressed.

"You'll not experience true fear until you hear the lot of them yell it as they spill out of their gunships to slit throats," Harkon said, chuckling. "Makes me freeze in my skivvies every time they practice boarding tactics on my hangar deck. Though I suppose since this raid is more an infiltration than a smash and grab, they won't be scaring the enemy with that heathen shout. Although I daresay Talo Haataja in full armor looming over me as I wake up would be enough to eject my soul from my body. Ah, here we go."

Harkon touched a screen in front of him, and the space doors on either side opened, replaced by shimmering force fields designed to keep the compartment pressurized. Then, one after the other, the gunships rose a meter above the deck and nosed their way through the energy barriers, half to starboard, the rest to port.

Dunmoore and Fennon watched until the last pair vanished before returning to the CIC and a relatively short wait that both knew would feel like an eternity.

— Fifty-One —

Command Sergeant Saari and his half of 1ˢᵗ Platoon were almost within reach of the wire-topped fence, hidden by folds in the ground and their armor's chameleon outer coating, when the mercenaries patrolling the perimeter stopped nearby. Both men flipped down the visors attached to their light-weight helmets and turned their backs on the camp so they could scan the night.

Saari, often called an artist with a combat knife by his fellow noncoms, was close enough to take either one with a thrown blade on the first try if necessary. But thanks to their almost preternatural alertness, his soldiers froze in place at the first hint something beyond the camp's perimeter was attracting the guards' attention. Saari listened intently, trying to discern what caused them to search the night but heard nothing more than the never-ending breeze rustling through the low scrub. Perhaps one of the remotely operated sensor suites atop the fence posts at the camp's four corners saw a non-natural shadow move and alerted the nearest patrol.

After a few minutes, the men flipped their visors up again, exchanged a few words — one of them shook his head — and they resumed their monotonous patrol. Three faint beeps sounded in Saari's ears, the prearranged signal signifying E Company's gunships, half headed for Ruby One, the other half for Ruby Two, were on final approach.

The brief message also told the two section grenadiers to prepare their breaching charges. These were long, flat, light-weight tubes filled with high explosives attached to tiny rockets that would drape the tubes over the fence and its deadly wire topping before going off and destroying both. Since the gunships would touch down inside the camp, 1st Platoon's breaching charges, due to go off just before Major Salminen's half of E Company landed, would serve primarily as diversions, to focus the guard detail's attention on the fence rather than the central square for a few crucial seconds.

Three long beeps came over the company push, just as Saari's trained ears picked up the faint whine of dampened gunship thrusters. Not even a second after the third beep faded away, two tiny sparks of light emerged from the dead ground on either side of him and skipped over the fence, trailing an almost invisible black string behind them. The sparks dropped to the ground and died out. Then, a pair of miniature lightning bolts split the night with a thunderous roar, slicing through the fence as if it were made from paper and creating two wide gaps. Saari's visor saved his night vision, but anyone not adequately equipped wouldn't be so lucky.

No sooner did the rumble fade than he saw four sleek, deadly silhouettes pass over him, thrusters whining and land where the deportees stood for evening roll call several hours earlier.

"Go, go, GO!" Saari climbed to his feet and followed alpha section through the breach to his right while bravo section took the other one.

The unearthly howl of an alarm siren split the air asunder, and powerful lights came on, illuminating every corner of the camp. They revealed four black gunships disgorging armored infantry soldiers who ran toward specific buildings with an easy, but determined lope, guided by their noncoms' hand signals.

The chameleon coating on their armor turned them into eerie shapes partially blending with their surroundings, not unlike human-sized earth clods. Until that is, they became strange bumps on building walls as the lead soldiers shuffled up to the mercenary barracks and what Saari had tagged as the headquarters.

His helmet's built-in friend or foe recognition receiver identified Major Salminen making her way toward the latter on the heels of 4th Platoon. The chatter of carbines on rapid fire showed the guard detail was finally snapping out of surprise-induced paralysis. The deeper cough of E Company rifles answered them almost at once, and yelps of pain rose above the din.

A pair of remote weapons stations opened up on either side of the breaches made by 1st Platoon. The initial bursts were badly aimed, then one of the troopers from 4th Platoon took a hit in the chest, mercifully absorbed by the armor, but he still went down under the impact. Moments later, bunker busters, shot by members of Saari's platoon took both of the RWS out of action. Those on the camp's far side remained operational, but their fields of fire were hampered by huts housing the precious workforce.

Two troopers took position on either side of the guard hut doors and yanked them open. Instantly, their fire team partners each tossed a grenade cluster through the opening. Five seconds later, the clusters exploded, spewing death. Then, the grenadiers stormed through the opening, weapons at the ready, followed by their wingers and the rest of 3rd Platoon. As they moved through, shouts reached Saari's ears while reddish light flashed behind plastic windows.

Meanwhile, the half of 4th Platoon that accompanied Major Salminen was carrying out the same sequence at the doors to the headquarters building. Although Saari would prefer accompanying either of his colleagues in dispensing death and destruction, his job was to protect the gunships, and he quickly dispersed his two sections around them. The soldiers adopted a kneeling position, rifle butts against the shoulder and heads on a swivel.

A new whine above them told him Gus Purdy's shuttle was now flying top cover over Ruby One, looking for mercenaries trying to outflank the attackers or outside reinforcements, improbable as they might be, after retrieving Vallin and Bergstrom. But the fight was over in minutes.

Forty mercenaries might suffice to intimidate four times their number into working the mine. They were, however, woefully unprepared for an attack by regular Commonwealth troops.

By the time Salminen called on the platoon leaders to report, the guard barracks and headquarters building were nothing more than empty shells, littered with the corpses of black-clad men. A quick count followed by a sensor sweep proved there were no survivors. Other than the trooper from 4th Platoon, alive but badly bruised by the direct hit, this half of E Company came through virtually unscathed, though several battlesuits would need mending.

Some prisoner huts, on the other hand, bore smoking holes, though no sounds came from inside to indicate wounded prisoners.

With the battle over, Salminen called on Saari to join her by the HQ building while 4th Platoon ransacked it, searching for intelligence.

"Show me again where the *Kattegat Maru* folks are housed, Karlo."

"There."

He pointed at the second last hut on the left.

Salminen switched to the company push.

"Okay folks, now comes the hard part. Separating our people from the general population without fighting off deportees looking for a seat on the gunships. I'd rather not hurt any of them. Arik, the location is as per plan. Secure, open, and confirm. Karlo, follow me."

"Roger."

With a few hand gestures, Command Sergeant Arik Ritland sent his alpha section to break open the designated hut's door. Two soldiers, covered by their wingers, made quick work of the lock and cautiously pulled it open a crack. One of them threaded a probe through the opening and glanced at his sensor screen.

"Clear. The inmates are mostly hiding under their bunks."

Salminen, with Saari to act as her cover, slipped into the building. Once inside, she said, "I'm a Commonwealth Army officer here to recover certain people of interest. My soldiers and I won't hurt you. I will call out names. When you hear yours, please stand, take your personal possessions and exit through the door behind me. If your name isn't called, stay where you are. We know what folks look like, so don't try a fast one. Once I collect those I want, I'll give the rest of you instructions."

She called the first name, Eugene Ross, *Kattegat Maru*'s second engineer. When no one moved, Salminen added, "Carrie's waiting for uncles Gene and Steph, who hid her in the shielded cubbyhole. Let's make sure she's not disappointed."

A ragged-looking man wearing the standard gray coveralls tentatively stood, followed moments later by another, older one wearing a short beard. Saari ran their faces against the images on record once again and nodded. Eugene Ross and Stephan Fennon.

"Over here, gentlemen."

Then, without prompting, nine more men and women climbed to their feet. The rest of the eleven from *Kattegat Maru*'s crew held in Ruby One, revealing themselves without being named, as Salminen had hoped.

"Carrie's here?" Stephan Fennon asked in a low voice as he neared the woman with a major's oak leaves and four-pointed star on her armored chest.

"Not on Hestia, but in orbit, aboard our ship. A Navy ship. *Kattegat Maru* is with us," she replied in a voice pitched low so only Fennon could hear.

Incredulity warred with relief in the merchant engineer's eyes.

"How's Carrie?"

"On pins and needles waiting for this mission to succeed. A fine young lady, your niece."

"What about the others? Aurelia — Carrie's mother — and the rest of our crew?"

"At the other mining camp. They're being rescued as we speak. You'll see them in orbit."

Salminen gestured over her shoulder, conscious of the deportees watching them intently, their fear ebbing with every passing second.

"Please exit this hut."

Fennon nodded once and led his relatives past Saari and out into a night air redolent with the scent of ozone, burned plastics, and charred flesh. When they were gone, Salminen spoke again.

"We can't take everyone with us, and for that, you have my apologies. But those who kept you captive are dead. This camp and the mine belong to you now. There are vehicles in the motor pool with which you can reach the free settlements where you'll be reasonably safe. Please do not interfere with our departure. Your fellows are still locked in, but you'll find opening their huts an easy task once we've left. Good luck."

She and Saari slipped out through the half-open door before any of the inmates could react. The pair standing guard outside slammed it shut, but didn't lock it again.

Out in the open square, Salminen's half of E Company, minus 1st Platoon, was hustling the eleven *Kattegat Maru* crewmembers aboard the gunships before jogging up the aft ramps themselves. The four that landed during the initial assault lifted off in a swirling cloud of dust, leaving Command Sergeant Saari and his soldiers to wait for Gus Purdy's craft.

It landed moments later as the first curious deportees crept out of the unlocked hut, but none dared interfere with Saari's departure. His last glimpse of the slave labor mine was a pool of light at the heart of an alien darkness on a planet far from his species' world of origin. And of tiny gray figures cautiously fanning out across the camp, wondering what their future held, now they were free.

Moments after Ruby One faded into the distance, Saari listened to Lieutenant Puro report his half of E Company, including Sergeant First Class Mattis' and her two sections, was extracting with the rest of *Kattegat Maru*'s crew. They took only two non-fatal casualties, both in 2nd Platoon.

The Ruby Two guard contingent, on the other hand, suffered one hundred percent fatalities. Saari settled back in the gunner's seat, a satisfied smile on his face — 1st Platoon would not be paying for the post-mission vodka. In fact, everything considered, his troopers deserved a double tot. Thanks to their recon, it couldn't have come off any smoother.

— Fifty-Two —

With *Iolanthe*'s space doors once more shut and the gunships settling in their usual spots, Petty Officer Harkon released the inner airlocks. Carrie Fennon, quivering with impatience ever since Major Salminen called to say E Company recovered every one of her relatives alive, if not in perfect physical condition, gave Dunmoore an impatient glance. Harkon, who caught the look, chuckled.

"I suggest you let the soldiers sort things out before you go running into the middle of it, Apprentice Officer," he said in a fatherly tone. "They'll not thank you for rushing their homecoming."

"A good suggestion, PO." When she saw the anguish in Fennon's eyes, Dunmoore relented. "We can go in and watch, but no more. A captain waits until her people report. She doesn't chase after them."

"Yes, sir. Understood."

Dunmoore led Carrie through the airlock, then assumed the parade rest position to one side. The young woman imitated her though she remained visibly excited.

Gunship aft ramps came down one after the other and armored soldiers trudged off with slung weapons and raised helmet visors. They wordlessly formed up by platoons at the center of the deck, between the rows of shuttles.

Meanwhile, Chief Dwyn and a few bosun's mates came through the airlock at the opposite end, ready to round up the rescuees and take them to sickbay for a checkup.

Dunmoore's communicator chimed for attention.

"Yes?"

"Holt, sir. Unless there's unfinished business on Hestia, might I suggest we break out of orbit and head for home?"

"Do it." The first gray-clad, unkempt, and thoroughly bewildered civilians emerged. "Dunmoore, out."

Dwyn, with uncharacteristic gentleness, did her best to round them up in a coherent group. Meanwhile, Salminen dismissed E Company to barracks and the inevitable hotwash, the Army's version of an after-action debrief.

A tall, thin, middle-aged, woman, the last of the twenty-five *Kattegat Maru* crewmembers, came out of Lieutenant Puro's command shuttle. As her inquisitive eyes turned toward them, Dunmoore saw the striking resemblance to Carrie beneath the cuts and bruises.

Unable to muster any further restraint, the younger Fennon, teary-eyed and sobbing with joy, abandoned her dignified stance and raced across the deck to embrace her mother. After waiting until both regained control of their emotions, Dunmoore gave Dwyn a nod to say go ahead with the rest, she'd take care of this one, and joined them at a more stately pace.

Carrie turned around to face Dunmoore. She wiped away a stray tear with her uniform tunic sleeve and smiled.

"Mom, I want you to meet Captain Siobhan Dunmoore of the battlecruiser *Iolanthe*. Sir, may I present my mother, Aurelia Fennon."

Dunmoore stuck out her hand.

"A pleasure, Captain. Welcome aboard."

"Captain." Fennon's hand was hard, bony, and dry, but her grip felt strong, vital, that of someone who never gave up. "Lieutenant Puro and my daughter tell me we owe you our deepest thanks. Ours and that of the unfortunates who took passage in *Katie*."

"It was a team effort, and if it weren't for Carrie's courage and determination, we might never have succeeded. Your daughter will make a fine officer once she sits for her examination boards. She's a credit to you and your ship."

Fennon senior glanced at Fennon junior and smiled although the split lip made it visibly painful.

"Carrie's good at seeing things through to the end. I suppose stubbornness is in the family genes."

"There's a long story behind our meeting here today, Captain, and I'll be glad to share it with you over a cup of something hot, or perhaps a glass of something strong."

"Or both."

Dunmoore nodded.

"Both it shall be. But right now, my ship's surgeon, Doc Polter, needs to give you a full checkup. Carrie can show you the way and stick around. After that, my people will bring you to a compartment we've set aside as temporary quarters so you can eat and rest."

"What about my ship?"

"We temporarily pressed *Kattegat Maru* into naval service as an auxiliary, so she isn't mistaken for a prize. But as Carrie can tell you, she's in the competent hands of a relief crew under my second officer, Emma Cullop, who was in the merchant service before the war and knows freighters inside out. Once Doc Polter pronounces you fit, we can discuss *Katie*'s immediate future. However, I would prefer if we retained control until we're out of the badlands and back where the Navy holds sway. Your ship remains a target for those who commissioned the piracy, and I won't rest easy until we've brought you to a naval base where your return home and *Kattegat Maru*'s handover will be formally registered."

"Why formally?"

"You were caught up in Enoc Tarrant's machinations and meant to vanish, leaving only an empty ship and a mystery, a plan you foiled by hiding Carrie in a shielded cubbyhole. Tarrant was working on behalf of a person or persons unknown, but who don't forgive failure, from what he gave me to understand. I'm sure they would dearly like to undo what my ship and I did to bring *Katie*, her crew and her passengers back into the land of the living. But neither Tarrant nor whoever hired him will try once the Fleet publishes your ship's return to civilian duty. Provided you stay away from outlaw colonies in the Unclaimed Zone, and more importantly, Kilia Station."

"What did Tarrant want with my ship?"

"We don't know, and probably never will."

"Yet he remains a threat to us?"

"Yes, which is why I'm loath to hand over control just yet. Better she remains in the hands of an experienced Navy crew as a Fleet Auxiliary."

"Very well." Aurelia Fennon's instinctive displeasure at not regaining her ship at once was clear in the way her lips tightened, but she nodded graciously. "As you said, there's much to discuss after I see your surgeon. Again, thank you for rescuing us. We owe you and your crew our lives."

"Take your mother to the sickbay, Carrie."

"Aye, aye, sir." Fennon junior came to attention and saluted, startling her mother.

"Did they press you into service as well?"

"No, mother. But Captain Dunmoore has been teaching me what she can about the attributes of a good officer. And perhaps a tour in the Navy would be a valuable experience. I understand they take merchant officers on a wartime short service commissions if they've passed their boards."

"We'll discuss that later," Fennon senior growled.

Dunmoore watched mother and daughter leave the hangar deck arm in arm, and felt just a tiny pinch of jealousy, one quickly pushed aside. Her own, now long-deceased mother was no spacefarer. Quite the contrary. Yet growing up without her had left a void she only rarely acknowledged. After a mental shrug, Dunmoore headed back to her day cabin.

Mikhail Forenza intercepted her inside the hangar deck airlock, proving he'd watched the return from the shadows, even though hiding wasn't necessary since his face no longer resembled that of Mostar Quantrill. Instead, he looked precisely like the man Dunmoore first met in the Cervantes system.

"I trust you didn't let on that this stemmed from a dispute between Commonwealth government agencies, Captain?" Forenza fell into step beside her.

"No need to worry. The names SSB and Colonial Office didn't pass my lips, nor will they. As far as Captain Fennon is concerned, this mess falls squarely on Enoc Tarrant and the unknown persons who hired him to commit an act of piracy for reasons we can't figure out. I don't want those honest spacers falling deeper into your rabbit hole, Ser Forenza."

A cold smile pulled up the corners of his lips.

"Honesty being a relative term since they traded with outlaw colonies and a known den of thieves."

"In part at the Colonial Office's behest, let's not forget." Dunmoore returned the smile. "But I'll bow to your greater knowledge of relative honesty."

"Touché, Captain. And thank you."

"For what?"

"For rescuing the innocent victims caught up in my sometimes deplorable line of work. You may not believe it, but I care about limiting collateral damage to the greatest extent."

She turned her head to study his guileless expression and snorted.

"I believe you're actually telling the truth, Ser Forenza. And for that, I'll buy you a cup of coffee in my day cabin. We still need to discuss a few details."

"Indeed. That we do."

They remained silent for the rest of the way, but once behind closed doors, Dunmoore said, "As much as I want to, we can't visit the other outlaw colonies with deportee labor camps, and free those. I'm sure you understand why."

"I do. Rescuing Captain Fennon's crew was a onetime thing, an operation carried out under the doctrine of hot pursuit. It was not in execution of Fleet orders under a policy of freeing involuntary colonists beyond the Commonwealth's legally defined sphere. That you released their fellow detainees and terminated the slavers, while a pleasing outcome, was incidental to your mission."

"Just so. But I will recommend the Fleet consider sending a task force to deal with Kilia and the outlaw colonies on humanitarian grounds."

"Which the government won't allow — *if* the Admiralty even makes such a proposal."

Dunmoore sighed.

"True. Unfortunately. Since I received orders to join a newly established task force and place myself under a rear admiral's direct command, *Iolanthe* won't be at leisure to carry out any unsanctioned missions as the privateer *Persephone*. In fact, technically, *Iolanthe* is already absent without leave since my reporting date passed while we were getting you out of Blayne Hersom's stockade."

"More's the pity. But even with the best will in the universe, you can't save everyone, Captain. Consider what you've achieved so far a significant victory against those who would use human beings as mere chattel. Destroying their Hestia operation will prove costly. The deportation scheme needs to finance itself because it can't be funded out of governmental coffers, so that's a considerable setback.

Then there's the small matter of setting me free to report back and offer testimony, which will have longer-term repercussions."

A skeptical smirk twisted Dunmoore's face.

"You think? Folks who can corrupt entire government agencies and hire powerful mobsters such as Tarrant will hide behind almost impregnable defenses."

"Almost, Captain. That's the operative word. Even the sturdiest walls can be breached by what is at first a mere trickle of water, entering invisibly through a tiny weak spot. Given time, that trickle grows and eats away at the foundations and one day, the entire edifice collapses. That's how things generally unfold in my world. We don't enjoy the luxury of solving problems with massive nuclear missile strikes and overwhelming gunfire."

She raised her cup in salute.

"Here's to hoping your trickle turns into a torrent with all dispatch."

"Will this rear admiral to whom you're reporting create any turbulence because of what you've done?"

"I don't intend to tell him anything more than what I've told Captain Fennon. Admiral Nagira already knows of the general situation, thanks to a private message I transmitted on our way back to Kilia from Temar. I merely need to send a follow-up with the remaining details before joining my new commanding officer and his task force. What Nagira does with the information is none of my business, and my new CO doesn't need to know anything beyond the rescue itself."

"That sounds like a remarkably sneaky runaround. Congratulations. If the Navy no longer suits you, look me up for a job."

"I'd make a lousy covert operative, Ser Forenza. You're aware of my old nickname, right?"

"Doña Quixote, because you're always tilting at windmills?" He indicated the old clock with the silhouette of a gaunt knight on its face. "That was perhaps partially true at one time, but you've changed. You're not even the same officer I first met on Toboso, and that's less than a year ago. For what it's worth, you've become someone capable of acting without mercy when innocent lives are involved. Or you always were, but taking *Iolanthe* into dark places brought it to the fore."

Dunmoore made a wry face.

"Thanks. I think. But if the Navy no longer suits me, or I no longer suit the Navy, something that has a greater chance of occurring, I'll find a captain's berth in a commercial ship. Or maybe even become a genuine privateer."

"Call me up anyway. The Colonial Office has its own starships. Perhaps I can persuade my superiors to arm one of them and use it to solve the involuntary deportee problem in the Unclaimed Zone."

— Fifty-Three —

"Thank you ever so kindly, Captain." Aurelia Fennon accepted a glass half full of amber liquid and examined its color before inhaling the rich, alcoholic aroma. A happy smile softened her dour expression. "I'd recognize a twelve-year-old Glen Arcturus anywhere." She raised it in salute, imitated by Dunmoore. "Your health. And once again, my most heartfelt thanks."

"Your health."

They took a sip of the smooth whiskey in silence, savoring the complex flavors, then Dunmoore put her glass down and sat. She examined Fennon now that Doc Polter had done his usual magic. The bruises would take a few days to fade, but already she seemed a different woman. Freshly washed and clad in black, navy-issue coveralls, Fennon was a far cry from the dusty, bedraggled slave worker who stepped out of Lieutenant Puro's gunship a few hours earlier.

"Fine stuff this." She set her glass on the desk as well. "Captain, my daughter's been talking nonstop since we left your hangar deck and I caught some of what happened between the time she crawled out of the cubbyhole and today. But her tale has a lot of holes in it, holes I'm hoping you'll be able to fill. For example, one of the passengers we were carrying seems to be missing. A Mostar Quantrill."

"You visited them?"

"Not exactly. Chief Dwyn was kind enough to allay my fears about their welfare by letting me take a peek via video. They might be in your charge right now, but they contracted with me to carry them safely, and by the Almighty, I aim to do just that once you return *Katie*."

"Ser Quantrill, unfortunately, took ill from something he caught in the prison where he and the others were kept. My surgeon tried his best, but in vain. He never discovered the origin of the disease, except that it was from an alien source."

The lie came as naturally as any truth she'd ever spoken, and Dunmoore thought back to Forenza's earlier comments about her having changed.

"So he's dead?"

"Yes. We buried him in space."

Fennon studied her through narrowed eyes in which disbelief warred with confusion.

"Shame. Lieutenant Polter struck me as a competent doctor, but I suppose even the best can lose a patient." She picked up her glass and took another sip. "You made quite an impression on my daughter. Carrie swears by your forthrightness and integrity as a Navy officer. Did you know?"

"I'm flattered, but all I did was try to act in *loco parentis* and mentor her as much as possible."

"And I'm grateful, though her idea of doing a tour of active duty as a Navy Reserve officer once she passes her boards isn't filling me with joy. But she's a Fennon, with a Fennon's determination. May I ask who was holding my passengers and why?"

Dunmoore had expected a sharp turn back to questions about the abduction. She shrugged.

"Pirates associated with Enoc Tarrant, hoping to collect fat ransoms. Failing that, they no doubt intended to sell them on a slave market deep inside the Unclaimed Zone."

"Did you find out why they separated those poor folks from my crew and me?"

"Sorry, no. Enoc Tarrant wasn't inclined to talk beyond telling me where to find everyone."

"Oh, aye? And how did you loosen the filthy bastard's tongue?"

"I planted nuclear mines in Kilia's crust."

A bark of laughter erupted from Fennon senior's throat.

"Serves the bastard right. So we're left with a mystery. Someone pirates my ship, leaves it drifting empty, takes my passengers to one place, my crew to another, and no one knows why."

"That's about the size of it, Captain."

"In other words, don't pry, Fennon. Thank the Almighty everyone except poor Ser Quantrill is alive and carry on quietly once the Navy returns *Katie*. Is that it?"

Dunmoore took a sip of whiskey and smiled.

"Pretty much."

"Navy secrets? Well, no one said old Aurelia can't take a hint, not when her only daughter has a bad case of hero worship for the woman who rescued everyone. But answer me this if you would. Why did you decide to recover a few dozen insignificant civilians traveling a dangerous route along the wild frontier where folks take their chances and tough luck if things go sideways? Isn't there a war for you to fight against the damned boneheads, especially with a ship of this size?"

"If our job isn't to save human lives, then what is it, Captain?" Dunmoore asked in a soft voice. "We rarely get the chance to turn tables on pirates and put things right again. I could have returned to my patrol route after salvaging *Kattegat Maru* and justified it by arguing that the needs of the many I might save raiding Shrehari shipping outweigh the needs of a few dozens I might actually rescue in a war which has already cost millions of lives. Yet I know I can't save millions. Perhaps not even thousands. But I've come to realize the small victories, the handful of lives spared each time, they add up."

Fennon, studying Dunmoore over the rim of her almost empty whiskey glass didn't immediately reply. Then, she said, "Perhaps it's best I stop looking a gift horse in the mouth, lest I become a facsimile of the animal's aft end. Please accept my everlasting gratitude for saving my daughter, my ship, my crew, and my life. There's no profit, let alone honor in questioning your motives. Carrie is a good judge of character, like most Fennon women, and the Almighty save me if I impugn your integrity in her presence."

**

"How did Captain Fennon take it?" Holt asked after pouring himself a cup of coffee from the day cabin's urn.

"I don't think she believed the cover story, but appeared willing to go with it, especially if it helps get her ship back without delay. And apparently, young Carrie looks up to me."

The first officer chuckled.

"Young Carrie has a serious case of hero worship where you're concerned, Skipper, and everyone in *Iolanthe* has known for weeks. Except you, it seems. Speak with Emma when she's back aboard and ask her about her conversations with the girl when they were standing watch together."

"I'm almost afraid to."

This time Holt laughed outright.

"And so you should." He sobered and asked, "Are we making a dogleg for Kilia, to give Enoc Tarrant our love on the way home?"

"I wish, but no. It's best course for the nearest starbase so we can restore *Kattegat Maru* to her crew safely and set Skelly Kursu's mob loose. Then we need to make for the Task Force Luckner rendezvous. We're no doubt late enough to attract Rear Admiral Petras' well-justified ire."

"So you won't tell him about the illegal deportee scheme?"

"No. The ramifications are well beyond my pay grade. Admiral Nagira can decide what to do with that information. Petras will hear about our rescuing Fennon, her crew, and her passengers. No more. If it displeases Petras that I ignored his orders for the sake of seventy civilians, too bad. The worst he can do is enter a reprimand in my record. Relieving me of command is beyond *his* pay grade."

"Please don't take that attitude when you report to him," Holt said in a wry tone. "He might just decide you need a few weeks slaving away under his steely gaze as the task force flag captain, and then where will *Iolanthe* be? Stuck with Lena Corto as temporary commanding officer? Don't do this to me. To us."

"I promise I'll be the meekest and most repentant captain in the Fleet."

A snort.

"That'll be the day. Your loyal crew will be grateful if you merely succeed in not annoying him overmuch."

— Fifty-Four —

Siobhan Dunmoore, in naval uniform, met Captain Aurelia Fennon and her daughter, both properly dressed as Guild-accredited ship's officers, outside the starbase commander's office. The latter, an Academy classmate of Dunmoore's, graciously expedited *Kattegat Maru*'s return to civilian ownership and service. He'd also arranged for the release of Skelly Kursu and her mercenary crew without prejudice on the neighboring civilian orbital station, thereby fulfilling Dunmoore's promise.

Both *Katie* and *Iolanthe*, the latter in her battlecruiser incarnation, were docked with the spindle-shaped orbital station and while Dunmoore saw to Fennon and company, Holt was busy replenishing their stores and more importantly, the ship's missile stocks.

But now that the formalities were over and her storage compartments full, *Iolanthe* could no longer tarry. A message barely short of nasty from Rear Admiral Petras was waiting for Dunmoore when she arrived. It summoned her to join Task Force Luckner at the prearranged rendezvous forthwith and explain her absence.

"All done?" Siobhan asked.

Aurelia Fennon nodded once.

"Done. We're free to go with the Fleet's compliments. You heard most of my passengers elected to find berths in other ships?"

"I did."

"Can't say I blame them, not after what they've been through, although once you told them you were undercover Navy rather than a privateer, the loudest complainers calmed down right smartly. But *Katie* needs to earn a living. I'll be leaving for the commercial station within the hour so we can find more cargo and fresh passengers. Nothing that'll take me into the Unclaimed Zone, mind you. At least not for a while even if it means fewer profits. Your lot might guarantee we're registered as being among the living, at least where Lloyds, the Guild, and the Commonwealth government are concerned. But that doesn't mean Enoc Tarrant won't be looking for revenge."

"A wise precaution." They fell into step, side by side, headed for the docking rings. "I know taking on passengers rounds out your income, but you might also consider sticking purely with cargo for a while, in case someone sneaks an infiltrator aboard."

"I don't know... Folks wanting to travel with no questions asked, and no identities checked pay handsomely. Especially in the frontier sectors. And we can always use the extra profits, but I'll think about it."

"For Carrie's sake?"

Fennon glanced at the young woman.

"Aye. And I'll even think twice about taking on well-paying cargo that comes with a no questions asked clause."

"Thank you."

"It's me who thanks you, Captain." Fennon sighed. "Don't worry. I damn well know you won't be around to rescue us a second time if I unwittingly find myself at cross-purposes with one of Enoc's business acquaintances. Besides," she jerked her thumb at her daughter, "this one here will remind me every time I bid for a contract or think of taking on a paying guest."

They stopped at the lifts. *Iolanthe*, thanks to her size, was docked on one of the lower arms while *Kattegat Maru* rode higher up.

Dunmoore stuck out her hand.

"Fair winds and following seas, Captain Fennon. Take care of your daughter. She'll make a fine officer."

"I will. Good hunting, Captain Dunmoore."

Siobhan turned to Carrie.

"Promise me you'll study hard, stand those boring night watches in deep space, and pass your boards on the first try. If you apply for a tour of active duty as a naval reserve officer, send me a message through any Navy subspace node, and I'll put in a good word with the selection committee."

When she saw Fennon senior frown, Dunmoore added, "I believe it's not unheard of for family-owned merchant ships such as yours to place freshly minted officers in other vessels so they may gain valuable experience. Three years as a junior watchkeeper in the naval reserve, serving on a Fleet transport or replenishment ship will certainly do that, and better than in any of the larger shipping companies."

"I'll consider it. *If* Carrie passes her boards on the first try. C'mon, youngling. Let's put *Katie* back into service."

But before the two Fennons could step into the lift cab, Carrie impulsively flung her arms around Dunmoore's neck and squeezed.

"Thank you for everything." She released her, stepped back, then came to attention and saluted. "Goodbye, sir. Fair winds to you and yours."

As the lift doors closed on them, Dunmoore realized she'd grown fonder of Carrie than she was willing to admit. The younger woman seemed almost like the kid sister Siobhan never had, and she wondered whether their paths would ever cross again. Just then, Ezekiel Holt came around the corner at a fast clip and skidded to a halt beside her.

"I gather you saw the Fennons off, Skipper?"

"Yes. How did you know?"

"I see that look on your face."

She eyed her first officer with suspicion.

"Which one?"

"The wistful 'I wonder if we'll we ever meet again' look."

"Hilarious." She jabbed the lift controls with her knuckles in a brusque gesture. "Is *Iolanthe* ready to sail?"

"The moment you and I are aboard. I just came from the harbormaster's office. He agreed to send Admiral Petras a subspace message advising him we're on our way."

"We could have done that ourselves."

The lift doors opened.

"Sure, but this proves we actually docked at the starbase to complete our rescue mission. It might make Petras less inclined to tear a strip off you."

"Now who's being sneaky?"

Holt grinned at her. "Merely taking care of my captain, so she stays my captain for a long time to come. I don't enjoy the idea of breaking in a new skipper, especially if it's someone named Lena Corto."

"What about Forenza?"

"Happily ensconced in VIP quarters and waiting for the next aviso, thanks to the good word you put in the commanding officer's ear."

"Excellent. I don't think him traveling on a regular liner would be safe right now. Not when the SSB is still on the hunt for Colonial Office agents interfering with the involuntary deportation scheme."

"That means we can join Task Force Luckner with a clear conscience. Since Astrid already plotted the fastest route to the rendezvous, all you need to do is give the word."

"It is given."

— Fifty-Five —

"Enter." Commander Gregor Pushkin, captain of the Voivode class frigate *Jan Sobieski*, paused the daily stores report and glanced up as his first officer, Lieutenant Commander Trevane Devall, came into the day cabin. When Pushkin saw the unusually broad grin on Devall's face, his eyes narrowed in suspicion.

"What's up?"

"Task Force Luckner's laggard just dropped out of FTL."

"That quasi-mythical Q-ship? The sole reason for Luckner's existence?"

"Aye, though she's identifying herself as the battlecruiser *Iolanthe* right now." The grin widened until it almost threatened to swallow his aristocratic face. "Captain Siobhan Dunmoore, commanding."

"What?"

Pushkin half rose from his seat, incredulity quickly giving way to a smile of pure pleasure.

"Desk job indeed. It figures Admiral Nagira gave her the newest Q-ship in the Fleet."

"Should I set up a tight-beam link so you can chat before she makes her manners with the flag?"

"Yes, please."

Devall touched his communicator and said, "Put it through," confirming Pushkin's suspicion his first officer prepared things before telling him of their former captain's unexpected arrival.

Moments later, a familiar face, though with a few more worry lines around the eyes and a touch grayer, appeared on his day cabin's main display. Her smile, though, remained unchanged.

"Hello, Gregor." That well-known alto sent an unexpected shiver of recognition down his spine. "Fancy meeting you here in the back of beyond."

"Sir! What an unexpected pleasure. How are you?"

"Prospering, Gregor, and making sure the enemy doesn't prosper. How is *Jan Sobieski*?"

"A dream, sir. They classified her as a frigate, but she'd give a light cruiser serious pangs of inadequacy and could eat *Stingray* for breakfast."

"Understandable. The Fleet intends to reduce the number of ship classes and operate just a few core types, like the Shrehari. Give this war another ten years, and we'll be sailing heavy cruisers, oversized frigates and damn near nothing else besides the inevitable support ships. They already retired the last battle wagons and turned the carriers into command vessels, and now the Voivode class frigates are making the old Type 260 destroyers Admiral Petras scraped up obsolete."

"I'd rather the war didn't last another ten years, thank you very much," Pushkin replied in a dry tone.

"Me neither. How are the former Stingrays, Gregor?"

"Prospering as well. Trevane Devall is as solid a first officer as I could want. He anticipates my orders so consistently, it's eerie. Say hi to the captain, you paragon of virtue."

Devall leaned into the video pickup's range and waved.

"Hi, Captain. Staying one step ahead of the skipper is easy. You might remember he's something of an open book."

Dunmoore's lips twitched with delight.

"Considering he taught you everything you know about first officering, I'd say it proves Gregor is a fine teacher. And the others?"

"Guthren evidently taught Foste the fine science of being a coxswain," Pushkin replied. "She carries the cane of office with a gravitas that instills awe in even the most recalcitrant spacers, and I received my fair share of those. You'll also be glad to hear Jeneva Syten has lost the worst of her bad habits now she's responsible for *Jan Sobieski*'s entire deck department as second officer. And young Lieutenant Sanghvi is showing the makings of a first-rate sailing master. I'm sure they would love to see you, Chief Guthren, and Vincenzo again. If we find time to invite guests over for a meal and an evening of war stories during our cruise along the wild frontier."

"I'd enjoy that, Gregor," Dunmoore replied with a warm smile at the memories evoked by hearing names associated with some of *Stingray*'s most terrifying and exhilarating adventures. "And in return, I'd love to reciprocate and show you *Iolanthe* — time and Admiral Petras permitting."

Pushkin's face darkened at her mention of their commanding officer's name.

"You should be aware he's waiting for you with a certain degree of, let's call it impatience, to be polite. Petras is keen on putting this special task force through its paces and prove the concept he and Lena Corto sold to the Admiralty. But without *Iolanthe*, we're little more than a light battle group, good mainly for internal security tasks, and the occasional raid."

"Thanks for the warning, Gregor. I didn't expect him to be happy with the inevitable delay in our joining his command, but innocent lives were on the line. It's something of a shaggy dog story, which is fairly normal for a Q-ship operating undercover in these parts. You and I can talk about it in private at some point."

Pushkin saw the look in her eyes and understood there would be more to Dunmoore's delay than what she planned on sharing with Petras.

"Take care with the admiral, Captain. And keep an eye on Lena Corto. I think our estimable flag captain covets *Iolanthe* for herself. She is senior to you by date of rank, a fact she let intentionally slip at the last in-person command conference aboard *Hawkwood*."

"I will." Dunmoore's eyes slipped to one side.

"Speak of the devil, and he appears. *Hawkwood* is calling. Until later, Gregor."

Her image faded away.

"This promises to be interesting," Devall said in a soft tone. "Our Siobhan, who's been sowing terror among the Shrehari from the bridge of the Fleet's newest and most dangerous warship, tied to an admiral's apron strings. And not just any admiral but one whose last command in space dates back to when I was a callow lieutenant with delusions of adequacy."

"I know. Let's hope she still remembers how to cajole a flag officer without letting on that she believes he's a damned fool. Otherwise, the sparks we'll see won't be from Shrehari warships breaking apart."

— Fifty-Six —

"Kind of you to join us, Dunmoore."

Petras, an olive-skinned, hard-faced, fifty-something man with the two stars of a rear admiral on his collar wore an expression that exuded all the warmth of interstellar space. His emotionless tone might belie the sarcasm implicit in his words, but she nonetheless understood he was conveying displeasure.

"My apologies for the delay, sir. Our orders reached us while we were in hot pursuit of pirates who kidnapped the crew and passengers of a merchant ship. It took time to track them down and rescue everyone, but the mission ended well for all involved except the pirates."

"I look forward to your report on the matter."

"You shall receive it momentarily, sir. May I inquire as to my orders?"

Petras eyed Dunmoore with suspicion, and she wondered whether she sounded too obsequious.

"I'll be honest with you, Captain. *Iolanthe* was not my choice as the Q-ship attached to this task force. I was hoping for something smaller, more believable as a lure, and more maneuverable, such as *Ruddigore* or *Sorcerer*. Preferably both."

Dunmoore mentally winced at hearing the names of two frigate-sized Q-ships, converted from pre-war merchantmen and suitable only for anti-piracy operations in her estimation. Neither could stand to a Shrehari *Tol* class cruiser let alone wreck it in a ship-to-ship fight. And neither would survive even one of *Iolanthe*'s broadsides without suffering severe damage.

"With respect, sir," she replied in an even, unemotional voice, "you'll find *Iolanthe* to be as believable and maneuverable as any Q-ship, and her bite is more vicious than that of a *Reconquista* class cruiser. We also carry this task force's only infantry, a full company's worth from the Scandia Regiment. They proved their mettle more than once and are the equals of any Marines. And after our last engagement, we hold the record for combat kills of any starship in Special Operations Command since the onset of the war."

"Commendable, I'm sure." Petras sounded unconvinced. "However, this task force faces a very different war from the one you've been fighting so far, Captain."

"My apologies, yet I fail to see how deep raids by a task force differ from those conducted by a single Q-ship, except in magnitude and firepower."

"You're a tactician, Dunmoore, and by every account a competent one. But the deployment of Task Force Luckner is a strategic move by Fleet Command, and the tactics that made you successful won't necessarily work. I aim to disrupt Shrehari shipping on a grand scale, something well beyond the ability of a single Q-ship, even one capable of going toe to toe with a battle wagon. As I mentioned, my plans need a believable lure, and *Iolanthe* just doesn't fit the bill." He shrugged. "But since HQ won't entertain any notion of replacing yours with a more suitable vessel, I'll improvise."

"I can assure you we will make your plans a success, sir," Dunmoore replied, swallowing the unexpected surge of bile that threatened to choke her. "Our experience raiding deep within enemy space will compensate for what we otherwise seem to lack."

A frown creased Petras' forehead as if he sensed Dunmoore's mood. His next words intimated that he understood the latent hostility in her words.

"Take care you don't overstep your bounds, Captain."

Siobhan inclined her head in a silent apology.

"Of course, sir."

He studied her face for a little longer, then his stern countenance seemed to soften ever so slightly.

"Listen, Dunmoore. I understand your unhappiness at being tied to a task force after operating on your own for so long, and I'm sure your views of Q-ship tactics are biased toward solo operations. But it's our mission to make large-scale raids deep into Shrehari space work. If we can weaken their resolve by proving their rear areas are no longer safe, perhaps they'll come to their senses and sue for a ceasefire. Sure, I'd rather SOCOM gave me something other than *Iolanthe* as my Q-ship, and you'd rather still be running a solitary wild hunt, but here we are."

"Aye, sir. Here we are." She paused, then said, "Sir, if you plan to hold in person command conferences, I'd like to offer *Iolanthe*'s facilities. Unlike *Hawkwood*, we have the hangar space to receive every captain's shuttle, a large conference room with the latest technology and the ability to offer temporary accommodations for everyone concerned, should meetings run longer than expected."

Petras gave her a knowing look.

"Since, in my experience, captains rarely fall over themselves to host a command conference, I'd say your offer is at least partially driven by a desire to better sell me on your raiding experience and your ship's value to this mission."

She allowed herself a faint smile.

"Indeed, sir."

Without Mercy

395

"I'm sure Kirti Midura — *Hawkwood*'s captain — will appreciate your offer. Do you know her?"

Dunmoore shook her head.

"Not personally. I believe Kirti was two years ahead of me at the Academy. I've served with only one of your captains, sir, though I know the commanding officers of the other frigates and the destroyers either by reputation or through a nodding acquaintance."

"Ah, yes, Gregor Pushkin," Petras said. "I read both his and your service records, Captain. His performance as your first officer in *Stingray* earned him command of the first Voivode class frigate. Impressive."

"A fine officer, sir. I've entrusted both my life and that of my crew to his professional abilities and leadership on more occasions than I can remember."

"No doubt."

Petras' dry tone seemed pregnant with the insinuation that Dunmoore might be responsible for teaching Pushkin more than just the basics of captaincy. Such as her tendency to defy doctrine and her superiors when she believed she knew better. Perhaps Petras was among the few who knew of the Corwin affair and its sad end, or the truth about the more recent Toboso incident.

If he enjoyed Admiral Nagira's confidence to the point of being given command of this experimental task force, then he could be familiar with the classified part of her personal file. Or she might just be feeling paranoid because Petras somehow irritated her.

"I shall accept your invitation," he continued, "and instruct Lena — that would be Lena Corto, my flag captain — to convene a planning session aboard your ship. A member of my staff will be in touch shortly. Are you acquainted with Lena?"

"No, sir."

"I'm not surprised. She graduated from the Academy before your arrival." He fell silent for a few moments, then said, "Unless there are pressing issues you wish to discuss, I'll release you to your duties. There will be ample occasion to speak over the coming days, and I look forward to a tour of *Iolanthe*. One can peruse specs and images for hours and still not appreciate the nuances of an unusual ship such as yours. I'll give you a chance to convince me. In any case, welcome to Task Force Luckner, Captain. Petras, out."

The day cabin's main display returned to its standby image, the Furious Faerie, leaving a puzzled Dunmoore to stare sightlessly at the starfield display on the far bulkhead. Before she could wallow in her thoughts, an insistent chime claimed her attention.

"Enter."

The door slid aside, admitting *Iolanthe*'s first officer, who, after taking one glance at his captain, immediately headed for the coffee urn and poured two mugs.

He handed her one and said, "You have the face of someone who needs a little pick-me-up. Was it that bad?"

"Strange, rather than bad."

After taking a few sips of the hot brew, she recounted her conversation almost verbatim, leaving Holt to contemplate her with raised eyebrows.

"He doesn't pussyfoot around, does he? I'm curious about his proposed strategy and tactics if he so casually dismisses *Iolanthe*'s formidable powers to confuse, mesmerize and destroy."

"I suspect that he sees Q-ships as adjuncts or props rather than full-fledged combatants. Lures to his destroyer and frigate powered fishing rod."

Holt made a face.

"Which is curious if he's been riding a desk in Special Operations Command."

"We aren't your average example of the breed, though. He'll be familiar with the limitations of our smaller brethren and draw conclusions appropriate to their capabilities. But *Iolanthe* is the first purpose-built Q-ship with the heart of a battlecruiser rather than that of an up-gunned merchantman."

"I wonder if it's dawned on him or his staff that we carry the heaviest broadside, both in guns and missiles, of this entire task force."

Dunmoore made a face.

"Intellectually? Sure. But perhaps they can't yet see beyond the sluggish bulk carrier envelope. People will listen to their prejudices rather than face facts contrary to long-held opinions. And the Fleet has never considered Q-ships as true men-o-war."

"Until *Iolanthe*."

"With our existence, never mind our deeds still tightly held secrets, I doubt we'll see a change in the general attitude soon."

"I'd say our attachment to Task Force Luckner just blew a big hole in the notion of us remaining a riddle, wrapped in a mystery, inside an enigma."

"To a point. Shrehari intelligence isn't what you might call highly effective. As long as we keep striking and vanishing as we did up to now, they won't add us to any Fleet order of battle."

Holt sighed.

"I guess that depends on how Admiral Petras intends to use the old girl."

Siobhan nodded in agreement.

"Aye. And that'll become my dilemma if his intentions risk blowing our cover."

"The boneheads are bound to wise up someday, so I wouldn't make it a fall-on-your-sword issue, Captain."

"I won't, I promise."

"And as to Petras rubbing you the wrong way, I'd wager the feeling is mutual."

"Really?" Dunmoore raised a skeptical eyebrow. "And why would that be?"

"You know why as well as I do, Captain, so there's no use belaboring the point. Now, should I pull out the good silver and prepare *Iolanthe* so we can receive a dozen senior officers in style? It'll make a change from our usual pretense of being scummy privateers interested mainly in plunder and sowing mayhem."

"If getting out the good silver means making sure both ship and crew shed their usual informality and do honor to our beloved Navy's most exacting traditions, then yes. And see that Major Salminen's troops practice the proper ceremonial to receive visiting captains and flag officers. We'll do this with the painfully correct protocol one expects from a starship of the line."

"I'm glad you're taking this in the right spirit."

Dunmoore gave Holt a curious glance.

"And what would that be?"

"Selling *Iolanthe*'s qualities and acting like a team player rather than locking horns with the admiral because you know this sort of warfare better than he does. Forenza wasn't blowing smoke when he said you've changed. Maybe mentoring a young apprentice officer helped you as much as it helped her."

"Perhaps." Dunmoore's eyes slipped back to the starfield display on the far bulkhead. "Or it could just be that I finally reached the point where I understand the adage old age and treachery will beat youthful exuberance every single time."

"In which case, may the Almighty help Admiral Petras."

About the Author

Eric Thomson is the pen name of a retired Canadian soldier with thirty-one years of service, both in the Regular Army and the Army Reserve. He spent his Regular Army career in the Infantry and his Reserve service in the Armoured Corps. He worked as an information technology specialist for a number of years before retiring to become a full-time author.

Eric has been a voracious reader of science fiction, military fiction, and history all his life. Several years ago, he put fingers to keyboard and started writing his own military sci-fi, with a definite space opera slant, using many of his own experiences as a soldier for inspiration.

When he is not writing fiction, Eric indulges in his other passions: photography, hiking, and scuba diving, all of which he shares with his wife.

Join Eric Thomson at: www.thomsonfiction.ca/

Where you will find news about upcoming books and more information about the universe in which his heroes fight for humanity's survival.

Read his blog at: www.ericthomsonblog.wordpress.com

If you enjoyed this book, please consider leaving a review on Amazon, at Goodreads, or with your favorite online retailer to help others discover it.

Also by Eric Thomson

Siobhan Dunmoore
No Honor in Death (Siobhan Dunmoore Book 1)
The Path of Duty (Siobhan Dunmoore Book 2)
Like Stars in Heaven (Siobhan Dunmoore Book 3)
Victory's Bright Dawn (Siobhan Dunmoore Book 4)
Without Mercy (Siobhan Dunmoore Book 5)

Decker's War
Death Comes but Once (Decker's War Book 1)
Cold Comfort (Decker's War Book 2)
Fatal Blade (Decker's War Book 3)
Howling Stars (Decker's War Book 4)
Black Sword (Decker's War Book 5)
No Remorse (Decker's War Book 6)
Hard Strike (Decker's War Book 7)

Quis Custodiet
The Warrior's Knife (Quis Custodiet No 1)

Ashes of Empire
Imperial Sunset (Ashes of Empire #1)

Printed in Great Britain
by Amazon

46461670R00225